SPECTACULAR PRAISE

Donna Levin and

THERE'S MORE THAN ONE WAY HOME

"*There's More Than One Way Home* is that rare thing — an original story. In an extraordinary setting, the deepest human emotion and fears come to the fore in a curiously **captivating and unexpected** way."
— Jacquelyn Mitchard, author, Oprah Book Club® Selection novel, *The Deep End of the Ocean* (Penguin Books)

"[A] mother questions her relationships with family and friends after classmates accuse her autistic son of murdering a student.... Through her fast-paced prose, engaging plot, and sharp insights, Levin underscores how intolerance and ignorance can cause difficult situations to spiral out of control.... A **witty**, modern voice delivers a **captivating** tale about a mysterious death that feels like a light read but soon submerges the reader deep into the throes of substance."
— *Kirkus Reviews*

"At the heart of Donna Levin's novel, *There's More than One Way Home*, is the narrator's search for autonomy ... The novel's strength lies in its ability to go beyond superficialities.... *There's More than One Way Home* deals substantively with issues like autism, and by doing so, stands to appeal to a broad audience as a worthy entry into popular fiction."
— Geraldine Richards, *Foreword Reviews*

"A complex protagonist trapped in a tragic circumstance that affects so many.... A book that **most readers will devour** in a weekend."
— Donna Gillespie, author of the *The Light Bearer* and *Lady of the Light* (Berkley/Putnam)

THERE'S MORE THAN ONE WAY HOME

A Novel

Donna Levin

ISBN-10: 0-9913274-6-2
ISBN-13: 978-0-9913274-6-1

Front cover illustration by Kelly Airo and book design by Daniel Middleton, Scribe Freelance

Chickadee Prince Logo by Garrett Gilchrist

Visit us at www.ChickadeePrince. com

First Printing

DONNA LEVIN

There's More than One Way Home

Donna Levin is the author of two acclaimed previous novels, *Extraordinary Means* and *California Street*. She has also written two books on the craft of writing: *Get That Novel Started* and *Get That Novel Written.*

Her work is included in the Howard Gotlieb Archival Research Center at Boston University and in the California State Library's collection of California novels.

She lives in San Francisco.

Visit her at *www.DonnaLevin.com.*

THERE'S MORE THAN ONE WAY HOME

A Novel

Chickadee Prince Books
New York

For William, Sonia, Elena, and Anna

Children leave their mommies

They waddle down the street,

And mommies look so wistful

It's really very sweet.

I pity them, I really do,

I only wish they'd find

The time to look around to see

  The child who stays behind.

AUTHOR'S NOTE

In 2004, when *There's More Than One Way Home* takes place, autism as a spectrum disorder and Asperger's Syndrome were still widely misunderstood, in spite of the increasing numbers of diagnoses. This story reflects an earlier time, before the autism research and recognition of today.

Donna Levin
September 2016

PART ONE

CHAPTER ONE
A TEACHABLE MOMENT

MAY 2004.

"Welcome to Minotaur Island."

The park ranger stamped my hand as I stepped off the pier, the last of our group to do so.

Just in time. The kids were getting tired of Jack's autistic parlor tricks.

At the head of the group Kristin Scarborough shrieked, "Hurry! We're behind schedule already! Go straight to the picnic tables!"

Poor Ms. Scarborough. She could have had a fulfilling career in the 17ᵗʰ Century. "Wanted: woman to accuse neighbors of witchcraft. Inquire Salem. Massachusetts driver's license not requ'd." Instead she was trapped in the body of a fourth grade teacher.

I'd spent the past half hour as her hostage, confined to a rotting wooden pier above the murky waters of San Francisco Bay with my son and his classmates. Jack and I had spontaneously volunteered as the entertainment, and he had played his part with goodwill: rattling off the names of vice-presidents in alphabetical order and calculating which days of the week various holidays would occur on in the year 2022.

But as we stepped on the shore, Jack announced, "I have to go to the bathroom. Bathroom...."

Jack often repeated the last word or phrase of his sentence in a squeaky, sing-songy version of his usual speech. He also liked to locate the bathroom in any new location we visited. He'd just used the head on the ferry so I was pretty sure this was part of his routine.

"Can you wait a few minutes? 'Til we get settled?"

"I guess so ... so...."

I pulled him gently along with the other children.

Our troupe inevitably mingled with the two public school classes that had arrived with us on the ferry. Jack's class numbered fifteen while the other teachers were each responsible for thirty students. It was like navigating Macy's the day after Thanksgiving.

"Stay together!" Ms. Scarborough walked backwards so that she could face us, motioning with both hands to follow. "Anna!" she said, addressing me. "Can you please divide the kids into groups? Or do you have your hands full with Jack?"

"Don't worry, I can do it." *One of these days, Kristin....* If the other moms had liked me better I would have recruited them into a fragging plot. You see, it was all right for me to become frustrated with Jack. No one else had better try it.

***

The benches of the redwood tables were rough through my slacks. I never missed a field trip, but I preferred indoor destinations, like the Asian Art Museum, where I could wear Prada kitten heels without getting them stuck in a divot in the grass. Today I compromised with stacked heels on black suede boots.

Ms. Scarborough had placed a mound of stapled pages in the center of each table. "There aren't enough for everyone! You have to share!"

"Now?" Jack wondered about the bathroom. "Now...."

"But we're supposed to do the project." I pulled one of the stapled packs towards us. Each page depicted an endangered species of the region, drawn in outline.

Emily Batarski reached to touch my wrist. "Oooh, what a beautiful bracelet!"

"Thank you, dear."

Emily was the alpha female of my Gal Pal Gang, four little girls who had attached themselves to me in kindergarten when Jack joined the school. Her mother, another chaperone, was next to her, and she shot me a venomous look.

I avoided her by turning to Jack. "Can you do some coloring first, hon? Just a couple of minutes."

"I have to go. Go...."

No, I did not like field trips. Forget the Asian Art Museum — I wouldn't have enjoyed going to the freaking Gershwin Theater with this crowd. I came along in part because Kristin ("Teacher of the Year") Scarborough seemed convinced that Jack would set fire to the school bus seats if not guarded on either side by an adult with a fire extinguisher.

Thank God the school year was almost over. Third grade had been far less nerve-wracking, as we'd had a much more understanding teacher. And the fifth grade teacher was supposedly one of the most laid-back. So Jack's dad and I had chosen to tough out fourth grade. But Jack's dad didn't have to go on field trips.

"...Go...."

Maybe he really did have to go by now.

That was when I made my mistake. All I had to do was to go with him.

But I didn't, because I wanted Ms. Scarborough to see that he could be trusted to go to the bathroom by himself.

"All right," I said. I pointed to the wood-shingled administrative building I had seen when we disembarked. It was the only man-made structure in evidence and I assumed it was where there would be public bathrooms. Jack would be in my line of sight except for the time when he was actually holding his penis in his hand. "Be careful, okay?"

Jack's Asperger's Syndrome diagnosis put him at the higher end of the autistic spectrum. At home he was just Jack: an easy-going kid if you followed his rules, which wasn't difficult in a big house with three adults and only one child. Everything he did, from talking to himself to leaving toothpaste where no toothpaste had ever gone before, was normal — for him.

I watched as he waddled across the meadow with his jerky gait, legs sticking out at 45 degree angles behind him, until I was distracted by Ms. Scarborough's next announcement. "It's time for the lecture!" I hoped she'd brought her Robitussin. "I want you to listen to Candy!" was how she introduced the island's resident ecologist.

Jack would have been obsessed by the coincidence if he'd stayed: he usually had a personal aide in the classroom whose name was Candy, but I'd given her the day off.

Ecologist Candy was very young, with a pert nose and blonde hair that danced in the wind. She was also tragically unequipped with either microphone or baseball bat, and so she, too, had to shout if she wanted to be heard by all three classes in attendance. Still, she lectured passionately about our overuse of pesticides and preservatives, our failure to recycle and to compost, our essential heartlessness. She was addressing the earth's last hope: the generation that must call forth unprecedented wheat from the fields, must sew closed the gash in the ozone layer, and finally harness the power of the sun.

I knew Jack's M.O. He would hide in the bathroom until exactly time to eat lunch. *Not on your life, Boychik.* I'd go after him before that.

***

But somehow — and this was unlike me — I lost track of time.

Emily and her sidekick Sophie told me about their new heroine, Tyra Banks ("She has her own TV show now!"), until Emily's mother interrupted. "You're getting all the wrong values from her."

The pronoun "her" struck me as ambiguous.

Laurie Batarski was also an alpha female, but of a less appealing sort. She was Ms. Scarborough's chum, and also a cruelly inventive fundraiser who could have demanded parents' help in selling chocolate to diabetics, and she had a chokehold on classroom politics.

I remembered her censure later, but not much else; although I must have checked my watch repeatedly, because I always did, the numbers didn't stick with me. I helped a couple of other boys and then began filling in the wings of a California least tern with an improbable violet, when suddenly Kristin Scarborough was screaming, "It's time to clean up! If we don't eat lunch now we won't have time to hike to the top and back!"

While Kristin ran around our table like a sheepdog, barking orders and collecting art projects, I beat my crayon against my palm a few times before announcing to no one in particular, "Jack went to the boys' room. I'm going to go get him."

God only knew what he was up to. Staring at the graffiti on the wall. Or maybe he'd never found the boys' room, even though I *had* seen him disappear into the side of the building. At any rate, I had to find him. So I put my purse on my shoulder and trekked across the meadow. If I had to stand at the restroom door and shout his name, it wouldn't be the first time. I had been proud of him when at age eight he had refused to go into the ladies' room with me. I worried about his safety, but any move toward independence was worth some risk.

I weaved my way through the milling public school classes, now breaking up for their own lunch. Jack's dad and I had toured a number of special needs pre-school facilities, which were understaffed, and which we rated about a notch above the state prison system in aesthetics and upkeep. And so we squeezed Jack's octagonal needs into the pentagonal hole that was the Pathways School, with its small class size and expensive computer lab. But the public school teachers, with classes twice as large as Pathways', had better control over their students.

The bathrooms were just where I thought they'd be: on the side of the office, hidden by an L-shaped wall creating a semi-private passageway to two doors. I knocked on the door of the men's room. No answer. I knocked again. This time a gruff male voice called back, "It's open."

"Are there any kids in there?" I asked.

A moment later the ranger who had greeted me at the shore emerged, zipping his fly. "Not that I saw. You know, y'all shouldn't let these kids run around unsoopervised if they can't go to the john by themselves."

"I — I'm sorry," I said.

His grouchiness dissolved. "They's slippery devils, ain't they?" He had red veins in his nose and crowded, yellow-stained teeth. "Well, he can't get far 'less he has a canoe. What's he look like?"

"Small for his age, black hair, pale skin, big eyes. Grayish."

"Looks like you, then," he said. He winked, but then he passed me with an impatient grunt, and turned into the administration building.

The next place to look was among the other schoolchildren. That would be like Jack, always eager to introduce himself to new people. Suddenly I saw the naïveté of my frequent warnings about strangers.

"Anna!"

Raven Fernandez was jogging toward me, crossing the grassy divide between the schools. Raven was the third chaperone mom, and one of the few women at the school I counted as a friend. Most of the others were cowed by Emily's mother, Laurie, who hated me both for bringing the stigma of autism to the school and for being the only woman who didn't wear jeans every day. I was too busy to serve on her committees and too proud to kiss her behind.

"Scarborough's having a meltdown," she panted. Raven was in remission from breast cancer, but she was still weak from chemo and lost in clothes that had fit her not long ago. "But with good reason for once." She stopped to catch her breath.

"What is it?"

"Three of the boys are missing. Tyler, Dylan and Cesar."

A ball dropped from my throat down to the bottom of my stomach. Raven must have seen what I was feeling in my face.

"Isn't Jack with you?" she asked.

He was not.

CHAPTER TWO
IT'S A JUNGLE OUT THERE

"Okay, so it's Tyler, Cesar, Dylan and Jack." Raven pulled down on the bottom of her sweatshirt.

She had to be relieved that her own son was not on the MIA list. But for me the news wasn't necessarily all bad. If Jack were missing, that was a disaster. If *four* boys were missing, that was misbehavior — misbehavior that Jack had been invited *to join*. But I didn't expect Raven to understand the logic of the Asperger's Syndrome mother.

"Ms. Scarborough told me that we should talk to the rangers," Raven said, pointing to the lodge behind me.

Making the boys absent status official put a large dent into my fantasy of Jack's sudden acceptance into the fraternity of mischief-makers.

"Is there a problem?" A long-legged teacher from one of the other schools came over to us. He had a plaid Thermos in one hand, the detached red cup in his other.

"Four of our boys are missing," Raven said. I wished she'd stop using that word. Every other Lifetime movie had the word "missing" in it.

The teacher tucked the Thermos under his arm, and drained the cup in one swallow. "I'll come with you."

I was grateful for his help but didn't like the tone of his voice. Too concerned.

The three of us went into the lodge. Inside, there was a bulletin board covered with flyers, and a plastic rack filled with brochures advertising other national recreation sites. A bosom-high counter separated this outer area from a gum-chewing secretary in the olive green park ranger uniform, who was typing on an IBM Selectric.

"Can I help you?" she asked in a voice that implied that she hoped the answer was no.

I let Raven do the talking.

"How long have they been gone?" the secretary asked. *Crack,* went the gum.

It couldn't have been more than a few minutes since Jack had left for the bathroom. I wouldn't have let him out of my sight for longer than that. Would I? I squeezed my forehead. Time was both distended and compressed. All I could think was, *I don't know where he is, I don't know where he is.*

Out of the secretary's view, behind the barrier, Raven squeezed my arm. "A little over an hour," she said.

"Then we have to go to search party status." The secretary yanked the paper from her Selectric and then, in the manner of a waiter avoiding customers at a table, she walked without looking at any of us into another room. "It's almost always a prank. Caregiver error."

"I'm not sure it's been that long," Raven admitted in a whisper to the other schoolteacher. "But I didn't want them to make us wait, you know, if there's a minimum time before they initiate some protocol or something."

He nodded and unscrewed the Thermos cup again. "Want some coffee? Some baby carrots?" He reached for his back pocket and withdrew a Ziploc bag. Raven and I simultaneously shook our heads, though I almost never refused coffee.

"I feel guilty," the teacher said. "I thought I saw some boys wander off towards the trees a little while ago, but I wasn't paying that much attention. I'm really sorry. I was pretty busy with my own class." He munched thoughtfully on a carrot. "I have so much respect for you parents. At least I get summers off. The pressure never lets up on you. Even when they go to college — "

"My friend does need coffee," Raven interrupted him. "But we can't take *yours.*" She plucked at the sleeve of my blazer and, with the charming chutzpah I always admired, pulled me into the room adjoining the main office, though it was obviously not open to the public.

It was a rustic lounge, and there was a coffee pot there, but the muddy brown contents sitting at the bottom looked as though it would have made a viable substitute for Ipecac.

Raven didn't want coffee, though: She was trying to protect me from Ms. Scarborough, whom she'd seen approach, and who burst into the main office at just this moment. "What's going on?" we heard her shout.

"I've called the police," the secretary said wearily.

"I don't want my name on any report!" Ms. Scarborough wailed.

"I can't do anything about that, Ma'am," the secretary replied.

A final squawk: "I told the principal last fall that it was a mistake to keep that Kagen boy on!"

Raven shuddered on my behalf. "Never mind Scarlett O'Hatred," she said. "This island is reeking with bad karma."

"What do you mean?"

She was going through the motions of looking for cups. "You've heard that story, haven't you? About the cult that lived here in the eighties."

I was having a little trouble accessing my personal hard drive. Then I remembered being let out of school early one day, back in tenth grade. "The Healerists," I said. "They occupied the island like the Native-Americans did Alcatraz."

"What was the guy's name?" Raven asked herself, pounding her fist against her scalp, where her hair was starting to grow in again. "Merrick. Theodore Merrick."

"I remember," I said, to keep up my end of the conversation. "He only had about thirty followers."

Raven found a mug on a corner table but after peering over its rim put it back. "The ATF came out and blew 'em all away," she said in that hushed, triumphant tone in which people sometimes spread scandal. "They were supposed to have a big cache of weapons but it turned out that they were unarmed." She went rambling on, nervous and trying to distract us both. "This Merrick, the Healerist honcho, was just a preacher and writer. Kept mountains of journals. Then supposedly he brought a heroin addict back to life after he O.D.'ed and a bunch of people flocked around him. You know what I think? I think it if it hadn't been for the Jonestown massacre, the shoot-out never would have happened. Merrick was almost an idiot savant." She threw out her arms in frustration at government screw-ups, and then, in this crucifixion stance, she froze. "I'm sorry," she said. "I didn't mean — "

"No, of course not." If I took offense at every inadvertent remark I'd have to live on an island myself, if not under a rock.

"It's good they've called the police," Raven said.

The police. Yes. Good. The San Francisco police department had jurisdiction, although it was Federal land. But now, God forgive me, I thought, *Alex will know.*

Alex was Jack's dad and, for better or worse, my husband. He'd be sitting in his wood-paneled office, under the seal of the consolidated city and county of San Francisco, at his huge oak desk, flanked by the California and United States flags. A team of ADAs, men and women alike in drab single-breasted suits, would be forming a semi-circle around him, holding their breath until he took off his reading glasses to signify that he was ready to comment on the documents he'd been examining.

But I told myself not to panic about him yet. It was on a floor below that the police dispatcher listened to incoming calls. By the time someone that far down in the food chain made the connection of the name "Jacob aka Jack Kagen" to *the* Kagen upstairs, Jack would be found.

"Let's go talk to the ranger again," I said.

The ranger was just hanging up the secretary's phone. "Damn budget cuts. You better start callin' them parents. I'll find out the names."

"Okay, Ed." The secretary sighed deeply, removing her gum to wrap in its birth foil.

"What budget cuts?" I asked.

Ed was deliberately nonchalant. "Oh, it's nothing. The department don't have a helicopter no more." Help, he explained, would have to come by boat — one of the Marine Units that patrolled San Francisco Bay within a one-mile radius of the county's edge. Depending on where the boats were, it could be an hour, or....

When Ed told me this, I squeezed my eyes shut.

He abruptly changed his estimate. "Aw, they'll be here in forty minutes."

Behind my closed eyes I heard Alex's Columbia School of Broadcasting voice, explaining to a rapt and heart-broken audience how those budget cuts *in law enforcement* had cost him the life of his only child.

But however angry Alex would be with me for letting this happen, I needed him here. Alex could frighten the sea into giving up its dead; he could certainly force this island into giving up its children.

Ed addressed Raven. "Ma'am, you look like the lady to help me organize the search party. Let's show those bums with badges what citizens can do. This thirty minutes right now makes all the difference."

Ed was not, as I had first thought, a civil servant coasting toward retirement. Underneath the straining buttons of his shirt was the intuition that came from having seen campfires become blazes and finding bodies dead from exposure. It had had him zero in on Raven as his best available deputy, and then, within a short time, it had him lining up every single available adult across the western meadow of Minotaur Island.

He gave us instructions in a deceptively avuncular tone. "We call it working the grid. Think of the island — "

I realized that I was wringing my hands, my fingers so tightly entwined that when I pulled them apart they ached the way my jaw did sometimes after a night spent grinding my teeth.

"Keep walking straight ahead — "

Just that morning I had resented so much about Jack: the inflexible bedtime routine that kept me chained to the house at night, the headlock I had to use to brush his teeth, the constant stimming. Why hadn't I realized how much worse things could be, just the way everyone was always telling me?

"They's only two real trails — "

Laurie Batarski switched places with another volunteer which put her within my hearing distance. "It's such a sad situation. That poor boy. It's just too bad that he has to expose other kids to danger."

Ms. Scarborough was hanging back from the group, biting on her index finger. "Ma'am, take your place in the line," Ed ordered her. "We need everyone. "

"Everyone" ranged from a gray-haired, weather-beaten man who looked like an extra in a John Ford film to Candy-the-ecologist, hardly old enough to bear a child, to the long-legged teacher. Scarborough, now with two fingers in her mouth, and Laurie Batarski, looked put-upon and smug.

Minotaur Island couldn't be more than a few square miles in area. But were there poisonous reptiles out there? Tree branches so high that a child who managed to reach one could fall to his death? Even child molesters who'd been here since Merrick's day, hiding in one of the caves that gave the island its name, living on squirrels and stolen school lunches?

At Ed's signal, we started marching east.

***

I no longer looked at my watch. I only knew that time was passing.

But soon our group had reached the end of the meadow where dense shrubbery marked the beginning of the forested area, and where the ground began to incline steeply. After that, I quickly lost sight of the others; my last glimpse of Raven was her loden green sweatshirt, which blended immediately into the surrounding foliage.

Suddenly I, too, was encased in trees: eucalyptus, acacias and pines were the ones I recognized. I had to squeeze between them, or go around them, and I tried to keep track, to zig and then to zag, but after a while I gave up and just pushed forward.

My black suede boots no longer seemed like an assertive fashion statement but yet another symptom of everything that was wrong with me as a mother, for it was hard to keep from slipping on tree roots, and I could feel the points of rock through my soles. I tried not to think, which made me think all the more — thoughts such as how, when the boys were found, Jack and I would be blamed for whatever had started this mess.

Anything to keep from thinking about *not* finding the boys.

I tripped but caught myself with my hand against the bark of a tree.

Thoughts of the other boys. Cesar, Dylan, Tyler. I knew all of them well from the unending stream of plays, songfests, recitals and art shows, where Jack drifted in and out at the edges. In previous years Jack's teachers had done their best to create the illusion that he was participating, and in fact he *had* participated a little more each year....

Cesar ... Dylan ... Tyler.... Actually, I did not know Tyler well, since he'd joined the school so recently, when his family moved to San Francisco. He was a frail-looking child, with translucent skin that revealed a network of veins. In the mornings I saw him hesitating before taking a showy jump from the running board of his mother's black Porsche Cayenne, and she called out to him, "Be careful!"

Dylan.... His birth mother had neglected him until the state had taken him away at age four, when Celia and Ron Shumacher had adopted him. They were in their early fifties and childless, but instead of taking out a second mortgage so that Celia could pump herself full of hormones and carry a donor egg fertilized by Ron, they went out and adopted this high-risk baby, accepting him as a mission from God. Then Dylan surpassed all expectations, growing into a dark, handsome boy with suave manners; the tallest, and most physically developed in the class.

Pine needles poked through the sleeves of my blazer. I wanted to take it off. Didn't want to carry it.

Cesar.... Cesar was gifted. In first grade I'd seen him win a game of "twenty questions" by playing the role of Copernicus. He'd already skipped a grade, but his mother, who believed that Chinese astrology had guided her in his conception, told me that she hesitated to put him another year ahead because he would miss his many friends.

Cesar and Dylan were an unlikely pair, but seemingly inseparable; I always saw them together.

The tip of a thin branch scratched my cheek.

Cesar, Dylan, Tyler ... and Jack. Dylan and Cesar were clever, competent boys. They would protect him. Except that bad things happened to kids all the time — and not all those kids were autistic. *Most* of them weren't.

A thicker branch tip tore a gash in one of my sleeves. The pony holder that I had twisted into my hair at the beginning of the search had slipped away and there was hair in my eyes and hair stuck to my lipstick and when I tried to hold it back with my hand I heard that I was panting. *I should be in better shape than this. Dear God, help me find Jack and I will go to the gym every day.*

Someone was screaming Jack's name. It was me.

Why am I screaming like this? the unscreaming part of me wondered. Then I pressed against two tree trunks, like Samson pushing the pillars of the Philistine temple.

I heard other garbled voices. Were the police finally here? Had another searcher found the boys?

"Mommy!"

He was all I saw at first, twenty feet away, in a tiny patch of sun.

Until then I hadn't let myself think about him dead. I thought I had, but I hadn't.

Again. "Mommy?"

"Jack!"

So I had another chance. To keep my temper, to love him as he was, to remember not just that things could be worse, but how much worse.

Jack came toward me. He was leading the others.

He stumbled on a rock but he, too, was able to grab a tree trunk to keep from falling. One of the boys behind him snickered but quickly caught himself, and Jack's smile was solar-powered.

I registered the other boys: hulking Dylan, and Cesar, smaller, brown-haired and blue-eyed. But Tyler wasn't with them.

Then I was hugging Jack, and thinking of nothing but his still-soft boy flesh in my arms and against my cheek. Dylan and Cesar looked away at this mushiness. The stereotype has it that autistics fear touch. Jack had always been a cuddly boy.

I released Jack and promptly realized that I was lost. "How did you find me?" I asked him, since it was obvious that he was the one responsible for that.

"I smelled your perfume," he said cheerfully. "Dylan and Cesar are my friends," he added.

"You smelled my perfume," I echoed. "You're amazing." But when I looked at Dylan and Cesar, above Jack's head, I knew immediately that something was wrong. "A lot of people are looking for you boys. We'd better let them know you're okay."

"Not everyone's okay, Mrs. Kagen," Dylan said, in a guarded version of his usual *politesse.*

"Why?" I settled my weight evenly. "Who's not okay?"

As if I couldn't do the math.

Jack kept smiling, while Cesar looked worriedly at Dylan — who kept his eyes fixed on me. "We'd better show you." Dylan said. "We'd better hurry." He frowned and then nudged Jack — just a little roughly, I thought — on the shoulder. "C'mon."

Suddenly we were no longer alone. Perhaps drawn by the concentration of our voices, other searchers were finding us. Ms. Scarborough, Raven, and Park Ranger Ed were among them. We all stood about awkwardly, trying to get our footing on the uneven terrain.

Jack didn't greet the newcomers, as he usually would have. As our numbers increased he lost the cheerful demeanor he'd had when he'd first found me. I tried to cling to the first euphoria of finding him, but it was slipping away, like the pebbles on the hill under the soles of my boots.

"C'mon, Jack," Dylan prompted again, in a fatherly way. He nudged him again with his elbow, this time more gently.

Jack turned and began heading back in the direction whence they had come. Dylan and Cesar attached themselves to him, one on each side, but a little behind, as the way was so narrow. I immediately inserted myself behind the three of them. The other adults trailed after. I wished I could brag about Jack finding his way in this baffling territory. He could distinguish among the subtlest design of branches, or remember the tiniest weed. He'd remember on which tree two of the Healerists had carved their initials.

The sun grew brighter, as the trees suddenly spread out. Ahead there were two or three yards of rocky, bare yellow earth, spotted with a few stubby wildflowers, some fallen branches, and then a sharp incline. I was disoriented, looking across the valley ahead with no sense of how steep the drop, or how far away the other side was. I clutched Jack's hand. And then I was being jostled, and a horde of people in navy blue appeared out of nowhere, bringing an oceanful of static with them. As the crowd grew denser, I fought the urge to flee with a dreadful need to know, and moved, with a few others, like Raven and Ranger Ed, toward the abyss. Dylan and Cesar were creeping toward the edge, too; the depth of what lay behind was further obscured by a few rocks large enough to be called boulders.

I gripped Jack's hand more tightly. He was talking to himself wildly, and more loudly than usual. I was surrounded by police officers now, overpowered by the static from their radios, broken by crisp, authoritative words.

I started to lean over the boulders, which weren't high enough to offer any protection, just to partially block the view. The descent was neither sharp nor deep after all. It wasn't an abyss, just a shallow scoop in the ground.

"Nuh-nuh-nuh-nuh-nuh-nuh." Jack's speech descended into nonsense sounds, while I let out a breath I hadn't known I was holding.

But Ms. Scarborough screamed. She screamed loud and long, drowning out static and Jack's babbling alike.

At the bottom of the gully lay Tyler, face down. Several people, including me, shouted his name, but he didn't move.

***

Three of the police officers skittered quickly down the incline. "I know CPR," Ed shouted after them.

"We've got it, sir," said one of the cops who stayed behind. I inferred that he was the one in charge since, instead of a navy blue uniform, he wore a light blue shirt and tie, with a holstered weapon and a large badge on his belt. He called out, "LaShane, you take it."

But the black policewoman he addressed had already rolled Tyler over and was checking his mouth for blockage to his airway.

"Hey, I know you," this head cop said, looking at me. "You spoke at the Police Education Team banquet a few months ago."

LaShane pumped air into Tyler's mouth while pinching his nostrils together.

I went blank for a moment, and then I remembered. I sometimes took over for Alex when he had to make a speech.

"You're Kagen's wife, aren't you?" He was short and olive-complected, with a moustache and unibrow. He pondered me. "You were good," he said. "You talked about that policeman in your neighborhood who kinda kept an extra watch on your house after — uh, after your dad left."

I didn't remember any of my speech at that moment, but I murmured, "Thank you. I'm glad to get a chance to meet you personally." I stuck out my hand, a politician's wife to the end.

"I get sick of hearing all the ragging on cops. You understand. But hey — work to do."

"Yes, Officer —?"

"Lieutenant Robbins. Jerome Robbins."

"You're kidding," I said. "Any relation?"

"To whom?"

"It's not important." I dropped his hand, because mine was so damp that I was embarrassed.

Lieutenant Robbins turned to a clean page in a notepad he had been holding, and called down to LaShane, "What response?"

"Nothing."

"Why aren't paramedics here?" Robbins asked irritably.

"They're on the fire boat," another policewoman said.

"Well, *that* was smart," Robbins barked. "What genius arranged that?"

There was some throat-clearing. Someone positioned a safe distance behind us offered, "We didn't know there was a medical emergency."

Robbins moved on. "I want the scene secure," he commanded. He turned to me again, as though having seen me before made me the resident expert. "Were you all up here for a field trip?"

"No," I answered, glad for the necessity of conversation. "I mean, we were down at the picnic tables, three fourth grade classes, and several of the boys wandered off. We called you and then — " I didn't want to rob Ed of his due, and I pointed — "the park ranger here called the SFPD. My son turned up with the two other boys just a few minutes ago."

Robbins had opened his notebook again. "Okay. Ennis, Wesley, get tape. Give me a thirty foot perimeter, and everyone else out so we don't lose any more footprints. Or get any we don't want. Move it! You say some boys wandered off, Mrs. Kagen?"

Kristin shoved her way through the crowd to my side, "It was her son," she said shrilly. "He took the boys off."

"You don't know that!" I snapped. Just a few feet away Dylan and Cesar stood. Dylan's black eyes were disturbingly composed. Next to him, Cesar looked small and too frightened to speak.

"Lieutenant!" I heard the policewoman call from below. "I'm still not getting a response."

"Where are those fucking paramedics!" Robbins burst out.

"They'll have trouble finding us," Ed grumbled.

"I can tell you what happened, Officer," Dylan said.

Jack's safe. Jack's safe, I told myself. And the paramedics would have all those injectable things that brought people around. No one could die from skidding a few feet down a 30 degree slope.

Kristin was taking it hard. After singling me out she had stepped back and shoved a record three fingers in her mouth.

"All right, son," Lieutenant Robbins said. "Bring it."

"Lieutenant!" the policewoman called from below us. The word ended in a sob.

"What's your name, son?"

"Dylan Shumacher. I'm ten."

Robbins raised his unibrow at this claim but kept writing.

"We came up here — "

"We came up here," Jack repeated. "Up here...."

"All together," Dylan went on, with an impatient glance at Jack. Then he shook his head sorrowfully. "Tyler took Jack's pawn away."

"Huh?" was Lieutenant Robbins's response.

"Jack has a chess piece he carries in his pocket," I told him.

This must have been a new one. "Why?"

"He's — he's — " I didn't want to say it in front of so many strangers. I hadn't had "the talk" with Jack about his disorder. I was planning to — when he was thirty. "Jack has Asperger's Syndrome," I explained. "The chess piece calms him down. He keeps it in his pocket and — "

"Mrs. Kagen, I'd prefer you let Dylan tell the story."

But he won't tell it right. At the same time I was relieved that I didn't have to give a seminar on self-stimulation. Having the pawn to rub helped Jack focus energy that otherwise would express itself in whole-body movements.

"We told him not to." Cesar spoke for the first time since the boys had reappeared.

"We did," Dylan agreed, folding his hands in front of his belt buckle. He was wearing a black turtleneck. He must have been hot as hell in it. "Tyler teased him with it." Dylan demonstrated, dangling an invisible pawn in the air and snapping it out of reach.

Down in the gully, policewoman LaShane was crying and her two fellow officers were comforting her. Lieutenant Robbins flipped closed his notepad and took the slope in what seemed no more than four strides. "Officer Hodges, if you could let me see the boy."

LaShane Hodges wiped her cheeks with her cuff and un-straddled Tyler. Lieutenant Robbins respectfully patted him down. Even as a layperson, it was obvious to me now that he was dead. His eyes were open, staring. There was no soul in this body, and nothing to inject to bring it back.

The full horror of that would take a while to sink in.

"Is this what you're talking about, son?" Robbins asked. He held up the black pawn.

"Yes, sir," Dylan called back. "We're here to help, sir."

"We tried to stop him," Cesar piped up again.

"My pawn!" Jack shouted. "Pawn...."

He started to run down toward it but another police officer grabbed him by the arm. "Stay here."

I wanted to lash out at the policeman but I held back. Serious shit was coming down now.

Dylan went on, apologetic but composed. "So Tyler was, well, he was holding out Jack's pawn there and then pulling it back. Over and over again. Jack started crying."

"What're these for?" Another office pointed to three branches, arranged in a neat triangle.

"We were going to use them for walking sticks," Cesar explained.

"We were getting tired," Dylan said.

Then both boys hesitated.

"Jack tried to attack Tyler with his stick," Cesar finally admitted. He looked at Dylan.

"We got it away from him," his friend said, shrugging modestly. "But Jack pushed Tyler real hard. I didn't know he was so strong."

As Dylan said this last he looked straight at me. I became aware of the absolute stillness among the entire group. Cesar's eyes looked unusually big in his face. Lieutenant Robbins had stopped writing. There was no more sound from the gully.

I heard the yank of yellow police tape from a roll, then a bird chirp. I felt the wind go across my neck and welcomed the momentary coolness.

"Tyler rolled down the hill," Dylan said. "We didn't think Jack had killed him."

CHAPTER THREE
THERE'S GOLD IN THEM THAR HILLS

Nearly an hour had passed. Jack and I sat next to each other in the employee lounge in the ranger station.

"I need my pawn back!" Jack cried yet again. "Pawn back...."

His hand fluttered away when I tried to take it.

The paramedics had arrived on the fire boat. Even as Dylan had been accusing Jack of murder they'd been hauling their equipment up the hill. When I saw them coming I'd commandeered this space for Jack and myself with the help of both Lieutenant Robbins and Ed, expressing my fear that Jack might be subject to a major meltdown as the scene got more hectic. Whatever shame Jack and I had brought on the great name of Kagen, for the time being that name still had sway.

Lieutenant Robbins had even used another private moment with me to express his appreciation for my involvement with the Police Education Team. "We didn't think you'd be so young, or — " He interrupted himself to return to the crisis at hand.

Now Jack was sinking deeper into the fantasy world of his favorite television show, *Crime Conquerors,* and private jokes. I wasn't doing much better. There was a mural on the wall across from us, depicting the Bay with its islands in lushest, variegated shades of green.

Then Alex filled the doorway.

I felt my thighs tense, but I didn't get up.

I wanted to throw my arms around him, but I knew I couldn't.

I wondered if he were thinking about how this would affect his re-election in the fall.

Alex stood a mighty five-ten to my five-three. I had married him when he was a vigorous forty-one, not just the heir to prestigious fortunes made in white bread (father's family) and leather goods (mother's), but an assistant district attorney who was on the Democratic Central Committee and whose political future shone like one of those searchlights that draw you to a big auto sale in the suburbs. He was my criminal law professor for the six weeks that I endured law school, before abandoning it to pursue a Masters in psychology.

But time had wrought changes in us both. Alex's hairline remained untouched, and only two flags of gray had appeared at his temples, reminding me of Hermes's winged cap. But his face was becoming jowly, and there were bags under his eyes. Those eyes were chronically bloodshot; his workaholic schedule had increased while the hours of the day had not. The most striking change was the thirty pounds he had gained since we met, though he carried it well.

He was still an attractive man. The problem was that I was no longer attracted *to* him. Not physically. His physical attractions had never been the main draw, though. I had always suffered from the female equivalent of the Madonna-Whore complex: the Daddy-Stud complex.

A Dad was a pal, and they made good boyfriends. In my undergrad days I'd had my share. Today we would have been called "friends with benefits," even though the benefits accrued, if they accrued at all, to the men. I was in it for reasons more spiritual than temporal: The lure for me was companionship, someone with whom to debate the merits of new Broadway plays, and to have a date to bring on occasions when a date was indicated. Like the short-bearded philosophy grad student who was my TA sophomore year. We didn't have intercourse often, but he was so … sensitive.

Sex with a Dad-type was unimaginative and as un-messy as possible. Dad-sex didn't need to be frequent. It didn't really need to happen at all: It was just for form's sake.

Studs were strong but dangerous, and not very endearing. Studs didn't converse much, not because they couldn't, but because they didn't come to philosophize. They came to fuck.

They never stayed the night, and I didn't want them to. And after we fucked, they left.

My undergrad boyfriends may have filled the Daddy role, but they were weak. The real Daddy would make me whole.

I thought it was Alex. He was the ultimate daddy: older, rich and well-connected. I'd had enough of Studs. If I wanted an orgasm I knew how to get one, and I liked having sex with Alex well enough. He made no bizarre, impossible requests like anal sex or having one of my girlfriends join us. I liked to sense his satisfaction afterwards, and to feel that I had, at the end of the day, (literally) done something for him.

But after Jack sex was never the same. Although it would be more than another two years before Jack's diagnosis, by the time he was six months old our unease had begun, a nameless anxiety that seeped into all our relations.

Alex said now that he knew about Jack from the beginning, but that was because he could rewrite history better than the old Politburo. The way I remembered it, *I* was the one who predicted disaster, but like Cassandra, would not be believed. I didn't blame Alex. I hadn't wanted him to believe me. I wanted him to talk me out of it.

It wasn't until Jack was almost three that I took him to see the good Dr. Wolichek, who cast the deciding vote. One of her staff called later to see if I wanted to volunteer Jack for a medication study. My, "No thank you," was a polite version of, "Go fuck yourself."

During work hours Alex usually had two assistants with him, treated not as servants but as mentees. If they brought him coffee which he drank black and to excess, or took notes for him, it was usually because they anticipated his need or responded to the most discreet hint.

But he had come to Minotaur Island alone.

Jack jumped up and ran to him. "Daddy, they took my pawn!" he said. "Fix it...."

"Sounds like there are a lot of things to fix," he said grimly, looking at me over Jack's head as he ruffled his son's hair. "I talked to the police out there." He made a line of his thin lips.

"You don't believe those boys' story, do you?"

"I don't know what to believe yet." His eyes scanned the dilapidated lounge, as if checking for wire taps. "They're treating us pretty much with kid gloves," he said. "Jack, and — uh, my position...." He coughed into his fist. "All those officers out there know they'll be dealing with my department for a long time to come."

"Why don't we ask Jack what happened?" I snapped. *Now that it's quiet he'll be able to focus ... I hope.*

"Fine." He tugged his trouser legs up and sat. "What happened, Master Jack?"

"Tyler took my pawn," Jack said plaintively. "I want it back. Back...."

"I'll get it back for you," Alex said firmly. "You've got to tell me and your Mom why you went up there in the first place."

"My friends asked me to. Dylan, Ces — "

"Start from the beginning. Where were you?"

"Dylan, Cesar, Tyler...."

Tyler. I shuddered at the memory of the small body, covered with dust, with the policewoman pumping his chest.

"Where were you, Jack?"

"In the bathroom. Dylan, Cesar, Tyler...."

I half-expected Alex to explode at me, "You let Jack go to the bathroom by himself?" He and I had agreed that this was acceptable policy, but this was another piece of history he could easily rewrite. Alex, though, was keeping his eyes on the prize, the prize being the facts, ma'am, the facts. "You were in the bathroom."

"Dylan, Cesar, Tyler — "

My head was starting to pound.

"—came in and asked me to go with them!"

"Why?" Alex leaned forward, supporting himself with his hands on his thighs.

"It's supposed to be a secret. Secret."

Alex looked over Jack's head at me. We worked so hard to help Jack understand the social niceties. Only after becoming his mother had I learned how impossible they were to codify.

"This isn't a secret," Alex said firmly. "This ... is ... *different*."

I saw a way in. "This is like when you hid Daddy's glasses."

Jack was startled to attention. Alex had never come closer to spanking him than on that Sunday night, when he had to be in court the next morning at 9 a.m. for the arraignment of an alleged serial rapist and had no back-up pair. Now he kept two extras, hidden and locked up.

Alex clasped his hands between his knees. "Start with why you and the other boys left the class."

"We went to find buried treasure," Jack said. "Dylan said pirates had left it!"

That was typical of the kind of puerile story that would appeal to Jack, and it could well be what the other boys had told him. Maybe they were going to take Jack out in the woods and leave him stranded there.... No, they'd know that he was the one who could find his way in *and* out. But they might have planned....

"So Dylan asked you to go." Alex picked up the thread.

"Yyyeessss." Jack had found a pencil somewhere. He quickly turned it into an airplane.

"Dylan or Cesar? Or Tyler?"

"Yyyeessss."

"Alex." I put my hand on his knee. "You're not trying to trap a suspect."

Alex tapped his knuckles against his teeth.

"There's gold in them thar hills!" Jack erupted, following this outburst with his own brand of wild giggling. I sighed, remembering the school play from a few months before about the California Gold Rush.

"There's gold in them thar hills!" had been the one line that Scarborough had condescended to give him, though he memorized better than anyone in the school. "Where's my pawn? I need my pawn! My pawn...."

He's regressing. Well, it was normal to be traumatized. Everyone was traumatized. The problem was that Jack didn't deal with stress the way other kids would, let alone adults. His reaction was normal but he always expressed his reactions, good and bad, *abnormally,* scaring people who didn't know him. Outside I was certain that the adults were scrambling through pockets or purses for pills, or even flasks, or falling into each other's arms and crying, while the children got into unprovoked fights. But no one else was barnstorming for invisible crowds with a pencil-turned-biplane.

"Tell me about the gold," Alex tried.But before Jack could answer — if he had been going to answer with anything new — I heard a clearing throat and a light tap on the open door. Lieutenant Robbins stood in the entryway.

"Mr. Kagen." He had been deferential to me, but he addressed Alex with outright awe.

Alex stood immediately. "Is the crime scene secure?"

"Yes, sir."

"And what about — " Alex's glance darted over to Jack who was staring cross-eyed at the pencil. Alex was never embarrassed by Jack's stereotypical behavior; he wore his son like one of his many dark Brioni suits. "Can we step outside?" It wasn't really a question.

"Of course, sir. You all right, Mrs. Kagen? I'm sure we could get you something."

You wouldn't have a Valium on you, would you? Once in a while I dipped into a small, secret stash. "I'm fine. But thank you." Then I stood, too. "Jack, will you be okay for a few minutes?" I knew that the menfolk would be talking about what happened and I wasn't going to be left out.

"We have to be home for *Crime Conquerors.*"

"You know Mairead will tape it for you." Mairead was our nanny.

"I need to see it! Montel will be fighting Deathtania...."

I didn't know what it meant for feminism that the worst evildoers on *Crime Conquerors* were female. Overall I judged it a lateral move.

I rubbed his back. "I'll get you home for the show," I promised. I had resumed my careful clock-watching. It was only 1 pm — earlier than I would have thought given all that had happened — and surely we'd be back well before 4:30.

Jack trusted me to come through. Enough so that he dropped to the grimy linoleum floor where the pencil and a newfound penny became

Max and Morgan who, along with Montel, were two more of the five fighting Crime Conquerors, chosen by the Mighty Quaso to defend the earth.

When Jack had first started using action figures, shortly before turning six, I was thrilled. Representative play! It was another year before I learned that his meticulous re-enactment of that day's episode of *Crime Conquerors* was called "preservative scripting," and was a classic feature of Asperger's Syndrome.

I stepped out of the ranger's lounge to see my husband and Lieutenant Robbins talking at the far end of the administrative counter. Two other officers were talking on cell phones and through the screen door I could see a rectangle of people, many in a variety of uniforms: navy blue, olive green and khaki.

Alex's back was to me but Robbins's eyes moved over to mine and then dropped guiltily. "Maybe you could explain to Mrs. Kagen."

Alex turned to me slowly. "We have to put a 5150 hold on Jack," he said.

The Lieutenant probably hadn't expected me to know what that was. A "5150" — the number came from the section in the state criminal code — was a provision that allowed certain authorities, under certain circumstances, to commit a person to a psychiatric facility for up to 72 hours. I myself was licensed as an MFT, a Marriage and Family Therapist, and as such I had the authority to put a 5150 hold on a client.

"Are you kidding? You can't put him in a psych ward!"

"It won't be as bad as it sounds," Alex said, which meant, *Don't make trouble.*

"Now, Mrs. Kagen," Robbins began soothingly, "it's partly for his own protection. *We* know he's not a danger to himself or others — "

"Or *gravely* disabled," I interrupted, invoking the third of the three criteria listed in the California Welfare and Institutions Code.

"But the truth is, and I'll be blunt, this crowd wants something done." Robbins indicated the restless people outside the station, which suddenly felt very isolated and thinly built. "We need to get him out of here, I think, and it'd be much better — "

"Than taking him downtown," Alex finished. "It'll be a formality. We can take him to St. Sair's, can't we, Officer?"

"Of course, Mr. Kagen. Since you have private insurance."

"He'll come unspooled!" I protested.

Alex patted Robbins on the arm. Then he added conspiratorially, "Let me speak to my wife alone for a moment, Lieutenant." *You know how women are.*

Alex drew me next to one of the windows.

"Do you know what's going on out there?" He tugged my elbow, forcing me to look outside.

"I have a pretty good idea," I said.

But I hadn't. Now that I had the full view, I saw that the western side of the island that had quietly waited for the arrival of schoolchildren a few hours before had become a chaotic gathering of parents, reporters, firemen, and rangers. Two SFPD boats were docked one either side of the pier, while a Coast Guard cutter floated some distance away.

I could easily imagine how a spontaneous phone tree could have brought out parents from other grades, their friends, and people who knew Tyler's family, the Gaineses, from outside the school.

The new wave of police had brought with them portable metal barriers with which they were improvising a roadway across the meadow to the dock. Two uniformed officers were fully engaged in herding the looky-loos behind the barriers. *Damn it all,* I thought miserably. *If they don't clear this island in another hour people are going to be selling logo t-shirts.*

"They're putting a ten-year-old boy in a body bag," Alex said. "Even as we speak. And Jack might be the one responsible for his death."

"You can't believe he killed him."

I kept my voice down, but Alex shushed me anyway. "I think the worst case here is involuntary manslaughter."

"*What?*"

"No, of course I don't 'believe,'" he snapped. "Now listen to me. I'm trying to keep control of the situation without appearing to use my influence inappropriately. Can you follow that?"

"Of course I can 'follow' that! Would you stop — " I had been going to finish *treating me like a four-year-old* but I saw how counter-productive it would be. "I'm sorry. I trust you."

That placated him enough to whisper, "It's to keep him from something worse."

It was then I saw the body bag he'd spoken of. It was the color of an avocado peel. It lay on a gurney which a fireman pushed from the rear.

Following immediately behind were a man and woman, the man in black pinstripes and the woman in an ivory suit with a peplum and vertical piping on both the jacket and skirt. I remembered it from the Saks catalogue that past fall. Valentino. This was an impromptu funeral procession, with several doleful, bureaucratic types following a few respectful yet close steps behind: a man in a clergyman's collar, an older woman wringing her hands, and another woman I hadn't met before in the park service uniform.

"Look at that," Alex said sternly. "You think we can just take away the TV from Jack for a week, call it a 'consequence,' and forget about this?"

My face must have been visible at the window, because four girls dashed away from the group. It was Emily in the lead, with Sophie, and the two other girls who formed my Gal Pal Gang. "Hi, Jack's mom!" Emily shouted so that I could hear her through the window. She tapped on the glass.

"Get back here!" Kristin Scarborough snarled, uglier than ever.

I nodded. "Go. You'll get in trouble."

Scarborough was chasing after her. Emily laughed and motioned to her friends. They split into pairs and cut a swath around Kristin, disappearing into the mass of children.

I turned back to the procession boarding the boat. Now only the Gaineses were visible. I knew so much about them just from seeing them from behind. Not only were they well-dressed, but they walked calmly and upright, conveying more grief in those dignified poses than if Mrs. Gaines were sobbing and Mr. Gaines were ranting at the sky. I knew so much about them just because they had a child, like me. They must have identified the body; heard the exact time that their son was declared dead. I was sure they wouldn't have been told over the phone. They must have ridden the across the rocky slate water of the Bay with hope.

I would learn more about them before long, including that their gait was misleading. But for that day, all I knew — and this was the only part that never changed — was that Alex and I were the lucky ones.

CHAPTER FOUR
MY FUNNY VALENTINE

There's gold in them thar hills.

During the drive from Fisherman's Wharf to St. Sair's, Jack sat in the rear seat, subvocalizing, and occasionally erupting with the old '49er rallying cry.

"We're getting the V.I.P. treatment." Alex could be as perseverative as Jack, and he kept repeating different versions of this statement, from his first "kid gloves" remark through a muttered "it's all who you know," and a more cheerful "the right name at the right time." Meanwhile, I was almost too preoccupied to ignore his more-than-usually aggressive driving: He seemed to have forgotten the existence of his rearview mirror.

"We've got to get home in time for *Crime Conquerors!*" Jack called out to us.

It was now obvious that we wouldn't. But Lieutenant Robbins had apparently made it clear that it had never been an option to take him straight home, even if Alex were, through an indirect chain of command, Robbins's boss.

This was what Alex had passed on to me as we ferried back apart from the others on the SFPD's marine unit boat. I could see that he was at a bit of a loss. He'd never been involved in a situation like this at such an early stage. Even as a rising lawyer in the D.A. office's homicide division, he was called in after the police filed their reports.

It was hot in Alex's Cadillac, and I turned on the air conditioning, though Alex didn't like it when I fooled around with his control buttons. "Jack would be in police custody under ordinary circumstance. They're trusting us to bring him to the hospital."

"What are we going to do, board a freighter for Argentina? My passport's in my other jacket." We were, in fact, heading south along the Bay, where the ships docked.

"That's just the kind of thing I was talking about," Alex said darkly.

"I'll miss *Crime Conquerors*! Call Mairead! Mairead...."

"What thing?"

"Don't go into your *act*."

"When I'm nervous — " I began apologetically.

"Well, don't be. I've got it under control."

One cruise liner shone bright white against the drab container ships. If only there *were* a way to flee the country, escape to a foreign land where autism really was "a different kind of normal," the way I had recently read someone describe it.

"If it looks like we're getting special treatment, there'll be backlash, against all of us." Then, without either turning on his directional or looking behind him, Alex hopped lanes. Behind us I heard the screech of brakes, then a sharp grind. "Mother-*fucker!*" the other driver shouted. Alex didn't seem to hear.

***

His belief in his own immortality got us to St. Sair's just behind the cops.

In the emergency room, the chief of police, Fred Hsu, shook our hands and mumbled sympathetic but vague remarks such as "unfortunate necessity," and "we'll expedite the process."

We were on a first-name basis from the political circuit, so I pressed him to see if Jack could come home with us soon.

"We'll have to see, Anna," he said.

St. Seraphina's Medical Center, locally known as "St. Sair's," was one of San Francisco's older hospitals, but back in the 90s it had been heavily remodeled in mauve, the color of nasturtiums and yuppies. It was a small hospital for middle-class diseases. The emergency room had newly upholstered chairs, fresh magazines and at least a partial view of the hills rising to Pacific Heights.

Fred left us with the promise to check back soon.

Robbins and the rest of the Marine Unit were already gone. I watched Alex fill out paperwork on a clipboard. Then there was a nurse in pink scrubs, wearing her surgical mask as if Asperger's were contagious.

I got down on one knee to talk to my son. Alex rested a hand on Jack's shoulder. "Jack, we're going to wait for you while you talk to a doctor," I said. Alex and I had divided the labors of raising him mostly by tacit agreement, and though Alex believed that psychotherapy was about as effective as bleeding patients, he left such things as "little pep talks" to me.

But as was so often the case with Jack, the usual tools of my trade didn't work. So when I said, "Just be yourself," it was really for the sake of the nurse in pink scrubs, because the phrase would be meaningless to Jack, and even I thought it was extremely hypocritical. In how many situations and with what people can one actually *be oneself?* At work? At big family dinners?

Pink Scrubs took him behind double doors that led to the back, and we settled in for the wait.

The focal point of the ER, besides a couple of crying babies, was a young woman who must have strained her back, for she was standing slightly bent over, propping her head on the end of a roll of paper towels. *No one has suffered as I have*, her expression said, while her husband stroked her arm.

Alex sat with his briefcase on his lap. The silence between us was Pinteresque: dangerous and hard to fathom. But it was less than five minutes before he got out his cell phone and went out into the ambulance entrance. Through the plate glass window I saw him pacing up and down the driveway.

After the third phone call he wandered back into the waiting room. "They're taking statements from the boys. That big one — Dylan — he says they did ask Jack to come with him in the bathroom."

"Which means?" I prompted.

"Not much. But we'll get more," Alex said. He would rarely discuss Jack's social isolation with me, as if the other boys weren't having parties and sleepovers. Often I still felt like Cassandra. It wasn't that Alex didn't think anything was amiss with Jack, but I could see so many things that he, my stubborn Hector, attributed to my being "hysterical and overreacting."

But he wasn't so far gone that he couldn't see that an invitation from other boys constituted evidence. "Why did they include him?" he wondered aloud.

There's gold in them thar hills.

I didn't answer because, again, it wasn't a question. I looked away, at a reproduction of Wayne Thiebauld's painting of a steep San Francisco hill.

Alex turned his back to me, his phone open and pressed to his ear. Then he snapped the phone shut. "Bingo."

I came to attention.

He lowered his voice. "They were looking for marijuana."

"Marijuana? Ten year olds?"

Alex punched the buttons on his Blackberry. It was a cutting-edge device that year, but the buttons were too small for his uncorrected vision and fleshy finger pads. "Maybe you'd like to come down to the office one day," he replied. "Look through some of our files." He put the phone to his left ear, the one with sharper hearing. "They say they got the idea from the ecologist when she was talking about endangered plant life, that there was marijuana on the island."

"*Did* she talk about plant life?"

He paused with one finger on a number, staring me down. "You were there."

"I don't *think* she did...."

"Well, have him call me back," Alex said authoritatively into the phone. To me again: "Cesar and Dylan swear they just wanted to see the plants. Just curious. No intention of 'harvesting' them — Cesar's word, apparently."

"Why would they want to take Jack?"

"They say he overheard them and begged to come along. Always wanted to be included, Cesar said. He's doing the talking now. They get all this from 'medical marijuana,' you know," he nearly spat. "It sends such a rotten message to kids. If pot isn't a gateway drug, I'm George Bush."

"The Shumachers are such nice people." Teetotalers and church-goers who hovered over Dylan. Rumor had it that they were Republicans.

"Try to stay on track, Anna." Alex put the phone back up to his ear. After a moment I realized that he wasn't talking to anyone.

I reached for the armrests to squeeze, missed, and felt my acrylic nails digging into my palms. They would be doing an autopsy of Tyler's body. *He* would have gone to San Francisco General. Not that it would matter to him. All I knew about autopsies was that they started with a Y-shaped incision and that they weighed organs on an old-fashioned produce scale. "Alex, they can't really bring charges against Jack, can they? I mean, you're the D.A. *You* get to decide these things."

"For God's sake, Anna. You know how it works."

I did: when there was a conflict of interest within the District Attorney's office the State Attorney General took over the case — investigating and deciding whether to seek an indictment.

"The Attorney General is Marianne Pasquale!" She was a former San Francisco D.A., with whom we also socialized. "She won't prosecute!"

Two frown lines shot up Alex's forehead. He had only gotten what he deserved when he took on such a stupid wife. Henry Higgins married Eliza Doolittle but after almost twelve years she still couldn't sing "The Rain in Spain."

What I *could* do was fool myself, for a moment, that Marianne could drop a homicide investigation to ensure her slot on the invitation list to Alex's next office Christmas party.

***

Freud said that boys liked to imagine that they were secretly the sons of kings. But Freud had it backwards. It's the parents who imagine their sons to be Moses, Jesus, Luke Skywalker. Alex and I were no different before our fall from grace. Now we had to imagine our child not another Moses but another Einstein, patron saint of the autistic spectrum. Einstein, who couldn't utter a word until he was four, five, nine. In my support groups the legend of Einstein grew. Each year his academic record was worse (first he failed math, then geography, then — was it German or English?) and his speech more delayed, so he could remain our hope and hero.

Another hour passed.

Whenever the double doors leading to the back opened, releasing a staffer in a white coat, I stopped breathing until he or she went to speak to one of the intake staff or to someone else in the waiting room. The cycle of anxiety and resignation repeated itself until I didn't expect anything different.

So when a very young man came out I hardly registered that he was in a white coat, until I realized that he was coming toward us. Everything slowed. I felt like Ray Milland in *The Lost Weekend,* just before he starts seeing bats. But he must be coming for the woman with the paper towels! I frantically searched for her.

No.

He settled two chairs away from us, put one ankle on the opposite knee, and balanced a clipboard on the triangle his limbs created.

"Mr. and Mrs. Kagen," he said, pointing a pen at us. "Right?"

He was smiling as if he'd just remembered that we'd all met at a mutual friend's wedding. He had Native-American features: high cheekbones, an aquiline nose and a broad forehead, startlingly combined with golden-brown curls and tanned skin that made his eyes cerulean. Those eyes were slightly small and close set but that gave him an intelligent expression. Laugh lines starting at the outer corners told me he wasn't quite as young as I'd thought at a distance.

"Yes," Alex said.

I opened my mouth and let it hang.

"Well, I've had a good time with Jack," he said. "I'm going to recommend that they release him to your custody right away."

I splayed my fingers over my eyes. Finally I stopped shivering enough to say, "Thank you."

"Then we should see him now," Alex said.

"Unfortunately, I don't have the final say," the doctor qualified. He used his pen to beat out "Smoke on the Water," after giving me one of the shortest reprieves from worry in recorded history.

"Who does, then?" Alex demanded.

I squinted to see the name on the I.D. badge clipped to the doctor's breast pocket. **ALEX VALENTINE, PH.D**. My magical thinking gears were grinding at full speed. First two Candys, now two Alexes. This had to be a good sign.

"My supervisor." Dr. Valentine flicked his hand as if brushing a fly from his knee. "He'll be out in a minute. Jack's very sorry about what happened. Though he doesn't really grasp how serious things are."

"Dr. Valentine," I began, "could I ask you something in confidence?"

"Of course."

"How could just a push down such a small slope kill someone?" It had bothered me from the beginning, and more and more during our wait. "I mean, he shouldn't have had more than a few bruises, don't you think?"

"I'm sorry, Mrs. Kagen," Dr. Valentine said regretfully, "I'm not a medical doctor, as you can see." He held his I.D. badge out at an angle.

I had another, equally pressing question. "Wait a minute — *Crime Conquerors* was on an hour ago. Didn't Jack freak out about that?"

Alex looked curious, too.

"Oh, yeah, he was having kind of a rough time," Dr. Valentine acknowledged lightly. "We went into a staff room with a TV and watched it together. He told me a lot of interesting stuff about the show. I'm sure you know he knows the title of every episode and the date it first aired."

I sighed. I wished I could say to all the so-called experts we had seen, from Jack's two shrinks to the legendary Dr. Wolichek, You see, *this* is how it's done. Treat a kid like Jack like a real kid, not a case study.

"How long have you been at St. Seraphina's, Dr. Valentine?" Alex asked.

"Just a few weeks, actually. And you can call me Val, if you want. Everyone does." He winked at Alex, whose nostrils flared.

"We may not see you again after today," Alex said dryly.

Val let this pass. "You're a psychologist, too, aren't you, Mrs. Kagen?"

"Please, call me Anna," I mumbled. I was glad he had called me "Mrs." instead of "doctor," so that I didn't have to choose between correcting him and passing as the Ph.D. I wasn't. All I had was that master's degree.

"Well, I was starting to say before that Jack doesn't understand consequences very well. But I'm sure you know that, too." Val slouched back in the chair, stretching his legs out. He was wearing brown corduroy pants and loafers. "You guys have had a rough day."

"I suppose you could say that," Alex agreed, with a distinct chill.

A gruff voice: "Doctor."

It took me a moment to focus on the new white coat, this one belonging to another tall, angular man. This man was bald save for a fuzz of gray hair around the lower part of his scalp that matched the gray suit under the coat.

"Hey, Mark," Val said, without looking up from his clipboard, where he was writing something.

"May I speak to you?' Dr. Mark White Coat had gone from gruff to commanding.

Val rose but followed his superior at a slow pace that left the older man waiting several seconds at the double doors, and once there he ignored Dr. Mark's motion for him to pass through. Dr. Mark mumbled. Val's replies were inaudible but his voice was higher-pitched in protest. Then, quite clearly, "*You* tell them."

Dr. Mark slapped his own clipboard against Val's chest, shoved his hands deeply into his pockets, and marched back to us. "Mr. and Mrs. Kagen, I'm afraid Dr. Valentine was premature in his assessment. We need to keep your son overnight."

"What? Alex — "

Alex stood, and assumed the posture of the Man Who Knows What You Did at that Intersection. "Are you sure that's really necessary, Dr. — ?" The pause was deliberate, as he used it to take two steps toward our new adversary, on the pretense of reading his name tag. "Dr. Thorndike. My wife and I can keep him at home supervised twenty-four-seven." Alex couldn't carry a tune, but his speaking voice was a powerful bass. "We have a full-time nanny, and my wife is quite hands-on — "

The shake of Dr. Thorndike's head was definitive. "I have a set of rules to follow."

"With all due respect, sir." Val came up behind Thorndike. "You also have a lot of discretion."

Dr. Thorndike spoke with a Boston Brahmin accent. "Dr. Valentine, you're out of order here. Don't you have another appointment?"

Val conspicuously ignored him.

Alex said, in an even deeper bass, "A 5150 has very specific criteria, and in particular is very narrowly applied to minors."

"We have a criminal investigation — "

"A *possible* criminal investigation," Alex interrupted sharply.

"In any case the staff here at St. Seraphina's has to take every precaution."

In other words, cover your ass, I thought. "You don't understand," I said, counting it a victory that my voice only quavered. "We've never spent a night apart. He has a bedtime ritual that if I don't adhere to — " I stopped because I didn't know what exactly would happen. I knew it wouldn't be good. "We've never spent a night apart," I faltered again.

"There must be some protection for a kid like this," Val interjected. "It's not like we found a knife tucked in his belt. And I can vouch for him — he doesn't have any violent fantasies...."

"We can't keep him here," Dr. Thorndike cut him off. "We don't have a locked psychiatric ward."

"Then you *can't* keep him," I concluded. And if they couldn't keep him here — no, no, they would *not* send him to juvenile hall, that was *why* Alex had gone along with — perhaps planted the idea of — the 5150 hold. Not every kid in Juvy was packing a shiv made out of a toothbrush, but Jack, uncoordinated and lacking in strength even by the standards of a ten-year-old, would be lucky to survive physically unharmed and would never emerge without emotional scars.

"So we have to transfer him to another hospital," Dr. Thorndike finished. "Since they closed Langley-Porter it's very challenging. There's no facility left that treats minors in a locked ward, so we'll have to send him out of the county."

I couldn't get a hold of the words that followed. *We have to transfer him to another hospital* echoed in my brain a few times until I heard Dr. Thorndike say, "Sometimes there's a wait for beds."

Behind Dr. Thorndike, Val made a slick "cut tape" motion under his chin. DON'T WORRY, he mouthed.

"So Dr. Valentine will be in charge of placing him," was the next thing I heard Dr. Thorndike say. "Then we'll transport him by ambulance — "

Alex interrupted to announce, "We'll go with him."

"No, I'm afraid that's not possible. He'll be under our supervision. We'll assign him a one-on-one at all times, but that requirement could be fulfilled by the ambulance driver."

An ambulance ride with nothing but the back of a stranger's head to look at, maybe in the dark, would scare the living shit out of Jack.

"In the morning a psychiatrist on the staff at whatever facility he goes to will take another look at him." A psychiatrist was not only trained in mental disorders but had the imprimatur of a medical degree.

Thorndike abruptly repossessed his clipboard from Val, lifted up the top page and skimmed. "Everything will be fine," he said vaguely.

"Fine! How can you — *ow.*" Alex had placed his arm around me, which I took as a protective gesture, until he took advantage of it to pinch me—hard.

Dr. Thorndike turned to go. Val called after him, "I've had a tough time finding anything this week."

"Better get on it, then."

The double doors swung open and closed.

Val made fists and let air hiss through his teeth. "Asshole." He plunked down to my left so that I was between him and Alex. "I see what he was up to now."

"And what was that?" Alex asked.

Val sighed. "All right, I kind of got here by accident. You know that counseling center down the hill?"

I nodded. It was part of a medical building which in turn was linked to the hospital by passageways on various floors.

"Okay, well, I'm working there temporarily. I've been filling in for a friend on paternity leave. So Thorndike probably figured I could do the grunt assessment work and then he could do what he planned to do all along."

"Which was — " I prompted.

"Well, he was never going to let Jack go," Val grumbled. "Are you kidding? He just needed to be able to say he had a mental health professional look at him before he farmed him out somewhere else. He didn't figure on getting me," he finished disgustedly.

Alex thought he was being so clever, coming to St. Seraphina's, and he'd just gotten us into this mess. Thank God or luck we'd found Val — or he'd found us.

"What do we do?" I begged.

"I can't send him home with you," Val said. "Not yet. But I can keep him here, so that you're close by, and I'm even closer."

That was much, much better. Because I could mistily picture Jack in a white hospital room forty miles away, getting an injection of a new psychotropic that would cause such a bad reaction that they would give him another drug, and the second one would make him violent, and then they'd have to inject him with something stronger, approved by the FDA but not for kids, and sure as hell not for autistic kids, and before the night was over he'd be pronounced a chronic patient. If we could keep him here, we'd get him through. Maybe.

"And how exactly are you going to pull that off?" Alex asked irritably. He was usually the one who got to solve problems.

"Well, I've never had to do this before," Val admitted. "But I know what's involved. You heard the doc. I'm supposed to call around the other counties 'til I find a facility that has room for him. I have no idea what it's like out there tonight."

"You told Thorndike you'd had trouble finding beds all week."

"And would you believe — " Val pointed an index finger to the ceiling — "that I haven't had to look for one, like, ever? I told him that so he'll believe me when I say I can't find anything."

I certainly didn't want to argue, but I didn't completely understand, either.

Val bent forward, and whispered, "What I'm going to do is to *pretend* to make phone calls. I'll do a lot of demanding and pleading with a receiver in my hand and no one on the other end." He sat back with a satisfied smile. "We're coming up on a shift change, and they tell me that Thorndike wouldn't stay late for his dying mother. I'll keep a close eye on Jack and keep stalling until I can spring him. There's one thing you can do to help me, though."

"Anything!"

"He keeps asking for his pawn."

CHAPTER FIVE
ESCAPE FROM PACIFIC HEIGHTS

I took the replacement pawn from Alex's hand when he got back from the house.

"He'll know it's not the same one," I said wistfully. It was a cheap plastic piece from an extra set that Alex kept in his study. In the fading light from the window I saw how smooth the surface of the new plastic was; Jack would remember even a tiny scratch from the original.

"And what am I supposed to do about that?" Alex demanded. "Go down to the evidence room and see if they'll let me borrow his 'special' one for the night?"

"Honey, it was just an observation."

He took his seat. It seemed to have become a tighter squeeze in a mere hour.

"I brought back *Harry Potter*," he sulked. He looked hollow-eyed and defeated. He had skipped his usual five p.m. touch-up shave which meant that his face was showing what on most men would have been a two-day growth. "I suppose you'll tell me it's the wrong one, too."

"No, no, it's perfect. *Prisoner of Azkaban,* just like I said." Five pages of *Harry Potter* was an integral step in Jack's bedtime ritual. Jack had calculated the date on which we would finish each of the existing volumes, but he couldn't follow the story any more than he could summarize Alex's legal briefs. "I appreciate it, dear."

Above Alex's head I saw the eastern sky growing dimmer, while the setting sun in the west set fires in the windows of houses and apartment buildings.

"I called Hyun-KiYe and explained about the dinner. He's fine with it."

We had been scheduled to attend the Korean-American Democratic Club annual dinner that evening.

"I'm glad," I said. "I'll — " I almost said that I would miss the kimchee.

"I was going to listen to the news on the way back here," Alex said, staring in the direction of the double doors. "But when I turned it on, it was Radio Disney."

"Because we had it on for Jack before."

"...they were playing *Who Let the Dogs Out.*"

"My God, that song is like Rasputin."

"I just kept listening. *Who, who, who....*" he imitated the Baja Men.

I was worried about him. I was worried about myself, too. Usually I would have felt much safer in a situation like this if Alex were nearby to throw his weight around, metaphorically speaking, but I'd have Val.

"Alex, you should go home. I'll call you if I need any help."

"I should be here."

The waiting room was less than half-full, and quiet except for a grade-school age brother and sister rolling around on the floor in a wrestling match that was going to turn from game to tearful argument any minute. I had seen a couple of ambulances come in, but their human freight would need too much care for a stopover in this upholstered art gallery.

"Let me do something for him. You're always the one."

Alex groped for the edges of the armrests. "They could take him away," he growled.

"You'll only be a few minutes from here. Just keep your cell phone next to you on high."

"Do you have my office pager, too?"

"Yes, yes."

By clutching the armrests tightly he freed himself from the tight grip of the chair. He wanted out of there very, very badly but three times after starting for the exit he dived-bombed back, making sure that I had extra cash, the pawn, the book, the mayor's phone number.

The moment he left I thought of other things I should have asked him to bring me: a book to read, my new iPod, the Godiva chocolates I'd hidden from him and Jack. Alex had told me that Mairead had made a batch of chocolate chip cookies to welcome Jack home. When Alex returned alone she packed them up for him to bring to the hospital, but he'd forgotten them. There was a cafeteria but I didn't dare leave, lest Jack vanish in my absence.

Though if Alex could have brought me just one item, I would have chosen a Valium.

Val didn't come out again for a long time after that. The fluorescent lights of the waiting room blinked on, and a woman helped an old man with a walker. The woman with the strained back had left hours ago, still bent over and looking really pissed off at God.

When Val did re-emerge it was dark outside. He sat, sighed, raked back his thick curls, and explained that one "Nurse Ratched" was insisting they give tranquilizers to the boy sitting on the gurney in the hall and demanding television. "It must be getting near his bedtime."

"It's past his bedtime," I said, looking at the clock on the wall, then at my watch, and then repeating the process.

"If he calls too much attention to himself...." Val fretted. "Or to me...."

On some level I had always known that "control of the situation" was an illusion, but that nameless hospital in the other county was a concrete evil I must avoid at all costs. That hospital with its own Nurse Ratched, who had a syringe of Just-Approved-PsychoZine and who knew how to use it.

"Go for it." As a member of the Blue Sisterhood, I didn't see much harm, though I imagined that many of the same parents dosing their children with Ritalin, Prozac and even Risperdol would condemn me. "Just watch the dosage — you know, he's small."

"Don't worry, I'll be careful." He frowned.

"What's wrong?"

"I'm not supposed to give meds," he reminded me. "But I don't think anyone's going to notice."

He didn't say more and I knew better than to ask.

An hour later Val reported that Jack was asleep, and I tried to make myself comfortable enough to attempt the same. By that time Val had spirited out a pillow and blanket, over my protests — he told me he had everyone on the new shift feeling sorry for him, stuck here after hours, saddled with Thorndike's work, trying so hard to find a place to send the boy, but too noble to take help from the busy staff.

***

I woke up at 2 a.m. That is, the clock told me that I had slept. But I had spent three hours dreaming that I was in the emergency room trying to sleep, lying on the armrests, which dug into my neck on one end and my thighs on the other.

I'd pulled the blanket higher over me and tucked the pillow farther under my head. But the blanket was thin from a thousand washings, the nap eaten away by disinfectant, and the pillow small and hard-hearted.

Val's head, upside down, came into focus. "I didn't mean to wake you up." He rubbed my arm. "But I'm better off out here now. I've got him in the bed at the end, with the curtain pulled back just enough that no one will look further. They've got enough on their hands. He's hidden in plain sight. Unless we hear three sirens come in at once, we're good."

He was in the chair behind my head, and he bent over my face to whisper, "Don't worry. I read to him. Five pages. I told him you were very close by."

Reassured for a moment, I said, "You're sitting like a shrink."

"Beg pardon?"

"Come on, you know, like a psychoanalyst. Me on the couch, you behind me."

"Oh, right." He made a soft noise at the back of his throat. "Psychodynamic therapy, okay. The strict Freudian stuff is a little heavy for me."

I stared at the acoustic tiles on the ceiling. "I don't know. It's like Churchill's worst-system-in-the-world applied to therapy. Everyone wants to swallow a pill now — " *including me* — "but what's worthwhile that's easy?" I hesitated. "I was in analysis myself." I admitted this tentatively. Psychoanalysis smacked of the 1950s, as surely as the McCarthy witch hunts and turquoise, Sputnik kitchens.

"How did that happen?"

I shrugged, bumping the armrests with my shoulders. "It's a long story."

"Seems like we have some time."

So I told him: I took a psychology course to fulfill a breadth requirement and chose the final project that seemed the easiest: spend some time in therapy and write about it. Almost as a prank, my then-boyfriend and I went to a local psychoanalytic institute where we could get nearly free "treatment." They love the medical paradigm, those analysts.

I'd expected to write a defiant exposé on the money pit and ludicrousness of going three-to-five times a week to lie on a couch, but instead the slightly built, prematurely balding *nebbish* who only occasionally voiced his opinions helped me to recognize some patterns in myself that seemed painfully obvious once discovered.

I stayed for two years.

I started to see those patterns in others, I explained to Val (while surprised that he would listen and wondering if he really were): The friend who saw conspiracies everywhere. The roommate who believed that everyone wanted to sacrifice to help her. I wasn't so sure that I cared whether people led better lives as I was fascinated by finding the patterns in others that my own analyst-in-training had found in mine.

"So...." I hesitated a long time. "I wanted to get a Ph.D. and become an analyst myself."

"But you already said you were a psychologist," he reminded me cautiously, as if wondering if he could trust me after all.

"No, *you* said I was a psychologist and I didn't have the heart to tell you the truth, not right then. All I have is a master's degree, so I'm a therapist, but not a psychologist, let alone an analyst." That required even more years of apprenticeship. "I promise, from now on, no more lying."

"It's what you know that counts, not what you hang on the wall," Val said. He squeezed my shoulder from behind. "I'm sure you're good. People don't care about the letters after your name."

"*I* care. I wanted to go the distance, for myself." That was true, though I had wanted the prestige of those letters, too. Not telling him everything wasn't the same as lying.

"What stopped you?"

What stopped me? I was at work when I went into labor, having passed the MFT licensing exam in my third trimester. In California, at least, that was the license one rank below official psychologist. MFT stood for Marriage and Family Therapist, which was a misleading label, since one was not restricted to marriage counseling or family therapy.

I'd planned to go back to school after the baby, but Jack needed me with him more than I'd expected. So when he was three I got a part-time job, instead of re-applying to the Ph.D. program I'd been accepted to before Jack started reciting *Thomas the Tank Engine* scripts from memory.

Was it survivor guilt? Disillusionment with the "talking cure" that failed Jack?

"It doesn't matter tonight." I twisted around and saw that Val had removed his lab coat, the better perhaps to pass as a waiting family member. He had traded it for a chocolate brown jacket lined with lamb's wool. On impulse, I caterpillared up twice, until my head was beyond the pillow, and rested my cheek on his thigh. "It doesn't matter when we're all going to die."

"Whoa, Anna." He stroked my hair. "It's going to be all right."

"Like Thorndike said?"

"Shh, forget about that putz. I'm here now."

"But what if — "

"I won't let them take him. If I have to smuggle him out under my coat, I won't let them take him. I promise you, Anna. I've been in tighter fixes than this." He stroked my hair again. "I've been at 25 thousand feet and run out of oxygen."

"When Jack's grandmother died, I told him she went to heaven. He seemed to believe it."

"That's what he told me about Tyler when we first talked."

"Why — why doesn't he feel worse about it?"

"Maybe because he believes you. About heaven. Sounds like you don't."

"I don't know." I rotated my head to stare at the ceiling again. "No."

The only light in the waiting room shone over the intake desk. Val and I were safe in the shadows.

"But I want to. I really want to. Life is just meaningless otherwise. If we all just disappear in the end, like Alka-Seltzer in water."

"Shh."

"Then at least I suppose it doesn't matter if Tyler's dead or Jack ends up homeless."

It did matter than Tyler was dead. He was still a child, not an 87 year old man. But Jack was my son and I couldn't help but end up with the image of him bearded and filthy, holding a dented and dirty cardboard cup out to the drivers exiting the Union Square garage.

"He's not going to end up homeless."

"I worry." None of his grandparents had lived to see sixty, except for my mother-in-law. Alex was an only child, and my sister, if left in charge of Jack, would spend his last dollar on mascara. "If Alex and I don't get him on his own before we're both gone — "

"You, my friend, are having some very dark thoughts."

He had no idea.

***

We talked a long time then, in hushed voices. He succeeded in distracting me from those dark thoughts, and I was getting drowsy when a baby's wail reminded where I was and why.

"How about some coffee?" Val offered. "I'm never going to sleep. Not like this, anyway." I was still taking shameless advantage of his lap. I couldn't let *him* sleep; I needed him to be awake for Jack.

"Sure." I was a bigger coffee junkie than Alex. Sugarless black was my least favorite but like any addict, I'd take it in any form necessary.

Val exchanged his jacket for the lab coat again, then walked with long, bold strides to the double doors.

What the hell do you think you were doing? I asked myself when the double doors slammed behind him. *Your head in a strange man's crotch?* I immediately came up with a dozen excuses — the stress of the day, the Platonic rapport that had sprung up between us — each excuse lamer than the one before.

Val came back empty-handed. His lips were puckered. "Everything still okay back there?" I asked.

"Yeah, fine ... but uh, I think we'd better plan on blowing this popsicle stand." He tugged on the lapels of the lab coat to re-align the seams with his shoulders. "How is he if you wake him up a little early?"

"Well, he gets up pretty early anyway, you know, six a.m., sometimes five-thirty, to get some extra TV time behind my — "

Val swung his head to check the clock on the wall. It was only four.

"We gotta chance it anyway."

"What's going on?" I pressed.

He spoke softly but quickly. "Okay, most of the people here are cool. But someone I know just came in from downstairs, a Thorndike clone — let's leave it at that."

"But don't we need — " I was about to ask the obvious: a signature from a real doctor — a psychiatrist? That was always why Thorndike was going to send him away. God, when I thought how I was always accusing Alex of denial.... But a doctor could give verbal permission to release a holdee, too, and if Val said that he got that over the phone....

"No big dramatic reunion, okay?" Val instructed. "Not 'til we hit the road."

***

Fifteen minutes later we were in the getaway car.

Our direction was the teal sky in the west. Traffic lights had not yet resumed their normal rotation but instead flashed a constant red or yellow, and the loudest noise was the shriek of birds, unheard during the day.

I suspected that Val had dug a little deeper into the bottle than he would have admitted when he pumped tranquilizers into Jack, who was slumped in the seat behind me, half dangling out of his belt. But we never would have made our escape otherwise, for the drugs kept him subdued when we hustled him, yawning in yesterday's rumpled clothes, through the ER and into my van, which Alex had arranged to have moved from the wharf to the St. Sair's parking lot during the night. When I clicked the seatbelt he complained groggily, "You never read to me, Mommy! Read to me...."

Adrenaline kept me awake until we were almost a mile from the hospital. Then I began to sway with fatigue. Which kept me from thinking about how hungry I was: I hadn't eaten in almost a full 24 hours. Fortunately, Val was driving.

"So you work in the clinic in the medical building," I said, in part to keep myself alert.

"Yep."

"With ASD kids?" Autistic Spectrum Disorder.

"No, no. It's a mix — people who can't find love or work and people who hate the work or lovers they found."

"Sounds like you don't like it much."

"More people should visit refugee camps in Pakistan."

I looked behind us, over Jack's drooping head, to the street behind, where I expected to see a patrol car, lights flashing. Empty.

Val had had even less sleep than I, but he was handling it better. "How do you know so much about ASDs, then?" I asked.

"I did an internship at FARE one summer," he said.

"Really? I know the woman who started that. Lourdes de Leon. Oh! Turn right here." My unbrushed teeth were coated with film, and I might have worried about my breath, except that my immediate problem was that my eyes were about to roll back inside my head.

I finally asked, "What's Thorndike going to say when he comes in today?"

"'When' he comes in?" Val snorted. "Try *if*. There's a golf course somewhere with his name on it."

"But...."

I stopped. Val knew what I was asking, though: Wouldn't someone notice Jack missing? His absence was as loud as his presence.

"I took care of the paperwork," Val said. "Ask me no questions, I'll tell you no lies."

After a short detour we were heading west again, now on Jackson Street. Alex and I had shortened "Jacob" to "Jack" before we moved here, and for years he had been alternately obsessed, amused, and anxious about being "Jack from Jackson Street."

When I pointed out the house to Val, he whistled between his teeth. "Some crib." It was, indeed, "some crib": brick, wreathed in bougainvillea, four storeys if you included the garage level, half of which was a one-bedroom apartment for Mairead. But it was the house for the life I'd planned, not the life I lived, and on a daily basis we huddled in just a few of its many rooms.

Still, I was desperately glad to see it now.

I was just as glad to see Mairead, who let us in. She'd been waiting at one of the ten-foot multi-paned windows that flanked our front door.

"God love you!" she cried, racing to Jack, still sullen and silent. "Sure, you must be exhausted." She hugged him possessively.

I smelled yet another fresh batch of cookies; in the midst of fatigue and worry, my stomach cramped for them. Had Mairead been up all night, too? She was already dressed in a lace-trimmed blouse and a cardigan knitted by her mother.

"You must be Mairead," Val said. "I've heard a lot about you from Anna *and* Jack."

Mairead could blush as I'd never seen another person blush, a maroon shade that clashed with her mountainous waves of nearly orange hair. Both colors set off her pale green irises. I saw that the rest of her eyes were red. So she had been up all night ... or crying.

She still ignored Val. I understood that it was a shyness that bordered on the pathological, and I wanted to step in, but I was functioning on no more than two cylinders, so I did not interfere when she said, "I've got him," and steered Jack in the direction of her territory: the kitchen and family room. "I'll scramble you eggs right now," she babbled, "just the way you like them. I think we have some bacon. And I'll put on the kettle."

Tea. The Irish chicken soup for the soul.

"She's something," Val observed, arms akimbo.

"She — she saved my life," I stammered. I told myself that if I hadn't been so tired that I wouldn't have let her take over that way.

We were standing at the bottom of a giant staircase, built to resemble the Beaux-Arts one at City Hall. Dark maple, heavily carved balustrades, the bottom treads spreading out like a waterfall frozen in wood.

Val folded his arms across his chest, now focusing on the big staircase that disappeared into darkness. "What MGM sound stage did you steal *that* from?"

I managed the first tread. "Come up and I'll ... show you ... the rest...." I bent over the banister until my forehead touched the cool wood.

"Not today, huh?" I felt him massage the dent between my shoulder blades. "Tell you what. Jack and I talked last night about maybe me teaching him how to ride a bike."

"Really?" I hadn't quite heard him.

"Yeah, sure. I'm a cycling nut."

"I can't ask you to — " *do whatever it was you just said you would do.*

"You didn't ask me. Saturday? About ten?"

"Ten...."

His voice was fading. "Call later.... Help you to bed now...."

Later I only had a vague memory of him doing just that.

CHAPTER SIX
THE ART OF THE POSSIBLE

I showered; then, once I was finally in fresh clothes, I heard the thump that sent me racing to Jack's room.

He was in full scale tantrum mode, throwing DVDs off the shelf, screaming, "Where is it? Where is it?"

Mairead was already there, trying to get some kind of grasp around his flailing arms. She was a big-boned woman, much stronger than I, and she knew, as we all did by then, that Jack, in this state, needed the comfort of being restrained — not by a straitjacket, but by reassuring arms. "He's missing a tape."

"The *Crime Conqueror Omega* season!"

"We'll find it, we'll find it." I added my un-heartfelt reassurances to Mairead's, as I joined her struggles to stop his thrashing. I thought the soothing tone of my voice might help Jack, even if my words were incomprehensible. What else was there to do?

If I'd had any idea of trying to get more information from Jack about what had happened on the island, now that we were home, that was a non-starter. If anyone could see this — a social worker, a judge — they would have said that he was belligerent, out of control, and definitely "a danger to himself and others."

"Wait — is this it?"

Without releasing Jack, Mairead stuck one foot out and kicked loose a DVD from the pile that Jack had made on the floor. She wriggled an arm free so she could pick it up, and she handed it to him triumphantly.

He was still upset, protesting that burglars had moved it, that others might be missing, that he had to reorganize the shelves, but the fever had spiked and broken.

"Why don't you go put it on the TV?" Mairead suggested.

Jack quieted completely then, and he slipped out to "Chillville." That was the nickname I'd given to the media room down the hall.

Left behind with Mairead, I slumped down on his bunk bed.

"Ah, don't be worrying too much about him, Anna," she said. "After last night, you know he's going to be having a tough time."

"I was waiting for this," I agreed. That tantrum had been a way of him crying, "Don't send me back!" At ten, he couldn't articulate that fear any more than most kids his age.

Mairead gathered the DVDs along with the many action figures he had scattered during his tantrum — always risky, since they might "belong" in the place where Jack had left them.

"You don't have to do that," I told her. We had a cleaning lady four days a week.

"I don't mind."

Jack's suite was three rooms connected to one another; these I referred to collectively as "The Briar Patch" because sending him here was more reward than punishment. I had immersed myself in the plans for this palace apartment when I was pregnant. But his personal playroom and library usually sat empty, while he confined himself to the throw rug next to his bunk bed.

"Don't you need to be going to work? I'm glad to have Jack home."

I would say that I loved Mairead like a sister, but it would be a backhanded compliment. I simply loved her, and my gratitude was even greater than my love. She was the one who taught him how to tie his shoelaces. She was the one who convinced him to take a different route home from the park, after he had decided that there was only one way home.

Sometimes I felt just a little jealous.

"I called in sick today," I said.

"That's not like you."

"No." I picked at a cuticle. I'd gone in after many a fight with Alex or upsetting call from the school, but today I judged myself unqualified to separate home and work adequately to see clients. I stretched out on the bed. "Rusty was cool about it. That's not like *him*."

The director of the Minerva Center, where I worked, was a demanding boss, though he surrounded himself with hip, laid-back trappings, such as the bean bags on his office floor. His idea of an excuse to miss work was a burst appendix. He would never let us miss a session, and he insisted that we achieve closure with clients before their insurance ran out Above all, we must "keep the therapeutic frame secure": do not reveal any personal information; do not have any contact with clients outside the office. But that morning Rusty had been exaggeratedly sympathetic, protesting that I needed not just a day but at least a week off. Alex would say that I was being paranoid.

I didn't think so. San Francisco was a very small city, and it took just one call from the wrong person to the right person for rumors to start.

***

Alex came home unnervingly early that night: 6:30. I was in the kitchen, cleaning up with Mairead while Jack finished dinner, and as I squeezed out a sponge, I wondered if this meant he had news.

Mairead, Jack, and I formed a mirror family, spending much more time together than the three actual Kagens. It was as if Bertha Rochester came down from the attic and found Jane Eyre a good companion. When Alex was home, he usually holed up in the "Batcave" (my nickname for his study), and he would ventur out only to watch sports or news, or to wolf down one of Mairead's giant pasta dishes.

So when he traveled all the way to the kitchen and dropped his briefcase with a resounding thump, I knew that if there were news, it wasn't good.

"Daddy!" Jack shouted. "Daddy...." He had a fork clenched in each hand, and he made them into pistons, pounding them on either side of his plate.

He was much better. Once again I was dealing with the logic of Asperger's. Behaviors that had disturbed me before Tyler's death were reassuring now because they were normal for Jack. He'd had another tantrum after the DVD mishap, this one because I wouldn't take him to school. He kept insisting that his friends were waiting for him, that they were going to play dodge ball at recess. But he wasn't in any more condition for school than I was for work. He finally napped and then, as dinnertime approached, he focused on that, pestering Mairead about the menu. I liked to say that Jack never met a meal he didn't like.

"Good evening, Mairead. Hey, there, Master Jack." After a quick ruffle of Jack's hair, Alex turned to me. "Can you be ready to go out in fifteen minutes?"

"I won't have time to shower." I put a plate in the dishwasher.

He appraised me briefly. "You look fine. Just change."

"Cocktail or business attire?" I asked edgily.

"Business," he said absently, with his back already toward me.

When in doubt, go for a black suit. I had a classic Piazza Sempore that would work for a wedding or a funeral.

An hour later we were at the Boulevard St. Michel, a hotel just South of Market, which not long ago had been one of the classier venues in the city but was now in need of a facelift. Alex threw his keys and a ten dollar bill to the valet. I hobbled behind him, in a skirt too tight around my knees.

In the lobby Alex's campaign manager, Madeleine O'Reilly, waited for us. She wore a long Chinese red dress, and her fingers on her clutch bag twitched with longing for a cigarette. She had solid white hair to her shoulders ("It makes me easy to spot in a crowd") and thick streaks of eyeliner that gave her already-tilted eyes an Asian look. She was fifty, and for her it was not the new forty, not after three decades of cocktail parties, late-night strategy meetings and heavy smoking. But Alex knew how to surround himself with people who balanced him, and Maddy had a track record that could have landed her a job with Huey Long.

The white of Maddy's hair and the red of her dress had indeed drawn my attention immediately to her. A moment later I saw that she was flanked by Sherri Pechner and Paul Deschiens. Sherri was a local publicist who hoped to get work with Alex's re-election campaign. Paul, the new ADA in Alex's office, was his latest protégé. A college diving accident had left Paul a wheelchair user.

Just as I was about to hail the threesome I saw Bo Hanks and Ray Shimmie emerge from the lobby bar. Political consultants: The best could win you an election. The worst were bottom-feeding slime.

Bo and Ray were somewhere in between. Ray was a broad-shouldered, six-foot-five African-American, almost as muscular as when he played football for USC fifteen years before. A soul patch graced his chin. Bo had long sideburns and a big, Tony Orlando moustache photocopied from the late 70s.

"Let's get it over with," Alex said gruffly. The meeting rooms were only on the second floor but Alex led us to the elevators so that we could accommodate Paul without singling him out.

Our party was packed close together in the elevator, making it easy for me to put a hand on Maddy's bare arm. "What's going on?"

"D.C. Washington's announcing her candidacy tonight."

The "D.C." stood for Decorrah Catherine. "That's all? She announced her candidacy two months ago." Along with a couple other of the usual suspects. "Treasure Chest," a local female impersonator, was a perennial candidate for mayor.

"That was before."

"Before what?"

Maddie kept staring at the elevator doors.

"Before...?" I prompted.

"Things have changed, all right? After — " She cleared her throat. "So she's reannouncing, you could say."

"And why are *we* here?" Attending a rival's press conference wasn't standard operating procedure.

"Your husband wants to hear it all. He wants *us* to hear it all." She meant herself and the other politicos. She could tell I was nervous because she added, "There's going to be a big crowd. We'll blend in."

Once we spilled out of the elevator I did not have to search an event menu to see where we were headed. The double doors of the Redwood Room were opened and a horde of people had been forced out into the hall and into a scene that would have made a fire marshal weep.

But Paul, in his new pimped-up Wijit DBS with the ultramarine trim, could easily part the crowd for us. And then people began to recognize Alex and spread the news that the incumbent D.A. was here. "The Enforcer," as he was known in certain circles.

Had I been the type to suspect the worst of others, I might have heard people whispering, *what's* he *doing here?* But at Alex's side I did not feel as vulnerable as I did when alone. So I mentally plugged my ears like Odysseus against the sirens. It was ostensibly still a free country, after all.

With Alex and Paul as our advance men, five of us were all able to get in the back. People would avert their eyes from Paul's wheelchair and thus help us remain anonymous. Meanwhile, Bo and Ray were happier outside anyway, where they could work the bystanders without having to pretend to listen to D.C. Washington's announcement. I scanned the room, looking for people I could identify. Was this a big turn-out of shills — Decorrah's friends, aunts, and cousins — or real politicos?

The press, I saw, was here in as ample force as on Minotaur Island. Tonight, though, it was the political team in attendance, reporters with whom I was more familiar. I recognized half a dozen immediately from the *Chronicle*, the *Examiner* and the *Bay Guardian*, among others, and there were crews from two of the local TV stations. They had set up in front and extra lamps stood on poles on the side of the narrow room.

"We should have gotten here earlier," Alex grumbled, just loud enough for me to hear. "I can hardly breathe."

He could have come here straight from work, and arrived earlier. His Bryant Street office was only a half mile away.

He came home to get me.

"This won't take long," Sherri said soothingly, stroking Alex's back. Maddy had made Sherri *her* protégée when the latter first arrived from Boston, and the two women were still ostensibly friends, because most members of the political scene know better than to let personal feelings enter into their relationships. But Maddy had said to me recently, "Keep an eye on that one, sister. You can't trust her."

Sherri had glossy black hair that she liked to move from shoulder to shoulder in equine tosses, nails like garnet knife-blades, and a store-bought tan. But if Alex abandoned me for another woman he'd leave me sitting pretty on Jackson Street, where I could finally have the remote control — *the one in the bedroom* — to myself. He'd do all the logistical things he did for Jack now, but I would be free of such public duties as tonight's — not to mention that one very private duty, even if the private one was becoming less frequent.

Watching Sherri's hand go up and down Alex's back I did not feel so complacent.

"I still don't understand why she's making a big deal about her candidacy now. She's been on the ballot since March," I said to Paul, disingenuously. Alex was more likely to confide in him than in me.

"I don't know much," he said evasively. Paul was an Ivy Leaguer from a very old Eastern Seaboard family. He had a thatch of canary yellow hair and the undernourished look of *really* old money.

It was hard to see the lectern from the back of the rectangular room, and some attendees were even standing on chairs. But by craning my neck and shifting around I was able to make out the imposing figure of Decorrah Catherine Washington.

"D.C." Washington, like Moll Flanders, had been born in prison. Her mother was serving a year for credit card fraud, but it was her drug use that labeled her daughter unadoptable and condemned her to the foster care system, where she remained until her eighteenth birthday as a ward of the state.

Now, ten years later, Decorrah had done everything but win the Pulitzer Prize. She was a Phi Beta Kappa graduate of Stanford and had been editor of the law review at that same institution's law school. She was nearly six feet tall, full-breasted and wide-hipped, with a massive honey-colored weave, now swept up high on her head, and skin the gleaming copper of a new penny.

Decorrah Catherine embodied the idea that the disadvantaged needed only to work hard to achieve the American dream. "See, look what you can do if you just avoid the temptation of drugs, don't get knocked up, stay in school." But the argument was spurious, because

D.C. had preternatural gifts. Had she been born with Jack's mis-wired brain she might well be bouncing between the street and whatever programs the county could provide.

After graduation, she and two former classmates had founded a non-profit agency to act as champions for "invisible children," lost in the file cabinets of Social Services or living with biological parents who couldn't care for them. Children such as she had been. The organization's name was ChildCARE, with "CARE" standing for "Child Activists RE-act." Their motto: "Children Should Be Seen *and* Heard."

Decorrah was an out and proud lesbian, as were her two associates, one Caucasian and the other one quarter Navajo. The latter had taken the name Soaring Eagle, though she had been born Mary Ann Evans. I never could remember Whitey's name.

"I'm looking out here and I'm seeing the real San Francisco," were the first words I heard Decorrah say. She had a sweet, child-like voice that did not match her build.

D.C. had not begun with political ambitions. The gossip according to Maddy went like this: One afternoon that spring the ChildCARE triumvirate of Decorrah, Soaring Eagle and Whitey appeared unannounced at the D.A.'s office to complain of a case that CPS had failed to investigate. They never reached Alex, who had no memory of their request to see him, but instead were turned away. That night, after two glasses of wine, Soaring Eagle and Whitey persuaded D.C. to run for District Attorney.

Within days Decorrah's friends had gathered signatures in a hail of surgical strikes at the entrances to cafés and grocery stores, and Decorrah filed. But she had no personal experience in criminal law, and her only appearances in court had been in the role she trained others for, as child advocate. Neither was she one to bear a grudge. So after that she let her campaign stagnate. She had done no fundraising and had no campaign headquarters besides the living room of her apartment in the Western Addition.

After tonight things were going to be different.

"You are the people who want change at the heart of the system," she praised us.

No, I thought, *we're your competition, Alex and I and his entourage. And half of the rest of the room are the caterers and graphic artists and event planners, the cottage industry that feeds on the likes of you.*

Alex was tugging at his collar, reluctant to loosen his tie and reveal any sign of stress.

Among the reporters I caught sight of were the devil twins, Perry Millard and Adrian Rotwell. Millard and Rotwell wrote a political column for the *Chronicle* three times a week. While they portrayed themselves as old-fashioned muckrakers, they had destroyed as many careers on a whim as they had unearthed genuine scandals. They had not yet paid any attention to Decorrah Catherine, and I did not like their sudden interest.

Decorrah, up in front: "Statistics can be as criminal as any terrorist group."

She'd gone record time before dropping the word "terrorist." As for "statistics," she was referring to how, under Alex's watch, the crime rate had dropped across the board, and most sharply in the area of violent crimes — homicide, rape, domestic violence.

Alex succumbed and unfastened the top button of his shirt.

Decorrah's voice hit an even higher register. "Yes, *in toto* violent crime has been reduced. But hidden within that misleading number is another, terrifying fact: the majority of crimes against children go unreported...."

I was getting a headache from the noxious combination of odors: tobacco smoked outside, armpits, and a mix of colognes, including my own.

"...and *those* heinous acts, if appropriately calculated, would tell a very different story...."

Decorrah was flanked not just by her adjutants but by two towering stands of helium balloons in blue and gold. I saw some movement behind one of them just as Sherri exclaimed softly, "Look who's here!" She pointed — discreetly, with a crooked finger — to where I had been looking.

"...and we're learning that the real criminals wear the most expensive suits, sometimes under the black robes of the judiciary, sometimes *hiding behind the mandate of justice itself...."*

I followed the line of Sherri's arm and saw that lurking next to Soaring Eagle, almost hidden in the balloons, was a man I knew, a man whose hair belonged to him, but not in the sense that it was growing out of his scalp. He would be in a shabby beige suit with an open-collared shirt. His striped tie would already be loosened, and he would be wearing scuffed brown wingtips.

Patrick Riordan.

Patrick was a washed-up political consultant whose washing up he blamed solely on my husband Alex.

Patrick was an alcoholic. He had succeeded in spite of his problem, relying on intelligent ruthlessness, with a little luck thrown in. Then one night he showed up drunk at one of Alex's own fundraisers. At the time Patrick was campaign manager for Robbie Chang, a political ally of Alex's who was running for a seat on the Bay Area Rapid Transportation board. Alex had spoken to Robbie; Patrick had been fired.

"...because this, my friends, is entirely a class issue...."

Patrick couldn't get another job that season, and by the end of the year he was spiraling down at 3Gs. He discovered cocaine, lost his house, and then his wife, who left him for one of his partners. He nominally had joint custody of their two sons, who attended Pathways but weren't in Jack's grade, but rarely saw them. He'd spent the past four years selling office furniture.

"He's sober," Maddy said. "They say."

"We could at least give him the benefit of that doubt," I replied. I had no reason to think otherwise; he must be very steady on his feet, keeping himself so well-hidden behind the balloons.

I calculated now that he had not been completely isolated at his day job, on the floor of Desk 'n' Chair World. Sometime early today one of the sympathetic contacts he retained on the inside — maybe someone in the D.A.'s office where Alex would be disappointed to learn that not everyone looked up to him — had told Patrick that opportunity was tapping lightly on the display window.

I could imagine Riordan talking to Decorrah Washington within the hour of hearing of Alex's own misfortune. "Kagen is vulnerable now. I can make this happen for you." *And make it happen for myself. Get back in the game. Get back at that fat, self-righteous bureaucrat.*

I'd tuned Decorrah out for a minute, distracted not just by Riordan's presence by several shoves from new arrivals.

But her next words got my attention again. "That's why I'm re-committing myself to this campaign tonight. Because, my friends, criminals don't all wear ski masks or even carry guns. Their weapons are the law books written by better men and women and a patriarchal system that can be corrupted with cash."

I hadn't had the nerve to look at Alex for several minutes. Now I did. His face was dark red. I thanked God that the TV cameras were up front.

"...Underclass parents are continually being scapegoated for their children's difficulties — while their minds are made feeble by the lead painted by slumlords, their pockets are drained by those who seduce them with lottery tickets.... They *want* to reach out for help for their children.

They try to reach out for help for their children." Her voice cracked. "But the oligarchs shut them out. They can buy private schools and luxury cruises for their offspring...."

From opposite sides, Maddy and Sherri each put a hand on Alex's arm.

Now Decorrah had her prey in her crosshairs, and she was about to blow it away. "These oligarchs — the entitled classes — can shield their own youth from the consequences of their crimes — even murder."

I had had no idea how noisy the room had been. Now I heard what was no longer there: the whispers, the *eergh* of metal chair legs against industrial carpet, the scattergun shots of private laughter.

"A little boy died just yesterday afternoon. A little boy whose death remains unexplained...."

My stomach cramped at the memory of that little boy's dust-covered body.

"...A little boy who didn't need to die. But will anyone be held responsible? No — because his killer has the protection of his class. The imprimatur of respectability, the illusion of innocence."

Just in case there was still any confusion about the identity of the evil genius masterminding the class conspiracy: "And sometimes the established power structure is represented by the exact men entrusted...." She glanced at the tower of balloons on her right. I stared hard at the same tower, and sighted bits of a beige suit in between two blue balloons. "...with the duty of protecting them."

Then bulbs started flashing, and the simultaneous clicking of cameras ended the silence.

"So now, with the help of my better halves — " she grinned as she linked arms with her comrades — "I have a new mission. And that's to be a champion for the victims of a corrupt entitled class, like — just as a recent example — Tyler Gaines."

Applause from her now-riveted audience.

"Children should be seen *and* heard!"

Patrick stepped out from his partial hiding place. His oiled rug was slightly out of alignment, yet he looked smug and, yes, positively sober. I squinted at him, no longer willing to give him the benefit of anything. He wasn't a recovering alcoholic, I decided, just a dry drunk.

Decorrah wasn't finished yet. But Alex, like the rest of us, had had as much as he could stand. He grabbed the nearest arm. It was Sherri's. "Let's get out of here," he growled.

***

Alex, Maddy, Sherri, Paul and I went straight to the lobby. Bo and Ray finally joined us — probably after sounding out other consultants about whether they should jump onto one of the lifeboats now, before the SS Alex Kagen sank.

The six of us walked out onto Ellis Street. As soon as we hit the sidewalk Maddy lit one of her Virginia Slims. *I've come a long way, baby,* was her flippant response to anyone who remarked on her habit. Sherri waved her hand elaborately in front of her face, and Maddy blew smoke right toward Sherri's palm.

"I told you not to get Riordan fired," Maddy said to Alex, blunt as always.

"I only did what was right," Alex said, resting his case beyond a reasonable doubt. "It isn't as if I were spreading rumors." *Like you do, Maddy,* he left unsaid. "I saw Riordan break three glasses and almost start a fist fight, and he was going to bring Robbie Chang down with him. It didn't exactly help my campaign, either."

"You won, didn't you?" Maddy fired back. She could stand up to him as well as anyone. "Huh. Patrick sure knew to head right to D.C."

"Well, it's easy," Ray said. "You just turn your back to the ocean and go straight." Then he snorted, "Of course, go straight is the one thing she can't do."

I cringed. Alex had little respect for either Bo or Ray, both womanizers and heavy drinkers, but they could call in favors with groups beyond — or below — his reach.

"And what is she, twelve years old?" Bo lit a cigar, puffed, then handed it to Ray. Sherri coughed meaningfully while Bo lit another for himself.

"How long has Riordan been sober?" I asked Maddy.

"I don't know — what time is it now? Four months, tops."

Paul sounded plaintive. "You can still win, Alex." He tightened his grip on the Wijit levers. "I'm not going to let it happen any other way."

Alex put a hand on his shoulder. "It's not ethical for you to campaign for me since you work in the office. I just thought you'd want to join us here tonight." He made a seal-like bark, as if he were trying to laugh off the evening.

Paul looked up at me, searching for support. "There's plenty I can do without doing anything wrong. We know you don't like doing anything wrong, Alex."

"We've got to be at another event," Bo announced.

I put my own money on that other event being The Recount, a pub near City Hall that was a popular haunt for consultants, publicists and their comrades.

"Yeah, we gotta book," Ray said, clapping Alex on the back, at which my husband frowned.

"We'll meet tomorrow to plan our next move," Sherri informed him imperiously.

Underneath my cashmere coat I was cold, and feeling the pinch of black patent on my toes. Though we all wanted to retreat to our separate corners, we each, if for our own individual reasons, wanted to see Alex beat this rap. I felt a protectiveness toward him that was unsettling in the old and new feelings it aroused. He and I waited at the corner while our group dispersed — Sherri after a peck on Alex's cheek — so that we could return to our car in private.

I tentatively broke Alex's no-public-displays-of-affection rule and slipped my arm around his. "I don't want to lose my balance," I said, trying to appeal to *his* protective side.

He did not reply but I felt the need to keep talking. "It's good timing. Home before Jack's bedtime. I wouldn't want to see him miss that two nights in a row."

"That bedtime routine is a bigger sham that what we saw tonight," Alex said.

"Nice of Mairead to — I beg your pardon?" I released his arm.

"It's bullshit."

"What?" He almost never cursed.

"You say it's for Jack. It's for you. It screws up some of my most important appearances. It's so hostile. I'm surprised you don't see that, being a so-called shrink."

"You always bring him home from baseball games — "

"I wouldn't have to take him to day games most of the time if you didn't have him trained to hold us all hostage."

"Reading to him at night is at least one thing I can do for him," I said calmly. "Don't take out what happened tonight on me."

Alex handed his tag to the valet.

"Talk to me," I begged. "Let's deal with this together."

"I'm not much in the mood to talk."

The wind blew through me. The wind never stopped.

It was spring in New York, though. I hadn't been there in many years. I loved the theater, especially musicals, and there was so much playing I'd like to see: *Avenue Q* for starters. It had just won the Tony for Best Musical.

In my other purse, at home, was a walletful of credit cards in my name. The bills went to Alex, but with them I could draw over $100,000 in cash advances from San Francisco banks. Pretend money, for someone would have to start repaying it, and soon, but that someone wouldn't have to be me, because once it was in my hands I would purchase a plane ticket in cash and disappear. I supposed that Alex could subpoena the airlines for their manifests, but I'd have a head start. Maybe he wouldn't even come looking.

CHAPTER SEVEN
I DON'T CARE IF I NEVER GET BACK

When I opened the door to Val the next morning, he nearly blinded me with his casual handsomeness. He had come, as promised, to teach Jack to ride a bike, and in snug-fitting cyclist-wear, I saw that he had a build to match his hospital tales of athletic adventures: slim through the torso, with muscles that pressed against the cotton of his yellow t-shirt.

For a moment (maybe more than a moment), I wished he had come to see me, rather than Jack.

"What's wrong?" were his first words.

Once Val had gotten Jack out of St. Seraphina's, I'd become confident that no case against my son could materialize. The autopsy would reveal the cause of death and Cesar and Dylan's crazy story would go away. Now I had to accept that if Alex's opponent were turning this into a *cause celebre* that this was unlikely to happen.

"I doubt you follow these things. But what after our little 'trouble' on Minotaur Island, Alex's re-election is looking iffy." I gave him the shortest possible version of the night before.

"Well, I'm glad he's got his priorities straight," Val said, clearly referring to the *sine qua non*: Tyler's death.

Yes, Alex had to face a real campaign now, but that was what he chose when he went into politics. Jack hadn't had any say in that.

"He's at a strategy meeting now," I said. "More like damage control."

"Well, it's not your problem at the moment." He slipped inside the house, tucking a sleek, metallic gray helmet under his arm. "Get in your happy place. Can I fill my water bottle?"

Something about his to-hell-with-it air made me put my troubles out of my mind.

"I'll do it." His large sports bottle boasted the logo of the previous year's AIDS ride. "Did you go on this?"

"Hey, it'd be pretty obnoxious carrying this if I hadn't." He tipped the bottle into this mouth and polished off the last swallow. I watched him run his tongue over his lower lip to suck up a couple of drops that remained. "You know I came back from Mexico just for that last year? I'm signed up to ride again next month."

"You're like the Albert Schweitzer of San Francisco." I'd learned a lot of Val's history during our vigil. He not only adored travel, but travel in the rough, even though his journeys had left gaps in his resume. He'd even visited the hospice that Mother Teresa founded. But I suddenly feared he might misinterpret my remark. "Sorry. Sometimes I sound sarcastic when I don't mean to be."

He tucked a loose wave behind my ear, and I shivered. "I know," he said softly.

I rushed off quickly to refill his bottle.

When I returned Val had made himself at home with Jack in the east parlor, a room large enough to host a wedding reception but furnished only with two oxblood suede sofas and two chairs, one on each side of rectangular glass coffee table. From a distance the seating arrangement looked as though it were afloat, so I had dubbed this room "Gilligan's Island."

"Do we have the house to ourselves?" he asked, reaching for the bottle. "Where's Mrs. Danvers?"

"You mean Mairead? At church."

"On Saturday? What is she, a Wiccan?"

"Hardly. She goes to Sunset Word of God. It's Pentecostal. They're having a bake-and-rummage sale today."

Val fingered one of the remaining leaves on the sweetheart orchid plant that graced the table. I wondered if he guessed that I had plucked it nearly clean while Jack and I restlessly waited for him to arrive.

"Really? I just assumed, being Irish — "

"Oh, she was raised Catholic. In a very traditional family that believed Vatican II was heresy." Bible study groups and gospel sing-a-longs seemed to suit her better now. Happily, she was a naturally tolerant soul and not only didn't proselytize but joined us to light Chanukah candles before returning to her Christmas tree below stairs. That only left me to envy her her faith and hope that she'd meet someone equally devout at Word of God — a man who wouldn't mind sharing her with Jack and me. "I suppose living with us with drive anyone to religion."

Now that neither Val nor I were focused on Jack, he was doing airplane-in-a-dive spins. Val noticed and waved to Jack.

"You ready, Pal?"

"Bzzz-bzzz — ker-pow!"

***

I had had some crazy idea that I would spend the time they were gone in Chillville, watching *So Proudly We Hail* on our 62 inch plasma TV, but as soon as I picked up the DVD remote, I heard Jack shouting: "Mommy! Mommy! You won't believe it! Believe it...."

Jack and Val waited at the bottom of the stairs. He and Val reached up to take off their helmets in a synchronized movement.

"Tell her," Val said.

"I rode the two-wheeler!"

"That's just great, dear." I looked questioningly at Val.

"I'm an eye witness." Val tossed his windbreaker over the banister.

"I have to check something," Jack said. He ran behind me, up the big staircase.

"He's going for the TV," I said. "How did it go, really?"

"Great. It went great. You were right, the bike's too small for him."

"We bought it when he was seven," I explained. "We hoped — "
That he would learn a skill that he could share with other boys.

"It's just as well for now, because he feels safer that way," Val said. "You're too hard on him, Anna Banana."

"You're a fine one to talk about bananas," I laughed. "That shirt — " It was the brightest yellow I'd ever seen.

"Yellow means caution." He pinched the material. "Besides, it beats being run over at night. But I take it you don't like that nickname."

"Your usual perspicacity, Dr. Valentine. All women named Anna seemed destined to be linked to tropical fruit."

He narrowed one eye. "Petite Anne Banane. Does it sound better in French?"

I considered. "Yes, actually. Much." I'd been a flirt since puberty, which I'd hit like a speeding motorcycle hits a brick wall. It was not only harmless, but Alex liked it. He knew he could trust me, and it flattered his ego, to think that other men might find me attractive.

"We really did get the training wheels off."

"You're kidding!"

"I'll have him doing the Tour de France by next summer," he said. "Speaking of French. Hey, how 'bout some more water? I used mine up already."

I led him back to my Kitchen of the Future. Granite countertops and gleaming black built-in appliances, including a six-burner gas oven and a Sub-Zero refrigerator. A greenhouse window over the double sink.

"You must love to cook," Val said.

"Uh.... Not really."

"I do." He pointed to his chest. "One taste of Lasagna Valentine and you'll never go back."

I got him fresh water from the dispenser to which I added ice from the automatic ice maker. "Sorry I can't offer you a beer." Neither Alex nor I drank. We did keep a few bottles of white wine for the occasional guest. Guests were very occasional.

Beneath us the garage door rattled open. We needed to replace the motor; the sound reached as high as the second floor. I could picture the white Cadillac slide into its spot on the far right of our three-car garage.

"That's Alex," I said, hearing my own disappointment. "He's taking Jack to a baseball game this afternoon."

"So you said. May I have that water or does it have to breathe for a while?"

"Water. Right." I handed him the glass. "I'm proud of him. Alex. He's never ashamed to take Jack places like this. There'll be lots of 'petty poobahs' at the park tonight, but Alex … stands *by* Jack. You probably think he's a cold fish."

"That depends. What fish live in arctic waters?"

"Be nice." I grabbed an errant tea towel and swiped at a clean counter.

"They go to a lot of games?"

"Jack doesn't follow them. But he loves being with his dad. And the hot dogs. I wish Alex wouldn't let him eat all that junk food, though. Ice cream. Deep-fried chocolate-covered peanuts." *You're rambling, Anna.* I wasn't doing any better with the tea towel, either, which I was using to swipe at every surface within reach.

Val, by contrast, was very relaxed: He propped his elbow on the kitchen island and glugged so fast that he finished with a burp.

Alex came up from the stairs that led to the pantry. I hated him on sight. I knew that last night he had been displacing his anger on me. But why did I have to be both analyst *and* scapegoat? People with Ph.D.'s got $300 an hour for that. It wasn't the analyst's paycheck I envied. It was that their patients went home.

As usual, Alex was panting from the climb up from the garage. Fifty-three in October. *Men his age die of heart attacks.*

"Yo, Mr. K.," Val said. He burped again.

A strange silence fell.

"Dr. Valentine," Alex said, as chilly as the arctic waters Val had just referred to.

I wondered how the meetings and interviews had gone; knew not to ask. It must have cost him great effort to cut them off to keep his commitment to Jack. Why couldn't I love him for that? I respected him for it. That would have to be enough. No New York escape for me. The marriage contract was sealed when Jack landed on my belly after emerging from my womb, because a minute later Alex held him as if he were the first thing of value he had attained in a life of privilege and achievement.

I squeezed the water in my own hand so tightly that I thought I heard the glass begin to crack.

"You won't believe this," I said. "Val took Jack out this morning to teach him to ride a bike. They finally got those damn training wheels off."

"You should be proud of him," Val said.

But Alex wasn't looking at either of us. "I suppose I have to change," he said absently, making a fan out of his suit jacket by flapping one side. "Dr. Valentine, it was nice of you to come by. Mrs. Kagen can show you out."

If I were Mairead, I would have turned deep red. Instead I felt the heat in my chest. "Hey, Val," I said, deliberately casual, "let's go see if the Jackson Street Jumpers have picked the lock on your bike yet."

Val started to follow me but he stopped at the kitchen door. "Catch you later, Alex," he said.

Alex ignored him.

In the foyer I clutched at Val's arm. "He's under a lot of pressure, and he keeps it bottled up — "

Val was strapping on his helmet. "Don't think I'm that sensitive, Anne Banane. He can kiss my ass."

"That's 'tuchas' to you."

I trudged back to the kitchen, still furious. How dare Alex embarrass me that way? I had my opening salvo prepared but Alex got off the pre-emptive strike. "What in God's name are you thinking, letting Jack go out with that man alone?"

Both human and animal response to an attack is "fight or flight."

"What the fuck are you talking about? If it weren't for him Jack might have spent the night with Walter Freeman!"

Walter Freeman invented and then indiscriminately practiced the lobotomy. I doubted Alex knew who he was, and calling attention to something he didn't know was the sharpest arrow I could shoot at him.

"Good God, you are dramatic." Alex swigged Coke in front of the open refrigerator door.

"He stayed for hours, when he didn't have to, and finessed and finagled — " I noticed that I was standing next to a large wooden knife block. The black handles showed above an inch of luminous stainless steel. We rarely used them, so they must be very sharp.

"Huh. A man who works overtime. I'm *very* impressed." He slammed the Coke can back on the refrigerator shelf. "Did Jack wear a helmet?"

"Of course he wore a helmet!"

"Did you check his driver's license?"

"Whose? Jack's? Val works at St. Seraphina's!"

Alex had never closed the refrigerator door. Here he was about to go to a baseball game and rummaging around for a snack to tide him over the three miles to SBC Park, where he'd eat nachos with something squishy and orange that the vendor called cheese, with garlic fries on the side.

I couldn't stay quiet. "So that was the result of your strategy meeting this morning? Take up the cause of children who need better bike-riding instructors? Think that will get D.C. Washington off your back?"

Alex very, very slowly raised his head from behind the refrigerator door. He looked past me — at the knives, I was sure. He knew from homicide investigations exactly where the carotid artery was located.... But no, his method of murder was the slower kind, a process already begun, a process that would take years.

He closed the refrigerator. "I'm leaving."

***

As soon as I heard him go I went up to the room we shared, stretched out on the bed, and cried.

Never mind New York with credit cards. Just let me the hell out of here, and I'd get a job. But I couldn't, because I couldn't get Jack to stop putting his hands on women's breasts as a form of greeting but I *could* keep his family together.

Yet another irony: a different kid, a "neuro-typical" kid (which was the PC way of saying "not on the autistic spectrum"), might well be better off if his parents divorced, but Jack was happily oblivious to the shaky rope bridge slung between me and Alex. We didn't shout in front of him; we shared a room and a bed. As far as he knew we were just any Mommy and Daddy from TV.

How would Jack go from my house to Alex's, carrying every *Crime Conqueror* DVD in his collection and 2,300 action figures two times a week? How could he go through a day that didn't begin with Alex ruffling up his hair and end with me reading to him?

Look how he smiles at you! the second grade teacher said on his first day. *I thought autistics didn't form attachments.*

And now he needed us together more than ever.

***

I realized that the doorbell was ringing. It had the persistent, irregular screech of a bell that someone had been pushing for a while. I had stopped crying. That was why I finally heard it. I saw a smear of black on the gray-and-maroon squares of the duvet cover, and I knew that it was from my mascara. The doorbell-ringer might be delivering a package from Saks, or Bloomie's. But no, it was Saturday, so —

I was probably too late. I prayed for the bell to ring again as I raced down the big staircase.

Our front door was inset with colored glass in an abstract design. It fragmented any visitor's face into a Picasso-like rendition of itself. But I recognized Val — red, yellow and purple — immediately.

I knew he'd come back. I had already learned that he was the one person who would never abandon me.

When I opened the door, he looked dramatically over each shoulder, then cupped a hand around his mouth. "All quiet on the Western front?"

That forced me to smile. I stepped back to let him in. "Where have you been hiding?"

"I disguised myself as a bike messenger and infiltrated the Clay Street Venture Capitalists. By the way, my street name is Big Wheels. That was my handle on the inside, and it just sort of stuck."

"Big Wheels? Damon Runyan would be proud." Damn, no Kleenex in my pocket. I swiped at what must be the smudges under my eyes with my index finger.

He took his thumb, gently inserted it under my lip and touched it to my tongue. Then he pressed it against the same spot I had just wiped. "Don't cry anymore."

"I wasn't crying. I'm going to be a raccoon for Halloween."

"Here." He surprised me with the handkerchief he pulled out of a zippered pocket in his shorts. Then he stepped back out of the house, and pulled his bike into the foyer. Was he hiding the evidence of his visit?

Apparently not. His next suggestion was, "Let's go for a walk."

I was still pulling myself together, literally as well as figuratively, tucking in my blouse where it had come loose. "I don't know, I — "

"A woman like you should be outside," he said. "Showing off her beautiful face."

"But I...."

"Yes?"

"I need to change shoes."

***

"You know," Val said casually as we walked along, "it would help if you didn't blame yourself for everything."

"Easier said than done."

"Betelheim has been discredited."

"I know I'm not 'cold and rejecting,'" I said. Bruno Betelheim had asserted that autism was caused by a "refrigerator" mother. Once a god in the psychoanalytic community, his name was now used as a curse among the mothers of ASD children. Some aging psychiatrists still subscribed to his theory. And sadly, in extreme cases, abusive caregivers *could* cause autistic symptoms in a child. But the frantic grief-stricken parents I knew would have to be suffering from dissociative identity disorder if they were subjecting their children to anything harsher than depriving them of sugar.

"But — ?"

Shoving my hands in my pockets, I took a few steps until I achieved a rhythm in my walk that would prevent me from stepping on a crack. "But I don't always accept Jack."

"That's not always so easy to do."

"I still keep asking myself, what did I do wrong?" I hadn't left him with a sitter for an evening the first six months, but by then I was sympathizing with Andrea Yates. Was that just too soon for some kids? Or had I succumbed, when pregnant, to some arcane craving, like colored marshmallows, that were dyed with the chemical that would soon be isolated as the offending trigger?

This wasn't purely self-torture. When an identical twin was autistic, nine times out of ten, the other twin was, too. But what about that tenth time? Who was to say that the cause wasn't a pink marshmallow?

"You should know better. You've done a fantastic job with him. If it weren't for you and Alex he wouldn't be where he is now."

"But where — " I was going to ask in rhetorical self-pity, *Where is that?* No. I'd given myself an entire night to wallow in front of Val.

"I've seen a lot of kids like him," Val went on. "I won't lie — I haven't followed a single kid on the spectrum over a period of years. After all — " he caressed his hair in a parody of vanity — "I'm not old enough to have been in the field that long."

I heard panting behind us. We both slowed to let the heaving jogger pass: a forty-year-old dot-com billionaire, owner of a twenty-million-dollar mansion over on Pacific Avenue.

When there was a safe distance between us, Val went on, "But the bottom line is you just don't know what's going to happen. It's all about hope, Anna. That's all we have. It's all we need."

I broke my "no wallowing" promise to myself after a record ten seconds. "What I hate the *most* is when people say stuff like, 'As long as he's happy.' I think Jack's happy most of the time. He doesn't know the other kids are making fun of him behind his back. He wanted to go to school yesterday. He kept saying his friends were waiting for him." That was puzzling, for while he didn't seem to know they were making fun of him neither did he usually seem to imagine a closer relationship with them than he had.

"To paraphrase the old expression, 'I've been happy and I've been unhappy, and happy is better.'"

I countered, "Who's really involved in life who's happy? It means you're not striving for anything."

"You and I must have very different ideas of 'happy.'" Val said. "Or of life. Or of something."

"I bet you were happy traveling around Europe. Though sleeping on a train with my head on a backpack ain't *my* idea of happy." That was another story I'd heard during our night in the ER.

"I was happy, yes."

"But you came back because you didn't want to spend your whole life wandering around just being 'happy.'"

"Why do people litter like this?" Val picked up a cigarette butt. "Call me a one-man clean-up crew."

"I met a woman at a fundraiser once whose thirty-four year old son lived in group home in Hayward. She said, 'He's always eager to go back at the end of the weekend. He's happy. What more do you want for your children?'"

"Marlboro," Val read off the butt. "Well, what more?"

"What more?" I demanded. "Are you kidding me? A home? A job, maybe? A family? Friends?"

"You don't know what it's like for him. You think too much. Oh, good, there's a trash can." We were nearing a corner.

"I don't 'live in the moment'?" I asked wryly.

"Anne Banane, I have never met anyone so far fucking removed from the moment as you. You are at *least* in the Eastern Time Zone. Maybe you have your own time zone."

That actually made me laugh.

We had encountered other pedestrians: every one was jogging, walking a dog, or pushing a stroller. Every one carried a bottle of water. Now a woman came toward us who was doing all four.

"Permission to speak freely," Val said after a moment.

"Uh.... Granted?"

"You remind me of the ancient Mariner."

"'Water, water everywhere'?"

"No."

As he slowed to toss the cigarette butt in the trash bin, I saw how he had had to cut his own stride in half all along to accommodate my shorter legs. I slowed more and let him get a few feet ahead. He quoted, "And 'til my ghastly tale is told/This heart within me burns."

He turned deliberately back to look at me. I stared back defiantly.

He either didn't detect my shields going up or didn't care. "Get off the subject and the subject will get off you," he said.

I'd found someone to unload on, covered him with my mental refuse, and now he was throwing it all back at me.

"I think I'll go home now," I said hoarsely. *And take my marbles. What's left of them.*

His cocky smile vanished. "Anne Banane." He came back to me and reached out as if to hug me. I took a step back. I would have pulled my hand away when he reached for it, too, but he was an athlete, and quick. "I wouldn't hurt you for the world. I — I've really enjoyed getting to know you," he said, "and if something I said got in the way...."

I did pull my hand away then, and he looked sincerely hurt.

Then I wanted to apologize and tell him I knew, I knew, he was right and I was wrong, but I was so, so tired of being the one who was wrong.... For once I was going to take something out on someone else instead of being the takee. At least I thought so until I saw how he was backing away from me, and how, after a few steps, he stumbled backwards into the street.

"Be careful!" I cried out less than a second before I saw the black Lexus SUV jump the opposite stop sign and speed through the intersection, in a game of Bowling for Pedestrians. It whizzed not more than six inches behind him while the driver pressed her horn in an unbroken, triumphant war cry.

I ran to Val as he jumped back on the sidewalk and threw my arms around him. "Jesus, you idiot!" I cried. "Just backing into the street like that — without looking!"

"Faster than a speeding driver on a cell phone!" he boasted, completely unfazed. He pushed a flopping wave of my hair back from my face. "Friends?"

I nodded, trying to find breath.

Val did not let go of me, but looked up and around. I followed the direction of his gaze and simultaneously we saw that we were at Divisadero Street, the first significantly trafficked street we had crossed — or tried to cross — since leaving the bounds of Presidio Heights.

"Checkpoint Charlie," Val said.

"I didn't know we'd come this far," I replied.

***

We turned back. I had to make the most of the time we had left. The return trip always seems shorter than the outgoing journey, when you didn't know what or how far away your destination was.

In August Strindberg's play, *The Ghost Sonata,* one of the characters says of his father, "Like all of us he was surrounded by a circle of acquaintances whom he called friends for short." Strindberg had described my current life. I was surrounded by people, *bombarded* with people: moms from the school, with whom I had nothing in common but being a mom, and parents of ASD kids, with whom I had nothing in common but ASD kids, and Alex's sprawling political crowd ... with whom I had nothing in common.

But friends? People to talk to without censoring myself, without reviewing the checklists I had memorized for a hundred others: their hobbies, names of their children, acceptable subjects, topics to avoid?

The unspoken understanding between me and Val on this walk home was that we would speak neither of Jack nor Alex. But even after our hours together in the hospital, we seemed to have unlimited topics to discuss. And we agreed on so many: the folly of the second Gulf War, how the feminist movement had been set back by our generation because women didn't understand what the world had been like before 1967, how Critical Mass hurt the have-nots more than the haves ... and for him to say that as a devoted cyclist was saying something....

And recent movies. Thanks to Mairead I was able to go to matinees. Val and I both liked *Catch Me if You Can. Napoleon Dynamite* was delightfully off-beat but the subject matter (a teen misfit) was uncomfortable for me. *Million Dollar Baby?* Could you believe that ending? That life isn't worth living with a disability?

And what the fuck were they thinking with *Vanity Fair?*

I sat through *Cheaper by the Dozen* simply because I didn't want to go home, but I drew the line at a Jennifer Aniston flick.

I went to these matinees alone. I didn't ask with whom he went to the movies.

When I didn't go alone I took Jack. He loved the movies, and I loved taking him now that he was a little older and didn't run up and down the aisles so much of the time. *Finding Nemo* had been our most recent excursion. Before that: *Brother Bear, Treasure Planet, Monsters, Inc., Atlantis.* We'd go to the same movie six times, which was my tipping point into madness, in spite of the mini-flashlight and paperback in my purse. Jack memorized the dialogue but couldn't talk about the storylines.

"I like classic movies the best," I said.

"'They don't make 'em like that anymore'?"

"No." The wind was coming up, as it reliably did in the afternoon, and I grabbed a fistful of my hair to hold at the back of my neck. "The old ones seem better because it's the good ones that've survived." I pronounced sententiously, "Time is the only film reviewer that counts."

"What's your favorite movie ever?"

"There are a lot ... *Groundhog Day.*"

"Not *Casablanca*?"

"Please. So predictable. Besides, it's about a woman losing her true love forever. *Groundhog Day* is about starting over."

"How about the most romantic movie ever?"

"Just 'cause I'm a girl you think I like romantic movies?" I asked.

"Busted." He punched me — lightly — on the arm.

I was too embarrassed to tell him that I did have an opinion on romantic dialogue. It was from the first and easily the best of the three versions of *A Star Is Born.* Fredric March, in a movie-within-the-movie, says to Janet Gaynor, "I've loved you my whole life." When she protests that they only met three days before, he replies, "That's when my life began."

***

We were silent for a while, on my side because I was trying to think of a way to suggest we go to one of those matinees together. *Are you ever free in the afternoons? Would you like to do a lonely woman a favor?*

The return walk *was* shorter; I knew exactly how many houses remained, because Jack had counted them on each block, and with each house we passed (though they were enormous homes that took more than a few steps to pass) I knew that my time was running out.

Two houses to go when I heard someone call my name.

My next door neighbor, Mrs. Dr. Marjorie Mitchell, appeared in her own front doorway. She was the middle-aged lady with short rust hair, papery skin and thin, painted lips, who was the only person I knew who was more dressed up than I even when there was nowhere to go.

"Anna!" she called again. She started toward us, which looked like a treacherous process, as her spindly legs teetered on heels as high as any I had in my closet. The actual doctor in the family was her plastic surgeon husband, a man with an eerie resemblance to Mark Twain.

"Hi, Marjorie," I said tensely.

"I am so sorry about what happened," Mrs. Dr. Marjorie Mitchell said. She was from Minnesota, near the Canadian border, and which she revealed in her "aboot"s.

I had a long-standing resentment of Mrs. Dr. Mitchell. Like Sweeney Todd, I had a little trouble with forgiving and forgetting, but even Mairead, who would have volunteered for a face with a dozen cheeks, sympathized with this one. Our neighborly relationship had soured about a month before Mairead moved in, one night when Jack was having so loud and uncontrollable a tantrum that Mrs. Dr. called the police and reported suspected child abuse — even though we'd warned both her and her husband about the possible noise.

The other residents liked Mrs. Dr. for acting as both watchdog and hatchet woman. She would run screaming across the road at a driver leaving his or her car even a few inches past the curb cut of a neighbor's driveway. But this phone call could have had serious consequences. Alex was only an ADA at the time, still beneath gossip columnists Millard and Rotwell's notice, but in his first run for office they would have uncovered any scandal from the past.

We were fortunate, though: Mrs. Dr. had not only used up a lot of her goodwill with the Richmond Station that patrolled Presidio Heights, but the officers who came by our house knew and liked Alex. Back then, already prosecuting violent felonies, he was also already picking up the soubriquet, "The Enforcer." Besides, it was pretty obvious that Jack was in mental, not physical, pain. The police left us with a sobbing child but filed no report.

Since that night, Alex had won a prestigious public office. And that had won Mrs. Dr. over far more than Jack's growing into his sunny self. He always greeted Mrs. Dr. Marjorie on the street with the announcement, "You live next door!" and she always replied, "What a charming young man."

"She's going to show her solidarity now," I muttered to Val, since we were still safely out of hearing. "Against welfare moms and their progeny." Marjorie must have read about D.C.'s speech the night before.

"Lean on me," Val said.

"Dr. Mitchell and I were just *stunned*," Mrs. Dr. said. She was silent for another two steps until she joined us on the sidewalk where, being ladylike in the superficialities, she lowered her voice. "We must have been up half the night talking about it."

"I appreciate your concern," I said, as lightly as I could. Half the night? "The election is still a long way off. I think the voters will decide on the merits," I added, using one of the shopworn phrases of my husband's profession.

"I'm not talking about the election," Mrs. Dr. said, rubbing her hands together, either gloating or commiserating. "I mean the Pathways parents meeting. Anna, I do hope Jack isn't — charged with anything."

The muscles in my face froze in their former position of subdued politeness.

"What meeting?" Val asked sharply.

"Well — " Her expression registered curiosity about Val. "I mean the Pathways parents' meeting tomorrow morning. I'm bringing baklava. I brought you some as a house-warming gift when — " She cut herself off, putting her finger tips to her mouth, where lipstick bled into the tiny lines surrounding it. "Oh, my. I just assumed you were invited."

She made it sound like a cotillion ball.

"What's it about?" Val asked coldly.

Marjorie backpedaled furiously. "I really don't know," she said, her voice rising an octave. "I just got a call from Delight de Bruin, I know her from the Symphony Guild, and she said they were meeting tomorrow morning at the Gaineses', did I need the address— "

"I thought you said it was a Pathways parents meeting." I finally found my voice. Val squeezed my hand. I knew Delight de Bruin, too — well enough to know that she had no connection to Pathways.

"Well, it is, or it was, or that's how it started, but — " she shrugged insincerely. "I guess I'll have to go to find out."

"What else did this 'delightful' woman say?" Val demanded.

I tugged at his sleeve. "Never mind," I said. "We've got to go, Marjorie." I started abruptly for the house, knowing Val would follow. I no longer cared what anyone would think about my being in his company.

"You don't want to find out more?" Val asked me as we mounted the porch.

"Of course I do!" I snapped, without turning back. This was my punishment for letting myself have a good time for a few minutes. "I just didn't want to find it out from Gladys Kravitz." I turned the key and then raised my voice over the BEEP-BEEP-BEEP of the burglar alarm as I punched out the code. "She already thinks I'm a witch. I've got a better idea."

I marched toward the back of the house, through the kitchen and into the family room, which was where Jack struggled with his homework under one of a quartet of adult supervisors (Alex, Mairead, his tutor or me) and which also served as my headquarters for all matters related to his school. From the hutch above my desk, I took down the Pathways roster and looked up the number for Raven Fernandez, my one real friend at the school.

I was lucky to find her home. But after I relayed Val and my encounter with Mrs. Dr. Mitchell she was silent. Then, "I'm going to switch phones." I heard her speaking to her partner, Janis. "Ms. Scarborough wants to put the parents in Renaissance costumes for the May Faire. Could she be any more last minute?" Raven was unofficial seamstress for the entire school.

Val hovered at the rear kitchen door, dangling his foot over one of the steps that led down into the room. After a moment Raven came back on and continued in a hushed voice, "I thought you knew about it, too, or I would have called you myself."

"No, somehow I didn't hear about this." Through the bay window of the family room I could see not just the deck but beyond, to a small but well-tended backyard with a custom-built wooden play structure.

Raven's silence acknowledged that this was not a good sign. Finally she said cautiously, "I didn't realize that this had gone beyond the Pathways bunch. I just got a call from Laurie Batarski — "

Laurie Batarski, she of the unkind remarks meant for me to overhear, and the mother of Emily, my little friend from Jack's class. Laurie Batarski, she of the Scarborough Mommy Mafia, the raffle ticket sales quotas and the bi-weekly student car washes.

"I know, I know." Raven shared my opinion of Laurie. "All she said was that we were having a meeting about field trip safety. It seems like someone named Patrick Riordan got this going. Do you know him? He's got a second-grader and a sixth — "

"I know him." Of course it was Patrick. I looked over at Val.

"Both boys. Since neither of them is in fourth grade, I was surprised — "

"So Laurie Batarski called you," I interrupted. "You know, I always wondered why I never got a Christmas card from her."

"She must have switched her own Rosemary's Baby in the hospital for Emily," Raven sympathized.

What frightened me most was my sense that a Mob was forming. A Mob could be far more powerful than the sum of the bigotry and cowardice of its members — and some bigotry and cowardice lived in most of us. A Mob lynches a man before trial. Erects a guillotine in the square. Kicks a kid out of school because he's HIV positive.

"Listen, Raven," I began. "I know they don't want me there, but right now it's just as well. They'll speak more freely. Will you go and tell me what went on, I mean after?"

"Don't worry, Anna. I've been playing 'I Spy' with Philip practically since he was a day old." She lowered her voice. "I'm not surrounded by happy campers right now. I'd better go."

"I owe you one," I said.

I hung up and covered my face with my hands. "I guess you got that," I said, speaking through the gap between my palms.

"The salient parts," he said. Suddenly I felt his two fingers press against my exposed lips. "Don't assume the worst," he said softly.

I leaned against him. My head fit exactly in the valley created by the gentle slopes of his chest. He wrapped his arms around me and bowed his head so that his cheek rested on top of my hair. We swayed together as I cried, clinging to him. I hadn't cried so much in one day since the early years with Jack, and I was embarrassed. But if only he could zip me up inside his yellow shirt and carry me around like a kangeroo's joey....

After a moment Val moved his arms so that he could stroke my back with one hand and caress my waves with the other. "Come on," he said finally, as my weeping subsided into sniffles, "let's get you comfortable. Do you want to lie down?"

I thought of the wide four-poster bed and I wanted to sink, sink, sink under the gray-and-maroon duvet that would still have mascara marks on it. So I nodded, rubbing my face against his yellow spandex shirt. When I pulled away I saw that I had left a black mark on that, too. "I'm sorry," I mumbled, touching it softly. It was actually three tiny black marks in a row: the imprint of a small animal's paw.

Then I felt his lips reaching down for mine from above. *No, I thought, this isn't where I want this to go.* Sure, I'd been admiring him on our walk, but the way I admired the Art Deco design of the Shell Building. Sure he was attractive. Sexy. But I knew a lot of sexy men. I saw them behind the counter at Starbucks on a near-daily basis: chatting with their colleagues, talking about clubs and bands with their co-workers....

This was crossing a line.

But his lips were already crossing the line of my lips and onto my tongue.

Val was wrong. I could be in the moment. I was in the moment then: feeling our mouths merge and his arms around my back and my arms around his back and we were one body.

But then he relaxed his grip, and I repossessed my body. What was happening? What was I let happening?

I didn't want sex. When had I wanted sex? Ten years ago — maybe. Now I wanted someone to hold me. The way he just had.

We were standing near the switchback staircase that led to the second floor from the kitchen. The house had more staircases than an M.C. Escher print, and this one dead-ended next to the master bedroom. We'd have some privacy there, to talk some more.

I pulled Val up the stairs as easily as if he were a helium balloon.

But at the threshold of the bedroom I stopped. If we went inside that room we were going to do more than talk. I might as well have heard a policeman with a bullhorn in my head announcing, "Step away from the door! Let me see your hands!"

So I pulled on Val again, this time taking him two doors down the hall, to the place I called Chillville.

The media room's walls, sponge-painted in pale gold, hid the wiring to the speakers to the 62" plasma TV. It was uncluttered except for the days between the cleaning lady's visits, when Jack crammed empty Fritos bags between the sofa cushions or the dregs of my last cup of coffee rested on the sole end table.

Jack had spent a good chunk of his childhood parked in front of that 62" screen, flapping his hands and shouting in purest delight. But when he was out — at school, with Mairead, or at therapy — I was often lying on the long sectional couch, either parallel to the screen or perpendicular, if I chose to stretch out on the attached chaise.

But Alex never set foot here. He hadn't wanted a TV in our bedroom ("it sends the wrong message") — as if we were going to have close personal friends take a tour of the place where we slept. First we would have to have close personal friends. In any case his resolve had only lasted six months: He had to be able to watch the news, not to mention the SFGOV channel.

And so I felt safe.

Val and I sat. I clasped my hands between my knees and mentally tried to rehearse my speech about how I wanted us to remain friends. I'd never cheated on Alex. I'd never *considered* cheating on Alex. Besides, what would be in it for me? Sex I didn't enjoy, gifts I didn't need? I'd wanted to murder Alex on more than one occasion, but had never hatched a satisfactory plan.

But before I could open my mouth to talk, I had opened my mouth to receive another kiss. After that I didn't try to speak. Kissing wasn't cheating. All of us on the political circuit kissed one another in greeting — air kisses, perhaps, but sometimes two in a row.

No one at political gatherings, though, kissed the way that Val and I did that afternoon. We kissed like teenagers, holding each other's heads, and I was the one who first groped under his yellow shirt. I discovered that his chest was almost smooth: there was only faint 'n' feathery golden brown hair, which I detected by running my fingertips northward over its hills and valleys.

After that he unbuttoned the champagne-colored silk blouse that I was wearing. He started from the top, and I started from the bottom, and then the blouse was on the floor. *Nothing else will come off,* I told myself, as I started to pull him down on top of me. We were kissing. Just kissing.

And then I heard the rattling of the garage door, two flights below.

I froze with my hands on his face. There were patches of my Murderess Red lipstick on his cheeks and chin. *They're home. They're home!* How could they be home? Did the Giants pitch a shut-out? Did Jack have a meltdown at the ballpark?

Val moved to nuzzle my ear.

"Up! Up!" I insisted, trying to wriggle out from under him.

"Why?" he asked lazily. "What's wrong?"

"They're back!" I pushed on his shoulders and he finally rolled up to sitting, only to regard me with drooping eyelids and a satisfied smile.

My own eyes landed on the crumpled silk blouse on the carpet. Val's Nikes were on the carpet. When had he taken them off? Had I asked him to? My shoes, too....

And the crumpled champagne silk blouse.

The rattling stopped.

Val calmly slipped his shirt back on over his head. "Comb your hair. We've been talking, that's all."

"No, no, no." I shook my head. "He'll know." The inevitable misbuttoned and now-wrinkled blouse, my customary make-up rubbed away.... "You have to take this seriously," I said. "For my sake. For Jack's."

"Okay, hon. Let's think." He rapped his fist against his forehead in a comic gesture. You had to admire a brave man. Val could take three Alexes in a boxing ring — but Alex was the D.A., and I had a feeling Val had inhaled.

I was beginning to panic when I saw how easily Val slipped into his Nikes. As if he were used to quick getaways.

I shoved my blouse under the couch. If I put on a bathrobe I could pretend I'd been in the tub. No — the tub would be dry, there'd be no towel in the hamper.... *Yes, think like a prosecutor....*

But first just get Val the hell out of here.

The front stairs. They were such a magnificent sight when one opened the front door; now they might save my marriage — at least for the weekend. Alex would come up with Jack through the garage, up the stairs that led into the kitchen. Then he'd come up to the second floor the same way Val and I had, the shortest route to leaving Jack with me on the way to his study.

But Alex moved slowly up stairs, and by that time I could have *So Proudly We Hail* on and have covered myself with a blanket. There was an extra blanket here somewhere.... Yes! In that closet where Fatima kept the ironing board and....

I had maybe thirty seconds to get Val down the front stairs and out.

I sprinted back to my bedroom where one of our three burglar alarm panels were installed, and turned it on. "We'll hear the beep when he opens the basement door," I said. "That's your cue to race down the front stairs. And I mean *race.*"

Val was double-knotting one shoelace. "I don't like this, Anna."

"I don't, either," I said petulantly. "I don't like myself right now very much, in fact."

"And how do you feel about me?" He drew a calm thumb and forefinger down a few strands of my hair.

"Go! Go!" I shoved him.

"Not until you answer."

"Okay — I — I want to see you again."

His laugh was sudden and confident and loud.

"I love you, Anna. See, it doesn't hurt to say."

No you don't love me. We just met. You want to have sex with me. "Stud," I said aloud, thinking that he would take it as a compliment rather than the insult I knew it to be.

"For Jack's sake, I'll sneak out."

After that, he moved like a rabbit.

CHAPTER EIGHT
FIRST THEY CAME FOR SPONGEBOB

I avoided Alex for the next several hours. I didn't know if he were doing the same to me. He said good-night to Jack and disappeared into the Batcave, but that was standard operating procedure.

At 10:30 I knew it was now or never. So I made the long journey down the hall, a dead woman walking, and knocked very, very quietly.

"Mairead?"

She was theoretically off-duty on Saturdays but if she weren't at church or perhaps on the phone with her family in Dublin, she seemed happy to step from the mirror and enter the "real" family, playing the role of Mammy in our modern recreation of the fantasy that Margaret Mitchell had created. Ironic, in that I had vowed not to fall into the trap that so many society and professional moms did, and pretend that their nannies "were part of the family," who would have performed their duties gladly without pay.

But I'd broken more solemn vows since then.

"N-no, it's me," I said.

"Oh." Alex's disappointment was muffled by the thick door. "Sometimes she brings me coffee."

Another wife might have been suspicious about such an arrangement, but Mairead's Christian principles were as much as part of her as Asperger's was a part of Jack. Obviously I had adultery on the brain. *I didn't commit adultery!* I shouted at myself. *I can be proud that I stopped things before they went too far!*

This was as lame a defense as any Alex had ever heard in court. *But I had stopped in time,* I thought. *It's not too late to make things right.*

"Well, come in, then," Alex said irritably.

I opened the door and there he was, crammed behind his desk, but looking so solid, and almost handsome in a Perry Mason way.... I *had* stopped in time. It wasn't too late to make things right.

...even though I was still feeling Val's skin against mine....

That would be my punishment, but enduring it silently would be part of making things right.

"Maybe *you* can make me a pot of coffee," Alex said, digging through a stack of files. "Don't you usually have some around now?"

The Batcave smelled of real wood and Lemon Pledge. It was overcrowded with Chippendale furniture and lined with built-in bookcases, each packed with volumes shelved sideways on top of the ones shelved vertically. The only light came from a desk lamp. "How was the game?"

Alex swiveled to the chess table next to his desk to brood over the black and white pieces that remained standing. He'd been playing a game with ADA Paul Deschiens via e-mail. The antique Italian chess table, a gift from his father, was his most beloved possession: It was topped in marble and inlaid with scenes of Rome: the Coliseum, the Pantheon and Vatican City among them.

Alex put his hand on the tip of his remaining white bishop. He'd lost one to Paul the day before Minotaur Island.

"Anna, I have work to do."

My promise to myself to make things right hadn't eased my guilt. Every word Alex spoke was a lash of the whip, and I welcomed them. How could Mairead have drifted from the Catholic church? I would have loved to have been a Catholic, to go confession for absolution and most of all to pray to the Virgin Mary. She would understand how I felt about a lot of things.

"I ran into Marjorie Mitchell today," I began.

"I know all about it," Alex cut me off.

"You do," I breathed. I wasn't surprised, but I was still relieved. I had dreaded the responsibility of telling him myself.

"Shouldn't we go?" I asked. "I'm sure you don't want to see Tyler's parents up close any more than I do, but we can talk to them — "

"They don't want us there."

"It's Riordan who doesn't want us there. That's his whole strategy. You know how the mob mentality works. These are the people who'd follow Hitler even though they're good people. They get swept up in the rhetoric whether it's for genocide or sending money to the March of Dimes."

"Good people who'd follow Hitler," Alex echoed. He sidled up to his keyboard. "You make a man proud."

"Okay, not *good* people. Typical people. That's what I was trying to say. Did anyone stand up against the Japanese-American internment?"

"We're getting rather far afield here." He tapped at the keyboard, eyes back on the monitor.

"What have we got to lose by talking to the Gaineses?" I pressed. "We don't know them. Maybe they're the kind of people who'd want the truth more than they'd want revenge."

Alex kept typing, but didn't respond.

"And think," I went on, "we could start a memorial fund for Tyler. Or how about...." I loved my next idea. "How about if we build a special reading room at the main library in his name?"

Alex stopped typing. He turned from his computer monitor, stripped off his glasses, and after a perfectly timed pause asked, "Are you *insane?*"

"We know that Jack couldn't have killed Tyler," I insisted. "What about Dylan and Cesar? Haven't they said anything else to the police?"

"I can't talk about it."

He cut me off so sharply that I didn't dare pursue that line any further. "If only Jack would tell us more!"

"Let it go, Anna."

I told myself to leave, but didn't listen to myself. "I know it's awfully awkward, but maybe the Gaineses are not vindictive people." I paused, too, though not for effect. "Maybe they're even intelligent people. Intelligent enough to not want D.C. Washington to exploit Tyler's death for the next five months just so she can get herself elected."

"Oh, God," he moaned, rubbing his eyes. "I cannot listen to this anymore."

"Okay, maybe I *am* insane, but if you and *I* could just talk — we could come up with something."

"Just ... shut ... *up.*"

Telling your wife to shut up, at least not when one is under a great deal of stress, probably isn't on a par with making out with another man. But where *I* came from (a therapist's office) this was verbal abuse, and it stamped out any guilt I felt for the early evening. I started to walk out, afraid I might hurl one of the heavier volumes at his head.

"I'll tell you what they get out of it!" Alex yelled after me. "Maybe a few million dollars or more!"

Keep walking, I told myself, but instead I turned back to sneer, "Is that what they'll get for their story for the *National Enquirer?*"

"Probably." He was standing behind his desk now, randomly shuffling papers. "After they get it from us in a wrongful death suit."

***

A long Sunday morning, wondering what was going on.

But finally it was two p.m. and time for the Raven Report.

I had never been to the Gaineses' house, though I knew what block it was on: Their address was in Jack's class roster. I knew that Tyler's father, Jimmy, was a real estate venture capitalist with an interest in several San Francisco restaurants. He collected modern art, so I pictured his walls covered with huge canvases, painted with colorful abstract shapes.

I'd seen him, so I also knew that he was a short, balding man with doughy skin and watery blue eyes. As for Margaret, Tyler's mother, the only image I could conjure of her that preceded my view of her straight, grieving back, was that of a woman's form silhouetted in the black SUV. I had heard from an awestruck classmate of Jack's that besides the Porsche, the Gaines' fleet included a Beamer z8 and a Mercedes convertible.

I told Raven to tell me the worst of the worst. I wanted to know what we were up against.

So this was how it happened, according to her: a large front room with a bay window, where a baby grand piano took center stage, and chairs brought from all over the house that still left many people standing. Raven said there were fifty or so attendees, but when pressed she admitted it was more like a hundred. I reassured myself that not all of them wanted to lynch Jack yet: Alex would have his own moles, and from what Raven told me, people had brought out-of-town guests.

About half of the school administrators and teachers were present, including Dr. Yeung, the principal. It was Patrick Riordan who chaired the meeting, in contrast to the furtive role he had played at D.C. Washington's speech, and he filled his shiny new black oxfords well. He never mentioned D.C.'s campaign, but he did manage to make relevant a series of conversations he had had with Michael Dukakis in the 1988 Presidential race, when Patrick would have been 24 years old.

After dwelling on his own resume long enough to provoke some coughing from Jimmy Gaines, Riordan positioned himself for the attack on Alex Kagen, District Attorney, and father of a juvenile offender. Riordan quoted statistics about how many of these juvenile offenders grew up to be career criminals. Jimmy Gaines sat on the edge of the piano bench with his head in his hands.

After that it was difficult for anyone to gather the courage enough to speak out for *my* son. Ms. Klein, his teacher from last year, made a final plea. She didn't think Jack capable of intentionally hurting anyone.

She had never seen him lash out in the way Dylan described. She doubted that he would have the bodily strength to shove another child off his feet, even another small boy like Tyler.

"Is his physical education teacher here?" a woman demanded. "Wouldn't he or she be the person to judge that?"

Raven couldn't identify the speaker, who was in the back of the room. Her "chemo chic" look (as she called it) also helped her blend in with Laurie's followers, who were strongly encouraged to adopt Laurie's aggressively no-style style.

Meanwhile, a cry went round the room to find the P.E. teacher. But she wasn't there, and her absence, when discovered, abruptly mobilized the Pathways parents as a separate group with their own grievances. "After what we're paying in tuition, you still send home those catalogues at Christmas and expect us to spend a hundred dollars on crappy Santa mugs!" "You promised you'd offer Italian to the middle schoolers — " "I've explained to Ryan's teacher that it's not my fault if my ex doesn't get her to school on — "

Mrs. Dr. Marjorie Mitchell, holding her proudly baked baklava, was shrill when she interrupted the barrage of complaints. "This isn't about your school. This is about a danger to our neighborhood."

Riordan strategically intervened. "I'm a Pathways parent, too!" he declared, "and I'm chairman of the Pathways Parents Committee." (There was no such committee.) "We all have our concerns. We'll work together to solve them. Our focus today is Jack Kagen."

Raven described the tableau in detail: Tyler's father with his plump white hands placed on his white scalp. Grandfathers visiting from out of town inspecting the disappointing refreshments. Rabid mothers in the back, rocking or jiggling their own new babies even as they denounced Jack.

Then someone whispered to a seatmate something about Jack being "a sweet boy," and the fuse was lit. When the flame reached the dynamite of Jimmy Gaines's temper he not only rose to his feet but actually jumped on the piano bench like a deranged Harold Hill. He cursed, "You assholes at this *school*, this *excuse* for a school — you think I don't know what's going on? You put all these kids at risk, but *my* son paid the price."

He swept the huge, crowded room. "How much does Kagen pay you to warehouse Ted Bundy, Jr.? I'm going to sue every last fucking one of — "

"Jimmy," Patrick Riordan said, pulling him carefully down from the bench. He murmured in Gaines's ear, and the man contained himself with effort.

Patrick kept steadying hands on Jimmy while he apologized for him. Mrs. Gaines, he reminded them, was too distraught even to join them. "Close your eyes. Imagine it was your child. He's gone forever. You will never talk to that child again. You will not watch him grow up, get married, have his own children. All that is gone, irreversible — his body dissected, buried in the ground — "

All that Raven actually told me was, "Riordan got up and, I admit it, he gave a pretty emotional speech about what it must be like to lose a child."

I'd thought about that when we were searching the island, and so, while I didn't know exactly how articulate Riordan had been, I filled in his speech with my own words. I now understood, a little, why Alex had been angry at me the night before, when I put forth the fantasy of going to church with Tyler's parents to sing "Amazing Grace."

Whatever Riordan's exact language had been, his speech touched off a firestorm of fear. This time everyone from the Pathways administration was permanently silenced, but the others had plenty to say. While a few of those out-of-towners and curiosity-seekers returned to the buffet to munch cheese and crackers like Madame Defarge knitting at the guillotine, others poured forth stories of sinister, drooling autistics.

"This girl my niece used to babysit would just go through her purse."

"My friend finally had to put her older son away when he left out a knife and the baby — "

"There was a boy in the group home in Berkeley who smothered an infant. Just held a pillow over his face and — "

"I knew one who would smear — I'm sorry, I can't tell this."

"They let them ride public transportation! One of them sexually harassed my daughter — "

"The police won't even prosecute a rape if it isn't 'politically correct.'"

"The *police* would, if they could. It's the D.A.'s office that decides whether or not to press charges."

Riordan had been fingering the piano keyboard. Now he slammed down the cover. In the brief startled silence that followed he reiterated, "Someone just said it. It's the D.A.'s office that won't prosecute these crimes."

***

Patrick Riordan's reminder of the identity of the real villain only kept people silent for a moment. Then the stories started flowing again, more sickening, about setting fires, about torturing animals and eating their flesh, about ritual murders....

"That's all," Raven interrupted herself. "I can't stand to talk about it anymore."

"I get the general drift."

Raven sighed. "I'm ashamed."

"Why?" I asked. "I wanted to hear it all." I needed to thank her for being so observant, but—

"First they came for SpongeBob," she said.

"Uh ... I beg your pardon?"

"I saw it on a bumper sticker once. Don't you know the poem?"

I did. Martin Niemoller: *First they came for the Jews, but I did not speak up, because I was not a Jew. Then they came for the Communists, but I did not speak up, because I was not a Communist....*

When they came for me there was no one left....

"I just stood there," she said. "I was scared, Anna."

I remembered things Raven had told me about growing up gay in a small town ("You just need to meet the right man"), about raising a non-biological child ("Your son must look like his father") and even the banal act of appearing bald in public ("Is it AIDS?").

"There wasn't much you could have done," I consoled her. But then I concluded bitterly, "I assume they're going to meet again."

"Yeah." Pause. "I'm so, so sorry."

I had to reach down deep to cheer both of us up. The best I could offer was, "First they came for SpongeBob, but I did not speak out because I was not a cartoon sea creature."

***

By the end of the meeting the group had given itself a name: PROTECT. People Resolved Only To Empower Children Today. Acronyms are what separate us from the animals.

After talking to Raven I wanted nothing more than to talk to Val. He'd calm me down; he'd give me perspective. In fact, he'd tell me that I was "hysterical and over-reacting" — but in language that actually did calm me down and give me perspective rather than adding a layer to my own guilt. It would be the difference between a root canal with nitrous oxide or without it.

I might have succumbed and called him, but I didn't have his number.

CHAPTER NINE
DEATH IN THE AFTERNOON

"Our first commitment has to be to the safety of the student body," Dr. Yeung said.

The Pathways principal was half-hidden behind a barricade of framed photos facing inward. They would either be of his family or his sailboat, the *Grade Point Average*. He looked out at me and Alex over the top, a knight peering over the battlements, assessing the attacking enemy.

His speech was speckled with a nervous clucking of the tongue, but his meaning was clear.

Even Alex was stunned into silence.

But I made an attempt at reasoning. "Dr. Yeung, you've known Jack since he was in first grade. You must see the panic that's building around this."

I heard the tapping of a pencil somewhere behind the wall of photos. Dr. Yeung looked down. "There have been specific accusations."

"Which are — ?" Alex asked.

Yeung clucked a few times. "Torturing the class hamster."

"Jack is afraid of the hamster," I snapped. "If you go observe him in the classroom — "

"Sexual harassment."

I sucked in my breath. I *had* seen him put his hands on women's chests. But he was so obviously clueless about its meaning.... "Of whom? The hamster?"

"Aggressive behavior."

"Please be more specific," Alex said through tight lips.

"During recess." No more hesitation in Yeung's voice. "Hitting the other students in the head with a basketball."

"Jack can't throw a basketball more than two feet!" I scoffed. I was bitter that I had to defend my child by disparaging his skills.

"*Dr.* Yeung," Alex began — he considered anyone other than a physician who used the title a fraud — "in my line of work, a defendant has the right to face his accuser."

I pounded a self-righteous fist on my thigh to emphasize my husband's statement.

I heard Yeung's pencil rapping again. His voice was stripped of hesitation now. "Threats."

"To do what? Recite the TV schedule for the night?"

The rapping stopped for emphasis. "To kill classmates."

I opened my mouth. *Anything you say can and will be....* "Sometimes he does say, 'I'll destroy you.' He's just quoting the Crime Conquerors monster...."

Dr. Yeung rubbed his hand over his chin until the skin around his jaw was flaccid. "In particular, he's threatened to stab fellow students."

"With what?" Alex asked.

"Pencils," Yeung said. "Ms. Scarborough's pointer."

The sticks on Minotaur Island. My heart raced. Was it possible? No, it wasn't. I couldn't let myself get sucked into this.

"I've had fifty calls this morning from parents who are going to take their children out of the school if — " *cluck* "— Jack isn't terminated immediately."

"Terminate?" I mimicked. "The governor is out of that business."

"I mean, his enrollment terminated."

"That's a relief."

Dr. Yeung shrugged. "I don't have much choice."

"The air must be pretty thin up there," I said.

"I beg your pardon?"

"The moral high ground."

***

It had started to rain while we were in the principal's office. Water came down hard around us as Alex and I stood under the green awning that extended from the school's entryway. The rock in my stomach was as weighty as a dead infant.

Expelled. Something so final about it, much greater than Jack leaving Pathways. Here I thought myself too wise for denial and yet — when Jack was away at school I could, and did, often pretend that things were just fine.

This wasn't even the first time. We had put Jack on the waiting list for the toniest San Francisco pre-school the day we got his birth certificate. Before he was old enough to attend he had started to go south on us, but when we went to Orientation Night and saw the artwork in Jack's future classroom, Alex must have looked at it and imagined that

Jack, like him, would want so badly to be the *wunderkind,* that somehow he would just snap out of this ridiculous phase of lining up toys and talking nonsense to himself. That night I said to Alex, "We're living in a dream world," but Alex said, "Let's see how things go." Poor Cassandra, never believed. She had to watch her family come apart, too.

Within a month, the admin called us in and threw us out. When I asked what they thought was wrong, where we could go for help, the Executive Director shrugged. She had the pointy end of a pencil stuck into the corner of her mouth and I hoped she died soon after from lead poisoning.

I had never quite forgiven Alex for putting Jack — and me — through that. But this afternoon I knew he was suffering, too. I slipped my arm through his. "How did this happen so fast?" I sighed.

"My God, did you have earplugs on? Yeung said they had calls about Jack all day."

I let my arm slip out again. Puddles were forming on the sidewalk. It was late in the year for rain.

"I mean, what were you expecting when he called us in?" Alex wanted to know. "The Congressional Medal of Honor?"

I stared at him a moment before I observed, "Sarcasm isn't your best weapon. It only really works if you have a sense of humor."

"You never should have sent him on that field trip."

"Excuse me?"

"A dangerous place like that."

"You knew about the field trip. You never said anything."

"You get hysterical at every suggestion I make."

"Since when is anything you say a suggestion, *mein Fuhrer*?"

"Is that all you have?"

At first I thought he meant weapons with which to argue, but as the wind slapped a handful of new drops into my face I realized he meant my newest black coat of pure, comforting cashmere. He was wearing a Burberry trench. His long black umbrella, closed, was tucked under his arm. "Yep, this is pretty much as good as it gets," I said. I had neither umbrella nor scarf.

"Honest to God, sometimes I don't know what you're thinking." He held his hand out just beyond the rim of the awning. "Don't you see how soaked you're going to get? I check weather-dot-com every morning before I even come downstairs."

"No wonder you hold public office."

"We'll just have to make a run for it. You can have the umbrella."

"I can think of something better for you to do with it," I said sweetly.

"We don't need you sick. Take my raincoat." He slipped it manfully off his shoulders.

"No. Thank you," I said, although the chill was penetrating my skin. I took a deep breath and rushed into the downpour. I heard the piercing snap of Alex's unfurling umbrella behind me as he pushed the release button. I ran toward my car, knowing that his Cadillac was parked in the opposite direction.

***

The phone woke me eventually, but I was still groggy. Valium again. I'd never taken it more than once in one week before.

But something bad had happened. I couldn't remember what, and then I remembered.

I answered just before the call went to voice mail.

"Anna?"

My chest tightened. "Yes?"

"Are you sick? You sound — "

Now my chest sagged. It was Rusty, the director of the Minerva Center. I had thought it might be Val. "No, I'm fine."

"This is going to be hard, so I'm just going to come right out with it."

"Okay." What day was it? Tuesday. Where was Alex? The last time I remembered seeing him was under the green awning in the rain. He would have gone back to the office. But he came home sometime after I went to sleep, because there was a dent in his pillow.

"So you see, I don't see how we can keep the therapeutic frame secure.... Anna, are you there?"

I turned over Alex's pillow. Yes, the odor of Clive Christian cologne and soap. He scrubbed himself like Lady Macbeth. "Yes, I'm here. I wasn't coming in this week anyway, remember?"

"Y-yes — " He hesitated a long time, but then finished. "And we miss you already!" I'd never heard false cheer from him and false cheer had never sounded so false.

I smoothed the wrinkles out of the sheet on Alex's side. *Two and a half days ago already.... Val has my number* ... wouldn't he want to know how I was doing? Couldn't he hear me call through the fillings in this teeth? No, he didn't have fillings in his teeth.

He said he loved me.

"Anna?"

Rusty. Minerva. "I don't understand, then. Are — are you giving me two weeks' notice?"

"No, Anna," Rusty said, brusque now. "I don't think you should come back in at all."

"But my clients — "

He shifted tactics again, and chuckled. "It's that natural empathy you have that makes you so good. But I have interviews lined up for today...."

"Not come back in at all?" I echoed him. "You've got to be kidding. You're firing me, just like that?"

"I don't see how we can keep the therapeutic frame secure," he repeated.

I believed in that myself, just as passionately as he, which was why I said, "I still need at least a final session with everyone so we can get some closure. You don't want me, fine. But they deserve that."

"Some don't want a final session."

"That doesn't sound right. Who?"

"I'm not at liberty to say. The therapeutic frame — "

I interrupted to thank him and say good-bye.

So Minerva was done with us, too.

I sat for a while with my hands between my knees.

How could so much hysteria spread so fast? In a sociology class at Berkeley we'd studied the Bucky-McMartin Pre-School case. One woman — a *schizophrenic* woman — had started a witch hunt the likes of which the country hadn't see since Joe McCarthy, when she accused a pre-school teacher of sodomizing her son. Innocent people spent years in jail. Journalists later accused the District Attorney's office of withholding evidence from the defense. I supposed I didn't have to worry about that, at least. Alex ran a clean ship.

My nightgown was long and trimmed with white lace, showing off my bosom but still modest enough to meet Alex's standards: A married woman shouldn't look like a Victoria's Secret ad. A Victoria's Secret ad shouldn't look like a Victoria's Secret ad.

I thought of calling my sister Darya, who was not coincidentally also the source of my Valium stash. She'd say, "So, he's another asshole like all men. What did you need that job for? You have it so good, not having to worry about money."

I had that job because part of me still believed in psychotherapy. I needed that job because clients had problems, and then along came Anna, who might be able to help, not like at home, where she was useless.

Now I saw that it was all a scam. What would I have said to myself if I were my own client? Exactly what I didn't want to hear now.

But scam or not, I needed that job because I wanted something of my own.

But now I had no job and Jack had no school. Where could we send him? There were just a few weeks left in the academic year. The apocalypse had come: I had no options left but homeschooling.

But for today.... This wasn't a test of the emergency alert system, it was a real emergency, and the test was how I would navigate this empty landscape to which I had no map. Dress in heels and pearls and get out the vacuum?

He said he loved me.

At least I could spend some time with Jack. My job had taken me away from him so much of the time, and going on field trips or shopping for school supplies to donate didn't help him — it just kept me busier.

With new purpose, I put on my white terrycloth bathrobe, the one I had ordered from the New York Palace.

Down in the kitchen, Mairead, wearing her green apron with "Smile, Somebody Loves You" embroidered across the front, swept up Cocoa Krispies. Jack, smiling enormously, ate pancakes dyed dark brown with syrup.

"We're just having breakfast," Mairead said. She brushed the last of the black crumbs into the dustpan. "God love him, Jack was just getting himself some cereal when I found him — "

"Mairead made pancakes!"

Two lines of syrup ran down his polo shirt. "We'll be changing that, sure we will," Mairead assured me.

"Why can't I go to school, Mommy? School...."

They don't want us, the pricks, the bastards.... But it's not you, honey, it's what happened, and it wasn't your fault....

"Isn't it nice to have Mam here this morning?" Mairead asked buoyantly. "Anna, do you want some pancakes? There's plenty of batter."

"Uh ... no, thanks." I loved Mairead's pancakes, but this morning the thought of sitting down to eat them made me feel as though she were babysitting me, too. When I had a job I had an excuse to rush out the door. I could pretend that, if I didn't work, I'd be making the pancakes. I didn't have to justify leaving; a modern woman was entitled to a career. I couldn't face the knowledge that I would have rushed to any job, from bagging groceries to mopping the emergency room floor at St. Seraphina's, just to get out of that house.

"And we'll be taking out the books pretty soon," Mairead warned Jack. To me: "He has some of his textbooks here at home. In fact, I went through his backpack and I think he has most of them?"

The perfect rhythm of her Dublin accent had been thrown off by one Californism: ending statements with the inflection of a question. She didn't wait for an answer in any case, but smiled as she picked up the mixing bowl. "You sure you don't want pancakes, now. Last chance. I've had mine."

"You've had yours," I echoed.

When the doorbell rang I jumped up. "I'll get it."

But Mairead clicked her tongue. "In your nightclothes, now," she teased, which was a ruse, because she really did disapprove. "Not even slippers. I'll go."

I sat down next to Jack. We rarely ate together, and on the infrequent occasions that Alex, Jack and I sat down to dinner — well, that was when we needed Mairead most. "What do you want to do today, Boychik?"

"Mommy?"

"Yes?"

"I want to live on Saturn."

"I wish we could, sweetheart."

"Mighty Quaso lives on Saturn."

"I know."

"Why can't we live on Saturn?"

"Uh … it's too hot. No, wait, it's too cold. Venus and Mercury are too hot because they're closer to the sun."

"My Very Educated Mother Just Served Us Nine Pumpkins. Are you educated?"

"Yes," I asserted. "Not as much as I want."

"So what can she serve us now that Pluto isn't a planet?"

"How about … how about just 'she served us nachos'?"

Jack laughed. It was a series of very loud, high-pitched, *ho-ho*'s. But just as I put my fingers on the back of his hand to quiet him, as I had learned from Mairead, he stopped himself and said, "You're funny, Mommy. Nachos, nachos, nachos...."

Then I smiled. I loved to entertain him.

"Mommy, why can't I go to school?"

My heart was breaking for him, a pale little boy who couldn't keep up with the other kids, who'd stand out all his life, who was covered in syrup now. I started to say, "Because they're remodeling," but then I thought, *no, no, this is an opportunity.*

I'd tried many times to get Jack to talk about that day, but he continued to insist that it was a secret. I thought by now he'd either become confused or didn't have the language. Or both.

But maybe the fiftieth time would be the charm. "You can't go back until they figure out what really happened to Tyler."

"Tyler died."

I cringed again at the memory of the dust-covered boy. Well, the best I could do now was find out what really happened. "I know, and it's very sad — "

I heard Mairead returning. Once again I'd assumed it was a package; I'd been self-medicating with shopping more than I had with Valium. But someone was following her.

"Val!" I was back on my bare feet. He was in his lambs' wool-lined jacket, the crease of his khaki pants pressed to the sharpness of a knife-blade. He carried a large cardboard box.

"You were expecting maybe the Fuller Brush Man?" An embarrassing attempt at a Yiddish accent.

"Oh, please don't do that," I begged, laughing witlessly.

Mairead gave me a look that reminded me stingingly of one of Alex's. *Bad enough you were going to go to the door in your nightclothes,* I could hear her scold. *Now there's a man in your house.*

In my own head I answered her, *mind your own business, woman,* but I also scolded myself: *You as good as an adulteress, just like your mother, and what did you think of* her? At least if I had to wear a scarlet "A" on my chest people might think it was a monogram.

"Val!" Jack cried. "Can we go bike riding again? Mommy won't let me go to school! School...."

"They're never too young to start blaming you." Val grinned at me. To Jack: "Next time, Pal. Today I came over to see your mom about *getting* you some schooling." He inclined his head toward the box. "Got some homeschool basics here."

"How did you know — " I stopped.

"When you said you had a meeting...." He shrugged.

My skin itched with paranoia. Were people gossiping all over town about Jack being expelled — the day after it happened? No — Val was just that intuitive. We'd talked so much that first night, and I'd been half-asleep through most of it. I was sure now that I had told him about hard Alex and I had searched for the right school, and how our final choice had still left us dissatisfied.

Mairead was clearing the table. "We had plans for studies this morning?" she said.

"Can I put this thing down?" Without waiting for an answer Val eased the box onto the granite-topped table. Then he said to Mairead, "You shouldn't have to worry about that. Anna tells me you help with his homework, but — " he laughed condescendingly — "I doubt she pays you enough to be a one-woman teacher, nanny *and* housekeeper."

"Mairead isn't the housekeeper," I said quickly. "Mairead and I are more like partners, really." I would have gone to put my arm around her if she hadn't been so shy.

But there was no rewinding that tape. As Val spoke, Mairead wiped the granite with a sponge. Her apron covered her blouse, and her broom still leaned against the table; all she needed was a little white lace cap. She lowered her head but couldn't hide the blush.

Val kept smiling, as if he deserved applause for his *noblesse oblige.*

Mairead wrung out the sponge, then poured out the freshly made pot of coffee, from which I had yet to drink. "While youse all talk, Jack and I will be going to the park."

Then she had Jack by the hand, while he asked her why he couldn't go to school. I watched them go out sadly, guiltily, but my heart racing at the thought of being alone with Val.

"Well." Val rubbed his hands together, and picked up the box. "Where can we spread out a little?"

Spread out. Was there a double-entendre there?

"We can take it in the dining room," I said, double-knotting the belt of my bathrobe.

The dining room was paneled in Victorian Gothic, with a chandelier worthy of *The Phantom of the Opera* hanging above the long oak table. Val carried the box easily but I could see how heavy it was from the way the veins in his hands stood out, and from the thump it made when this time, instead of sliding it on the table, he let it fall. I looked over the flaps and confirmed that it was full of books. I could see three titles: *Homeschooling without Hassle*, *The Spirit of Learning*, and *What my Child Taught Me.*

No double-entendres there. Val was all business now. He settled into the nearest chair and I sat down next to him, biting my lower lip. "So you think this is it now?"

"Anne Banane, what are the alternatives? Maybe it'll be temporary."

I dreaded the thought of homeschooling: Interviewing tutors. Jack home all day. Me on the phone, begging for playdates.

And the advice. "If I were his mother, I'd...." "What worked with my son was...."

I traced the grain of the wood on the table. I often saw faces in wood grain — distorted, ghostly faces: spirits trapped in pine or, in this, case, oak. "I guess I needed a reality check."

The real reality check was how he'd put our little encounter behind him as thoroughly as I'd thought I'd wanted him to. He was here to help. What Stud had ever done that for me before?

Val stretched his legs out under the table, his knees brushing my robe in the process. He leaned back, lacing his fingers behind his head. "I know you hate the whole New Agey thing, and I don't blame you, but maybe — don't jump on me now — maybe this was 'meant' to come out of this? You know a lot of Aspie parents swear by homeschooling."

He softened me with his use of the term "Aspie," now beginning to emerge online, which had a take-us-or-leave-us ring to it.

"Yes, I do know. They make good points, and Jack is like a lot of their kids. Some of them are really academically advanced — Jack isn't, but he learns way, way better in a one-on-one situation."

"So? What's the problem?"

"The problem is that I can hire the best tutors in the nine counties who'll 'teach to the test' and probably get him to score in the 90th percentile." That might have been a slight exaggeration. Or a flagrant one. "And it means nothing, because once you take him out of this dining room, or wherever you set up, he doesn't pick up a book. He doesn't count his change at the store. He goes right back to *Crime Conquerors* and his stupid websites." I was instantly ashamed to have spoken of him that way.

Val tapped his thumbs together. "He doesn't generalize," he observed.

"Yes — it's like if he learned to drive a car, but he could only drive that one car."

"The generalization might come, though, eventually."

"But meanwhile, there's the other big problem." I put my head down on my folded arms. "The whole socialization issue. I had a friend a few years back — I guess we're still friends — but she's one of the ones who kind of likes to play 'my disabled child is progressing faster than your disabled child —'"

"I think you might be a little sensitive," Val interrupted.

I raised my head with effort, pushed my hair out of my eyes, and suddenly remembered that I hadn't looked in the mirror since rolling out of bed. "So, in first grade, she says, 'you know, we just had Heidi tested and she's at age level with everything but speech and social skills.' "

"Well ... good for her?"

"Speech and social skills *are* autism!" I pounded my fist on the table hard enough to hear the books shake. "I don't see how we can help our kids unless we face the reality of where they are. Do we have to pretend our kids are angels to persuade the world we love them? To persuade ourselves?"

"Maybe that's the only way we *can* help our kids," Val said softly. "Denial has its place. Even competitiveness, if that's what it takes for some people. Even ruffling the feathers of *ma petite Anne Banane*."

I closed my eyes. "Well, forget everything I said about her. That is my problem. But as far as homeschooling goes — okay, Pathways was a mistake, but you can see what we were going for. The best of both worlds. He has an aide to write down the homework, and a tutor or Mairead and sometimes even me to help him do it, and then he also has NT peers to emulate."

"NT" was the abbreviation of "neuro-typical."

"So?" He threw up his hands. "Playgroups."

"Right. Right," I agreed sarcastically. "You sound just like his shrink. Integrated playgroups. You get some ASD kids playing with NT kids, with every interaction micro-managed by a professional, but then when you put the ASD kid back on the playground, with just regular teachers or the afterschool counselors — "

"Okay. Disaster." Val sighed. "You might never speak to me again after this, but I'm going to say it anyway. You talk about your friend not wanting to face her daughter's autism. So what do you and Alex do? You send Jack to a private school and hire that aide so he can get by. When someone asks you if you have any children you can say, 'oh, yes, a son,' and 'he goes to Pathways.' No one probes any further."

He was correct. So correct, that I wasn't sure if I *would* ever speak to him again. "We're totally 'out' about Jack. Saturday Alex took him to a goddam baseball game. What are we supposed to do, put up a gold star in the window?"

Val had a gift: He could not only calm my anger, but earn my immediate forgiveness. "We don't need to argue about this, because it's all academic. Huh — academic? Get it?"

"Huh."

"The school year's almost over. So, you have three, four months to experiment with a homeschool program." He slapped the side of the box. "Anne Banane, I didn't lug this over here for exercise."

"Okay," I agreed, as if I were doing him a favor, "we'll give it a try. I even have a place to use."

***

Val climbed the kitchen stairs. His hair burned gold in the sun, which filtered into the room through the skylight.

Painful as it was, I did see how hypocritical my martyrdom had been. The unhappy wife living for her son, absorbing the blows of her unfeeling husband, Rapunzel in this very comfortable tower and yet with hair too short to let anyone in. Val had shown me I was playing the same game as the online cult heroine-mom who blogged about "Josh's Special World."

"Whew," Val wheezed when we made it to the second floor. "You must have an extra room up here we can use."

"*Au contraire, mon frère*. There's a third floor. Can't you tell from the outside?"

"Damn it, Jim, I'm a psychotherapist, not a real estate agent."

The third floor was only partly furnished. The original destiny of these rooms had been to serve as private apartment for my mother-in-law, and she had moved a few of her larger (and more hideous) pieces up here before she died. She hadn't liked me very much, as I was of East European, rather than German, Jewish descent. By the time she died, she didn't like Jack very much, either, even if he were the long-awaited Kagen heir. Lucky for her, because I did have a couple of practical murder schemes, each of which would have been less pleasant than the stroke that carried her off so quickly that her housekeeper found her motionless over the sling back she was buckling.

By the time Val and I reached the top of this staircase the box fell by itself. Thanks to Val, some of the pain of Jack's expulsion had fallen away, too. Kids got expelled for all kinds of reasons: cheating on a test, selling drugs. I wasn't the first parent to cope with this.

"How did you get this stuff together so quickly?" I asked Val.

"My buddy came back from paternity leave yesterday, so I am now officially unemployed."

"Like me," I commiserated. "My boss came back from sanity leave."

Val shrugged. "You've got other things to do." He made himself at home; he disdained mom-in-law's horrific French empire settee and instead settled on the floor with his back against the wall. "Me, I've got to find something different than that St. Sair's gig."

I hesitated, but then lowered myself down next to him, cross-legged, keeping the box between us. "What was wrong with it?"

"I need a job that means something. Like with children. Or anything that helps people who couldn't get help otherwise." A sly smile. "But at least I got to meet you at St. Sair's."

I stared at the picture of the happy blonde grade-schooler swinging on the cover of one of the books. I found Val's messages mixed. Since he had entered the kitchen and re-entered my life, I'd tried to work up the nerve to talk to him about Saturday. At shrink school they teach you to be "honest about your feelings," but I'd never found that that principle applied to real life very well, and now I could think of what to say to him. "I'm awfully glad to see you," I finally choked out. That part was honest.

"Me, too. I mean I'm glad to see you, not me. I mean, I'm glad to see me, too, but — " .

I shook my head in feigned exasperation. He'd given me courage. "I can't — you know, we can't — "

So much for courage.

Val tucked my ever-errant wave behind my ear and I shivered. "I know," he said softly. "We blew it the other night. Okay. I've looked deep into my heart and find it difficult to locate regret. But — being involved with a married woman does not make me like myself very much."

Involved? I almost echoed. We weren't involved, we just … what was the difference between first and second base again? It wasn't an issue I had examined in close to two decades. I had retained my "technical purity," in the words of that great feminist, F. Scott Fitzgerald. It would have to do.

Besides, I could live without sex. Hadn't I been living without sex since the memory of man ranneth not to the contrary? Not completely, but I might as well have been. *Close your eyes and think of the next election.*

"*Could* we be friends, do you think? I'd much rather have a friend for life than a lover — " the word slipped out, so I coughed quickly — "for a month."

What I wanted, what I needed far more than I'd known, was someone who could make me laugh. Someone I could talk to. Mairead came the closest, and my sister Darya, with all her own neediness and quirks, shared my past as no one but a sister could. But neither of them were Val.

"I don't see why not. You're just as fascinating in a vertical position as horizontal."

I didn't care for how he reduced our little make-out session to geometry. Putting aside a physical relationship wasn't as easy as I had anticipated, and when he took my hand and stroked it, it seemed nearly impossible. I had a normal sex drive, more or less. It was just that I'd never met the man I want to befriend *and* fuck.

"I'll just be like Cyrano de Bergerac," Val said, "and worship you from afar."

Cyrano was one of my favorite plays. "You know, I always wondered, if Roxane were so in love with Cyrano's *soul*, how did she hang out with him for fifteen years and not realize she was in love with him, and not Christian?"

Val ran his hand around the collar of my bathrobe, folding it down evenly. "Because we really choose who we love," Val said. "It just doesn't feel that way."

"Am I disturbing anything?"

My body jerked so fast that I bumped my head against the wall. Alex. How could such a heavy man approach so silently?

"What — " I stopped. "What are you doing here?" A horrible thought occurred to me. "Did someone else die?" *Tyler's mother committed suicide; his father went on a shooting spree.* I couldn't think of any other reason for Alex to come home on a weekday.

"The autopsy results are in," Alex said. He did not acknowledge Val; he did not look at me, either. "I thought you might want to see them." He swung out of the room.

Val and I both stiffened, and instantaneously Alex put half his body through the door again. "Perhaps you'd like to get dressed," he suggested.

My hand flew to the collar of my bathrobe.

Val and I sat motionless another moment, and then I said, "He'll be going to the Batcave. You'd better go," I finished dully.

He tilted his head. "You need some alone time with your better half?" he asked archly.

"Didn't you hear?" I asked sharply. "The autopsy?" But I couldn't help but think, *he's jealous.* "I'm afraid this won't be pretty."

"He'll go back to the office after, though, won't he?"

"You catch on fast."

"So come to my apartment when he leaves. I mean, you might need moral support."

I glanced toward the door. Alex would be getting irritated with the delay. "I don't know where you live," I said.

*** *

I did get dressed, as quickly as I could, yet still taking enough care to tie a red-and-gray patterned silk scarf over my bosom to pull together a red cashmere turtleneck with a gray herringbone skirt. Val had offered to let himself out.

Even in daylight hours Alex's study was gloomy, with its dark wood paneling. That was why they called these rooms "dens." No one could approach except through the one door, and he always sat facing it, like an animal guarding itself against predators.

I went in without knocking and pushed his blotter a few inches in his direction, creating just enough of a ledge on which I could rest one buttock. "Talk to me," I said. *Because this is your last chance.*

Alex reached down beside him into his briefcase. I imagined him reaching down to withdraw a Hydra-like creature whose heads would each represent one of his complaints against me, and which, as I defended myself against them one at a time, would grow back as two.

As it turned out he brought out only one of his drab, ubiquitous accordion file folders. He heaved it against my thigh. I saw a thick sheaf of pages inside, bound together with industrial staples. I could read the cover.

Tyler Christopher Gaines
Autopsy Report

And below: "Submitted by Irwin Green, M.D., Deputy Medical Examiner"

I had to lick my finger to get enough traction to turn the first page.

I performed an autopsy on the body of Gaines, Tyler Christopher at the department of the San Francisco County coroner's office. Deceased is Caucasian male, 10 years old, weighing 70 pounds and measuring 48" from sole to crown.

"I can't read this," I said hoarsely. "Just tell me what it says. The important parts, you know?"

Alex cleared his own throat. "The M.E. found no cause of death."

"Oh, Jesus. I suppose you're going to tell me he was killed by the *Avada Kedava* curse." That was the spell in the *Harry Potter* series that caused death without leaving any signs. "You could have told me this upstairs."

"I would have if you'd been alone."

Ouch.

"These are an awful lot of pages for a document with no answer." I snapped a chunk of them against my thumb. "I've never heard of this happening."

"In your wide experience with autopsies?"

"Alex, please."

"It happens rarely, but it happens. It's never happened on my watch."

"I've got news, then. It just did."

His smug expression disappeared. "I swear to you, Anna, I called in Marianne before we left St. Sair's." He covered his eyes. "Okay — maybe it was when I when home to get Jack's pawn. I can't remember now. It was like — "

"Being in a black-out," I filled in.

He leaned back resignedly in his chair. "It wasn't clear there would be any fallout. I didn't need her administrative assistant running to the likes of Millard and Rotwell with an item, if I could handle it on my own."

"I see."

"Marianne's office told me just to stay out of it. If I'd kept calling her it would have looked bad — and anyone who ended up in charge of the investigation could subpoena any phone records, even my cell. I thought of driving to Sacramento. I didn't want to leave you and Jack. Now I wish I'd just gone. I didn't know until this morning that our own M.E., the county M.E., had done this. It was probably a mistake. Bureaucracies work on autopilot, even my department...." He rapped a knuckle hard against his teeth. "After everything that's happened the last few days, I'm feeling paranoid."

"I know that feeling."

"Can't you hear people asking, 'Isn't it just perfect that the autopsy reveals no cause of death?'"

"Oh, Alex, honey." He would never tamper with evidence, not if his own life were at stake. "It just takes one dirty look.... I've been there." With the moms at the school who didn't want Jack there even before Minotaur Island. At the first pre-school, where they couldn't kick him to the curb fast enough. Even at the Montessori pre-school that warehoused him for us, and where everyone "celebrated differences."

"The A.G.'s office came in and confiscated all the files. They acted as if it were a raid." His eyes darted from books to chess table. If this were how it felt for him when *I* was falling apart, then I understood better why it was so difficult for him to watch. "The A.G. will do a second autopsy, of course."

"Alex...." I was afraid to ask. "They can't really charge Jack with murder, can they?"

He slid the autopsy back toward himself. "I haven't wanted to scare you. But there have been cases like this.... Kids as young as eleven tried as an adult."

"But that's — "

"Conviction thrown out. But he still got five years on retrial." He spoke absently, caressing the title page of the autopsy.

I sputtered, "But Alex, he has — he has — "

"Asperger's Syndrome?" Alex looked up at me calmly. "Would you want that established as a valid affirmative defense? 'I'm not responsible because I'm on the spectrum?'" He steepled his fingers and as he stared at them he seemed to be going into a trance. "Advocacy groups don't *want* it used as a defense. It means that Asperger's — autism — is a mental disorder, not a learning disability, or...." he cleared his throat, "'a different kind of normal.'" He smiled benignly, but didn't look up. "All we can do is wait."

I slipped off his desk, afraid not just for Jack but for my husband. "There's something else, isn't there?"

He was organizing pencils in his World's Best Lawyer mug, as carefully as the most expert flower arranger. "I understand that Tyler's father is getting ready to file a wrongful death suit against us."

I had hardly forgotten Alex threatening me with that the night before the PROTECT meeting. But I had decided to believe that it was just that: a threat meant to punish me by giving me something else to worry about.

I slumped on his leather sofa. "Is that all? Let him have some money if it makes him feel any better. How does that compensate him for the death of his son?"

"He's going to ask for sixty million dollars."

"Sixty million?" I echoed. I wouldn't give Jack's life for a billion, but.... "Can he get that?"

"You never know what a jury's going to do. That's the first thing you learn in a courtroom. You never know what a jury's going to do," he repeated to himself.

Now I was the one knocking my thumb knuckle against my teeth, a habit I'd picked up from him. "He can't get that. He can't get that. Besides ... we have a personal liability policy for this kind of thing, right?"

"There have been wrongful death settlements for over a hundred and fifty million. Sometimes they're reduced on appeal, but — "

"But we have a personal liability policy, right?" I asked again.

"Yes," he said. "For ten million dollars."

The house alone was worth seven, eight million. I didn't know how much money Alex had, but it wasn't any sixty million. "Why so little?"

"That was what my father had," he said decisively.

"When, during the fucking Depression?" Sixty million minus ten million....

"Anna," he said, very calmly, "you know I don't like it when you use language like that."

I forgot the lawsuit for a moment, remembering the scene in *Gone with the Wind,* the movie, when Vivien Leigh realizes that her father has lost his mind, while Alex went on in the same disturbingly composed manner, "I'd appreciate it if you'd join me at Robert Britteridge's office at the end of his work day. Six o'clock."

"Of course. If my being there will help Jack." Robert "Bob" Britteridge was our family attorney.

Alex carefully positioned a stray pencil flush against the blotter's edge. "Well, if you don't mind, I'm going back downtown. Voters didn't put me in office to gossip the afternoon away at home, right?" He smiled.

I was only too glad to escape that gloomy den, dark before its time.

CHAPTER TEN
BEHIND THE GREEN DOOR

I knocked on the splintery wood of the pale green door.

I'd fled here like a refugee, not concerned with my destination as long as I could escape the danger at home. Val had written down his address using a page torn from one of the spiral notebooks he had included among the school supplies — "stocking stuffers," he'd called them. And that was just what I did with the slip of paper: stuffed it between my breasts, where my bra held it in place.

He's not here, I thought, after my first knock. *This is a sign. I'll go home.*

I turned my back to the door and looked up and down the street. Once I'd wondered how people could bear to live with a cancer diagnosis, the onset of blindness, the kidnapping of a child. I'd heard people glibly remark, "Oh, I'd just kill myself if that happened."

But you don't.

Behind me, the door opened, and when I turned around, Val did not look at all surprised.

"You said — you said I could come to talk."

"And I'm a man of my word." He stepped back and ushered me in with a sweep of his arm.

"N-no. It was a mistake."

"A bigger mistake to just stand out here," he said. "Broad daylight. Many neighbors."

I bowed my head when I shuffled in. "So this is Aunt Patsy's place." I had to say something.

"M'm h'm."

It was the lower unit of a duplex, very much of the 70s, with a shag carpet that had once been emerald, but had faded to tourmaline. Val had been traveling just six months ago, when his aunt's terminal illness brought him back to the States. "It was time to get back on the career track," he had said, "but I'm sorry it had to happen that way."

Aunt Patsy had owned the building, renting out the upper flat, and now her daughter let Val stay in the lower unit for a while, hoping that the elderly upstairs tenants would move out (or move even farther "upstairs") and that she could sell the building with two empty apartments.

"You can sit down," he said. "I mean, just until you leave again."

The sofa was covered with strawberry blonde hairs. The sight of them triggered the smell of urban dog, a mix of animal, gasoline and pigeon droppings that no amount of bathing could entirely remove from a pet in the city.

As if on cue, a Golden Retriever bounded in.

"You don't mind *les pooch-ays*?" Val asked. "Jack told me he was scared of them, that first night at the hospital."

It was true. A Chihuahua could drive him into traffic.

"Otherwise you would have met her already. I don't usually go out without her on weekends."

"No, no, I don't mind." I scratched her head between her floppy ears. She had a thick, feathery saffron coat and white forepaws.

"Elsie, this is Anne Banane." He scratched her neck hard, his hand near mine. "I know you don't like to share, Elsie love, but let's all try to be friends, okay?"

Elsie squeezed between us, wagging her tail possessively. "How long have you had her?"

"Oh … we go way back. When I came home I — " he laughed, self-consciously, I thought. "You might say I got her in a custody battle." I quickly changed the subject. "What happened since I left you?"

I told Val about the suspect autopsy and Gaines's lawsuit.

"I know why Alex never raised our personal liability coverage. He never wanted to admit that anything could happen to him. Now he's weirded out on me."

"You mean, more than usual?"

"This is serious. I'm scared." I didn't like Alex but I needed him. And I needed his money to take care of Jack. I needed money for private schools and someday, if we were lucky, a private college, but if not, then whatever else he needed to help him find a way to blend into the community. I couldn't take care of him alone. Mairead and Alex did that. All I did was read to him at night and live with his lousy father.

"It was always his pattern to take out his anger on me. I hated it but this is worse. What if he cracks?"

"He's not going to crack," Val said with regret. "You'll see. He'll be back to his usual asshole self by the time you get home."

I sank against his shoulder. "If anybody'd told me I'd feel better knowing that my husband was going to revert to his jerk self — "

Val tilted my chin up with a crooked forefinger. "Why do you put up with it?"

"You've seen him at his worst. We haven't had much of a marriage, but most of the time we leave each other alone."

"Even at all those parties you say you go to?"

"Especially there."

He put his arm around me and leaned his cheek on my head. And from there it was inevitable, or so it seemed, that his lips reach down and mine reach up until they met and then crushed each other.

We'd been here before. The very day before. I was not yet a cheater. An adulteress. A bitch. A tramp. A whore.... Not yet.

Alex would never cheat on me. But that was only because it was Against The Rules. *What rules, whose rules? Since we've gone this far, what difference does it make if we go a little further?*

And everyone else is doing it. Half the male elected officials in the county have girlfriends. It isn't just the men. Bob Britteridge and *his wife are having affairs. 30% of "dads" are raising non-biological children!*

Such is the power of rationalization. Such was the power of his kiss.

***

The inevitable buzzkill came when Val, forming a plank above me and resting his entire weight on his arms (which trembled not at all), asked, "Do I need a condom?"

"No," I said, "I haven't used birth control for years." I had what was called secondary infertility. It was an unhappy thought, but it passed quickly into another thought: *He has condoms here.* That meant he was responsible. That also meant other women.

But a moment later he was inside me and I was only thinking that it was pleasant and that I was so, so happy to have sex with someone I liked. But I lay passively. It had been so long since there had been anyone else that I didn't know what to do. Val didn't speak. He kissed me, his hand resting on my cheek. But then he put his mouth on my breast, and an electric current passed from my nipple to my groin. I was passive no longer. I grabbed at his hair, pulling until I heard a muffled "yow." He thrust harder, but without separating his mouth from my breast. He arched his back in what looked like a painful position, but I clutched his hair more tightly and now thrust my hips up to meet his. A few seconds later a mighty orgasm hijacked my body, spreading through my torso and limbs. It was the first orgasm I had had during the actual act of intercourse.

I turned away from him, rolled over on my side and curled up in a semi-fetal position. I covered my breasts with my arms.

"Are you all right?" he asked.

I could only nod. I wiped a little tear from the outer corner of one eye.

***

I drifted off to sleep then. When I woke, it was like waking up in a hotel room on the first night of your vacation, when it takes a moment to remember where you are. But this wasn't just a strange hotel. This was a different world, and not because I could almost feel the springs of the ancient mattress beneath me.

There was no going back now. Technical purity = history.

I still had my back to Val, and I pulled my knees up even more closely to my chin. Before this afternoon, I'd been unhappy, but I'd been safe. Perhaps I didn't know what unhappiness was.

I did know what ambivalence was: waking up with the man you are falling in love with when you know that his nearness hurts the people — the person — you already love more than anyone.

I leaned over the edge of the bed to see my red and gray clothes in a heap. I wondered if I had unconsciously chosen fabrics that didn't wrinkle easily.

Raising my eyes I stared at myself in the mirrored sliding doors of the bedroom closet.

"How 'bout some music?"

"Isn't that supposed to *put* me in the mood?"

"Anne Banane, if you were any more in the mood when you got here I'd be in traction by now."

That wasn't the way I wanted to see it, but I offered no argument.

Val got up, turned on an old-fashioned stereo that rested on the floor, and selected, from a low shelf in a corner, a Simon and Garfunkel album. He crawled back into bed and put his arms around me.

"Did you have a nice nap, Banane? I fell asleep, too. But that's a guy thing."

"M'mmm." I snuggled into his firm, downy chest. I might as well enjoy it while I could. He stroked my bare back with his fingertips. On the other side of the bedroom door, Elsie whined and scratched.

I raised my eyes again, this time over his shoulder. There was a window onto a little breezeway alongside the building. But it let in very little light and I couldn't get an idea of the time. "What time is it?" I asked.

When he didn't answer, I wriggled free of his embrace to look at my watch.

Val stretched. "*I* don't need a watch to tell me what I want when I want it."

I stared at my own, burning wrist. My watch was set to run twelve minutes ahead, but since I knew it was twelve minutes ahead, it didn't help me get places on schedule.

And at the moment, my schedule was fucked.

I brought the watch closer to my face as if that would make the numbers change.

6:22. That meant that it was 6:10 p.m.

"I was supposed to be downtown at 6:00."

Val mimed looking at an invisible watch. "Well, it's half past a little late for that."

I sprung upright. "Alex will kill me!"

"I doubt it." He pulled me back down, and nuzzled my neck. "Murder is a felony. I love your perfume, by the way. What is it?"

"Light Blue."

"It smells like you. An insouciant bouquet with a very sexy body and — " he raised his nose in the air and pinched the tip — "and as for the aftertaste … definitely wanting more."

I let my head fall back on the pillow. Val stuck his left arm under me and reached for my breasts with his right. I resisted the urge to shove him away. I left Alex on the verge of a psychotic break to visit my personal Fantasyland. Well, my vacation was over. "Help me think of a really good lie," I begged.

He propped himself on his elbow. "God, I don't know. I'm not a very good liar. Car trouble with dead cell phone?"

"Maybe." I didn't want to hurt his feelings by telling him that yes, that was fairly lame as lies went. Alex knew I was both more resourceful and responsible than that under ordinary circumstances. That was where I got into difficulty — the circumstances.

"Being late is better than not showing up," Val tried to reassure me.

As I got out of bed I immediately felt the stickiness begin to travel down my thighs.

"You'll be all right." He caught my hand, and kissed it quickly. "I promise."

***

I freshened up as much as I could before leaving Val's. There was no point in going downtown now, so I headed back to the house, amusing and torturing myself with fanciful tales. What if I put the blame on Pollutia, the newest villainess on *Crime Conquerors*?

No, unless I was spouting arterial blood when he first saw me, I was in trouble.

But this was not going to happen again. Never. Never, ever, ever. I'd been weak. But fear of repercussions with Alex was branding the lesson into my flesh. If I can just get out of this, I promised myself, I will have learned my lesson and never ever let it happen again. There had to be some statute of limitations, especially on a one-time ... encounter. Let months and then years go by and I could learn to forget. Forget....

I got home before Alex and I couldn't help but thank God for that. I took a real shower, using an exfoliating sponge and applying a heavier layer of Light Blue body lotion than usual. I removed what little remained of my make-up and re-applied. I put the same skirt and sweater back on, so that Alex would see neither rumpled clothes on my side of the closet nor an extra outfit in the hamper set aside for outgoing dry cleaning.

I repossessed Jack from Mairead and said my official good-night to her before she went down to her own apartment for the evening.

When the garage door opened at 8:30 the rattling chain tolled for me. But the moment Alex came into the kitchen, where Jack and I, over bowls of ice cream, were alternately discussing why he couldn't go to school and why we couldn't live on Saturn with Mighty Quaso, I knew that I was going to live to see another day.

"We didn't need you," Alex said before I even spoke. The dazed look was gone, replaced by satisfaction. He dove into the refrigerator. *"You load sixteen tons...."*

"I-I'm glad," I faltered. "I — " No. Stop. If he doesn't ask for an explanation, don't volunteer it.

"Did Mairead leave me something?"

"There's a Saran-wrapped plate," I said in a small voice, "right next to the Tupperware with the — "

He'd found it. I crunched down on my lower lip, to fight the compulsion I had to fill any silence with my own nattering.

"How was your dinner, Master Jack?" Alex boomed.

"Great! Great...."

"Glad to hear it." Alex set his own food on the table, then farmed a healthy crop of cowlicks on his son's head. "We've got to get back to the stadium pretty soon, eh?"

Something good had happened. And in the fading light of the late spring kitchen, we felt like a family. Father, mother, son.

"You know, Young Master, we've got to take Mom to the next Giants' game with us. What do you think?"

"Yeah! But you said...."

"I said she'd love the game," Alex interrupted.

"No, you said she...."

I rescued him. "You only have the two season tickets."

"Well, let's see what I can do." Alex winked at me. "I'll make a few calls." Then, to Jack: "Your old dad can pull a rabbit out of a hat when he wants."

"Can you really, Daddy? Can you pull a — a goose from the ground?" Jack laughed his signature shrieky laugh. "Can you pull a duck from the sky?"

Alex checked his watch. "Right now I'd settle for pulling victory from the jaws of defeat. Almost bedtime, isn't it?"

"I start getting ready at nine. Nine...."

Another fifteen minutes.

"Tell you what. Why don't you watch TV for a little bit and then your mom'll put you to bed?"

Jack scurried out of the room, and I was struck again by how normal we seemed. I got up to switch on the lights. When I turned to face Alex I saw he had an expression that Jack had sometimes: hesitant, looking for approval.

"Don't you want to hear what Bob Britteridge had to say?"

"Of course."

His own laugh was less perfunctory than usual. "He thinks we'll be fine."

"About the wrongful death suit?" I asked on an intake of breath.

"Yep. Too many hurdles for Gaines. The first is, he can't just sue us, he has to sue everyone from the Pathways board members to Ms. Scarborough. It's colloquially known as 'having no empty chairs.'" Alex looked down at Mairead's roast beef and mashed potatoes, but instead of stripping off the Saran wrap, he went back to the refrigerator where dished himself up a generous bowl of chocolate-chocolate chip ice cream.

"The deal," he began through his first mouthful, "is that if Gaines names only us as defendants the first thing we say is, 'hey, not our fault.'

Because Minotaur Island was dangerous and the school should have done more research. Ms. Scarborough didn't ask enough parents to help. Gaines is only after us because we have some money. We're 'deep pocket' defendants."

Scarborough wouldn't be worth suing. Neither would Ranger Ed, or even Pathways — they operated as a non-profit. "But the government has deep pockets, right?"

"The deepest," Alex agreed, without breaking the rhythm of shoveling ice cream into his mouth, "and they also have unlimited resources to fight back with. Case like that would take twenty years. No, Gaines has to focus on us if he wants money before he's in a nursing home."

He chuckled at his joke, but it felt good to be back in our teacher/student roles, where we had been happiest, back where we had started, and to watch him gratify his illusory appetite. "Gaines' only real hope would be a quick criminal conviction. If no charges are ever brought against Jack, then it'll be almost impossible."

We didn't think Jack had killed him, Dylan had said.

He's threatened to stab other students, Yeung had said.

Alex suppressed a burp. Now that the ice cream bowl was empty, he pulled Mairead's dinner toward himself.

"No charges," I repeated. "Do you think there won't be any charges, then?"

"Nooo," he drawled. "We'll be fine."

We'll be fine. Those three words were such a relief that I savored them for a few moments before moving back to the remaining problem. "Aren't there cases of defendants who weren't convicted in criminal court but who lost in civil courts?"

"But at least there *was* a criminal trial," Alex reminded me. There was a dot of ice cream at one corner of his mouth. "Gaines was counting on that to happen fast."

Alex's new outlook released the pressure from a house that had been ready to implode. So I didn't say aloud what I was thinking: that it all could still happen. I'd already been through the next ten, fifteen years in my mind: Jack in the "Conservation Camp" in Nevada City, trying to make sense of how to plant tomatoes, when he couldn't make a bed. I always tried to stop myself there and not think about the harder core urban detention facilities, about the older, bigger boy in the upper bunk, the pedophile hiding in the bathroom stall....

Because if the court picked up on this contagious perception of Jack as truly dangerous, they'd never let him stay with us — or even in foster care — while his case worked its way up through the appellate court system.

Against the specter of Jack's incarceration, Alex's bankruptcy did not seem devastating. But the possibility, that Alex was offering to me now like yet another fresh bowl of ice cream, that would we escape both scenarios....

Life hadn't really been that bad before, had it? Jack was so sweet, Alex let me buy all the clothes I wanted.... Why had I complained so much? Why hadn't I appreciated what I had?

And why, oh why, had I risked it?

I remembered my promise to myself in the car. Yes, it was over with Val. It was too bad, but it wasn't possible that no one else in San Francisco could teach Jack to ride a bike.

Alex shoved the empty ice cream bowl aside, then gazed at the roast beef and potatoes as if he hadn't seen food in three days. "Ahh.... Good old Mairead. I don't know how restaurants can get away with putting vinegar on weeds and calling it a salad. Not that your cooking isn't just fine," he added.

"You don't have to say that, dear. We both know I'm just a microwave jockey."

"You have other talents, then." He cut into the beef and began to eat without putting his fork down. He wouldn't do so until the plate was bare.

I was reaching for the ice cream bowl to put in the dishwasher when he burped and said, "I'm sorry about the way I've been lately. I could cut my tongue out sometimes."

The bowl he'd used was one of Jack's, depicting the cast of *Crime Conquerors.* "I, um ... it's been pretty hard the past week, hasn't it?"

Two more bites and he had scraped up the final knob of potato. He shoved back from the table and stretched out his arms. "C'm'ere."

He pulled me down on his lap. "I ran into our friends Millard and Rotwell."

"I wouldn't call them anybody's friends," I said. "Where did you — run into them?"

"They came to see me. At the office, before I went to meet Britteridge. They're onto Riordan. They know I did the city a favor when I benched him."

I nodded respectfully.

"So...." He took my two hands in his and pressed them together. "Tomorrow their lead item is going to be a little exposé of Mr. Patrick R. Nothing about Jack. Just a little 'graph telling the story behind the story.

How Riordan messed up and why he wants revenge — why it's personal with me."

I wriggled in his lap.

"They promised me they could give my whole campaign another jumpstart," Alex went on, "'in exchange for a little gossip.'"

"But Alex — "

"You know I wouldn't betray anyone's trust. I threw them a few crumbs and they gobbled them up." He mused, "Those guys are like Walter Winchell twice over. He was before my time, even an old coot like me. But you and Jack keep me young," he said fondly. "Do you know who Walter Winchell was?"

"Of course I do. You know what a nostalgia buff I am." I quoted, "'And all the ships at sea.' As a matter of fact, there was a musical, *Sweet Smell of Success,* just a couple of years ago, with a character named J.J. Hunsecker, that's based — "

"Tell you what." He put his lips right up against my ear. "Why don't you put Jack to bed and meet me in our room, say... how long does it take?"

My mouth was dry. "Forty-five minutes or so." It would be more like an hour. Maybe Alex would fall asleep before Jack.

"Good girl." He eased me off his lap and patted my behind.

CHAPTER ELEVEN
WILL OF IRON, LEGS OF STEEL, HEART OF GOLD

Is it *schandenfreude* or were we all hoping for Mr. Perfect, D.A. Alex Kagen, to take a fall? He'd counted on winning re-election on memories of the Gary Bryce Smithson case, but dear readers, Mr. Smithson was a man convicted before he walked into court, and there are still unanswered questions about interrogation techniques used by the police. Kagen, a shoe-in until he botched the investigation into criminal charges against his son, now faces an interesting race with fresh-faced challenger Decorrah Catherine Washington.

***

Alex swept his hand across the top of his chess table. Black and white pieces flew in the direction of the door. I ducked before the black king hit the wall.

"I'm going to sue the bastards!" He pulled down volumes of the California Reporter from his shelves. At first he seemed to be looking for a case, since he opened a couple of books, but the dismantling itself quickly became his only objective. They were heavy tomes and made a resounding *thump* as they began to make a pile on the carpet.

It had been the sound of the first of them biting the dust that had woken me up. When I turned on the bedside lamp I saw that it was 4:20 AM, which meant 4:08. Another thump. *Earthquake.* I was running toward Jack's room when I heard the noise coming from the Batcave at the other side of the house.

When I first came in, Alex was back behind his desk, his satin robe unbelted, revealing the plaid pajamas that only a grandfather would wear, his face dangerously red, his eyes darting madly around the room, his jaw slack. He pointed to the monitor of his computer. "This — this is what they wrote about me!" he sputtered.

"What?" I shivered uncontrollably. I had dashed here without my own bathrobe, and I crossed my hands over my chest.

I guessed what had happened. Alex had gotten up early to see the morning's *Chronicle* on the Internet. He'd done that before when he was waiting for a piece of special interest — coverage of an important trial or an article about crime rates in which he was quoted. This morning he must have arisen to see the plug that Millard and Rotwell had promised him — a plug so powerful that it came with a guarantee to put his whole campaign back on track. He hadn't seen what he expected.

"They lied to me! They swore to me! They lied *straight to my damn face!*"

"Shh, shh." I was too frightened and too smart to remind him that Millard and Rotwell were well-known for that strategy. Alex had just thought he was exempt from it.

I slid one foot along the carpet, not breaking contact with the weave. My arms remained protectively across my chest. "Everything'll be all right. You'll see. Everything'll be all right." I didn't know how to get him back under control. He was like Jack when he fell over the tantrum cliff, beyond the reach of reason. But Alex outweighed Jack by more than a hundred pounds — I was hardly going to restrain him physically.

He stormed past me and back to the bookshelves. "There's a case here on libel from just last year, I don't need any fucking Lexus-Shmexus to find it...."

I seized the moment to read the Millard and Rotwell paragraph. "*...until he botched the investigation....*"

They *were* bastards. No good to remember the others they had done it to. Like the county assessor who paid illegal immigrants less than minimum wage to remodel his bathroom, or the supervisor who used his ex-wife's address to establish residency in his district.

Alex, after all, never pushed the bounds of ethics.

Alex stomped back towards the desk, and this time I scuttled away like a terrified crab. I needed to maintain an escape route.

"Honey, come to bed," I pleaded. Just a few hours before we had made love there. "This is just one little paragraph. Everything will blow over. You'll see."

"*You* go to bed, if all you can think of is getting your damn beauty rest!"

"Alex, sweetheart, if you wake Jack...." Though Jack had returned to being his cheerful self most of the time, he still had the odd unexpected meltdowns, which I believed were triggered by flashbacks to his night at St. Seraphina's.

"To hell with Jack!"

He slammed his fist into the monitor of his computer. It toppled off the desk, landing on its back on the chess table. I heard the crack of marble.

He quieted. We both stared at the monitor. The screen was unbroken but after a moment the light flickered out.

Alex stared at me, panting. "Just get the hell out of here and leave me alone," he said.

***

It's easy to commit to a diet after a huge meal. It was the same with my promise that my first visit to Val's apartment would also be my last.

I released myself from that promise when Alex's computer monitor cracked his chess table. I didn't know if it could be fixed.

I went back the next day, and the next.

But marriages do survive infidelity. I could name several among our acquaintances, and I was certain that there were many more whom I didn't know about.

I'd never seen Alex lash out physically before, and that frightened me, but there were no more explosions, and I came to see it as an anomaly, a time when the heavily armed guard around his id was out on leave.

It was almost as if the rest of his so-called pyche was on leave, too, but unfortunately, not quite. On the rare occasions he came home, he disappeared immediately into the Batcave with a pot of black coffee, without even saying good-night to Jack. The last time he had retreated so far into himself had been after I came home from my appointment with Dr. Brenna Wolichek.

Now that I was unemployed and Alex no longer asked me to accompany him to fundraisers or speeches, it required very little subterfuge to get to Val's apartment. I did not try to rationalize our liaison; I knew it was wrong, because it could hurt Jack. But I also knew it couldn't last. I would find the strength to end it eventually, but most likely he would tire of me before that anyway. His ruling passions for helping others and for adventures in the wilderness ran deep, but in their micro-manifestations they burned hot and fast. It only stood to reason that his passion for women was the same.

Soon his life would be with another woman. And my life would always be on Jackson Street, in a big hollow house, with a boy whom I loved unconditionally but who also drove me crazy, a husband whose heavy footsteps I dreaded to hear, and an Irish nanny who moonlighted as Jewish mother.

But meanwhile, I kept going back to Val's like Robert Downey Jr. to rehab for the moments I spent enfolded in his arms, with our legs entwined together, Simon and Garfunkel on the stereo.

When Alex's cursing woke me at 2 a.m., I remembered lyrics from the original concept album of *Evita:* "I thought the more who loved me the more loved I'd be." Maybe the lyrics were deleted because most Americans would not agree with Eva Peron's dying conclusion about popularity contests — contests like Academy Awards and elections: "Such things cannot be multiplied."

***

If Val and I were destined to be together only for a short time, it would be tragic if our affair were discovered. So I wasn't just discreet, I was fanatical. When I went to his apartment, I parked three blocks away and walked to his door by different routes. I bought — with cash — two pay-for-minutes-in-advance cell phones. The phones were supposed to be untraceable and were the only way we communicated. The only further precaution I could have taken would have been to wear a Groucho Marx moustache and glasses.

The problem was that the longer we carried on (such an unfortunate term), the deeper in I got. The quagmire theory of politics applied to my love life. The irony was that I'd that I'd never had a real love life before. Yes, there was that short-bearded philosophy grad student who had no greater ambition than to remain a philosophy grad student, who liked foreign films and espresso, like *that* was something original in Berkeley in the late 80s, and I'd had professors before Alex: (supposedly) unhappily married men who crept into my bedroom after dark and left well before sunrise. Daddies and Studs.

But Val…. It was like putting vodka into a Virgin Mary and turning it into a Bloody Mary. There's no way to go back to being a virgin.

His apartment even began to feel like my own. From the basement of the house on Jackson Street, I unearthed *tchotchkes* that Alex hadn't allowed me to display: the pre-9/11 model of the World Trade Center that I considered a memorial but which he found offensive; the model of the Eiffel Tower that he simply regarded as tacky; the picture of myself with my mother and sister which he claimed was too blurry for display.

I arranged these in Val's apartment, and they contributed to the illusion that we were a real couple, which gradually overtook my common sense. As always, rationalization fueled my folly. But Val was my lover *and* my friend. He still wanted to help me launch Jack's homeschooling, and he persuaded me one afternoon to go to the Teachers' Supply Store with him. I agreed because Jack's education was stalled at home.

The store was in a quiet part of the Outer Richmond, warehouse-sized, and deserted during school hours. The multitude of long aisles with shelves reaching above my head made it feel even safer.

Val and I were leafing through workbooks when I heard a piercing shout. "Anna Kagen! How *are* you?"

Inevitable, maybe, but did it have to be Lourdes de Leon? *Doyenne* of the autism community and Filipina yenta?

Her hug was more like a tackle.

"Lourdes," I croaked, stuck in her python-like grip.

"How *are* you? You look so *tired.*"

"I'm fine." Set free, I pulled my sleeves down.

"No, really, you look like you haven't slept! If only you and Alex could get away for the weekend. You know, I could take Jack. Would he stay with me?"

I don't know. The Weather Channel doesn't report from Hell. Yet.

"If he would, then you and Alex could get away for the weekend. Maybe to the wine country. Or there's a bed and breakfast in Monterey that Craig and I...."

I looked at Val for help. He immediately thrust out his hand. "Hi, there. Alex Valentine. Call me Val."

Lourdes returned Val's vigorous shake. "Lourdes de Leon. But Anna, it must be awful for you. Weren't you there when that poor boy died?"

I tried to speak; failed. In that moment Lourdes' eyes settled on Val, then narrowed. "How do *you* two know each other?"

"Would you believe I met this little girl back at Berkeley?" Val asked, reaching around my shoulder and giving it an uninhibited squeeze.

"Really? You went to Berkeley? You must have known — "

She started spitting out names, but Val interrupted her. "My only memory of Berkeley is of little Anna Shapiro," he said wistfully.

I was grateful for his rescue but wished he would have a little less fun with it. Lourdes was a lot smarter than she seemed on brief acquaintance. She had founded FARE ("Families Are Really Equal") a non-profit group not dissimilar to Decorrah Washington's ChildCARE, but focused on ASD children and their parents, and much more successful.

"What are you going to do about school?" Lourdes asked me. "I heard Jack was expelled! Anna, I think it's so *unfair*."

"We're going to try homeschooling for a bit."

"I've been telling you for years that's what you should do! The Regional Center pays for us to homeschool Heidi. What have you got there?" She peered over the edge of our cart, the clucked. "No, you don't want that speller. There's a new edition, you can only get it on the Internet. I'll bring it over this afternoon."

"Not a good day," I said firmly.

"Well, then tomorrow. I'll bring Heidi, and then I can stay. Tell Alex to come home early so the two of you can at least have a romantic dinner out. I know the maitre d' at — "

"Lourdes, it's been real," Val interrupted again. "But if I don't get this little girl home, I know a man who's going to be jealous." He cupped his mouth and stage-whispered, "He's *so* possessive."

Val sounded very sincere when he said that. Very humble and sincere. I decided that we were going to get away with this.

"I'll come to a support group meeting soon," I promised Lourdes.

"Oh, no," Lourdes protested. "Don't come to the group."

For months, she'd been begging me to return.

"It'd be too much for you. Nothing but questions. You and I have lunch next week instead. What day is — "

"I'll call you." I put both hands on the cart and gave it a shove, bumping against her hip. "Oh, gosh, I'm sorry."

"No problemo!" But as she realigned the wheels of the cart she stopped me with a hand on my chest. "I just want you to know that I don't believe it for a second."

"Believe what, exactly?" I asked through a tight throat.

"That Jack was trying to stab that boy. I mean just because he has a history — "

"He doesn't have a history!" I burst out.

Val crouched a little, ready to pounce on her, a panther from a tree.

And Lourdes *was* smart: smart enough to retreat a step. "The attorney general will never get that indictment."

"What indictment?"

"You know. She wants murder one. Isn't that *ridiculous?*" Lourdes rolled her eyes. "It's just because she's up for re-election. She has to appease every right-winger in the state who thinks she's soft on crime — just because she's from San Francisco."

I shoved the cart forward again. Unfortunately, her feet were not in my way. Val did not follow immediately, so I motioned to him.

"I hope Alex isn't worried this will hurt *his* chance at becoming attorney general."

We kept walking.

"Call me!"

"I'll call you!" I promised sweetly, then added to Val, "I just don't know what yet."

                    ***

Lourdes's words clanged in my ears the rest of the day. The fact that she hadn't remembered Val from his stint at FARE — he'd been there briefly, he explained — was very little comfort.

Murder one. That was not possible. But an indictment, maybe, in spite of what Alex had said.... *He* wouldn't talk to me at all anymore. But there was Maddy — Lourdes's chief rival in women's freestyle gossip.

The next morning I called her. For her, morning began around noon, but I called her at 11:00 a.m. I couldn't tell if I'd woken her up, but I thought I heard the rustle of bedclothes before the more familiar-sounding *snap* of an old Butane lighter. After a couple of deep drags, she was ready to schmooze.

"Don't worry, honey, Marianne's going to stall as long as possible." She had the hoarse voice of the heavy smoker. "She thinks she's Elizabeth the fucking first." Her voice rose mockingly on "Elizabeth" and it made her cough.

"She can do that?"

"Damn straight she can do that. She can keep saying" — mimicking Marianne Pasquale again, if Marianne were an elderly society lady, which Marianne was most decidedly not — "'we don't have all the facts, dahling, we must continue on!'"

For now Marianne had the excuse of waiting for the results of the second autopsy, which was taking an unusually long time. Marianne was in a statewide race, and whether she indicted Jack for some level of homicide (murder one *was* ludicrous, Maddy assured me), tried to indict him and failed, or dropped the charges altogether, she would alienate a significant segment of voters. For outside of San Francisco, Jack's story commanded its share of sympathy. It was only in our own most liberal city that he was perceived as an actual danger, and Maddy blamed Riordan and Gaines for stirring up that fear.

On the other hand (Maddy continued to explain, between drags and hacks), there were those who said they were tired of miscreants of any age blaming their crimes on everything from poor nutrition to dyslexia.

For now, Gaines was stalling, too. He had not officially filed his wrongful death suit, because he was waiting for the Attorney General's office to do the work of discovery for him. He'd be able to subpoena that information and save thousands in billable hours.

"This all sounds encouraging," I said. *So why don't you sound encouraged?*

Maddy exhaled very slowly to postpone answering. "Hell, Alex commissioned that poll. I told him not to."

Alex's numbers were down. The numbers leaked, and Decorrah's campaign received a jolt of confidence. She was attracting more money and volunteers. But Riordan was spending it, Maddy suspected, not just to replace his worn-out wingtips but his Reagan-era suits. "If enough money comes in he might be able to finance a hair transplant," she cackled.

I tuned out for the rest, thinking of the phrase popular among Alex's colleagues: "There's only one poll that counts."

"And do you know what I heard about Sherri Pechner...?" Maddy said. I heard the *pop* of a cork, and the splash of liquid. Chardonnay was Maddy's drink of choice. If she were drinking this early in the day, the pressure was getting to her, too.

I didn't listen closely to Maddy's story about Sherri's fling with a county supervisor, but at some point I interrupted, "What can I do to help?"

"Send Sherri flowers and sign the supe's name," Maddy chuckled. "We don't want her to get any ideas about *your* hubby again."

Again? "No, I mean, help with Alex."

I heard her swallow. "Try to keep his spirits up. Try to keep everything 'up.'" She coughed on her wine, amused by her own joke.

"Right."

"Do something new for him. I'm serious. Doggie-style."

I spent the rest of the day trying to shake that image.

***

Short of giving myself dry heaves, there *was* something I could do to help Alex.

I had pictured Lourdes as the Hamster of Evil powering the rumor wheel, but the city was crawling with similarly inclined rodents, and the wheel could turn a brief extra-marital affair into a Satanic cult. One county supervisor had done six months for embezzlement when (according to Alex) all he'd done was borrow money for a taxi.

But if jail time were a bit of a paranoid fantasy, then making Alex look like a fool was not. So: give up Val, then re-attach myself to Alex (in public, at least), so that everyone from Millard and Rotwell (the biggest and fastest rodents on the wheel) down to the bus boys at the Fairmont Hotel could see us together.

But how do you give up smoking? Heroin? Sugar?

I had to. I would. Meanwhile, no more excursions to Teach Supply Stores or to cafés, no walks around the block — no trips anywhere, except from Aunt Patsy's bedroom to her tiny living room and back.

That wasn't a sacrifice. The television that Aunt Patsy couldn't take with her was too old to hook up to cable, but I brought in a portable DVD player. We alternated between action-adventure starring our very own governor, and film noir, while eating pizza or KFC. We had serious talks in his bedroom in the late afternoon, the sun a ripening peach in the May sky.

And in between the two … well, I'd discovered why there was so much fuss about sex. We'd be watching *Since You Went Away* and he'd put his arm around my waist and travel south and even though I had a mouthful of popcorn I didn't think, *oh for God's sake, not now, at least let's finish the movie*. We'd make love and return to the couch with as much to talk about as we had before: the deficit, the Middle East, healthcare, the origins of the Universe. We were both relatively ignorant about the first three, and as ignorant as everyone about the fourth, and so made a good team. We didn't need the Great Outdoors.

But Val often spoke (restlessly, I feared) of past adventures with friends with interchangeable names, climbing mountain peaks I'd never heard of, and whitewater rafting down obscure but apparently violent rivers. And one afternoon as I reluctantly gathered up my "intimate apparel," wishing that Val had his own washing machine, he said, "I love being outside and I love you. Can't we go to Golden Gate Park tomorrow, if it's another nice day?"

When he said "I love you," I always wondered, did he love me the way I loved him? Or did he love me as one might love a new garage band or inventive Ben & Jerry's flavor?

Whatever they meant, they were the three words to which no woman says no.

***

I knew that Val would have been happy if I, too, could discover the joys of hang gliding, bungee jumping and even wind surfing, but I was in love, not certifiable, and he accepted that Golden Gate Park was about as much wilderness as I could handle.

There are a few places deep in the park where you can believe you are not in the city, unless a car alarm goes off. Val had borrowed a bike for me from the smallest of his friends.

Almost no one else knew about this trail, Val assured me, which was hidden under a canopy of trees and barely wide enough for our two bicycles to stand side-by-side. Elsie followed resentfully behind.

Val was cycling; I was wobbling. Poor Jack. Val might have helped him master this skill, but now I was afraid to let Val come to the house.

"'S not very crowded today," I said.

Val put his foot down on the rocky earth to let me catch up. "My God, Banana Boat, you are the Patient Zero of worry. Who's going to snitch on you, a pigeon?"

"Sorry."

"You don't have to apologize, either." He patted the top of my ill-fitting helmet as I squeezed carefully up alongside him. "So what do you think I should do?"

"What? I'm sorry."

I usually hung on his every word, but for the past few minutes I had been too distracted by gravity to listen.

He didn't seem to care. He reminded me that he'd been telling me about the job he'd landed just that week, as head teacher at a daycare center in the Mission. With only two assistants to help he was responsible for nearly eighty children. After his interview, he'd compared the facility to a Romanian orphanage, with its broken toys and backed-up toilets.

"You know it's all about the staff," I reminded him. I was thinking of the pre-school that had expelled Jack: there was a computer for each child, but his teacher couldn't remember the kids' names. "You're the best there is, and that's more important than their supplies.

Parents magazine took a poll, and the most popular toy of the decade was the box that refrigerators come in."

Val grimaced and pedaled slowly on, so I went on, too: "Of course they didn't publish those results. They said it was the Tickle Me Elmo, but it was a cover-up."

Val let the distance between us grow again. Highly motivated to stay upright I tried to catch up. He slowed but kept looking straight ahead. "It's my boss. I got a funny vibe from her from the beginning but yesterday I overheard something."

"And — ?"

"She's busting the kids. Or their parents."

"For — ?"

"She's on the look-out for illegal aliens. Almost all the parents are from Mexico. Some of the kids were born there, too."

"So what did you overhear?"

"She was on the phone to the INS."

"God, I'm sorry."

"I heard her give out" — he choked up — "an address."

"Can you talk to her?" I'd never seen him upset; I had begun to believe him incapable of it. If only I hadn't had to grasp the handlebars so tightly to keep from falling, I could have put my arms around him.

He shook his head. "She'll fire me. And I need this job."

"Well ... stay on for a while. Get her to trust you, to give you a good recommendation, then when you leave...."

"I can never deceive people that way, even if it's for a good cause."

I was too ashamed to respond. I had revealed my own capacity for deception, showing no hesitation in laying out this scheme.

"I have to admit I'm looking forward to a break."

The AIDS ride. He'd told me he planned to go back on the day of his first visit to my house.

"...and when I come back, I need to get back on the career track...."

When he comes back.

I couldn't have both Val and Jack. I'd known that from the beginning. I prided myself on always being honest with myself: Val was funny. Val could hold me. While Jack could be irritating, frustrating ... boring. In my darkest moments I cursed him for the lifetime of worry he would likely cause me. And sometimes three more minutes in the same room with him threatened my sanity.

But he was my child. My son. He could have my bone marrow with five minutes' notice.

How do you give up smoking, heroin, sugar?

You just give it up.

I didn't want to do this for Alex or for his election. But I had to do it for Jack.

"I'll have a whole week just to be on the road and clear my head." At least, that's what I thought I heard Val say. He was facing away from me, talking into the wind.

And I'd have a whole week to go through Val-withdrawal. For me that withdrawal would be my skin left untouched. My jokes misunderstood. My thoughts unsaid.

And will you miss me at all? I wondered, and had to squeeze the handlebars even more tightly than before to keep from whining the words aloud like a child.

At that very moment he stopped again, one long leg balancing his own enormously tall bike, turned around and waited for me to close the gap again. "You know I'll miss you," he said, just as I came into alignment with him. "I'll miss you like a limb."

His smile. His handsome face. Those close-set, bluer-than-blue eyes. I'd never seen eyes that color outside of a magazine ad.

It's human nature to take for granted what one possesses. But at this moment of feeling that I did possess Val, he became more precious than ever. More precious than the night at the hospital, more precious than the time of our first love-making (for love-making it truly was, not fucking, not sex, not intercourse, but love-*making*)....

And being as precious as he was, giving him up was the motherly sacrifice I'd never made — the hours of ABA-style drilling I couldn't bear to spend with Jack, the times I couldn't keep my temper with him, the times I'd let Mairead take over.

Giving up Val would make me a good mother after all.

How do you give up smoking, heroin — food?

But at that moment, I made a bargain with myself and the God I did not entirely disbelieve in that I would give him up. *Next week. Next week while he's gone.*

The air traveling down into my lungs was made of cat's claws.

He broke eye contact first. "Race you to that big rock!"

"It's right in front of us!"

"I know! Catch me if you can!"

***

On the first Sunday of June I drove Val to Fort Mason, the Army base-turned-cultural center. This was the departure point for the AIDS ride.

If you love something, let it go. As b.s. went, that was about the b.s.iest. If I truly loved Val, then I'd want him to be happy, want to make it easy on him, right?

No fucking way.

But it wouldn't be hard for him. He just wasn't that kind of person. No matter how intensely he lived and loved, unlike me, he could live and love wherever he was. During the week we were apart, he'd be absorbed in an intense routine, surrounded by old friends, making new ones (perhaps female) — and I'd resume the lifestyle to which I'd become resigned.

By the time we squeezed into the last parking space, hundreds of cyclists and their friends were mobbing the lot. It was almost hard to believe that there wasn't someone from Alex's office here — any of these female jocks, with their brown ponytails sticking out of the backs of their baseball caps, could be an ADA. I stood out like a flag of surrender in my white linen pantsuit and high-heeled sandals. It would be exquisite irony for one of them to spot me *in flagrante* at this final moment in the affair. Another reason to get it over with quickly.

"Where are you?" Val asked.

"Admiring the view." We stood by the rail next to the bay, Val holding his Stumpjumper bike like a high-strung thoroughbred. The sun was brilliant, the clouds as white as a cleansed soul and the water a darker blue than Val's eyes, dotted with sailboats going nowhere. I wished it could be like this all summer, but in my neighborhoods, at least, these would be the final days of sunshine until after Labor Day.

"Me, too, then," Val said. He smiled down at me.

"You know...." I began.

"Yes?"

I suddenly felt nauseous. "I.... Uh.... I want you to know I respect the decision you made about your job."

He'd gone to the daycare center's board of directors and within 24 hours Boss Lady had fired him. She cited his tardiness and absenteeism. But it was clear now that the board had known and approved of her witch hunt for illegal aliens. Now he couldn't use Boss Lady as a reference or add such a brief stint of employment to his resume. She'd even stiffed him out of his final pay.

He looked amused. "I'll go job hunting after the ride."

The nausea was getting worse. "We have to stop meeting like this." I tossed if off as if it were a joke.

"You sound as if I'm not coming back." He freed one hand to gather my hair into a ponytail. "I'm going for a very good cause. You helped me get my best sponsors."

I looked past him. God, that was a beautiful bridge. Was there any human-made structure more beautiful in the world? "This is where it ends."

"The Western world," he agreed. "Out that way...." He released my hair, looked back over his shoulder and sighed. "Wouldn't you like to see the East someday, Banana Boat? China, India?"

"Actually, by 'it' I mean...."

"Indonesia...."

He might have been talking about a lost love.

"I mean us."

"What are you talking about?"

The metal rail was sticky under my fingers. "Don't make it harder."

"Oh, Banana Boat Bee. You're upset because I'm leaving, aren't you?"

"No — I mean, of course — but...."

I had made this promise to myself and just possibly God, so now, being given to magical thinking, I was afraid that something bad would happen to Jack if I didn't follow through with the break-up. I did have reason to believe that Marianne would continue stalling for now. Her sound bite for the press: "It's not responsible to bring an incomplete investigation to the grand jury."

"What future do we have?" I asked him. "Won't it just hurt worse later?" I was teary-eyed, and I hoped no one would notice. The risk of being found out seemed greater by the minute, even if the irony did not.

"But 'later' doesn't exist yet," he said. Val smiled indulgently. "Later is just something we imagine."

He kissed my forehead, and I flinched, thinking of those ADAs disguised-as-jocks, while simultaneous thinking, *you see, bitches,* someone *loves me!*

Then he leaned his bike against the rail and took me in his arms. "Who knows? Maybe I'll get shot by a crazed Central Valley winemaker on the way south."

"Don't say that." I sniffled. "You're not going through the Central Valley."

"You see my point, don't you?" he almost purred. "We don't have to make any decisions now."

I almost collapsed against him. *No,* I thought, *we don't. He'll be gone for a week; if my secret is safe it will stay safe. I don't have to let him go* today.

So with adolescent defiance I remained in his embrace, my hands against his back, feeling the hard rhomboid muscles between his shoulders.

Later. Later was also not now. Later I'd end it. Not today.

For the first time since our bike ride the air went all the way to the bottom of my lungs.

"I'll call if I can," he said. "C'mon," he said. "Big smile. Big hug."

"We're already hugging," I said into his chest, and he squeezed me harder. I didn't give a fuck who saw us.

I sensed from how his chin moved that something had caught his eye above my shoulder.

"Hey, Vince!" His shout bounced painfully off my eardrum. "And Chucko!"

I pulled away.

"Valentino Valderoo!"

"V-8!"

"Count Valenski!"

We were suddenly encircled by men in tank tops and spandex shorts.

Val replaced a proud arm around me. "Hey, dogs," he said.

Dogs?

"This is Anna. She — "

But one of them — Vince, or Jimbo, or Timbo, or Tank Top — couldn't control his enthusiasm. "Man, I am *psyched,*" he said.

He was followed by a chorus of agreement worded in the same vernacular.

"Oh, Dude, it's going to be *awesome.*"

That was Val talking. His vocabulary was shrinking faster than Alice on her first visit to Wonderland. The others were lobbing "pimped" "killer" and "hottie." But overarching concept here was definitely "awesome." Maybe because it could be found so early in the dictionary.

I took a few steps back. Val didn't seem to notice. "Freakin' awesome, Dude," he reiterated.

"I know you've all been looking forward to it," I said.

"Randy Andy brought those Downhill Rush bars, Dude," another of Val's friends said, ignoring me. "*Forty-fucking-seven* grams of protein. Killer."

"Awesome." Val's arm slipped absently off my shoulder.

"Well, I'd better be going," I announced. "Bravo is showing 'The Best of Evel Knievel.'"

Val gave me a kiss on the cheek that was possessive and dismissive at the same time. "I'll try to call. But I warned you about cell coverage." Then: "Dudes, have you seen the check-in lines?"

"Yeah, who we gonna blow to get cutsies?"

That was the last remark audible to me as I strutted toward my van, as determined as Orpheus not to look back.

And like Orpheus, I failed.

The crowd around him had swelled. He was high-fiving the latest arrivals.

Such a mistake, not to end it after all. But he'd be back in a week, as he kept telling me, and I could make it official then. I'd become another step in his karmic journey. I only wished I hadn't lost my nerve before his friends showed up.

I turned away from my lost Eurydice. My Town and Country was at the other end of the lot. Alex had picked it out: We had to buy an American name, whether the car was assembled in Fremont or Nagasaki. I aimed the remote keypad and punched the button as though firing at a target.

CHAPTER TWELVE
THE RIGHT OF THE PEOPLE PEACEABLY TO ASSEMBLE

From the window of my bedroom I saw two women standing just at the outside of our gate. Their hair was teased high and sprayed heavily, and they each wore Chanel knock-off suits, one in canary yellow and the other in lobster red. They were pointing at one of the parlor windows. The woman in red had a large street map.

They looked like tourists. Either that or ghosts from JFK's doomed motorcade.

"You were saying, Mrs. Kagen?"

"Right." I turned to my companion, Kelly O'Donnell. She was a new friend of Mairead's from church who was studying special education at San Francisco State, and Mairead had helped me recruit her to teach at Jack Kagen Elementary. I had filed our Form F-4 and was now running an official homeschool; the next step was to broaden our curriculum past the contents of the cable guide. "Well, the main thing is to keep him engaged. We've got the textbooks ... he'll need frequent breaks...."

The school year was officially over but I hoped that during the summer we could not only keep Jack engaged but perhaps makes some small progress on his lagging academic skills.

But I delivered my spiel on auto pilot as I looked down at the women below. The sky was the color of an oyster shell; the sun had followed Val on his travels. He'd given me the schedule; today he'd be cycling to King City. I'd hidden that schedule with my remaining Valium, in my lingerie drawer. *That* was one place Alex never went.

Fine. Let the Ride take him away from me, into his future and into my past. I only regretted that my final memory would be of Val as he had been by the waters of the Bay.

"...fine motor skills?" I heard Kelly ask. She was Irish, too, but from "the Nort'," and her cadence and vowels were subtly different from Free Stater Mairead's.

"Anything you can do on that, of course," I murmured. I was again focused on the canary and lobster of the strangers' suits: They were the brightest colors on view. Although I flattered myself occasionally that I had a kind of celebrity as Alex's wife, in my wildest dreams of grandeur I could not imagine tourists going out to seek the home of the District Attorney in the name of sight-seeing. Were these women spying on me for Alex? If so, he had chosen poorly, for they blended in about as well as two female Austin Powers.

"Mrs. Kagen?"

"I'm sorry." I dragged my eyes from the window. I was tempted to ask Kelly if either woman looked familiar, but feared that it would sound ... oh, a bit paranoid.

"We'll get started then?" Kelly asked tentatively. She searched my face a moment, sensing my anxiety, perhaps wondering if it was about her. She shared some of Mairead's diffident manner, but the resemblance stopped there: she was petite, with a constellation of freckles that stood out against milky skin. Her teeth were small, the lower ones crowded together.

"Please do," I smiled munificently, trying to reassume the air of the lady of the manse.

But as soon as Kelly went off to find Jack — probably playing *Crime Conquerors* under his bed — I opened the window. When I leaned forward my cable knit sweater rode up. I'd gained a few pounds from all the munching at Val's. It was annoying, but I hadn't let myself worry about my weight since I was a teenager and I wasn't going to start now.

The scrape of wood against wood was loud enough to get one of the women to glance up. She quickly looked down again as if trying to pretend that she hadn't seen me.

A black Range Rover coming down the street slowed and then stopped. The driver waved to the women. This lady, whose face was vaguely familiar, glanced up at me and away in much the same way as her compatriots had.

The rhythm of the next ten minutes was like the beginning of a party: The first three or four early arrivers show up with their bottles of wine and the hostess divides her time awkwardly between her final preparations and not leaving them to their own devices. After a few minutes, though, the next wave of guests comes in a big rush. Soon the hostess can flit from group to group, passing out food or drinks, now that there are enough people that the party can take on a life of its own.

And so it was down on Jackson Street. The driver of the black Range Rover started up again, creeping along on a road where most vehicles went nearly double the speed limit, and so indicating that she was looking for parking. She had just turned the corner when six more women turned the opposite corner, all on foot.

One carried a picket sign. I could not read it quite yet. But by the time the marchers had passed another two houses the red paint came into focus: "PROTECT" OUR CHILDREN. The cardboard poster had been attached to its wooden stick before the words were dry, and the letters dripped paint that reminded me inevitably of blood. The woman who carried the sign looked grim with the weight. The other women just looked grim.

I stood frozen as the numbers of protestors swelled with alarming speed. I found myself wondering whether they had walked from distant parking spaces or.... Had they arranged *carpools* for this? Had they taken taxis, or even buses? Surely not the people carrying the picket signs — for more of those were arriving, too. But one way or another, people had talked on the phone, maybe at their beauty salons on those damn earpieces, (suddenly ubiquitous that year) organizing transportation to get to my street, my house, and to hold up those posters with unimaginative but intimidating slogans like PROTECTION FIRST and MURDER IS STILL A CRIME.

There were some more specific and disturbing though: THEODORE MERRICK IS ALIVE AND WELL AND LIVING ON JACKSON STREET. (It took me a moment to remember that Theodore Merrick was the reluctant cult leader who died on Minotaur Island.) Still others played with the name Jackson, spelling it "JACK'SON," or "JACKS-OWN."

Later I liked to think that I stayed there as long as I did because I wanted to know exactly what I was up against. But it was pure terror that kept me immobilized. So far, the atmosphere was almost festive. Matrons passed out trays of food. There were mini-bagels and Levant sandwiches, crudités and ... dip, for God's sake. Then there was my neighbor, Mrs. Dr. Mitchell, with her famous baklava on a sterling silver platter.

But Londoners used to bring their lunches to public executions, too. A mob is a mob. Would they start throwing rocks through the windows? Would they burn a cross on my lawn? Or would they skip the formalities and just set fire directly to the house?

And the crowd was still growing. By now the roadway was effectively blocked with people, and SUVs and mini-vans had to stop at the corners to drop people off. Two black stretch limos pulled up together, and uniformed chauffeurs got out open the passenger doors.

What to do? Call the police? Call Alex? And what about Jack and Kelly studying on the floor above me? Our tiny front yard was bordered by a low, wrought-iron fence. No defense there. The police. No, Alex. No....

A white van with windows painted black and speakers atop its roof slowly turned the corner. The driver, a young Chicano man, leaned out the window and, amicably at first, but then more harshly, warned protesters out of his way in a thick Mexican accent until he could inch the van near our house, which was approximately in the middle of the block. He had barely come to a stop when a statuesque auburn-haired woman jumped out of the passenger side.

Laurie Batarski. Mother to "my" little Emily, the little girl in Jack's class who had attached herself to me. They shared the same birdlike features and auburn curls.

The rear doors of the van flew open at the same moment and two — no, three — lithe, dark men pulled out equipment with professional speed. With no more than a few grunts they set up a collapsible platform for Laurie to mount and gave her a handheld wireless microphone — likely connected to the speakers atop the van.

Laurie had exchanged her snug stonewash jeans for an ill-fitting black gabardine pantsuit. Her favorite snakeskin cowboy boots peeked from beneath the hems of the trousers. Cowboy boots with gabardine. *The school should have a fundraiser to buy her a mirror.*

She took the four foot platform in one mighty bound, her loose reddish-brown mane swinging behind her, all the while gripping the microphone. She had just graduated from the platform of the PTSA to a beer hall in Munich.

It seemed that most of the protestors had been expecting her, for they pulled back to make room, further encouraged by the men who now leaped from the hastily erected platform to create a wider zone of safety.

Laurie wasted no time.

"WHAT'S THE MOST IMPORTANT THING TO ALL OF US?"

"Our children! Our children!" Enough shills in the audience, probably among the early arrivals, had been coached in advance to start the responsive cry, which was immediately taken up by the others.

"WHAT DO WE WANT TO DO?"

"Protect them...." This time the response was fainter and more scattered, but as soon as the uninitiated caught on the rallying cry was repeated, this time louder. "Protect them!"

Riordan's group had been well-named.

"AND WHEN DO WE WANT TO PROTECT THEM?"

"Now! Now! Now!"

"Mrs. Kagen?"

Kelly stood in my bedroom doorway, with Jack in front of her, her arms encircling his chest. "Mommy? Mommy...." He was doing the Asperger's Dance. "Why can't I go to school? Whyyyy...."

The second "why" was shrill.

Be brave for him. "It looks like there's some trouble on the street. I, uh, think I'm going to call the police."

"Oh, I wouldn't be doing that," Kelly said, "don't you think ... well, it can't have to do with us, can it now?"

Although Kelly, like Mairead, had recently joined Sunset Word of God, she had not only been raised in the North but raised a Catholic, and she might have had some of that ingrained fear of law enforcement that had afflicted my grandmother. "Tell you what," I said. "Go down the back way and take Jack out in the backyard." *Why don't we have a bomb shelter when we have every other goddam thing you can add to a house?* "The police will break up the crowd."

"How do I get there?"

I delivered staccato instructions, but she looked confused.

"Jack, you can show Kelly into the backyard, can't you?"

"Of course I can!" Being responsible for Kelly made Jack proud. Thank God he didn't know how serious this might be. I kept listening for the sound of the first window shattering.

"Come along, lad." Kelly managed a kind tone in spite of what appeared to be growing terror. My unspoken fears probably wouldn't sound "hysterical and over-reacting" to *her.*

"I'll lead the way!" Jack declared.

Kelly didn't let Jack lead anything. She was already pounding down to the first floor, dragging him by the hand.

Thank God Mairead isn't here. I'd insisted she take the day off since she'd watched Jack when I was at Fort Mason. She'd be more terrified than Kelly.

If only Mairead were here.

The noise from outside abruptly rose and I was back at my reconnaissance post in two long leaps. There I saw that simultaneously, at either end of the block, where the growing number of spectators were beginning to clog the intersections, several more vans had arrived. Each of these was brightly painted with the logo of the TV channel with which it was affiliated. Satellite dishes crowned the roofs. Within seconds anchormen and -women were dismounting, already bearing their own wireless mic's, followed by cameramen carrying tripods in one hand and balancing video cameras on their shoulders. Still more techies carried weighty, charcoal-gray nylon satchels.

My stomach cramped. During the same years that I had learned to trust the police, as Alex's wife, I had also learned to fear the media. They were more likely to incite the crowd to vandalism or violence for the sake of their "film at eleven" than they were to try to maintain order. From among passersby who had stumbled on the event, there were already twenty hands in the air, filming the action on their cell phones.

"AND WHO PROTECTS OUR CHILDREN WHEN WE CAN'T?"

The "can't" was absorbed into the shriek of feedback. Someone in her van had turned her mic up too high. I pressed down on my ears while the crowd collectively groaned. But most had turned instinctively toward the TV cameras, waving posters if they had them. Others jumped in front of them, hoping to be captured on videotape.

"THE LAW ISN'T PROTECTING THEM! TYLER GAINES'S KILLER GOES UNPUNISHED WHILE A MAN AND A WOMAN IN VERY HIGH PLACES PROTECT *HIM*!"

That was it. I dashed for the phone on Alex's nightstand. On his direct line, voicemail picked up. I dialed the District Attorney's main line. A recorded voice gave me a string of menu choices, but "If protestors are gathering in front of your house, press...." was not among them.

Back to the window. I leaned out as far as I could without toppling. I couldn't make sense of all the things that were happening at once: people at both ends of the street surrounded the camera crews; more, newly arrived crews were setting up, and a third throng in the middle, still focused on Laurie's cause, pressed closer to her, while a squad of five thuggish escort-guards held them back.

When one of Laurie's bodyguards shoved a picket-holder who had apparently gotten too far up into Laurie's space, the picket-holder swatted back. Other scuffles broke out.

Laurie was appalled. "I need your attention, people! I'm not finished speaking here!" She spoke too close to the microphone, and the final words came out in an eardrum-pounding blare. "We aren't going home until I deliver my message!"

More brawls were breaking out. Laurie stamped one cowboy boot. "You are not going home until I deliver my message!" she repeated. Suddenly her face went blank. Then she frowned and said petulantly, "They will too listen to me." Pause. "They will *too*."

My suspicions were confirmed. I squinted and made out the earpiece that connected her to someone in the van, someone with Vitalis in his "hair." Two befuddled ladies with a map had turned into a mob on the verge of a riot in no more than half an hour. Where was Val when I really needed him? Or Alex? Was there a line of picketers at Bryant Street, too?

I lurched back to the phone. "911, what is your emergency?"

"TYLER GAINES DEATH IS NOT ONLY A MURDER, BUT A HATE CRIME!" Laurie had resumed her tirade, but now she was trying to harangue the crowd into listening. "WE DEMAND THAT THE ATTORNEY GENERAL TAKE ACTION!"

I couldn't get any words out. I was fighting nausea from the stress.

Then I heard the sirens. Two, from opposite directions. "Never mind." The phone slipped out of my hand. This time, halfway to the window, I had to stop to lean against the wall. The running had made me dizzy.

The patrol cars had arrived in my absence. I could see the flashing blue, red and yellow lights, and I never had been so happy to see the police in my life. Unless.... Unless Kelly and my grandmother were right, and they would join against us, on the side of the protestors?

No — I couldn't trust the police. I had to get Jack out, and Kelly, too. How? We'd be trapped in the backyard if I tried to go out that way. I could never scale that fence. I could never help *Jack* scale that fence. Maybe with a boost from Kelly....

I hurtled down the stairs. But instead of going down to the kitchen, I headed to the front of the house. *You're going the wrong way. Go back to Jack and Kelly.*

I flung open the front door.

In the yard, more than a dozen people had scaled the fence. Someone had dropped into the hydrangea. A few sat cross-legged on our tiny lawn, smoking cigarettes. Others merely wandered about, happy to have some space in which to move freely. Everyone ignored me as I rushed toward the gate, shoved several people out of the way, and jumped up on the platform next to Laurie.

"Get off of here!" Laurie waved the mic at me as if trying to swat away a bee.

I swayed and had to steady myself to keep from toppling off. From my new vantage point, I spotted a terrible number of people I knew. I might have been mistaken about some in the state I was in, but there were many about whom there was no mistaking.

Kristin Scarborough — holding a picket sign. No surprise there.

Dr. Yeung, our old principal? I wasn't sure.

Danielle Hardy. Wasn't sure there either but if so … she was in my support group, with an AS son born on the same day as Jack.

Lourdes de Leon. From the Teachers' Supply Store. No wonder she didn't want me to come to the FARE meetings.

I blinked and Lourdes and Danielle were both gone. Or maybe I just couldn't see them anymore.

Laurie had decided to ignore both me and Riordan in the van in favor of berating her recalcitrant audience. "You people are part of the problem if you can't see what Marianne Pasquale is all about! And she's working with Kagen and his … his *wife*." She said wife as if it meant "whore."

I tried to grab her microphone.

"Help!" she cried. "She's hurting me!"

"I'm not touching you!" I was close enough to the mic's mouth that my voice reverberated down the street in both directions. "How can you all turn on us like this?" I shouted.

Laurie tried to jump away, but I grabbed her sleeve. She was stronger, but I was the more desperate. "This is about *two* innocent boys!" I addressed the mob. "Jack Kagen *and* Tyler Gaines!"

With one sharp yank, Laurie freed herself. Then she slapped me across the face.

As I reeled back, my hand flying to my cheek, I saw Alex emerge from one of the police cars. *Alex, Alex, thank God.* The police were still on our side. Tears stung my eyes. I refused to wipe them. "You bitch," I muttered softly.

Unfortunately, the microphone picked up the words, just loudly enough for the nearer part of the audience to hear.

Yet another electronically amplified voice came from the police car on the eastern side of the block. "This crowd will disperse immediately."

Laurie was no longer angry; she was frightened. She tugged her ear. "We have a permit." Another tug. "We have a permit on file downtown and … with Richmond Station."

"Your permit to assemble is good for fifty people." The disembodied sound was threatening. "And you're creating a public nuisance."

Another incorporeal voice, from the opposite corner, this one thunderous: "IN TWO MINUTES WE WILL BEGIN MAKING ARRESTS."

At the word "arrest" the crowd was transformed from a single vicious entity into its component parts — mostly yuppie parents and middle-class busybodies — and everybody for themselves. People fled by the dozens, bumping into one another, knocking each other over, but no longer stopping to fight, only disengaging to get away. The passersby who'd joined from curiosity turned coward just as fast.

Mrs. Dr. Mitchell whizzed past me, almost twisting her ankle on her stilettos, and scrambled to the safety of her house. She dropped the last squares of baklava on the asphalt then held her silver platter to her chest as a shield. *Are you proud of yourself now?* I wanted to shout.

Next to me Laurie shrieked to her invisible partner, "Let's get out of here." Pause. "I don't care," she whimpered. "I don't want to go to jail."

And there was Alex, striding directly toward me, head up but not looking to either side of himself. Two policemen flanked him.

As the reporters hastily gathered their equipment I made one last declaration. "My boy is being scapegoated and you all know it!" But Laurie was already climbing into the van, and she had taken her mic with her, so only a few heard my voice.

Alex reached me faster than I could have imagined, and he held up his arms. I jumped into them, and he set me on the ground. The platform folded up almost magically behind me.

I sank against Alex as we headed to our own house, each of us still escorted by the policemen who had first accompanied him. Another policeman, and a policewoman, wrote citations for the few demonstrators who had not been quick enough to get out of our front yard. I recognized one sulky neighborhood teen whose parents had just brought him back from a year of studying in Germany. "Man, this sucks," I heard him say.

"Mr. Kagen!" someone called just as we reached our gate.

We both turned automatically, and a large square-topped microphone almost hit me in the nose. A diminutive Eurasian TV reporter asked, "What's your response to the accusations made by these demonstrators today?" Immediately behind her a cameraman looked into his viewfinder, holding the lens on Alex.

I gagged.

Alex gently nudged me to the side as the single microphone became a semi-circle of six. He caught the eye of the policeman who had been on my right, a barrel-chested man who was surprisingly tender as he pulled me away from the gate and onto the lawn. "Let your husband handle those vultures," he said. "You don't feel well, do you?"

"No," I shook my head. "Maybe — could you help me get inside to get a glass of water?"

"Of course, Mrs. Kagen. Can you walk?"

He had striking blonde eyebrows standing out against coarse, ruddy skin and strong arms. His uniform could barely contain him; he looked as though he could protect anyone.

"I'm just a little stressed," I said.

"When your kid has homework he can't do, that's stress. Your house was just surrounded by torch-wielding peasants."

"I appreciate that."

"You were very brave," he said. "I got here just as that woman slapped you," he added in disgust. "Here." He put my arm around his neck, and I had to let him, for my legs were shaking. "We've met," he went on. "You wouldn't remember."

I didn't, but took a guess. "Were you at that PET luncheon when I spoke for Alex?"

"Yes!" His face brightened. We stopped and he lowered his voice. "I have a son … a son like...."

"You mean a son with an ASD?"

"Yes. His name's Trevor. I'm Jason Armstrong."

I looked over at Alex. I could see the dignified set of his head and shoulders from behind as he fielded questions from a swelling crowd of reporters, including some who had come sidling back once the police separated media from mob. I heard him say, "Neither my wife nor I bear any grudge toward PROTECT for this morning."

"Don't worry about this pig-ignorant 'neighborhood' group," Officer Armstrong said. "They put the 'dog' in 'watchdog.' I knew there was going to be trouble with them as soon as we heard about it down at the station. Don't worry, we'll keep an eye on this street tonight. We'd better get you that water." He lowered his head to get a better look at my face.

"No! Stand back!" I shouted.

Too late. Though I broke free at the last second, when I vomited on the grass it covered both of Jason Armstrong's thick-soled shoes and at least two inches of his trouser legs.

CHAPTER THIRTEEN
GREAT EXPECTATIONS

The circle of light from Alex's desk lamp did not reach as far as my outstretched arm.

Still I could trace the blue of the veins through my skin. My head lolled to the side of his sofa; I had, as he required, removed my pumps before lying down.

It was only two in the afternoon, but it felt as if it were night, not just because of the persistent gloom of the Batcave, but because it seemed that it had been much longer than a few hours since my conversation with Kelly and my first sight of the two women with teased hair.

"It wasn't like this with Jack," I said. "With him it came on so slowly."

Wrong approach. Alex liked stoicism. "I know we weren't intending to have another child," I went on, moving back to the script. "But, uh...." I feigned a nervous chuckle. "Life is what happens while you're making other plans, right?"

"And what about the birth control pills?" Alex asked, as if I'd forgotten an item on our grocery list. "They've been proven to be, I believe, over 99% effective."

I started to wipe a sweaty forehead with the back of my hand, then remembered the handkerchief in my pocket. Alex believed handkerchiefs were more tasteful than Kleenex; I found them disgusting, at least once they'd been used.

"Well, I didn't even think it worth mentioning, but I lost last month's pack. So I just went that one cycle.... You're not supposed to be fertile for a few months after you go off.... And then, I was due to start another cycle last week, but my prescription had run out and I couldn't get it refilled 'til I saw Dr. Phelps for my annual...." I stopped myself again. Had I learned nothing from Alex's advice to the accused? *They should keep their damn mouths shut.*

Speaking of Alex, just how long could he go without blinking?

I turned my head back up to the ceiling and that twelve inches was a long journey. The ceiling was paneled with cherry wood tiles. *Keep breathing.* I saw how stupid all my lies were, but ... but there was a baby.

I'd wanted another baby since the moment Jack was born. You go into a hospital with cramps and — whoops! They take a human being out of your body. And then, too, I'd gone in expecting "to curse God and demand the sweet release of death," as Raven had described doing while giving birth to her son, but *I'd* managed it in two hours with merely some ladylike moaning. He was pronounced perfectly healthy.

For ten days I lived with him in a place where there was no time. The tingling in my breasts told me when to feed him; his body language told me when he wanted to sleep.

Then his colic began and I began to measure the hours — sometimes the minutes — in diapers, in naps that lasted no more than ten minutes, in the baths where he screamed.

And gradually, the real problems began.

But no matter how perseverative he became, no matter how sad I felt about the Gymboree classes he wouldn't participate in, and the Disney on Ice performances that terrified him, at the most unexpected times I re-experienced the transcendent love of his birth hour. It was the only time I felt better than I was, and I wanted to feel it, to be it, again.

Alex had never wanted more than one child, and after Jack's diagnosis his decision was non-negotiable. I had felt obliged to comply, because it wasn't right to force a child on someone.

Not to mention that he and I carried, hidden along the strings of our DNA, the risk of another autistic child. But my willingness to take the chance grew along with Jack. The odds were still on our side, and if we did dodge that bullet, then in a couple of decades there would be at least one close relative who might who look out for Jack when Alex and I were gone.

But I continued to respect Alex's wishes until two years before: The Night of the Pastrami Sandwich. I had been crying in the kitchen after catching two of Jack's Pathways classmates mimicking his echolalia. When I stopped them they looked at me silently with defiant eyes.

When I heard Alex pad down the back stairs, I raised my head. Maybe he'd heard me. If not, it would be obvious that I'd been crying, for my eyes had reddened and swelled.

But Alex, in his black socks and grandfatherly plaid pajamas, went to the refrigerator, and he slapped together a pastrami sandwich using the refrigerator shelf as a counter, and he silently returned upstairs.

After that I stopped using the birth control pills. He might be happy if I got pregnant. He might want a baby as badly as I; he might just need to be able to blame me if something did go wrong.

After a year without any results, I reconciled myself to the fact of our secondary infertility. By the time Val asked me if he needed a condom I believed I was giving him an honest answer when I said no. I'd always had a long cycle, often missed periods, and had been sloppy about birth control before meeting Alex. When I conceived the very first month of my marriage, Dr. Phelps, knowing my history, shrugged it off as fluke I should be grateful for.

These were all thoughts I had later because at that moment all I could do was grip the sides of Alex's couch. I understood why people give up state secrets, their loved ones, their religious beliefs, under torture.

My sister Darya was the first (and only) person I had called a couple of hours earlier when the home pregnancy test surprised me with a positive reply. This was her area of expertise. Darya saw no dilemma if I were serious about breaking off with Val, and I swore I was. "Tell Alex it's his. Men can't fucking count worth shit."

"You know I don't believe in abortion," Alex said now.

"You say you do," I countered before thinking, *shut up! You don't* want *an abortion!*

"I say I'm pro-*choice*," he clarified. "That's not the same as believing in abortion. I believe that women should have control over their own bodies."

I wasn't up to grappling with the political mind. He called himself pro-choice because no one who didn't could get elected in San Francisco.

I drew my knees up to my chest. "Well, then, we're going to have a baby," I said to the back of the sofa. I rubbed my cheek and forehead against the leather cushion for its coolness. "Look at it this way: By August I'll be starting to show. If that doesn't help you get re-elected I can't think what will."

He was silent, and I regretted what I had said. That last "joke" made him sound more cynical than he deserved. I was sincere when I went on. "It was an accident, but it'll be a good thing for us, honey. Maybe we can go back to some of what we had before … I'm willing to try, really I am — "

He was silent. I only heard the softest tap of an eraser-tip on his blotter.

"You know what I hate?" I asked the cushions.

"What?"

"The way in movies a woman throws up or faints once, and then the next time we see her, she's just fine."

"Of course. You never want to do the hard part."

I just had to take it. I had to take it for the sake of — of my children. *Children.* I loved it in the plural.

"That baby's not mine," I heard Alex say.

I stared at the button punched in the brown leather.

"What makes you say that?"

"Oh...." Papers snapping. Prolonged silence. "I had a vasectomy."

"What?" I would have sat up if I could. "When exactly?"

"Does it matter? It seems the issue is moot."

"Yes, it matters! To do that behind my — " I stopped.

"Feels different when you're on the receiving end, doesn't it?" he asked. "It was St. Patrick's Day, a little over two years ago. Mairead wasn't here and you were falling apart at the notion of being on your own with Jack for a few lousy hours."

That was just around the time when I stopped taking my pills.

"How could you do something like that without telling me?"

"I didn't trust you not pull some stunt like this."

I did remember that St. Patrick's Day. Yes, Mairead had Monday off. Now I had a memory of Alex limping up the stairs....

"Haven't you always been able to trust me?" I cried indignantly.

He let my words travel slowly around the study like heavy smoke.

"Get me some crackers," I said suddenly.

"We haven't finished discussing the current situation."

"Get me some crackers," I repeated, "unless you want me to throw up all over your beautiful chess table." Although Alex's computer monitor had cracked the marble, an antiques dealer had been able to restore it.

That would have required actual projectile vomiting, but I could accomplish a lot when I put my mind to it.

It seemed to take forever for him to return with a plate of six Saltines.

"Next time bring the box," I snapped, just before cramming two crackers in my mouth at the same time.

"Well." Alex squeezed himself back behind his desk. "I suppose Surfer Joe is the proud father. But he's out of town right now, isn't he? Have you been able to notify him?"

I stopped mid-munch and felt a couple of crumbs fall down into my bra.

That's your story and you're sticking to it, Darya had further advised. *He might suspect something. He'll go fishing. Stonewall.*

"Who are you talking about?" There was no way he could know. Not when we had been so careful. Or had there actually been an ADA at Fort Mason? Or had Lourdes—?

"Don't you think a husband has some instincts? A wife entertaining a male guest in her bathrobe?"

He sounded sad.

"You haven't been around much," I said. It could have been before Fort Mason, before the Teachers' Supply Store. Alex already had a team of private investigators gathering information on the Gaineses in order to defend us against their wrongful death suit. How hard would it be to add one more to the squad?

The crackers were gone. I tried to think how I might yet convince him that I hadn't cheated on him, then realized that it was a geometric impossibility. A: Your wife is pregnant. B: You are infertile. Therefore, C: the messiah has finally arrived (for the first or second time) or she has been in bed with another man.

"...I won't be as busy in the future. It looks as though my career in elective politics is pretty much over. Your little neighborhood group saw to that this afternoon — "

"How is it '*my*' neighborhood group?"

"—regurgitating on Officer Armstrong's shoes was a nice capper. I don't suppose you'd want to minimize the press coverage for your son's sake by any chance."

This time I didn't rub my face against the leather, I scraped it. Maybe Jack would be better off without me, too.

"All right," I said. "I fucked Dr. Valentine. You really are a sadist, you know. You could have just told me you — "

"*Doctor* Valentine, my ass," Alex said. "The man doesn't even have a college degree." He spoke with a precise contempt that made it clear that not having a college degree was a far greater offense than committing adultery.

"What are you talking about?"

"Oh, maybe he got some bullshit online print-your-own lambskin from someplace. I can tell you he's not licensed in the state of California."

"A lot of psychologists aren't licensed," I said. "It's not a regulated field."

"I'm aware, in fact — " he pressed his fingertips together — "that should I wish, I could hang out my own shingle. Alex Kagen, M.S., J.D. Specializing in pathological liars."

"All right, so it's not your baby," I croaked. "What do you want me to do?"

"If you promise — not that your promises mean much, but I can give you some assistance with adhering to this one — not to screw around with this schmuck any more, you can stay and we proceed with our lives as before."

Not screw around. Maybe it was over between me and Val, but it had been a true and beautiful thing — the first true and beautiful thing I had experienced since Jack nursed at my breast.

"This is where we started. I stay, and we pretend the baby is yours."

"With the small difference that you've admitted that the baby's not mine, as opposed to trying to sucker me in." He removed his reading glasses as he looked up from that damn endless stack of files. Even now — another trial on his mind. "*And* as opposed to you continuing to publicly humiliate me."

"I haven't told anybody."

"And no one would ever find out, would they? Studly Do Wrong isn't blogging about you this very night from his Blackberry."

I was having an attack of chills now. "Is this arrangement meant to be permanent? Or is it just so you can have a pregnant wife through the election, before you turn around and kick me out?"

"That is the way you think, isn't it. That I'm no better than Riordan, or Millard and Rotwell, or your gigolo." He put his reading glasses back on. His eyebrows were beginning to grow shaggy with age. "Of course you'd think that way, because those are the morals *you* have. You were the one pointing out the benefits to *me* of running for office with a pregnant wife."

It wasn't like that. I was desperate. I needed time to think....
Then I cracked.

"How long was I supposed to take all this shit? All these rules! My hair can't be too long. My skirts can't be too short. But it's okay for me to flirt with reporters, or *machers* with money, right? Then *you* look good because you scored a sexpot wife. You wrote the Wikipedia article on morality. If *you* do it, it's right. If you don't approve, it's wrong."

"I'm fighting for our son's life. Do you know how many phone calls I make every day, how many promises I've made, trying to make this go away?" By "this" he meant the A.G.'s investigation. "While you get pregnant by another man. And then I offer you a safe haven. But *I* have a distorted view of morality."

"I make one misstep — but it's the woman who gets knocked up, so she's the one who gets stoned to death."

"Stoned. All right. Now we on a subject you know something about, h'm?"

I sat up. "You knew who I was when you married me. I've had to change everything for you. It's been twelve years of hell — *hell*. The last time I remember being happy with you was waving good-bye to your friends before we headed off for the shortest honeymoon in history. How long were we gone — five fucking minutes?"

"We were there a full day," Alex corrected. "I suppose your spa appointment at the Inn at Pebble Beach was more important than a woman violently murdered at the age of 34."

"You were an assistant's assistant deputy schmendrick then! There were fifty other people in the office who could have handled that."

"*I'm* the narcissistic one. Listen to yourself, talking about a young mother who's never going to see her children grow up — "

"And listen to you, making your closing arguments."

"They needed me."

"And you're always there, aren't you, Counselor, unless I'm the one who needs you. Do you remember the day I saw Dr. Wolichek? I tried to get a hold of you all afternoon — "

"You know I was in court. And do *you* remember teasing the Public Defender about his daughter being named Miranda? Could it never occur to you that the Public Defender and the District Attorney need to keep a little professional distance from one another?"

"'The farmer and the cowman should be friends,'" I tried to sing, but my voice was a thin strain.

"What?"

"It's from *Oklahoma.*"

"Funny. Funny, funny, funny. Do you know that's still a big joke around the office? Which makes *me* a big joke."

"If you're a joke it has nothing to do with anything *I've* ever said," I fired back.

The bullets kept flying.

"…how many others times you've embarrassed me...."

"…made me kick my own sister out when she needed me...."

"...missed my acceptance speech...."

"…have the sense of humor of Heinrich Himmler...."

"…twenty-five pairs of identical black shoes...."

Magazines emptied, we reloaded and fired again.

"...feed Jack so much junk food that he's going to be as fat as you are by the time — "

"...dress him like a girl — "

"...gave up teaching him chess after five minutes — "

"The time when — "

"I'll never forget how — "

"You always have to — "

"And guess what?" My voice was getting hoarse. "Guess what? Once I met Val I did start using birth control again — but only with you."

"...have to ... what?"

"Once I met Val I didn't want to take any chances. I hated fucking you. Not that you bothered me very often, old man. You can get Viagra on the Internet now. Look into it."

He drummed his fingers on the desk. We were both exhausted but not out of ammo. Not even close.

"That's right," I said. "I slipped in a diaphragm with you. Couldn't you feel it?" I asked slyly, for I possessed no such contraceptive device. "Or doesn't Mr. Petey reach back that far?"

He was so repulsed by the details of female reproduction, that even in his fury he could question me no further. Our marriage had been a Cold War for a long time, but as in the final scenes of *Dr. Strangelove,* we had passed our "fail-safe" points, and all that was left to do was to plan for the post-apocalyptic wasteland.

But the next move was my own body's. I barely made it to the toilet. My stomach cramped and bits of Saltine came out of my nose. I held onto the towel rack hoping that after this I'd have a brief respite.

After I wiped my face and rinsed out my mouth I dragged myself back to where he waited, taking notes on what I suspected was another matter.

"So what do you see as the plan." I sat down but kept my back stiffly upright.

"Well...." He scribbled a few more words, then put the pen down. "I don't think we should make any announcement just yet, but just the right leak in ten days or so.... I'll see what Maddy thinks. She has a woman's perspective."

I frowned quizzically. Alex leaned back in his chair, looking up at the ceiling in thought. "I think it can only help us."

He was admitting something he'd just denied: that he would use my pregnancy for political purposes. But all I wanted now was to lie down and, God willing, sleep. "I think we should have separate bedrooms now," I announced.

"That's a good idea."

"I'll move into the guest room."

He glanced toward the door. "We need to keep up appearances for Jack."

"That won't be hard. The three of us are hardly ever alone together anyway."

He resumed writing. "Caveat. The 'no screwing around' clause is irrevocable."

"You have made that abundantly — " My indignant response was interrupted by my stomach and I was rushing to the bathroom again. There was nothing left. Still the cramps went on, but then they eased, and I was thinking, *Val and I made a baby*. He wasn't even making camp for the night yet. If I wanted to call him — ? No, no, no. It was over. *Don't remember him at Fort Mason. Remember him holding you and humming along with Simon and Garfunkel. Goodbye darkness, my old friend.*

I'll run away with Jack, tonight while the anti-Christ is asleep.

No, I'll never take him away from his father.

Creeak.

Oww.

I had fallen forward and slammed my forehead against the raised toilet seat. I rolled back on my heels, massaging what I knew would be a bad bruise. I looked up: I had wrenched one end of the towel rack right off the wall.

***

I told Mairead that I thought I had food poisoning. She'd heard from a very shaken Kelly about the demonstration and about my incident on the front lawn; she insisted on bringing me ice for the emerging bruise and tut-tutted about the towel rack.

Alex did not go back to the office even though it was only late afternoon. A couple of hundred people demonstrating in front of his house triggered the caveman in him, for Jack and for his home and, strangely enough, I thought, for me, too.

So it came about that we spent the longest uninterrupted period of time in the house together since the day we'd moved in.

***

I finally got into bed with my box of Saltines and a large bucket in case I didn't make it to the bathroom the next time.

Alex could have kept his distance while still staying home. But he kept wandering in. The first time was to interrogate me about the towel rack. I asked him for a wet washcloth. He got one for me. Sullenly — but a washcloth is a washcloth is a washcloth.

Half an hour later, when I finally felt as though I could sleep, he was back.

"Are you really that ill?"

I pretended that I had fallen asleep.

He wasn't fooled, but he wandered out again.

Half an hour later:

"I thought we were going to sleep in separate bedrooms."

"Give me one night. Maybe Mairead can help me move a few things tomorrow."

Twenty minutes this time:

"I just got off the phone with Fred Hsu. He's going to have a patrol car on the street tonight."

"Officer Armstrong said he'd see to it."

"Was that before or after you threw up on him?"

I rolled over. My pillowcase was wet from perspiration. I was very, very hungry, and weird cravings were flashing through my mind, from beef burritos to mussels. "Fred is trying to help," he persisted.

"I appreciate it. Do you think — do you think maybe Mairead could make me something to eat?"

"I told Mairead to go to the movies. She doesn't need to see us like this. So if you're too lazy to get your own food...." He trailed off, unable to produce the insult I deserved. "Besides, what's the point of eating if you're just going to throw up?"

"You have to trust me on this one," I groaned, twisting around, looking for the driest spot on the pillowcase.

"Well, I have work to do. I was in the middle of a staff meeting when I had to leave to rescue you."

Val wouldn't treat me this way.

Should I tell Val about the baby? He deserved to know. Or was that just a rationalization, because I wanted to tell him? Would he be happy if he knew? Demand a DNA test, fight for visitation rights? Or would he want me to have an abortion?

Don't ever tell him about the baby. Don't tell him about Alex's vasectomy. Let him think, for the rest of his life, that in his absence you re-discovered true matrimonial bliss.

Darkness came at last. Jack arrived to demand I put him to bed. Alex blocked his entry to the master bedroom door. I heard him say, "Mom's sick. Can't Daddy put you to bed for once?"

"No! I want Mommy! Mommy...."

They batted the argument back and forth a few times until I worked up enough momentum to propel myself out of bed.

"Oh, so this you can get up for."

"You sound like my grandmother," I said, struggling into my bathrobe. "Or Yoda. Syntax reversing your."

"You're never too sick to be a smart-ass."

***

Alex's visits came every fifteen, ten minutes now, as he harangued me about everything from how we were going to explain to people why we'd decided to have another child to what had happened to the cookie dough ice cream he'd had in the back of the freezer.

M'mmm ... ice cream....

"If I tell you where it is, will you bring me some?"

He walked out. I tried to imagine how I would feel if I'd found out he'd had an affair with Sherri Pechner, the sexy publicist who was still working on his campaign.

Yes, I'd be humiliated.

The only thing that annoyed me more than the treacly blogs by women convinced that their disabled children were angels in disguise were the blogs by the professional women who went to the other extreme, declaring, "If I'm not happy, my children won't be happy!" before they accepted the promotion that required them to travel two weeks a month. Children don't care if their parents are happy. You can be giving CPR to an unconscious swimmer when your teenage daughter calls — chances are that if she needs you to pick her up *right then* that she's not going to want to wait while you pump "just a little more air, dear" into the victim's lungs.

But this was not going to work.

I was reminded of another Strindberg play, *Dance of Death.* A couple is stranded on an island, where they engage in an exquisite ballet of two-way torture. This was going to make *Dance of Death* look like the happily-ever-after part of *Cinderella.*

***

Two hours later I was able to get myself something to eat, an apple that made a quick layover in my stomach on its journey from refrigerator to the San Francisco sewer system.

Back in my soon-to-be-former private bathroom I rinsed my mouth and wet my face yet again. If I were this ill I had to be six weeks along — maybe more like eight. But the risk of miscarriage was especially high for the entire thirteen weeks of the first trimester.

I looked at my face in the mirror, pale without makeup, paler from dehydration. When I got up that morning, I had worried about whether Alex really could pull enough rabbits out of his hat to keep Jack out of the youth prison system and, secondarily, to save our house. A short time later, I had envisioned a lynch mob setting fire to that house before the Gainses' lawsuit could take it away. In between, I'd pined for the days when Val and I were innocent lovers; the inevitable end of our romance only made it sweeter.

But right now all I cared about was staying pregnant.

In the mirror I saw Alex standing behind me. He looked as though his collar were choking him. But somehow we'd adjust. He was often home only an hour a day, if you didn't count the hours he slept. Once I got a few things into the guest room I'd have a place where I could shut the door, and then I'd become, to him, the file of a closed case.

Alex kept staring at me in the mirror. I turned around, patting my face dry with a hand towel. Maybe it was because of the brighter light in here but he looked entirely different from when we'd huddled in the Batcave and come to our unhappy truce.

"What — what is it?" I asked, when he kept staring at me.

He thrust a sheet of paper at me.

"Millard and Rotwell's column for tomorrow."

"Well, we both knew there'd be something," I sighed, reaching for the paper, "and something not good."

"It's the first edition of their *Chronicle* column for tomorrow. I printed this out."

I took it and read,

Are the streets of San Francisco still safe to walk, when our District Attorney has trouble with every member of his family? When some of Kagen's neighbors gathered peacefully to discuss the recent cover-up reported in this column, Mrs. Kagen physically assaulted their spokeswoman. That was before she called that spokeswoman a five-letter word we can't reproduce in print, but it starts with a "B." ...Spousal loyalty is sweet, but if she weren't Madam District Attorney, wouldn't she be spending the night in jail along with some of the concerned citizens who dared step on the grass of the Kagens' Presidio Heights mansion? We're guessing the city will bear the cost of the clean-up, too. ...

...Meanwhile, there's trouble in that paradise known as the Bay Area Rapid Transportation board, where some of Kagen's best friends hold office...

I thought I'd known how Alex felt when Millard and Rotwell had hit him with their first piece. This was the first time my name had come up, though, and the knife thrust much more deeply. I was determined to put that aside and to give Alex the extra sympathy I owed him from before.

"Assholes! No one was kept overnight," I said. "No one was booked for anything. Just taken to Richmond station and released."

"That's hardly the point, is it?" Alex yanked the paper from my hand. "I ask you not to swear at home, and you have to do it in public."

"Alex, you were there. I just whispered the word, and she slapped *me*."

Alex folded the page in half, then ran thumb and forefinger across the crease until the paper snapped.

"It's all lies, and you know it." I tried to snatch the paper back but he undid his own careful work by cramming it into his pocket.

"I can't bear to look at you," he said.

"I can see that you can't, but — you have a lot to blame me for, but you of all people know what it's like to be misquoted."

He turned his back on me. "You have to go."

"What? Go where?"

"Anywhere. Out of this house. I can't be the one to leave. Then legally I've abandoned you."

I wasn't too proud to beg. "Can't we talk about it in the morning at least?"

He pulled the now-crumpled paper out of his pocket as he turned away, and threw it over his shoulder at me.

"Read what you said. Read what you did."

"Alex...." I switched to the approach I used with my mother when she was drunk and was trying to shove me and Darya in the car. "You need someone here," I said kindly, "unless you let me take Jack with me. Why don't you? Then you can just focus on your campaign."

"You're a fine one to talk about campaigns." He whirled back around, fire in his eyes and blood in his mouth. "Get out of here before I throw you out on your sorry ass!"

***

Knocking on someone's door with a hastily packed tote bag in the middle of the night was my sister Darya's style, not mine. It had been less than a year ago, in fact, when she had arrived at my house unexpectedly, with her two children and ten suitcases. Alex had her installed at the Fairmont within an hour. Now she was settled in a borrowed home in St. Francis Woods.

But Darya, God bless her, smiled as if I were a welcome surprise. She was in a teal satin nightgown with black lace trim, but that was common daytime apparel for her as well. With her coltish limbs, angular features and apricot complexion she bore hardly any resemblance to me — a fact that a number of people had commented on over the years. Perhaps history was repeating itself.

"I guess my plan didn't work," she said when she saw me.

I shook my head. "No."

"It's just as well. It's about fucking time you left the putz."

"I shouldn't have left," I mourned. "I'm a coward. I'm worried about Jack."

"Do you want me to call the police? Holy shit." She reached to touch my darkening bruise, but I pulled back in time. "Has he been hitting you, hon?"

"No." Domestic violence, real or threatened, was the third rail of San Francisco politics. I didn't care about Alex's career but a police report right now could set off a domino effect that ended with Alex's (and therefore Jack's) financial ruin, and worse, more evidence that Jack was a killer. Violent father, violent son. "Run-in with a towel rack."

"That sounds like you." Darya reached to take my tote bag. "Ooops! That's heavy!" She tilted forward with the make-believe weight, giggled drunkenly, and then reminded me, "Honey, he loves Jack. It's you he hates."

She circled around, pushed me inside, and then closed the door with a shove of her behind. "You can sleep with Guadalupe." Guadalupe was Darya's newest nanny. "It isn't fancy-schmancy here like Lardo's place, but even we have four bedrooms. Can you find your way there? Lupe won't mind. Get yourself changed and you can tell me all about it tomorrow." There was black eyeliner and mascara smeared around her long, light brown eyes. "I'd like to talk now, but I've got company." She tilted her head toward the stairway. "He's a Libra, like you, and they do *not* like to wait."

"Go," I managed to sniffle. "Thanks for taking me in."

Darya pecked me on the cheek and padded back upstairs on bare feet. I stood trying to collect myself. I hadn't met Guadalupe yet, but I doubted she'd want a stranger crawling into bed with her. I wasn't super-keen on the idea myself.

I probably should have gone to a hotel, but I was self-conscious enough to care about how I reeked of illness, paranoid enough to imagine that the press (and thus eventually Millard and Rotwell) would find out that "Madam Kagen" had left her husband, and vulnerable enough to want to be with the only other family I had.

All the accommodation I really needed that night was the living room couch, where I lay down in my clothes. I had forgotten to bring a nightgown, but I had remembered to bring the untraceable cell phone, the phone that Val would call — if he called.

***

If Darya and I didn't look alike, then my niece and nephew looked as though our most recent common ancestors were Adam and Eve. They resembled their blonde, body-building Swedish-American father: He was a minor TV producer whom you could picture on a football field or in another woman's bed (which Darya had done more than imagine) more easily than in a director's chair. His children with Darya were Callaghan, five going on fifteen, and Kennedy, just about to turn three and going on something frightening.

At 10 a.m. Darya joined the four of us — by now I had been introduced to Guadalupe — in the kitchen, where I was swishing Cocoa Krispies in a bowl.

"Your cousin Jack likes Cocoa Krispies," I told her.

Darya went straight for the coffee that Guadalupe had already made. She wore the same teal nightgown, and she was still barefoot. She groaned as she poured. "Callaghan, can you ask Lupe to change Kennedy's diaper?"

Kennedy dashed from the room. Darya rolled her eyes.

"*Por favor, cambiar el pañal de Kennedy para Mami,*" Callaghan translated.

"She's speaking Spanish?" I asked.

"What's the big deal? She's been around Spanish-speakers all her life. I guess you don't shop at Target."

I doubted Darya was a frequent customer there either. "Still — "

"I'm sorry, honey, do you mind keeping your voice down a little?" Darya stirred her coffee even though she had added neither milk nor sugar. To me it smelled like diesel fuel.

Guadalupe started clearing the table, which also bore plates of congealing leftovers from the night before. Callaghan spoke softly to her. *"Mami tiene una de sus migrañas, pero yo credo que esta de cruda."*

I picked out "Mami" and "pero" easily enough. "Migrañas" I knew because I knew my sister. "Cruda" probably didn't mean either "crud" or "crude." But it wasn't anything good. *Note to self: Talk to Callaghan as soon as your own "cruda" lets up.*

"You're brave, Anna," Darya said, taking what looked like a brave swallow of the coffee. "I bet I know exactly what happened. You caved and told him everything, right?"

"Correctomundo." Ooops. Butchering Spanish in front of a native speaker was hardly polite. I had a real gift if I could offend people who didn't understand English.

"All you had to do was visit the doctor — poof! You could have gone to mine in L.A. if you were really that worried about Alex's spies. It works, trust me."

It worked for Alex. I was thinking of his vasectomy, but I'd already said far too much in front of my niece.

"You can stay here, hon," Darya said. She put down her coffee mug and massaged my neck.

"I wouldn't impose," I said, moving my shoulders to take better advantage of the pressure. "But I feel like I should lie low. I do have a key to — " I stopped again. I'd have to invent some reason for my visit for Callaghan's sake; meanwhile, I could circle around it. "Alex was having me followed, and I don't want to give him more ammunition by going — " I cast a sideways glance at Callaghan, and I stopped a third time. We'd just have to have this discussion later. "Anyway, thanks again, Sis."

***

Darya was still massaging my neck when we heard, from upstairs, a noise like shattering glass. Callaghan shoved back her chair, but Guadalupe was up first, and by the time the rest of us caught up, she was clutching a bleeding hand and biting down her lip hard. Kennedy had knocked over a row of picture frames.

Callaghan acted as interpreter. Guadalupe had cut herself, trying to clean up. Kennedy, unremorseful, scampered around the room, pulling other bric-a-brac to the floor.

Lupe refused to let us take her to the emergency room. Callaghan said she couldn't understand why but I was pretty sure that I had caught the Spanish version of the initials "INS." I told her to reassure Lupe that an emergency room would not report her.

Callaghan didn't cover for her brother. "Kennedy cut her on purpose, Mommy," she said sternly. "This isn't appropriate."

Lupe shook her head after Callaghan repeated herself for her. "No, Kennedy *es uno bueno nino.*"

We finally convinced Lupe to go. When we returned a few hours later, Guadalupe's hand was bandaged and the pain pills the doctor had prescribed had mysteriously disappeared from Darya's purse.

I went to unpack. We had decided that I would share quarters with Callaghan, and I had moved my tote bag into her room. When I walked in, though, I discovered Kennedy unpacking for me. He had already strewn the items inside, from toothbrush to panties, everywhere from light fixture to bed post.

At that moment, he was scaling a bookshelf on the other side of the room. On the top of the bookshelf Callaghan had displayed her collection of snow globes, many brought home from her father after filming out of town. Callaghan had wisely placed them out of her brother's reach, but Kennedy had gained more strength and agility than maturity in recent months.

I caught him around the waist just before he pulled the bookshelf down on both of us. Pushing as hard as I could I righted the shelf, which had just begun to tilt, with one hand. He howled and kicked me in the stomach while I gripped him with the other. A viscous liquid oozed on the hardwood floor.

I screamed. I was losing the baby.

As my nephew and I toppled backward on the bed I saw the broken snow globe. It was from Toronto, a low-cost shooting location.

Kennedy kept kicking, but now his heels were landing between my spread legs.

    ***

I believed that future civilizations would look back on my own as being as superstitious as the Middle Ages seemed to me. "In the 21ˢᵗ Century, people living in California believed that what they called 'stress' could cause everything from eczema to miscarriages."

But I *was* superstitious. And since within hours of my arrival at Darya's home, someone needed stitches, and I mistook the liquid from a snow globe for amniotic fluid, then I was experiencing a dangerous degree of stress. Maybe it didn't reach the level of being surrounded by "torch-wielding peasants," as the sympathetic Officer Armstrong described the protesters, but the fact remained that her house scared me.

I had nowhere else to go. So here I was in Val's living room, watching the light drain from his apartment.

I really had meant to end the affair with Val. Really. I hadn't even considered coming here when Alex ordered me to leave. But if Alex wouldn't have me, obviously he wouldn't have the baby either. And Val was the father. Maybe that would mean something to him. Maybe it was good that I hadn't been able to force myself to break ties with him. By definition, you can't get to know someone well in the course of an extramarital affair, because you see that person in such artificial circumstances. I had no idea what he was like as a brother or a son. As special education teacher and therapist, let alone lover, he was incomparable. Could I dare hope that he'd succeed as a father?

Whether he failed or succeeded, the baby created the same link between us that had kept me with Alex all this time. Now I didn't just want to be with Val for company, or cuddling, or sex, I wanted to be with my baby's father. How the hell was I going to work all this out...? But I could hardly think. I needed Val to help me think. According to the pamphlet he had given me, he was in Paso Robles tonight.

Jack was on my mind even more than Val and the baby. The night before, when Alex had thrown me out, Jack had already been asleep. But what about tonight? How would he cope without our five pages of *Harry Potter*? Would Alex have another violent fit of rage, as he had the night of the Millard and Rotwell item? *He loves Jack,* Darya had said. *It's you he hates.*

I called home from my regular cell; no answer. I left a beseeching message. I called Alex's cell. Another message, this time groveling. I went outside and walked down the street until I found a group of teenaged boys passing. I offered one $20 to use his cell phone so Alex wouldn't recognize the caller i.d. I got the machine.

I tried to think who could plead my case for me. Alex had never liked Darya, though rules concerning family duty had spurred him to help her financially on more than one occasion. Mairead was too shy to make eye contact with him. Maddy — she would believe me about Millard and Rotwell. But I couldn't get a hold of her, either, at least not before the youthful owner of the cell phone, laughing with his friends, demanded another hundred bucks.

Maybe tomorrow I'll feel better. I went back to the apartment, where I threw up once, then crawled under the white chenille bedspread.

Dark shapes on the far wall looked like many-fingered ghosts. I held the bedspread close to my chin, shivering until I realized that they were tree branches made into shadows from the streetlight a few houses down.

I'd never been here by myself, let alone at night. Was it possible that Aunt Patsy haunted the place, that she disapproved of her nephew's whore?

***

Convincing Mairead to let me see Jack was no small task. Alex had forbidden her to communicate with me.

But Julius Kahn Park was a safe place, I had argued. Jack hadn't been here in years, and a new generation of toddlers and caregivers had replaced him.

She agreed to meet me on Friday.

Julius Kahn was part of the Presidio, with tennis courts, state-of-the-art play structures, and a baseball diamond at one end of a large meadow. It was the meadow that had forced us to stop bringing Jack here, for though there was a leash law, it was not enforced, and there were always dogs of every breed and size running free.

Between the meadow and the play area was a clubhouse, where, on a picnic table bench I now sat "disguised" in the biggest black coat I owned, a floppy, wide-brimmed hat and oversized sunglasses, courtesy of Aunt Patsy. As a finishing touch I had wrapped a burgundy wool scarf that belonged to Val around the lower part of my face. I looked like Claude Rains in *The Invisible Man*. The only reason I didn't stand out more was because the temperature had dropped below 50 degrees. And for the first time since my first date with Alex, I was wearing gym shoes outside of a gym.

But what made coming here really misguided was that the park brought back too many memories. More than once back in those days, I encountered an Asian immigrant grandmother, caring for her grandchild while her own son or daughter pulled the eighty hour work weeks that would send that grandchild to the Ivy League. "He didn't get enough oxygen at birth," one woman said. "Sue the hospital. *Lots* of money."

Or, on another occasion: "Punishment from another life. Your husband must be bad man."

Cultural differences, Alex said. *Don't you dare repeat what they said to* anyone.

I had been waiting for a century (although my watch said twenty minutes), when I spotted Mairead's flaming red hair coming down the main road that bordered the park. No Jack. My heart seized up. Then saw that Mairead had four legs.

Jack, Jack! *Would God that I had died for thee.*

I held myself still so that I would not rush to hug him, afraid of scaring off Mairead. That was, until I started running. *Running is really easy in gym shoes.* Mairead cocked her head — until my hat fell off, and she recognized me. Then she let go of Jack's hand to cover her mouth. She was laughing.

"Mommy! You're back! Where have you been? Been...."

Little boy! My little boy —

"God love you." Mairead was hiccoughing. "You look a sight, sure you do."

— how could I have ever thought I wanted to be away from you?
"You're so handsome!" I cried.

"Mommy! Where have you been? Been...."

He threw his arms around me. I hugged him back and he said, "I missed you. You...."

I loosened my grip and kissed him on the cheek. Jack couldn't kiss me back. He couldn't pucker his lips enough to kiss or spit. But he said, "I'm a big boy now. I put myself to bed. Put myself...."

"Why don't we go in the clubhouse?" Mairead whispered. Jack was way ahead of us, as a small, shaggy dog of mixed breed was scampering in our direction. Mairead and I followed. Mairead giggled again briefly when I whipped off my sunglasses and unwound my scarf.

Other children played at various stations set up with toys and art supplies. We found some folding chairs and created a semblance of privacy in one corner.

"Dans un cercle." I heard a mother speak French with a thick American accent to her toddler daughter who was painting. "Et voila, tu as la tête."

"Mommy, where have you been? Been...."

"I had to go stay with Auntie Darya for a while."

"When are you coming home?"

"I don't know," I said evasively.

"He did get himself to bed without you," Mairead said. "We had a couple of pretty tough nights."

Oh, you did, did you? "What has Alex told you?"

"Just that the pair of you had come to a new understanding." Mairead lowered her eyes, turning nearly purple. "But I'm not supposed to talk to you or let you see Jack."

"So you said on the phone," I reminded her dryly. *Who's your friend, here, Mairead?* "Don't you want to hear my side of the story?"

Mairead tugged nervously at one ear lobe. "I don't think I should get in the middle."

"Fine." Just wait until she found out that I was pregnant. And by whom. "Though you know, it says in Proverbs, 'Speak up for those who cannot speak up for themselves.'"

She cleared her throat. "What are you going to do?" she asked.

"I — I don't know." The sight of Jack hurtled me back to Go. The moment I saw him I knew that I had to put everything into a reconciliation with Alex. But when I'd been throwing up that morning all I could think of was having Val hold my head.... "I just don't know."

"Mommy." Jack picked up two crayons from the floor and launched them in the air by turns with accompanying hissing sounds. "I want to have a 4th of July party."

"*Tu es très ... très ... talentée,*" the mother at the next table said to her daughter. She looked up at the three of us. Unlike Spanish, I knew a few words of French. "*Giftée,*" she tried, glaring at me.

Hoping for a few moments alone with Mairead, I said, "Jack, why don't you get some paper and draw a picture?"

"Okay. Ka-pow! Ka-pow!" He launched the crayon missiles again. "Can I have a 4th of July party? Party...."

"Why don't you talk to Daddy about it?" I said. "Tell him how important it is to you."

"We can have fireworks!"

"Right. Here." I ripped out a page from the notebook I carried in my purse. "Draw me a picture." I was ashamed of my next thought: *Be like the girl who's learning French.*

Jack took the jagged-edge paper and made slashes with one of the crayons. It was dark green. "When are you coming home? Home...."

"It really worked out," I asked Mairead, "Jack getting to bed?"

Mairead stammered over a few different consonants.

"*Ecrivons une… une* story *maintenant,*" said the woman, staring at us again. She had been silent awhile and I wondered if she'd been trying to eavesdrop. I glowered back at her until she looked away.

"Can I have a 4th of July party?" Jack persisted. "We can invite Sophie, and Emily, and Armen, and...." He named everyone in his former class. "…and Ms. Scarbo, and Candy, and...."

Mairead and I looked at each other wistfully.

"Did Daddy and you have a *fight?* Did Daddy and you…."

At least Alex must not have told him much about what had happened. I'd imagined him spinning tales about me that would make Heidi Fleiss look like a Carmelite nun.

"We did, honey," I answered. "Maybe we'll make up." Probably it was wrong to get his hopes up. *But this is Alex's fault.* I'd still come home if he'd let me.

"We'll have the party and you'll come to the party and you'll make up!"

Now Mairead looked sad. She obviously didn't think it likely that I'd be home anytime soon. "Anna, I'm just going to come out with it, is that all right with you?"

I doubt it.

"I have to move out."

"You can't!"

Jack kept making meaningless lines on the paper. He stayed with the one color. I should be glad he was drawing instead of stimming, but....

"I can't be living with a man by meself?"

"But Alex — the only women he makes eye contact with are criminal attorneys." *Or criminals.*

"It doesn't matter. I can't keep this from my parents, and they'd be on the next plane to collect me. I don't feel comfortable, that's the truth of it."

"You have your own apartment on a completely separate floor. It's no different than if the two of you were living in a duplex."

"He wants me upstairs at night now."

"But where will you go?"

"I'll be moving in with Kelly."

"And have you told — " I dipped my head toward Jack, still absorbed in marking up the paper. "Jack, can you try to draw me a real picture?"

That inspired him to attempt a loopy circle.

"No, and not Alex, either. It's going to be hard."

"I should think so." Did she have to pick *this week* to get over her savior complex?

"But I'll have to find the courage. I'm praying on it."

God had never failed her. She'd be gone soon. "You'll still come in days, won't you?"

"Of course! I wouldn't desert him." She put her arm around Jack's shoulder.

I didn't think there was a saint named "Mairead" yet. She was obviously bucking to be the first.

"*I* didn't desert him, I — "

"I'm finished with my picture! Picture.... "

I pulled the paper toward me. Among the slashes were some wobbly circles. "What is it?"

"Can't you see? Can't you see.... "

"*Très bon!*" As if on cue, the woman at the other table exclaimed over her own daughter's artwork.

I resisted all temptation to turn around, to see the watercolor of the Golden Gate Bridge or the city skyline. *I can't draw, either. You don't need to draw pictures to be successful in life. I worry too much. I can't make comparisons. He's on his own path. He's a happy kid. Isn't that what Val said was important?*

"It's beautiful, honey," I said. "I'll put it on the refrigerator."

"What refrigerator?"

"Uh...."

Mairead shook her head at my blunder. Then she bent over to Jack. "Tell you what, Handsome. We'll take it home and put it on *our* refrigerator."

I was suddenly and selfishly not so sorry that she was moving out. But I had to get past that. Jack needed her.

"No." I pulled Jack's scribble toward myself. "Boychik, I have a refrigerator — " a defiant glance at Mairead — "at the friend's house where I'm staying. I'll put it up there. I'll look at it all the time until we're together again."

Jack broke out into a huge smile, and I remembered that none of us could live without hope.

***

On Sunday morning I received a text message:
     mt me @ 111 Folsom 4p luv u trulee

It was the first word I had received from my baby's father in a week, sent from a cell phone number I didn't recognize.

111 Folsom turned out to be a mongrel structure of rotting gray shingles that might once have been blue. I parked my Town and Country in a yellow zone, with the front poking into a bus stop. But the bus stop was so covered with graffiti that I didn't know it was a bus stop until I had staggered too far away to care if my van got towed to Brisbane. Brisbane, Australia.

The organizers of the AIDS ride did not provide transportation back to San Francisco. Val had been vague about his return plans, and I hadn't pressed him — proof to myself that, before circumstances had intervened, I had been sincere about my intention to stop seeing him.

The first floor of 111 Folsom was a boarded-up storefront. Most of the windows of the second floor were broken, with some of the gaps covered with plastic. The moment I got out of the car I was assailed by heavy metal music. A staircase with warped, uneven treads led up to the front door. I picked my way through a dozen young men sitting with cans of beer, some showing signs of inebriation, others sober but rude, and a few both drunk *and* rude. "The opera house is down the street, bitch," belched one man, with a dirty blonde mountaineer's beard and dreadlocks down to his waist.

I ignored him and teetered up the steps. I should have worn the gym shoes from the park, but I wanted Val to see me as I'd been when he'd left.

Inside the music was louder, unbearably so, and the press of bodies was just as bad. Among the odors inside I inhaled the sweet, fecund aroma of marijuana. It had been years, but one did not forget. *This might be bad for the baby.* I needed to find Val and get out asap.

The smell of beer was everywhere, too. A couple of young men, friendlier than the ones outside, offered me large plastic tumblers foaming with it. The partiers were almost all male, and most looked under twenty-five. I saw one shaking as if with palsy, and my first, terrible thought was that he was having a seizure. Then I saw him rub the side of his nose. These weren't the socially conscious jocks from Fort Mason.

I started asking people at random if they knew Val, or Alex Valentine, but I got shrugs and blank stares from some, more offers of drink or drugs from others, and offers of more intimate interactions from a few.

Like a child separated from her mother at a carnival, I squeezed through the smelly, crowded and noisy rooms, sometimes leaning against the wall for support. I thought I heard someone say, "Stoned cunt" — but I wouldn't have been surprised if I imagined it.

"Anne Banane!"

Thank God. I fell into his arms. "I'm so glad I found you."

But wait — was it him, my Val? The smell ... all smells were strange to me now, and most of them were sickening — but Val always smelled like rumpled sheets on a morning when you can sleep in. And he always felt so soft, like your worn beloved teddy. This man was grizzled, and stank. Only his voice penetrated, and the familiar stroking of my hair calmed me.

"I've got the car out front," I said, my voice muffled by his t-shirt. It was red and bore the emblem of the ride. "Let's get out of here." I was sure I was going to vomit soon. "I have to tell you something. Important."

"Banana Boat Baby, it is so awesome to see you!" His enthusiasm was reassuring, and then disturbing: He'd been drinking. I hadn't smelled it earlier in the midst of the alcohol radiating off every other surface, animate and otherwise.

"I missed you *so* bad. I wanted to call, but my phone got lost at the first rest stop, then we found it at the next, smashed — we think someone took it, used up the minutes, then destroyed it — "

He was talking fast, but I was still focused on escape. "Can we go to the car?"

"Babe, it's a party!" He whispered in my ear, "Holy shit, I can't wait to get you home and into bed. But I want you to meet some dudes first so I can show you off. They've heard all about you."

"I'm going to throw up," I said baldly.

"Really? You been drinking? I've never seen you drink before!" He beamed as if I had just taken my own training wheels off.

"Can we please get out of here?"

"Sure, babe, sure," he nodded, though his lips briefly formed a pout. But I took his hand with as much authority as I could muster and fairly dragged him out of the house.

The fresh air was a relief, but after the journey down the vertiginous steps I finally did retch, on the sidewalk. The punks on the stairs laughed and pointed, and I heard the epithet "bitch" again.

Val, who had been holding my hair back, whipped around and started back toward them. "Is it on, assholes?"

Their laughter stopped abruptly.

"I asked you something, scumbags," Val reminded them.

I gripped the hem of his t-shirt. "No, honey, let it go."

Val stared for a moment at the evident leader, the one with the beard, who had taunted me about the opera, before turning around again. There was a snicker. This time Val was even faster. He grabbed a fistful of Long Beard's t-shirt, pulled him upright, and shook him until the man's beer bottle landed on the concrete, smashing into pieces. "My girlfriend doesn't want me to hurt you," he growled. "If you weren't feeling lucky before, you should start."

"It's cool, dude," Long Beard said edgily.

"You'll say you're sorry to my lady."

Long Beard tilted his head back defiantly, but that positioned his chin perfectly to receive the blow from Val's fist.

"Whoa! Dude!" The man's compatriots, who had been an amused audience, all shoved themselves upward two stairs. Long Beard swayed, his eyes rolling.

"I'm waiting."

"I'm very sorry, Ma'am," Long Beard gasped.

Val pushed him so that he landed with his back against the steps.

I felt brief, guilty satisfaction in Val's primal instinct toward me, then I pulled hard on his t-shirt again.

"My lady wants to go," Val growled. "You really are one lucky dude."

Val teetered as he followed me to the van, which had been ticketed but not towed. "Are you okay, Banana Boat? I guess you're not used to the brew."

"It smelled pretty bad in there," I said. As much as I wanted to get away from 111 Folsom, I didn't trust either of us to drive. So instead I opened the middle doors of the van so that Val and I could sit in the pilot seats and still catch a breeze. Fortunately, Long Beard's friends were helping him into the house. Not so fortunately, the music was as loud as ever.

The plane explodes
The people scream
Too many roads
It's all a dream

"I'm sorry you didn't get to meet my new posse." Val looked back at the empty stairs. "You were the most babelicious female human in the crib."

"There weren't a lot of female humans there," I observed smiling, and thinking, *I'm not sure there were a lot of humans, period.* "Val — what were you doing in a place like that?"

"You mean how'd a nice boy — "

"I'm serious. This was sleazy stuff. People were doing drugs." Marijuana was bad enough, but cocaine … I hadn't *seen* cocaine, but I knew what I knew.

Val laughed. "Here." He eased me halfway around so that he could massage my neck with strong and always-skillful fingers. "The dude I bummed a ride with took off without telling me five minutes after we got here."

"But you texted me this morning to meet you here."

"Ban-Ban, *relax*." He dug his fingers more deeply into my shoulders. "I just thought it was his apartment. I didn't know any of this stuff would be going on."

"Why didn't you call from the road?" I hadn't meant to whine.

"I told you I might not be able to." His fingers stopped working. I couldn't see his face but he sounded hurt. "I told you inside that I lost the phone." He was starting to sound sober now, too. "This isn't like you."

Well, things have changed. I was about to blurt out my news, but it hit me, and hit me hard, that I had an entirely different set of needs to impose on him. Needs that he hadn't asked for and for which he was unprepared. A week before I'd been ready to say good-bye — or so I'd told myself.

The nausea was returning. I fought it back down my throat. "Tell me about the Ride."

"What an awesome time!" He whirled me back to face him and held my face in his hands. "The first day — "

He launched into the tales of overused outhouses, of the Tentmate from Hell (no more trips with Randy Andy!), the trucks that created a vortex of air to drag you into the wrong lane as they passed you, honking. But then, the wrap-up meetings at the end of the day, seeing people from the year before, talking about the research they were funding just by getting on their bikes in the morning....

"There's one thing I want to do with my life," he said rapturously. "Leave the world a better place than how I found it. This was one small step." He laughed. "Or let's say, one long ride."

That laugh. How had I lived without that laugh? How had I thought I was *going* to live without that laugh?

"My turn," I said. I took a deep breath. I'd been rehearsing my announcement since I'd gotten his text message. Maybe it's just impossible for these moments to live up to one's fantasies. Maybe....

Maybe I didn't have to beg or sneak my way back into Alex's house. Maybe there was some other way. Val and I had so much fun together — watching DVDs on the portable player, listening to his vinyl albums, playing Yahtzee. Why couldn't we make room for Jack? There was only Alex's pride to overcome.

And Baby makes four.

Val had resumed his stories, but I hadn't been listening. "I know I'm rambling. It was just such an awesome — *journey,* especially after I was so bummed about losing that sorry-ass job — "

"I'm pregnant," I said.

"—and you're physically so ramped up, the endorphins are just flooding — "

"Val."

"I mean, it was awesome, and we were lucky with the weather, too...."

"*Val.*"

"Yeah, babe?"

"*I'm pregnant.*"

He stopped, pushed a hand through thick, damp curls. "My God."

My nails dug crescents into my palms. " 'My God what are we going to do' or 'my God I'm happy'?"

He unfolded my hands. "Oh, my sweet Anne Banane, how could you ever think I wouldn't be happy?"

Easily.

"It's a new adventure," he said, grasping my hands.

"And I've left Alex. I — I've been staying at your place." We'd never discussed this possibility.

"Then I'm ecstatic! We're getting you out of here." Val climbed into the driver's seat, an adventure in itself given his height. He seemed entirely sober now. "You stay back there, the middle row is safer. Everyone makes such a big deal about 'shotgun'? That's the suicide seat. So Elsie's going to have a little brother or sister!"

What is it they say in *Showboat*? There's Saturday night, and then Monday morning. Tomorrow was Monday.

"Oh, and we have to swing by Geoff's place to pick her up."

"Pick up — "

"Elsie, silly. You should have heard her bellow when I left her behind. But I didn't have a choice."

Across the street, someone turned the music up louder. It was nothing from *Showboat*.

The light at the end of the tunnel
Is really the tunnel to Hell.

"Do you trust me to drive now?" Val asked. "We're starting our life together, you know."

I handed him my keys. "You can take all three of us home."
Home.

PART TWO

PART TWO

CHAPTER FOURTEEN
LOVE IS A BATTLEFIELD

Monday morning came, and I was slapped with a restraining order. I was not to communicate with Jack via phone, e-mail, letter, carrier pigeon or skywriting. I was not to stand within a hundred feet of him. It was a felony to dream of him.

But now I was able to bear it because Val kept saying, "We'll make it right," reassuring me that we would find a way to make Alex relent about Jack and to become that happy family of four I had envisioned right before I told him I was expecting. Meanwhile he could help me through the physically rough days.

He brought me chamomile tea, read to me, massaged my shoulders. Neither tea, massage nor stories ease morning sickness, but they take your mind off it. A little. He insisted that he postpone his job hunt for a few weeks to care for me and to keep me company. "It's just like you have the flu," he said, adding, "*if* you had that flu that killed everyone after World War I."

"That was called the Spanish flu. Don't joke about it. Too soon."

On the Wednesday after his return he helped me get to my OB-GYN. Dr. Phelps, a walnut-skinned woman with close-cropped hair and gold wire-rim glasses, calculated my due date in late January, informed me that I was now a candidate for amniocentesis since my due date was after my thirty-fifth birthday, and told me to come back in a month. For this information, plus some blood work and a moment standing on a scale, I owed her $800. Fortunately, I was still covered by Alex's insurance plan. We were still married, after all. But I was sure he'd find a way to fix that soon enough.

And indeed, the day after that the papers arrived by certified mail, as had the restraining order. Petitioner (Alex) was seeking not only a dissolution of the marriage but sole custody of issue of marriage (Jack).

Wholly expected as it was, I took to my new bed and cried.

Later in the day, when Val left for groceries, I called Maddy, but as soon as she heard my voice she hung up on me. Over the next two days I tried three more times but she never picked up again. I left only one message. I knew better than to appeal to her woman to woman; for one thing, she heartily disliked children. She did not return my calls.

Val's aunt's newspaper subscription had run out and he had not renewed it. He preferred to buy what interested him on any given day, and suddenly he was not interested in the *Chronicle*. Campaign gossip, though it spread as fast as any broadband connection among political insiders, rarely merited television coverage, certainly not this early in the game. So after giving up on Maddy I spent two days almost entirely in bed, rising mostly to vomit, escaping in sleep when possible, grateful to know someone would be next to me when I awoke. Most of the time it was Val and not Elsie.

There were moments when I enjoyed the pleasant domesticity into which we had settled so easily. Yes, I had wanted to end the "affair," because the very word meant something time-limited and tawdry. But now Val and I had a "relationship." There was dog hair on the furniture, and a few dirty dishes in the sink, signs of a home in which a family-to-be lived. We would be a very different kind of family, a *real* family. And Val kept repeating, "We'll make it right."

* * *

Bay Area politics did merit some radio coverage, and on late Friday morning I remembered Perry Millard's regular spot on our local all-news station. For two hours I cuddled Val's transistor radio like one of the stuffed animals that Jack never really bonded with, listening to stories of random shootings, families made homeless by foreclosures, and the director of the Employment Development Department spouting predictions for the job market. I wondered when PROTECT would finagle its way onto one of the talk shows (which they might have already — for how would I know?), until the anchor introduced Millard at his 3:20 time slot.

Perry Millard. Half of the team that was the proximate cause of my separation from Jack. But was it Perry Millard's fault that I had gone to bed with Val? Had Perry Millard been on Minotaur Island?

"...our weekly check-in with *Chronicle* political insider...."

"...thanks Rebecca ... lots to tell about the D.A.'s race...."

Static. I tilted the radio, hoping for better reception.

"It was Kagen's to lose until...."

Crackle crackle crackle.

"...yes, it seems that his personal life...."

"...turn of events that just seem to get more bizarre every week...."

"...true about a civil suit?"

Crackle.

"...campaign staff have quit ... Bo Hanks and Ray Shimmie ... signed off as Kagen consultants...."

"...Marianne Pasquale has withdrawn her endorsement...."

"...I understand that her campaign is in trouble now, too...."

"...questions about the missing autopsy...."

Missing autopsy?

"...promised to locate the report or perform yet a third...."

Third ... autopsy?

"I understand that a neighborhood activist group has formed. Can they actually have an impact on this campaign?"

"Absolutely, Rebecca...."

I made frantic circles with the radio's antenna.

"...very ugly demonstration, but it turns out no one was cited...." *Crackle.* "...false report there! You have to feel sorry for the guy, Rebecca...."

A long arm stretched over my torso and pulled the little black radio from my hands.

"Media boycott," Val announced.

"Did you hear?"

"Some of it."

Millard hadn't mention that "the guy's" wife was pregnant, or that she had moved in with another man. Unless I'd missed it during one of the static attacks.

But a missing autopsy? *The second autopsy was performed and has mysteriously "disappeared."* That was all I could conclude. It must be a (misguided) plan to help Pasquale continue to drag out the investigation. Did she think it was possible to drag it out until after the November election?

And did this mean that they still hadn't buried the poor boy? The thought prompted a fresh wave of nausea. If I hadn't been so very certain in my heart that Tyler was someone else's victim....

I felt the mattress shift as Val climbed into the bed and spooned me. "Make room."

He didn't just mean in bed. "I hope you like this," I said, trying to accommodate him in both the physical and psychological sense. "In a few months it will definitely be the position of choice."

His own torso stiffened.

"You don't like that I've been through this before."

"No."

"I haven't been through it with *you*," I said. It's hard to compete with history. Val and I had to make our own, and it would take time. For both of us. I hadn't just imposed new expectations on Val; the baby had imposed them on me. "That makes it like the first time." Then I lied, "I think I'm feeling a little better today."

Val tenderly rolled me toward him so that I was on my back. There was bile at the back of my throat, but I had just said that I was feeling better, so I didn't complain. This was sign of our new level of intimacy: the closer a couple grows the more they have to hide from one another.

Val pulled up the big t-shirt I was wearing, borrowed from his drawer. "Can you feel it?"

"It's way too early for that," I chuckled.

He put his hand over my navel. "Why are you so flat?"

He sounded panicky, and I was ashamed to be pleased. "Because it's only the first trimester." Since I'd been so ill, I'd lost not only the pounds I'd gained early on but more.

Val traced a circle around my tummy, so lightly that his finger barely touched my skin. "And when can we find out if it's a boy or girl?"

"Do you care?" I asked.

"No. As long as — "

As long as it's healthy.

"I want a girl," I said. That was partly because of the enchanting little girls who had found their way into my life, not just Callaghan but the Pathways princesses, little Emily and Sophie, especially, of whom I often thought with nostalgia.

What I wouldn't tell him was the other reason: that ASD boys outnumbered ASD girls by four or five to one, depending on which study you read.

Girl or boy, I admitted to myself that I was glad that this baby had a different father. I knew a disturbing number of families with more than one ASD child, often affected at different levels. In my more generous moments I wondered if it really had been fear of combining our DNA again, not mistrust, that had driven Alex to his doctor's office for that vasectomy.

     ***

A few days later Val brought me the phone and told me it was Mairead.

"I'm in me own place now," she said. "With Kelly. I thought it would be safe to call. He wouldn't be tapping my phone, now, would he?"

"Even Alex couldn't pull that one off," I said. "He'd need to hold a Federal office." At first I was amused by her naïveté and then immediately had to struggle not to catch her anxiety. "We'll make it short. Just tell me how things are at home."

"Grand," she said. "We're splashing on a coat of paint in the bedroom — "

"I meant at home with Jack."

"G-grand." Pause. "Maybe not grand."

"Please tell me everything you can."

With Mairead out of the house, instead of a floor away, Alex needed help on nights and weekends. He had replaced me with two extra sitters. Mairead saw only the weeknight one: a tight-lipped woman in her fifties who wore a snug white uniform and the crepe-soled shoes of old-time nurses.

At first Mairead thought the sitter didn't speak English, but then she overheard her talking on her cell phone as she came through the front yard. Mairead rarely saw Alex. Instead he left her typed notes. "Your assistance is much appreciated in this challenging time," was how he signed off.

He never directly mentioned Jack.

"But he must see what's going on?" she said.

"What do you mean?" I asked.

"Wh-when I come in he's awfully... he's a little ... grubby."

"Alex?"

"N-no, Jack."

"How so?"

"You know the problems we always had with his hair."

His hair. His thick black wavy hair. Like mine. So much like mine. I buried my fingers deeply in my own, to remember the texture of his.

"You comb it when you come in, though."

"Of course," she said indignantly. "I give him a good scrub, too, and make sure his clothes are clean."

Jack always had food stains on his clothes within minutes of sitting down to eat. His table manners were appalling: He ate noisily with his mouth open, insisted on picking up food from the floor, and never used a napkin of his own volition. When Mairead arrived in the morning there was no food on the floor, but it didn't seem that anyone had touched Jack.

"Well," I tried, "it's nothing we can't turn around." Mairead was a bit overly fastidious, and boys Jack's age were supposed to get dirty.

"I j-just." Pause. "Worry?"

"Because...."

Longer pause. *Out with it, woman!*

"He won't go outside."

"At all?" Maybe she just meant the backyard. In Jack's toddler years it had often been difficult to lure him outside. He didn't have enough words then to tell us why, but some of the dangers were known to us: sirens, car alarms, dogs.

"No," she confessed. "He won't leave the house." Another pause. "I'm sorry."

She had always been the one who could coax Jack to take the different route home from the park, to pass the dog, to try walking in new shoes when the old ones became two sizes too small.

That brought back a memory that might soothe us both. "If you weren't there, he'd be much worse off. Remember Alison Baxter? How she had bought six pairs of the same shoes in ascending sizes so Logan could just keep growing into the same shoes over and over?"

"Logan always knew the difference, though," she chuckled.

There was no point trying to persuade her to move back in. Alex wouldn't want her. I didn't know if he had given her a raise to cover the added expenses she had brought on herself by renting her own place — he probably had, the generous bastard — but now that this much time had passed, he wouldn't want a single woman living in his house any more than she wanted to be there, because rumors would get around. If Perry Millard, Adrian Rotwell, Patrick Riordan and all their crew failed us, then we could count on Mrs. Dr. Marjorie Mitchell, watching the house from behind a raised corner of her drapes.

Mairead returned to the subject of Kelly. "She's read so much Irish history, she makes me ashamed of myself. But she loves my cooking."

I was happy for her. At least I tried to be. Finally a life of her own.

I knew she'd never bring Jack to me again, as it would be breaking the law, not just disregarding an order from an employer. But she could keep me in the loop. She owed me that much. So I pressed her for more details. But....

"Anna? I'd better go."

"Tell Jack I'm thinking of him?" I asked.

"He might tell Alex."

"Right." The receiver of the phone was sticky. "Will you call me again?"

"I'll try."

***

A few days more and the worst of my symptoms lessened. I could imagine, at least, a future without nausea and a pounding head.

One morning, Val awoke from our nightlong spoon and reached for my breasts. I feigned interest, rolling over to kiss him. But he stopped as immediately as he had started. Pushing hair off my lightly perspiring forehead, he said, "You're still not up to this. Don't pretend."

"I want to keep you happy."

"You have made me forever, permanently happy."

"But I've been — "

He could always read my mind. "I like taking care of you." He grinned. "But okay, I'm a guy. I like making love with you, too." He gave my cheek a resigned pat. "You just tell me when you're ready."

"I'm ready."

"Really?"

He said it so quickly and eagerly that I almost laughed. I wanted to do something for him, and a convenient element of being female was that one *could* pretend, up to a point.

"You mean I can have my way with you?" he teased, flicking his tongue against my upper lip.

Those words and the touch of his tongue sent an unexpected tingle through my groin. "Have away."

There was no need to pretend after all. A few minutes later, after many more tingles, I had another of the full-blown, body-rocking orgasms he had introduced me to.

I had never identified with the women in stories of sexual obsession in novels or movies, women so aroused that they could come with their backs pressed against the corner of a dresser, women who loved men *because* of sex. My desire to get in bed in the first place began with the kind of intimacy Val and I had achieved in the emergency room. If I had nothing to talk about with a man before sex, I had nothing to talk to him about after. Maybe, "Don't forget your contact lens solution," but that was about it.

I had finally met a man who was both Daddy and Stud, for Val and I had plenty to talk about afterwards. We even went for a walk that morning. I hadn't been out in almost two weeks, since my visit to the obstetrician's. The uniformity of my surroundings — so many hours spent looking at the same four walls — had affected my depth perception. When we first stepped out onto the sidewalk the world looked like a sound stage.

We strolled to Geary, holding hands, where passers-by, the battering noise of traffic, and Elsie's yaps re-oriented me. *There is life outside your apartment,* promises a lyric from *Avenue Q.*

"I'll even take you to Starbuck's," Val offered gallantly. He usually boycotted what his friends — for I had met a few more since moving in — oh-so-maturely called "Starfucks," having seen it put so many family owned cafés out of business in the neighborhood. I hated to see the small indy cafés go as well, but my guilty pleasure was Starbucks. I had been a caffeine junkie from adolescence.

My stomach was hardly ready for coffee, though. Maybe I could get through this pregnancy caffeine-free? I hadn't done so with Jack and I'd been waiting for ten years to learn that coffee caused autism. For today, I'd go for one of their strawberry frap's.

At the corner of 18th and Geary, with the ubiquitous green logo of a ship's figurehead just above us paying homage to the first mate of the Pequod, there was a long row of newspaper vending machines.

"I've never gone this long without reading a paper." I did not like the way I suddenly missed the pampered feeling of having three newspapers delivered to my door.

"No newspapers, and no more radio," Val reminded me firmly.

I dug in my pocket for change but came up short. "You're not going to make me panhandle for fifty cents, are you?"

Val tied Elsie's leash to one of the news racks before grimly handing me two quarters. He was an intuitive man.

The inside of Starbucks was populated by college students with their laptops and balding, middle-aged men who made ponytails from the hair that still grew at the base of their scalps. I sensed that more than one job interview was underway between young males and even younger females, with a resumé laid out between them.

I took a window seat while Val went to order. Outside, on the other side of the vending machine where Elsie sat patiently, was a woman shaped like the Michelin Tire man, who had fashioned sandals out of cardboard and string.

Val give me the thumbs up sign as he moved to the front of the queue. I returned the gesture and automatically turned to the Bay Area section of the *Chronicle*, the way you turn the corner toward home. Millard and Rotwell's column only appeared three days a week, and this issue was an M&R-free zone.

District Attorney Kagen sets goals for fighting hate crimes

It was the lead story. B1. Over the fold. Headline in big type. Even bigger: the picture of Alex in his Bryant Street office, three columns wide and in color. The California State and American flags hung limply, one on each side of his desk, just within the borders of the frame.

It was unnerving to see him, after three weeks, in a picture. I worked my tongue around the insides of my cheeks, trying to produce some saliva. The byline was Diana Levy's. She was a friend of Sherri Pechner's. They'd gone to Wellesley together.

Just the lead screamed puff piece: "Alex Kagen was a *wunderkind* who, unlike many of the breed, went on to fulfill his promise." The *wunderkind* had gone to Berkeley both as undergraduate and to study law. (He chose Berkeley over Stanford and Harvard to dramatize his loyalty to California's public University system.) The *wunderkind* rose meteorically up through the ranks of the D.A.'s office. Levy mentioned two early career-making cases but wisely neglected to remind us of his failed attempt to win a seat on Community College Board. Then she gave in to pure hagiography, the epic saga of Alex Kagen's First Term in Office. Great Moments in History — *and you were there!*

During Alex's tenure, the crime rate had gone down 37%. Yes, he'd be happy to break that down. Violent crime by 35%. Domestic violence 40%. Elder abuse 38%. No, neither the state nor the nation as a whole had experienced a similar decline. Yes, a big drop had occurred nationwide in the 1990s, but that had leveled off in 2000.

Not since Rudy Giuliani had simulated noon in Times Square had an elected official so spectacularly made the night safe for Joe and Jane Citizen. "My top priority for my second term is expanding the definition of hate crimes, particularly hate crimes as they relate to the disabled and to the homeless. Ranking crime according to heinousness is like trying to compare Hitler and Stalin to see who accomplished the most evil. Evil is immeasurable.'"

Sanctimonious prick. I raised my head so that I could breathe more easily. I saw Val hovering near the barista, looking over his shoulder, watching me. He raised his eyebrows. It made lines on his forehead.

I dipped down over the article again. I wondered what he was going to say about the little matter of Tyler Gaines. Levy would probably ignore the subject. For Jack's sake I hope she did.

"Anna Banana Boat." Val's voice was mild, but when he put my strawberry frappuccino down right at the place where I was reading, I barely restrained myself from knocking it over. With a downward glance he registered the cause of my stiffened posture. *"Don't turn the page,"* he stage-whispered, in a voice from a horror movie trailer. *"The call is coming from inside the house."*

"I'm going to read this whole damn thing." I lifted the plastic cup and set it down in the middle of the table, enough to spill several mounds of pink foam.

The second part of the article was even longer: two full-page columns on the right hand side. The headline:

Kagen knows what it's like to be victim, too

My eyes were drawn to the pull quote:

"My wife didn't mean to exacerbate our son's difficulties."

In the paper, Alex? In the Chronicle?
Inevitably the promise of the pull quote was fulfilled, and I read:

> Kagen's personal life has interfered with his campaign in unexpected ways. His wife recently left him after a citizens' group demonstrated in front of his house.

> "I think that pushed her over the edge. I've been trying to get her help since our son's diagnosis eight years ago."

> Kagen's son has Asperger's Syndrome.

> "I look at it as a challenge. He's a remarkable boy with unlimited potential. I'm dedicated to bringing out as much of that potential as possible."

After what Mairead told me? The newspaper rattled in my hands. *You call that bringing out Jack's potential?*

"The diagnosis put me over the edge, did it?" was all I trusted myself to say aloud. *In Starbuck's* everyone *can hear you scream.*

> Kagen says that his wife became addicted to prescription medication.

Darya's Valium. How did he know about that? *The lingerie drawer. Where I hid the AIDs Ride schedule. So that's how he knew about....*

> "I didn't realize until it had gotten out of control. Addicts are masters of concealment. I tried to get her to admit that she had a problem, but she was in serious denial."

I'll sue him. I'll sue him for libel, for harassment, for tricking a former student into marriage when she was too young to see through him....

> "If she reads this I want her to know that I still hope she gets help."

Val was not reading the article, only my face. "Enough. Please." But I read on:

What about Tyler Gaines' suspicious death?

I could hear Alex's peremptory tone:

> "My son had nothing to do with that." Kagen points out that no charges have been filed, and he stresses that he's confident that he can resolve the situation promptly. "If my wife had handled the situation differently when it first arose this would be settled already. Perhaps a young man didn't have to die."

I gasped so hard I thought I was going to choke.

I could see that there was more — a lot more — about my neglectful habits, from leaving Jack with unqualified sitters to imposing dangerous experimental treatments for autism on him. But I just lay my head on the newspaper, damp with strawberry frappuccino.

"Share it with me." I felt Val's hand on my shoulder. "Don't shut me out." Tentatively: "Isn't that what you said Alex always did?"

"Leave me alone." I raised my head too quickly, and it made me dizzy. "I suppose you're going to say 'I told you so' now."

"I wasn't going to say that," he said quietly.

"Well, get me a napkin anyway," I snapped. "Don't worry, crazy hysterical woman will pull herself together."

He walked off to the counter very slowly. Maybe giving himself time to think. Maybe giving me time, too.

It worked. "I am so sorry," I said when he handed me two napkins, using a third to mop the table. "I *did* just do to you what Alex always did to me. You took the bullet. I'm so, so sorry." I didn't know what else to say.

Val perched on the edge of my chair, carefully nudged me a few inches over and then pulled me onto his lap — a feat made possible by the fact that I was still in my first trimester.

"This isn't the place for this," I said, though I put up no fight. "The Laptops will be staring."

"You're my laptop." Val didn't embarrass easily. "Besides, everywhere is the place for this. Or it should be." He stroked my hair. I felt the waves spring back after his palm passed over them.

I blew my nose into the napkin. "Real attractive, isn't it?" I said, scrunching up the napkin and wiping under my eyes. I had no make-up on. Nothing to smear.

Val made a show of folding the newspaper up while surreptitiously reading what he could of the article. "Anyone who knows you is going to see right through this b.s. Besides, you know what Dr. Seuss said." He quoted, "'The people who matter don't mind and people who mind don't matter.'"

He was wrong. There would be more than a few people who both minded and mattered: the judge eventually ruling on custody, Tyler Gaines' father, the voters. But I'd taken enough out on Val for one day.

And on myself. Allowing myself one final glance at Alex's smug expression, I vowed that however he hurt me, however I panicked about Jack or grieved for Tyler — that whatever else happened, I was done with my crying.

Done.

Oh my God, how I wanted a Valium then.

After I'd learned I was pregnant, I'd flushed my remaining stash. I hadn't suffered any ill-effects from quitting, or if I had, they'd been masked by serial vomiting.

I didn't know if Alex really thought I had a substance problem or not. I didn't use the way he said. Nowhere close. But many addicts will tell you, and often correctly, that they only use occasionally. It isn't the amount that makes the addict. So to myself I acknowledged that I had been on the way to a pill popping problem.

But from now on I was going to fight instead, and live through whatever I had to live through.

Val was the only one I could rely on for some help. So I'd better not ruin that, too.

"Can we go out and come in again?" I asked timidly. "Forgive me?"

"Forgiven." He kissed my temple. "I can withstand a little displacement of anger." He nuzzled my ear. "Maybe I should make you show me just how sorry you are," he growled seductively.

Diana Levy's article — I was already thinking of it as *"The Interview,"* as in The Mother of All Euphemisms — would not be easy for me to forgive or forget. I had been dissecting it, putting it back together, and dissecting it again, like a mad pathologist. *He didn't say I was pregnant. Why not? It would have made me look worse. But made him look bad too.* He had not even said I had left him for someone else. I snorted. Make me out a weak drug addict, an incompetent mother — but never imply that someone might prefer another man to you.

"We've got to get your mind off this," Val whispered in my ear.

***

Our second sexual encounter of the day wasn't quite as pleasurable as the first. I was impatient, I confess, to call Raven Fernandez.

Her partner, Janis Song MacIntyre-Choi, was a family lawyer. I'd known I needed a lawyer the day the Alex filed for divorce but I'd been so ill that I'd put it off. No longer.

Janis said she'd been hoping I'd call. "I would have contacted you if it weren't ambulance chasing."

So I was encouraged but no less angry when I got to her office the following day. "I read the piece." She slapped the folded section of the Chronicle on her desk. "Typical," she spat.

"What can we do?" Relieved to have an ally, I seated myself without being invited.

"I've been planning just that." Janis came around her desk to sit on the edge with one leg dangling. She was all sharp angles, from the needle-like point of the scarf draped over her breast to the high arch of her eyebrows, which made disapproval her default expression. The arch was mirrored by the deep Cupid's bow of her small lips. "Are you familiar with the Greek prophetess Cassandra?"

"A little too familiar."

But Janis, I would learn, liked to explain things. "Apollo gave her the gift of prophecy but because she wouldn't give him what *he* wanted, and you know what that was, he cursed her so that she'd never be believed." She bent over until the point of her scarf touched my forehead. "Hence the Cassandra Phenomenon."

I thought I'd heard the expression.

Janis was still in lecture mode, pacing now. "The wife of an undiagnosed Asperger's man acts crazy, gets called crazy, when really she's just responding to the sadistic behavior of her husband."

Our conversation had veered off the road on which I had been speeding. I tentatively pressed the brakes. "He can be a sadist, all right. But he doesn't have Asperger's."

She stopped. "Oh, no? I've met him at the Korean-American Democratic Club. He never makes eye contact. He can only read from a script."

"We all have symptoms of everything if you look closely enough," I argued, so taken aback that I forgot she was on my side. "I can be moody, but I don't think that makes me bi-polar."

"Oh, really? But all right, all right." Janis held up her hands in surrender. "Let's say Alex doesn't have Asperger's Syndrome. Though you may be in denial about that." Her eyebrows rose even higher. "Do you know what the French word for lawyer is?"

She seemed surprised when I replied, "*Avocat.*" (I didn't tell her that the word always made me think of "avocado," as in "not yet, not yet, eat me, too late.")

"That's correct. *Avocat* — as in *advocate.*" A slow, feline smile. "Every client, civil or criminal, is entitled to the best advocacy possible."

She was right. What did I care if she convinced a judge that Alex, too, had Asperger's? These days professionals were handing out the diagnosis, like lollipops after a shot, to adults in their thirties and forties. Too often, in my opinion, it was to explain away aimless or eccentric lives.

"Raven's kept me in the loop. We'll show how your husband systematically tortured you psychologically *and* how he's therefore incompetent to be the custodial parent." She picked up a letter opener in the shape of a fencing foil and ran her finger along one edge.

That was what I wanted.

"If your son is dangerous, maybe he's suffering from the Cassandra Phenomenon himself," she continued slyly. "Responding to your ex-husband's confusing, Asperger's behavior."

"Jack *isn't* dangerous. That's the whole point."

She whirled on me so fast that I jumped. "I'm not just trying to help *you* here. I'm trying to help thousands, maybe hundreds of thousands — maybe *millions* of women who are victimized by creeps like Alex. You can be a test case. You can be the next Linda Brown — the next Jane Roe!"

"I don't want to be a test case," I insisted. "I just want my son back."

"You also want a lawyer *pro bono*, don't you?"

"Yes," I admitted, hating my answer. I didn't like taking things for free, but I didn't have much choice at the moment.

"Well, then." Janis positioned the letter opener upright by stabbing it into a pile of mail. "This is how you get them both."

CHAPTER FIFTEEN
SIBLING RIVALRY

Darya pleaded with me to babysit while she went out on a date with her Soulmate du Jour. "He's a Capricorn."

"Dolls, we have to have another talk about astrology."

"You are so closed-minded. That's why I lost Magdalena — she's a Taurus, and that says it all."

Val said that he would come with me. He was eager to see Kennedy for himself, to give me his own opinion.

At the last minute one of his "road dogs" called, stranded somewhere, with a flat tire and no spare. I was disappointed. But Val's love of rushing to the rescue of friends extended to rescuing me, too. I couldn't have that both ways, either.

Callaghan and I got out every board game in the house. I saw how my niece's shoulders sagged under the weight of just a few. "I wish we could play chess, Tia Anita."

"Who taught you to play chess?"

"Mommy's last boyfriend. I liked him."

"I'm sorry."

"His name was Dick and she kept saying it was the perfect name for him. What did she mean? I asked Magdalena if it meant something in Spanish but she said no. Does it mean something in French?"

"We'll play chess when Kennedy goes to sleep."

"Sleep?" Callaghan asked.

"Let me get five moves in before checkmate."

We made it to seven before Kennedy swept the pieces off. He swept cards, tokens and dice off of each game we took out — Clue, Sorry, Yahtzee. After several incipient tantrums, he broke out into a full-blown Tasmanian Devil rage, as bad as Jack in his younger days; he kicked the floor with his feet, pounded with his fists, and even — I had never seen this before — held his breath until he started to turn blue. I was on the phone to 911 when Callaghan brought out a fresh package of Oreo Double-Stuff. She poured the whole package over him and he caught them as they fell, cramming them into his mouth. The crisis subsided.

Preliminary damage report: a bruise on my left shin, another shattered piece of glass from a picture frame, a long trail of grape juice on a stairway with a runner that had once been white, and Oreo crumbs splattering the floor of almost every room like spent shells from a semi-automatic.

This was a typical evening at home, Callaghan informed me with a chilling lack of affect. She went to her room to read, and I thought I heard the click of a lock, but her room was far enough away that I couldn't be sure. Later I did hear her cry, but I couldn't go to her because Kennedy had just slipped out the front door. I remembered her skeptical echo: *Sleep?*

                    ***

Darya and her Capricorn tottered in a little before 3 a.m. Cap was wasted. He swayed off to another room before I got any sharper impression than the silhouette of a brawny Teutonic male cast in the mold of Darya's ex. Darya, as always, successfully imitated a person only tipsy instead of behaving like an overgrown teen celebrity a few hours away from choosing between jail and rehab.

"We have to talk," I said.

She responded with a passable Mae West impression. "I've got other things to do with *my* mouth." She turned sweet. "Thanks for coming over tonight, hon," she said, kissing me on the cheek. "Let me call you tomorrow."

"That boy needs help."

She resumed Mae West, this time striking a pose to go with it, hand on protruding hip. "Help is on the way."

I almost slapped her. Instead I gripped her arms.

"*Ow!*"

"Listen." If only she weren't drunk! "We almost ended up at the emergency room again."

She wrenched away. "What are you going to do, tell Mom?" She was all whiny little sister now.

"That would be difficult, now, wouldn't it?"

"Is this what they call 'tough love'?" she slurred. "I call it jealousy. I always got the guys and you were sixteen and still pining by the window, hoping Dad would come back — "

"This has nothing to do with — "

"I get out of a marriage when it's time and I get to keep my kids — "

I remembered those times with my mother again, but now Darya was our mother, with *her* children in danger. When my mother had us by the hands, dragging us toward the car, and sheer pleading hadn't worked, I tried patient reasoning. "Look, Darya, this might not be the best time—"

"You think?"

Patient reasoning hadn't worked with Alex. Come to think of it, it hadn't worked with my mother.

" — but I finally have the nerve and you just have to listen." I shoved her into the nearest chair.

"I don't have to do shit."

"*I tell you Kennedy needs help.*"

"He's *two*."

"He was three last month, and you're so loaded you don't even remember your own kid's birthday. He doesn't say a word, *and he's hurting your daughter.*"

"Einstein didn't talk until he was eight. Or ten, or something. Just because you have an autistic kid doesn't mean everyone's kid is autistic." She managed, after two failed attempts, to get back to her feet. "You can go home now."

"I never said he was autistic. But don't you see what's happening with Callaghan?" I pleaded. "She's seriously depressed. You have some issue with her I can't figure out. What is it? Did she tell you she misses her daddy? Did someone tell you that Callaghan had prettier eyes than yours?"

That was a stupid thing to say.

"You talk about my children?" she demanded. "*My* children? My children are both with me. Neither of my children tried to kill a little boy by stabbing him through the heart."

"Jack didn't — " But I stopped. I stood there until the tennis ball in my throat traveled down my esophagus and then split into two, and traveled down each leg, and into the floor. Then I left.

***

The truth was that there were many hours during which I did not think of Jack at all, such as when I lay awake in Val's bed — my new bed — with Val's forehead on my shoulder and with my hands on my stomach, waiting to feel the first flutters of the growing fetus. I was still in my first trimester, but a mother is supposed to feel the baby move earlier in her second pregnancy. Feeling the baby move was my favorite part of being pregnant. It never felt as though Jack were kicking; it had felt as though he were stretching, or shrugging his shoulders, or even clapping his hands.

Dr. Phelps let me schedule a sonogram to determine whether I was a candidate for CVS, chorionic villi sampling, a prenatal test that could be performed earlier than amniocentesis. If there were something wrong I wanted to know as soon as possible.

Val came with me, and now we sat in the waiting room holding hands. He had come to every obstetrical appointment with me, but he was particularly eager today, because we could find out the baby's sex.

"I'm so angry at her," I said. I'd been talking about Darya. "But I'm also worried about her kids."

"Of course you are," he sympathized. "I am, too. But what do you want, for the state take them away?"

I bit my lip. "Not until they're really in danger. But I'm not sure they're not in danger."

"Give it a little time," Val said. "Maybe we can figure out a way to keep an eye on them from a distance. You know you've got to keep your head low."

I saw Val's point. The only alternative to getting through to Darya was calling Child Protective Services, and I'd heard my share of stories of parents who, after one anonymous phone call, were pushed into a bureaucratic pit so deep that they never could climb out to retrieve their children. Some of these tales were urban legends, campfire ghost stories for the ASD parent set, but some were awfully convincing.

A nurse came in but called another name, and a woman either nearing the end of her term or carrying triplets, struggled to her feet.

Dr. Phelps was part of a big practice that catered primarily to the Hummer-driving jet skiers of Presidio Heights. These weren't my *companeros* anymore. I'd owned neither Hummer nor jet skier, but I wouldn't have minded a quick visit to the jewelry counter at Neiman-Marcus.

Finally: "Mrs. Kagen."

Val and I got up together.

"Mr. Kagen," the nurse greeted him.

Shit. Shit, shit, shit. There couldn't be more than three nurses still working at this office who remembered me from my pregnancy with Jack. I remembered her, too: Joni. She was one of the nicer women in this otherwise anonymous baby factory. We hadn't seen her on previous visits.

"I don't think we've met," Joni went on with a smile, addressing Val. "I hope you don't my saying, but you're not what I expected." Iron gray bangs hung over her forehead and she was plump in powder blue scrubs. "If I'd known the District Attorney was so young and handsome I might have wanted to get myself in a little trouble." She winked at me.

My luck was really flowing downstream today. Not only was Joni one of the few nurses who remembered me, she was apparently one of the five people in the city and county who didn't read the *Chronicle*.

The Val I knew would have let it go. But his face had an unfamiliar and disturbingly dark expression. Now was my chance to repay some of his generosity by showing my respect for him. I put my hand territorially on his back. "*This* is the proud father," I said, not obnoxiously loudly (like that other pregnant woman's husband, who had been bragging into his Bluetooth about a recent scuba diving excursion off the shore of Costa Rica), but not lowering my voice, either. "But he's not Mr. Kagen. Alex Valentine, this is Joni. I'm sorry, I don't know your last name."

"Pedroni."

"Joni Pedroni?" slipped out of Val's mouth.

"Mm hm. I should have kept my maiden name."

"I should have kept mine, too," I said, "as it turns out. I won't make *that* mistake again."

Val was disarmed. "Everyone calls me Val," he said, in the comfortable-in-his-own body way that always put everyone else at their ease, too.

"Okay, Val. Let's go see what your baby is doing in there, shall we?"

***

It was dark in the examining room, the better for Nurse Joni to see the screen. I had changed into a gown and was lying on the table, too nervous that Joni would find Siamese twins to indulge in the excitement of seeing moving shadows and being told it was a baby. At least I knew a sonogram would be painless.

While Joni adjusted dials Val leaned over the table, brushing my hair back from my forehead with one hand and holding one of mine with the other. He was tall enough that, when he bent over, his bottom stuck up in the air.

"There's a chair you can roll over, Mr. Kagen, if you want to sit."

Short memory.

But Val didn't seem to notice. Maybe he was just that excited. I hoped so. "I'm fine." His voice shook a little as if holding back tears. He cared. He cared that much. My own eyes misted over, and I felt a little of the happy anticipation I had experienced with Jack.

Joni turned the monitor to face us so that we could see the baby while she took measurements of its organs and body parts. "I still can't get over it," I said. "It just looks like spots to me." Later in the pregnancy I'd be able to see the general outline of a fetus but right now....

Thump.

Val's butt had landed on the floor.

"Mr. Kagen, are you all right?"

"F-fine. Just a little.... Fine."

Oh my God. Val was squeamish. Like Alex. "Maybe you could roll that chair over for him after all?"

Joni obliged, and we smiled conspiratorially at each other over Val's shoulder as she positioned the chair under him. She mouthed the word, "Men."

Val excused himself. "I ate something...." he faltered. "Uh ... I think the milk went sour, Anna. I had it on my cereal this morning."

"You don't have to stay for this," I said. It was amusing to try to reconcile the Val who had spent the night in an emergency room with me and Jack with the man who was made light-headed at a sonogram.

"No, no, I want to — just let me sit for a minute. Maybe — uh, maybe I should get out of your way." He rolled the chair to his right so that the screen would be out of view.

When Joni sat back down at her station I could see how she was trying not to laugh. But the work of recording data soon absorbed her, and I also went back to trying to see a baby in the shadows.

"It looks like there's a problem with CVS," Joni told me.

"Problem? Is something wrong?"

"No, no, no," she reassured me quickly. "But there's a second placenta in there, and Dr. Phelps doesn't like to do CVS on twins. Some doctors will, but I agree with her." She turned the screen toward me again but I still could make nothing out.

"You mean I'm having twins? Oh, my God!" Scary, but — I'd be the mother of three. Such riches! "And that would explain why I've been so sick, wouldn't it? The extra hormones."

"Extra hormones, yes ... but you don't have twins, Mrs. Kagen. I'm so sorry," she apologized at my obvious disappointment. "I shouldn't have put it that way. The second placenta is empty. You probably started out with twins."

"I — I don't get it."

She put her hand on my shoulder. "With this early testing we know now that about 30% of pregnancies start out as twins, at least by this definition."

"Oh." Well, twins would have been awfully hard to handle.... I was already worried about money.... It was one thing to be an unwed mother, but the unwed mother of three ... it would be harder on Jack, wouldn't it...?

Those thoughts were what they called rationalizations. Or maybe reaction-formations. I knew a defense mechanism when I heard it. They just never worked for me. I felt a loss and I would just have to feel it.

"You have a boy already, don't you, Mrs. Kagen?"

"Yes," I said absently.

"Well, I hope you'll be happy about this, then. It's a girl."

"Yesssss!" I squealed, making a fist and pulling my arm straight down in a gesture of victory, forgetting for the moment the empty placenta.

"Oooh, you've got to stay still for me, love."

"What did you say?" Val's voice from the corner was hoarse.

I turned my head to him. "You're happy, aren't you? You said you didn't care what it was as long as it...."

"—as long as it's healthy," Joni finished for me. She probably heard that a dozen times a day. "I'm glad you're pleased, Mrs. Kagen. I have a new granddaughter and she's delightful."

Val's face was only semi-visible, tucked beyond the reach of the fluorescent light panel.

"You meant it, didn't you?" I asked him. "About it being healthy?"

"Of course I did," he said.

But he didn't. He had told me the truth for too long that I heard his lie hit my ears like the first *ba-ba-ba-ba-ba-ba-ba-ba-ba's* of *A Chorus Line.*

"You wanted a son."

"I just said I didn't care, didn't I?"

I blinked half a dozen times and turned a falsely cheerful face in Joni's direction.

She must see this moment re-enacted pretty often, too. She feigned cheer right back at me. "Well, everything looks fine so far. Congratulations."

***

Val drove in silence down the hill from Dr. Phelps' medical building. This should have been such a happy time. I still could have made it so, at least for myself, if I had chosen to ignore his reaction. *I will make it a happy time. I would have been disappointed if it had been a boy — is that any worse?*

"You had a passel of brothers," I said. "I bet you wanted a son to go hikin' and bikin' with and to grow up to be captain of the football team. There's no reason why a girl can't do all those things."

He grunted.

"*I* wanted a boy, too, the first time — " I swallowed quickly — "I mean, I didn't want a son so much as I was scared of having a daughter, with all the Oedipal stuff that comes up, and then my own mother was—"

"So you've mentioned."

His tone implied that I had *kvetched* about my mother more often than he wanted to hear, which I probably had. But it was my turn to comfort him, no matter how my feminist feelings were hurt. I had always been impatient with the primal male urge to have a son "to carry on the name." Who were we, the Roosevelts? The Windsors? Of the three of us, it was Alex who had the most legitimate claim to being part of a dynasty, if one believed that such things mattered. If I had my way, this child would carry on the great name of Shapiro, subsistence farmers in the Pale of Settlement for generations. (What last name would I put on her birth certificate? Touchy subject and obviously not one for today.)

"Girls are an awful lot of fun, just like the nurse said. And they love their daddies. You'll see, sweetheart." *That empty placenta might have held a twin brother.... No,* I begged myself, *don't mourn something that was gone before you knew you had it.*

And just as there had been a reason, in my mind, for not wanting a girl before, there was a reason for not wanting a boy this time. It would be a betrayal of Jack, an attempt to replace him.

Val braked for a jaywalker, so fast that my seatbelt locked. "I just, you know, thought it was going to be a boy. In those World War II movies you make me watch, it's always a boy."

"I think that was unconscious on the filmmakers' part," I mused. "The whole country wanted to replace the men who were dying." But the announcement "it's a boy!" had been a cry of triumph across the decades — across the millennia. There was no denying that, not even in a city like San Francisco.

Val ran a stop sign.

"If it's okay with you, Anne Banane," he said. "I'm not in the mood to discuss how pop culture reflects larger historical events."

I gripped the door handle for the rest of the ride.

CHAPTER SIXTEEN
NO KIDS, NO PETS, NO VU

The pair who stood before me was a man and a woman. The man was very thin, with a long neck and pockmarked skin, reminders of serious adolescent acne. He was in a Rod Serling suit, black, with a narrow tie and white button down shirt.

The woman was in her mid-fifties. Her hair was a woolly mass of inflexible frizz, with just a few gray threads curling in their own stubborn directions on the top. The back of the hand that held the clipboard was bony. I made a bet with myself that she'd been to Woodstock but not come upon a child of God.

They showed me I.D., in addition to the plastic photos they had clipped to their respective lapels. They were from the Family and Services Division. Colloquially known as Child Protective Services. They introduced themselves stiffly as Mr. Flaherty and Dr. Ahrens. And so when Dr. Ahrens called me "Mrs. Kagen" as they entered I corrected her haughtily: "It's Ms. Shapiro now. Please. Sit down." I was determined to act as if I had nothing to be ashamed of or hide. That was going to take quite a bit of acting.

The worst thing about a spouse, when that spouse turns on you, is that he's seen you naked and knows where the bruises are. Even if Alex hadn't seen me naked in a while, he had known where to press, and part of me believed the description he had published, of drug-abusing, neglectful mother.

Okay, so if that was Anna Black, it was now my job to create for these intruders the persona of Anna White, a woman valiantly struggling to make a life that would include Val, Jack and my baby daughter. The bereaved Virgin Mary. Demeter deprived of Persephone. Donna Reed. Betty fucking Crocker.

"Please sit down," I repeated. Gracious. Undefensive. Almost welcoming. They had taken all of two baby steps each into the front room.

Mr. Flaherty wrinkled his nose. "I'm allergic to cats."

I hadn't noticed how much dog hair had recently accumulated on Aunt Patsy's sectional. And there was a coffee stain on one cushion. I would have turned the cushion over but the other side already had an even larger stain of unknown provenance.

"It's from our dog, Mr. Flaherty," I said. "Let me bring you a chair from the kitchen." I would have had to anyway since the sofa was the only place we could sit, unless I tried to move the heavy club chair, and the three of us squeezing torso to torso was an intimacy I doubted they wanted any more than I. "Can I get you anything while I'm up?"

Dr. Ahrens didn't answer. Mr. Flaherty sniffled.

"In fact — " Oh, God, what to call Val? Lover? Boyfriend? Significant other? My gaydar was beeping on Mr. Flaherty so I chose the word he might find the most politically correct. "My partner is out walking our dog right now. She's a beautiful, loving creature. A Golden Retriever. Elsie."

"I don't think I'll take a chance." He dabbed at his nose with a green-monogrammed handkerchief.

I went into the kitchen and slipped my arms around the chrome frames of two chairs. As I dragged them back into the living room, I concluded that they didn't know that I was pregnant, because surely one of them would have offered to help a woman in the family way with moving furniture. Maybe I shouldn't be too sure about that. I also wished that *I* could be "Dr." Shapiro. Fuzz-top probably had a degree from one of those private grad schools in Berkeley that gave doctorates in transpersonal psychobabble.

I let the chairs fall with a grunt, then seated myself on one. Mr. Flaherty flicked his handkerchief on the seat of the other, then lowered himself as if it were an outhouse at a cattle show.

"What brings you here today?" I asked pleasantly.

Dr. Ahrens crossed her legs. She was wearing a loose floral-print dress that reached mid-calf, and when one knee rose over the other I saw the band of knee-hi nylons. "We've had complaints about the living situation at home with your son."

Alex. Backing up his campaign for office and his campaign against me at the same time.

"And from whom have you received those complaints?"

"People who call Child Protective Services are permitted to remain anonymous."

In my tenure at the Minerva Center, I had a few times called CPS anonymously and been grateful that I could do it. On the receiving end, it didn't seem as fair.

"What complaints did you receive? The sixth amendment entitles me to know that at least."

They looked blankly one another. Score one for the lawyer's estranged wife. Dr. Ahrens recovered herself quickly and looked down at her clipboard. "You were frequently absent from the home."

"That's simply not true," I said matter-of-factly.

"On several occasions, you wouldn't let people come into the house."

"Dat always waises thuspicion," Flaherty said through his handkerchief.

"Jack was afraid of strangers for long time," I mumbled.

"But you let him go *out* with a total stranger."

The bike ride with Val, when Alex accused me of exposing Jack to pedophilia. This visit reeked of him as surely as he reeked of Clive Christian. "Mr. Valentine was not only not a stranger, he was the caseworker on duty when … Mr. Kagen and I both met him at St. Seraphina's Hospital." Was it possible that these were actors, posing as representatives of the county? No, Sarah Bernhardt and Lawrence Olivier couldn't have played these roles, down to Flaherty's tasseled loafers and Ahren's scuffed, open-toed black flats. (Yes, with knee-hi nylons.) I rose a few inches from my chair to see the top of the paper on Ahrens' clipboard. That was a reproduction of the City and County seal on top, all right. But then, Alex had a shelf full of stationery, at home as well as at work, with that same crest.

"Besides, I don't live with Mr. Kagen anymore," I said firmly. "So this is really all moot."

Tears were reaching critical mass in the outer corners of both of Mr. Flaherty's eyes. "You were living wid him until a short time ago.'

"As long as there's the possibility that Jacob could be returned to your care, even part-time, we have to investigate."

They thought he might be returned to my care. What an unexpected time to have hope — and from what an unexpected person to get it.

"For all we know — " Mr. Flaherty was beginning to sound like a foghorn, as his nasal passages swelled further — "you could waltz right back in with your husband tomorrow."

"My husband has filed for divorce."

"We see that you're expecting," Dr. Ahrens said.

Damn. "I don't see that this is relevant to the situation at hand."

"We have to make sure that you'll be providing a fit environment for that child as well. Do you own or rent this apartment, Ms. Shapiro?"

"I anticipate purchasing a home of our own soon."

"How soon?"

"Soon."

"May we take a look around?"

We didn't have any drugs or pornography, unless there were things about Aunt Patsy I didn't know. We had our books and our music and thanks to my last surviving credit card, a laptop computer. Most visible of all were a profusion of healthy houseplants, proof of our power to nurture.

At the moment, though, I could see the apartment through the eyes of Dr. Ahrens and Mr. Flaherty, and I did not like what I saw. During the first weeks I'd been too sick to do any housework. Although much improved, the smell of Ajax still threatened to make me vomit. And a vacuum would have been difficult for me to maneuver, even if Val had owned one.

But cleaning up dog hair, even with the Dustbuster I'd bought, was like holding back the Colorado River with my finger in Hoover Dam.

Now as Dr. Ahrens picked one of these "billions and billions" of dog hairs off her dress, I saw the apartment as she and Flaherty would. There were boxes stacked in the small, dark second bedroom. Open a closet door and you'd find clothes dating from the Eisenhower administration. Val had never fully unpacked his belongings after he took them out of storage, and you could trace his usual path from door to hall on the ground-in dirt on the carpet. Val and I would look not just like slobs, but squatters.

"I let you in as a courtesy." I rubbed my palms against my knees. "If you have any questions about the brand of deodorant I use, feel free."

Flaherty moved on. "Do you use recreational drugs, Ms. Shapiro?" he asked, gingerly removing his handkerchief.

"*No.*"

"Your estranged husband has claimed so."

"I guess it's his word against mine, then."

"Does your partner use — "

"No."

Dr. Ahrens picked up the interrogation. "Do you currently have other sexual partners?"

"No! For the love of God." This was too much. "Since when is this your business?"

"Does your — "

"Partner have other partners?" I was furious. "What do you think we're running here, Plato's Retreat?" *Don't make them mad. Don't make them mad.* I held on to my knees as if on one of those obscene roller-coasters that turn you upside down and shake you until your guts come out through your mouth. I wasn't going to make it through the next question.

I didn't have to.

"Honey, I'm home!" Val called out buoyantly, doing a perfectly timed early sitcom-dad imitation, a golden figure against the dark gray of summer. Elsie bounded in behind him, looking as big as a pony. She galloped up to Mr. Flaherty. He jumped up and took several steps back.

"Oh, she won't hurt you," Val said. "Will she, Banana Boat?"

"Wiwl this animal be wiving with you?" Flaherty had clamped the handkerchief to his face again. Never mind the allergies — he was terrified of dogs. *Cynophobia.* I had come across the term while researching how I might help Jack, and it always sounded to me like "fear of cyanide."

Elsie and I hadn't bonded as Val had hoped, but I was still indignant on her behalf. "You're not going to tell me that owning a pet is illegal now. Didn't they teach you at Gestapo headquarters how caring for an animal contributes to a child's development? Or did you miss that day in class?"

"Ban-Ban," Val warned, but he was battling a grin.

Flaherty remained in his corner. Dr. Ahrens appeared to doodle on her clipboard.

"C'mon, girl, let's go in the kitchen for some lunch," Val invited Elsie. Mr. Flaherty edged his way back to the chair.

Val was back in a moment with another chair. He turned it around so that he could sit backwards while facing Dr. Ahrens, a little close for her comfort.

"We have to ask you about sexual abuse, now, Ms. Shapiro," Dr. Ahrens said as Mr. Flaherty edged cautiously back to his own chair.

"Let me ask *you,* something, Ma'am," Val interposed. "Have you been giving my good lady a hard time?"

I had an uncomfortable memory of the stairs on Folsom Street.

"We are doing our job, Mr. — "

"No, I suppose we haven't been properly introduced." He didn't extend his hand. "Dr. Valentine. As in 'Be my.'"

"Well, my name is Dr. Ahrens and we're from — "

"1957. Just a guess."

I put my hand over my mouth.

"Dr. Valentine." Flaherty cautiously removed his handkerchief. "This is not a matter for joking."

"Who's joking?" Val squinted, the better to read Flaherty's badge. "Oliver Flaherty? It *is* a pleasure to me you." Val's register dropped an octave. Flirtatious.

This was dangerous territory. But it was my own fault for making him feel he had to rescue me. Again.

"And you — " he turned provocatively to Dr. Ahrens — "has anyone ever told you that you have a *beautiful* smile?"

Val....

"But." Val stood up and as he unfolded himself body part by body part he emerged even taller than his 6'3". "I'm going to have to ask you to leave now."

The representatives of CPS looked at each other, startled.

"It's been real," Val went on, "but — what was it again, Benson and Stabler? — maybe we'll see you around."

"We don't need a warrant to come in," Ahrens informed him

"And *we* have a right to refuse you entry. Put it in your report. We co-operated with you until you harassed us. That's going in *my* report."

"We're not finished here," Flaherty said, rising to take the clipboard from Ahrens and lifting up a few pages by their corners.

"Oh, yes you are," Val said. He held the door open. Flaherty looked nervously over his shoulder at Elsie, who loped from the kitchen to bark farewell. Ahrens had to pause to unhook her skirt from a splinter on the doorframe, and she released it just before Val slammed the door shut behind her.

"You shouldn't have done that. But I love you for it." I hugged him.

He squeezed back, but said, "I was protecting them from *you*, not the other way 'round."

***

The attorney general's office announced today that it will be unable to perform yet another autopsy on the body of suspected homicide victim Tyler Gaines. "The victim's body has been cremated," Marianne Pasquale said in a press release. "Mrs. Gaines acted without consulting our office. We are disappointed with what has been an ongoing lack of cooperation, yet our sympathy remains with the family." Pasquale declined to comment further.

So — to the scandal of the missing second report, Pasquale had added the foolishness of promising a replacement before checking the availability of a body.

I shuddered as I always did at the reality of Tyler's death, but I couldn't help but also feel some relief that this phase was finally over.

In a separate *Chronicle* piece, a "spokesperson for the Gaines family" reported that Tyler's mother had scattered his ashes on Minotaur Island. An odd choice, I thought, but since the Gaineses were new arrivals to the city, maybe it was one of the few that had any meaning.

As for why Jimmy Gaines never had a private autopsy performed the moment he decided to sue us: "That was the state's responsibility. I relied on them to do their job." And: "My wife needed closure after all this time." He was considering a suit against the Attorney General's office for infliction of emotional distress.

My own final memory of Tyler was on the Minotaur Island pier, shoving another boy. But we'd all been fidgety, crammed onto that narrow strip of wooden planks above the murky waters of the Bay.

***

Ahrens and Flaherty were just another skirmish in what was turning out to be a war of attrition.

Mairead called that very evening to say good-bye. Alex had fired her.

"He was very polite about it. He said it was because of the money, but he gave me two month's salary." She hesitated. "He found out that I called you last week."

The call she referred to had been the first I'd heard from her since before Alex's *Chronicle* interview. She'd spoken in a hushed voice from her new apartment, even though she was two miles from Alex's house: so softly that I could hear the banging of pots and pans as Kelly cooked them a late dinner.

"It's a good job he never found out about — well, I won't say more." She must have meant our rendezvous at Julius Kahn.

"How were things when you left?"

"Ah...."

But I dragged it out of her. Jack losing more language, adding new rules to his routine and throwing more tantrums again.

"It's the strangers in the house," she concluded, "making him anxious."

"What strangers?"

"They're there when I come to get Jack up. Alex talks to them before he goes to work."

Lawyers. Britteridge would have hand-picked a team of personal injury attorneys, headed by someone who handled wrongful death suits in particular. Alex wouldn't want to meet them at the office.

I had been served, as a party to Gaines' lawsuit, by certified mail, which was far better than personal service. I didn't want to see any more strangers at the door, either. Lawyers on both sides would probably call me in for depositions soon.

"As soon as I walked out of your house, I told meself, just leave the country."

All I had to do was to tell Mairead that she, too, might be deposed by the Attorney General or in Gaines' lawsuit and she'd find a way to hire a private jet. "Mairead, Alex has nothing against you personally, he just — "

"And then this morning Kelly's grandmother had a stroke. So we will be going back after all. To Belfast?" She was piously resigned when she concluded, "I suppose it was all part of The Plan."

Not my plan, I thought selfishly. The tight-lipped nannies or their clones would take over from the woman Jack had known and who had loved him since he was three. The woman who was his last link to his old life.

"I'm sorry about Kelly's grandmother." I'd never met the woman; for all I knew she was ninety-seven. "How serious is it?"

"I don't know yet." She paused, and then went on in a voice so soft it barely reached. "But if she, uh... passes while we're there, Kelly and I will go down to see my family in Dublin."

With a real friend instead of a little boy to keep her company, back in the land she missed, and no job here in the States ... would she ever come back?

"Send Jack a postcard," I said. "He'll get a kick out of it."

***

Val was in the corner of the front room, settled in his aunt's club chair, reading *Great Expectations* stockinged feet. The chair was positioned so that he could get to most of his own books by reaching over his shoulder. While Aunt Patsy had left a collection of hardcover romances, Val's library was one-third classic novels, one-third science fiction and one-third books that used the word "backpack" as a gerund noun, from *Riot of*

Passage: Tales of Backpacking 'Round Europe to *Allen and Mike's Really Cool Guide to Backpackin'.*

But he had the soundtrack of *Cabaret* on the phonograph. It was the Broadway cast album, and the landlady and her Jewish suitor were singing, "Married."

"I made plans for the afternoon," I said. "To look at apartments."

"What?" He looked up, marking his place with his finger.

"I've got to do something or I'll go crazy," I said, sitting on the ottoman next to his feet.

"If you want to do something, we can go for a bike ride." He looked to the window. "It's nice out for a change." He sighed. "July in the city is hard, isn't it?"

"I don't mean just to keep occupied," I said. "I want to get us *settled.*"

Since Ahrens and Flaherty's visit I had done what I could to clean Aunt Patsy's. I'd dusted, taken Resolve to the carpet, and even tried scrubbing the walls. (All while covering my nose and mouth Flaherty-style, to avoid inhaling the fumes of cleaning products.) But, although I was only in my second trimester, I still tired easily. And there was nowhere for me to put Aunt Patsy's boxes, which were stuffed with hats with veils and scrapbooks of newspaper clippings, turning brown as their edges curled.

I hadn't thought any less of Val for taking advantage of a free apartment; I thought it was a practical way to save money in a city where college students lived three to a studio. But it was also temporary. He'd made no secret of that; her daughter would claim it soon.

Yet again, I reminded myself that *I* was the one who changed the rules when I welcomed him back from the AIDS Ride with my news.

Still. We had to find a permanent place to live, line up jobs, and become a respectable family with whom a court would want to place a little boy, especially when compared to Alex, now an eccentric bachelor living like General Tilney in *Northanger Abbey*: a man who cared more for his dinner than his son, whom he left alone to wander the rooms of the manor, reciting the words of the previous day's episode of *Crime Conquerors.*

"I want to start getting on with our lives as if the worst had happened." But I wasn't imagining the worst; not even close. The furthest I would let myself get was picturing the two of us trying to live on the child support that Alex would eventually give me for Jack.

But Val seemed increasingly comfortable living without a job, and I was restless.

And very worried about money. I had *some* set aside — Alex never asked about my Minerva salary, and I had squirreled that away with small amounts that I skimmed from our household account. I had never asked myself why. It had never been enough to finance my fantasy getaway to New York, or even to Sonoma County.

"I don't know," Val said, turning the open paperback in his hands. "I want to find out if Pip is going to inherit all of Miss Havisham's money."

I seized the moment. "I set up some appointments with a real estate agent."

He dog-eared his page very slowly, to avoid looking at me.

"I'm in limbo here!" I threw up my hands. "I can't call my lawyer every hour — she's fed up with me. No one will talk to me — " I broke off and then broke down. "Mairead's gone. Oh, God, Mairead's gone."

I put my head in my hands and yes, I cried. *Big whiny baby. You promised you wouldn't do this again.*

"Ban-Ban," I heard him say before he pulled me toward him.

I recovered myself quickly. "At least it's something I can do," I repeated. "We could get kicked out of here without any notice. You said so yourself." Val's cousin would get tired of waiting for the upstairs neighbors to die; real estate was too valuable. "Then those CPS workers — "

"Those slimebuckets were just harassing us with everything they had. They're not going to hurt us." He stroked my hair.

I closed my eyes and nestled into his chambray shirt. "I'd just love to have a crib waiting for her when we bring her home from the hospital and not worry about getting thirty days' notice the next day."

"A crib for her crib?" He grinned.

And room for Jack. "If we can get just some kind of den, just an alcove I can put a curtain over, we might not have to move again for a long time."

"Okay," Val agreed indulgently. "Anything for my Ban-Ban. I'll think of it as a guided tour to bourgy-land." He twisted around to shove the book back in its place on the shelf. "Miss Havisham had it good. Big house, all paid for."

***

"I have never heard of anyone using a rental agent," Val said as we drove to our first stop. "You go to bulletin boards at cafés, or on Craig's list. Boy, you can take the girl out of Presidio Heights...."

I did have some bad habits to unlearn, minor daily expenses I hadn't had to consider since before Alex: ordering take-out, buying new shoes, replacing a worn-out tire.

Penelope, the rental agent, was waiting for us at the front door of the building at the bottom of Ashbury Heights. She was a buxom woman in high heels with pointed toes, and weighed down with over-sized costume jewelry, in bright colors and inventive shapes, such as a bracelet fashioned of large, red plastic hearts.

"So you're Anna. And you must be Val." To me: "Are you from New York?" "You look like you're from New York."

"No," I smiled, "though I consider it a compliment. San Francisco born and — "

"Brooklyn. Loved it. Miss it. There aren't any *seasons* here."

"Apartment?" Val reminded us.

The apartment had hardwood floors, high ceilings, and tall windows that made the whole front room seem part of the sky.

It was also on the sixth floor and there was no elevator in the building.

"Good exercise," Penelope panted, when she ushered us in.

"Sure is," Val agreed cheerfully. Six flights of stairs didn't even have him breathing fast.

While I was completely winded. "I don't see it with a baby and a stroller," I finally managed to gasp.

"Is she always this hard to please?" Penelope asked Val.

***

Next stop: The bottom unit of a triplex on a steep hill descending from UCSF Medical Center. I wondered if the rooms were legal to rent: these ceilings were very low, and the kitchen and bathroom were dug into the hill, and therefore windowless.

"It's awfully cold," I said.

"There's no central heating," Penelope admitted.

"We'll freeze."

"You've never heard of space heaters? I thought you said you grew up here."

"But space heaters and a baby — "

"You don't put the space heater *next* to the baby," Penelope said, tapping her pointed toe.

***

"Oh, God," I groaned to Val when we were back in the van and headed to our next stop. "I can see where this is going. I owe you a *big* apology."

"Don't be silly, Anne Banane. I'm having fun now."

I wasn't. I'd privately asked Penelope what the rent was on the first place we'd seen. When she told me, I'd tried to look as though it were in the range I had expected. It was three times higher.

The third stop was a live-work loft in "SoMa" — South of Market. The building was surrounded by warehouses. "It's becoming gentrified so fast," Penelope said. "The smartest thing you could do would be to get in now."

***

The place in North Beach had no garage.

"People *do* get residential stickers," Penelope said.

"I've lost a dozen friends to North Beach," I said. "It's the black hole of San Francisco. Once you get a parking space you get landmark status for it and never leave the neighborhood again."

"I don't get it." Penelope put out her hands, palm up. Her armfuls of bracelets made the gesture sound as though she were busing silverware. "Is she joking or what?"

Val smiled and shrugged. "Sometimes it's hard to tell."

***

The last place we visited was a studio apartment in a Nob Hill high rise.

"Something different," Penelope said smugly. "You give up some space but you get the location, the doorman — you don't see doormen out here much, do you?"

"We have a son, too, you know," I retorted. "He'll be with us part-time."

"A son, too?" Her tone implied that I had been very careless. "How old?"

"Eleven in September." I took Val's arm. "We need to go home."

Penelope walked us to the elevator, pestering us to make another appointment.

Val waited until the elevator doors were closing to shout, "Our people will call your people."

"I suppose I deserved that," I said, though I wasn't sure that I had. "It was a great idea whose time has not yet come." And would not come, until we had substantially more income.

Val opened the door of the Town and Country for me.

"Anna, did you ever think — I mean, just what if — what if you didn't get custody of Jack?"

"What do you mean?"

"I think you know what I mean," he said kindly. "Alex is going to fight you like a pit bull 'til the end."

"And you're going to help me fight back!"

He walked around the van and seated himself behind the wheel. After a moment I climbed in on my side.

"You know, babe," he said, "it's like shopping at Ikea. It doesn't come in one package. And then you have to assemble it yourself."

***

I heard Janis and Raven quarreling in another room. Then I heard a door slam.

This was not good. Janis had given me a good solid scare by calling me at 6:30 in the morning. At first I was relieved to hear her voice, because she wouldn't be the one to call me if Jack had had an accident. But when Janis demanded that I come to her home immediately, a good deal of my anxiety returned.

Muffled from behind the slammed door, I heard Raven's voice: "This is wrong and you know it!"

Janis's answer indecipherable, but angry.

At last she came out. She was in a fuzzy yellow bathrobe and bunny slippers.

"I didn't know this was formal," I said.

Janis yanked the belt of her robe across her waist. "Why didn't you tell me?"

"Tell you what?"

"About your past. About Val's past."

I riffled the edge of a pile of mail resting on the end table next to me. "I actually don't know what you're talking about."

"Oh, you don't, do you? I suppose it's your evil twin who's been coming to see me. We haven't met then. Let me introduce myself. My name is — "

I kept snapping my thumb against the pile of mail while Janis became Susan Brownmiller on steroids. The Nordstrom's catalogue.

Saks. Neiman-Marcus. Whoa — Bergdorf-Goodman. Someone had a serious habit, one worthy of an intervention.

A TV Guide near the bottom. Hidden. Alex didn't approve of them, either. Said they sent the wrong message.

"I had a chance to bring an important woman's issue to public attention. You ruined that — not for me, but for the wife whose Asperger's husband is forcing her to hang up his suits according to the date of purchase, the woman in therapy because her husband won't go, being medicated by another male psychiatrist — "

"That *would* be a nice closing argument," I said dryly when she paused for breath.

"I spent days researching case law, interviewing mothers who've lost custody of their children unfairly — I already wrote the first draft of a brief. These were billable hours!"

"Oh, *billable* hours," I said. "That does clarify matters."

"You know I agreed to take this case *pro bono* because I was going to make a name — make a *point* — "

I squirmed. I had hoped to pay Janis back eventually, but her regular fee would have wiped out my small savings in the first month. "Now that we're at the heart of the matter, maybe you can tell me what this is really about."

"I got up early this morning to review the paperwork your husband's attorney sent me yesterday. " She put her hands on her hips, loosening the belt of the bathrobe again, which then hung unashamedly open to reveal pajamas with yellow bunnies on them to go with the slippers. "Now I have to go to Judge Riggio to withdraw as your attorney of record, do you know how that's going — "

"I don't really care how it looks," I said. "At least not until you tell me the rest."

"Let me ask you something. You were married to Alex for *how* long?"

"Eleven years. Please answer my question." Raven had said more than once that Janis had a temper, but that she usually cooled off quickly. This wasn't my definition of quickly.

"You're familiar with the rules of discovery."

"To some extent."

"Then you *might* know that trials don't play out like they do on TV, with the witness breaking down to reveal the truth on the stand. Lawyers have to share what they know in advance." She stamped her foot. To make stamping your foot in a bunny slipper seem threatening is something of an achievement. "And you didn't tell me about Val's run-in with the law!"

"Wh-what was there to tell?" I grabbed the top catalogue, Saks, off the pile, and clutched the cover photo of a bosomless woman with arms like twine against my own chest.

"A conviction for drug dealing when he was twenty-two. Selling pot to a minor."

"Really," was all I could get out.

She nodded, and the nod spread to her upper body, until she was almost bowing. "Yes, really. Or no, let's say I invented it for entertainment value."

"Did he — "

"Did he what?"

"Go to jail?"

"Oh, *please* don't tell me you didn't know about this."

I jumped up, letting the catalogue slip to the floor. "No, I did not know about this!"

"He did community service," she said through a tightly clenched jaw.

"Is that all?"

"Is that *all?* Sure. He's an eagle scout. He could be a poster boy for Big Brothers of America."

"What does it have to do with me anyway?" *It's a lie. Alex's lawyer forged documents to scare Janis off the case.*

"What does it have to do with you? Nothing we can't handle. We just explain to the judge that a convicted drug dealer who's probably still dealing can provide a *stable, nurturing* environment for a child. A disabled child. He taught Jack to ride a bike, didn't he? It sounds as though there are a lot of things he can teach him."

"*I* can call him disabled if I want," I said automatically, "not you." But oh my God, now what was I supposed to do? I couldn't break up with Val — I'd be leaving my daughter without a father. And Val — how did he get hired working with children after that?

"Janis, Val doesn't use and he doesn't deal. I would know it if he did. And if this isn't some cockamamie story, and I bet it is, then it still doesn't change anything about what you wanted to say about me and Alex. You've still got your mission, right? About the whole Cassandra Phenomenon and victimized women?"

"Right, right, right." She rolled her eyes until they could go no farther back. "Listen, if you popped a few pills, I'll buy that Alex drove you to it. I don't suppose he drove you to Folsom Street, too?"

My legs wouldn't hold me, and I sat down again. Folsom Street. The blaring music and the trouble-makers on the stairs. Inside, people staggering when there was hardly room to move.

"Alex has people who will testify that they saw you and Val at 111 Folsom Street, snorting cocaine, smoking marijuana and drinking to excess. Of course, drinking is legal, even if you *are* pregnant, so they can't make too much of that. Whew!" Then she slapped her forehead, hard. "Oh, wait, I guess that's evidence that you're not a real responsible mom." She bent over to pick up the catalogue and replaced it on the pile of mail with a slap. "We can talk about compensating me for the time I already spent on this case later."

"Well, let's stop the clock running now, shall we?" I proposed sharply. The strength had returned to my legs. I grabbed my purse with one hand and the catalogue with the other. "Check out page forty-three. Nothing can heal the pain like a three-thousand-dollar tube top."

At least parting shots would never desert me.

***

Janis gave me her files on the case to take with me. The stack of folders was hefty and daunting. Still, I had to see it for myself. There must have been a mistake. I was in the bargaining stage. It was familiar territory.

Back in the van I got into the middle row to give myself room to spread out. There it was. *The People v. Alexander Valentine.* For the defense a PD named MacKenzie Yamamoto. And representing the people of California, a San Francisco ADA also named Alexander. Alexander M. Kagen.

A plea bargain, a brief court appearance. The two attorneys would have worked most of it out without Val being present. Val and Alex might have been in that courtroom together for all of ten minutes. As for why they didn't remember each other: Alex might have handled twenty cases like this in a week.

They wouldn't get the memo from me.

CHAPTER SEVENTEEN
PUT ASIDE CHILDISH THINGS

Val swirled his chopsticks around the chow mein noodles. They went straight from the carton into his mouth with nary a wiggle.

I was going off my pregnancy diet for the night. The man who had taken our delivery order over the phone had promised me there was no MSG, but I was not going through a very trusting period.

"I thought you were so hungry," Val said.

"I was. Not so much now." There weren't butterflies in my stomach, there were B52s. "Val. Janis told me about your drug conviction today." *Please tell me it isn't true.*

"Oh, yeah?" Not a wiggle in this next bite, either. "You know, it wasn't as bad as I thought. I got to paint over graffiti. My worst nightmare was having to pick up trash on the freeway in one of those orange vests."

I let my fork clatter to the plate. "How could you?"

"How could I what?" He stopped with the chopsticks poised three inches from his lips. "Do something that someone I met ten years later wouldn't approve of?"

"But *dealing....*"

"It didn't quite come down the way your friend described it." He resumed eating. "I was at a party and I shared a joint with some kid who was in my econ class. He knew I was broke, said he had lots of money from a trust fund, begged me to sell him a bag. Turns out he's a sixteen year old narc."

"I believe you," I said after a moment.

"You *believe* me?" He held my gaze without effort. "Have I ever lied to you before? Can you see me crouching behind a dumpster, asking some poor kid if he wants 'a taste'?"

I looked down at my hands, folded over the little basketball that used to be my lap. "You must have lied about it on job applications."

"I didn't have much choice, did I?" He looked at me slyly. "What would you have done in my situation?" He didn't wait for an answer, which was good, because I didn't have one. "You told me yourself you smoked pot in college."

"In my freshman year!"

Val rested one cheek on his hand, but he did not put down his chopsticks. "Banana Boat, according to my calculations, that means I quit two years after you. I wouldn't say there's a yawning moral abyss between us."

"You should have told me about it once Alex asked for custody!" I pointed my fork at him. "If I'd been honest about it up front with Janis, maybe she would have kept me on."

The bullets bounced off his chest. "I wasn't covering anything up. I thought the records were sealed at twenty-one."

"Eighteen. And it doesn't happen automatically." But maybe it *was* an honest mistake.... I drew the nearest carton toward me. Pale soggy beef sank into a swamp of onions and bell peppers. When the food arrived the smells were intoxicating, but just as quickly they decomposed into rotting flesh and chemicals.

"I don't know what to do with a person who doesn't regret past mistakes," I said.

"Learn from him," Val replied.

I pushed the Mongolian beef away. Val had reloaded his plate and was attacking orange chicken with gusto.

"You can't lie about it again."

"Have some of this." He tilted the carton of orange chicken toward me. The chicken skin was oily.

I stabbed a piece.

"How is it?"

"Good." But I stopped eating again to massage my eyes and forehead. The conflict between us remained unsettled in my mind, but other thoughts were crowding in. "You know, I called the Minerva Center yesterday. I thought maybe they'd let me work part-time until the end of the year. No dice."

"You can't work now. You're pregnant."

"I was at work when I went into labor with Jack."

"You're the *uberfrau*," he beamed.

I made circles in my own chow mein noodles. "Rusty is still onto his 'therapeutic-frame-secure' line."

"They have a diagnosis for that in the DSM. It's called 'Stick up the Butt.' Boss Lady had it. Remember her?"

"We're going to have to get some money coming in soon."

He fiddled with the soggy tabs of the carton. "I thought you had some saved."

"I did. It's not going to last much longer, even if we keep living rent-free."

"But Alex — "

"Is rolling in dough, yeah. And if I get a divorce he'll have to support me in some fashion. If I get just some custody of Jack, he might have to give me child support. For his son, not for our daughter." *Unless you were expecting that, too. That's if I get custody, and if....*"

"If — ?"

"If he has any money to give me."

He quietly pushed the tab of the carton into the greasy slot.

"You don't need to stay home to take care of me anymore," I said. "Maybe — maybe you could start job hunting." It was long past time to bring this up. As I recalled, he'd been in the same room with me when we conceived the baby.

"You are right, Anne Banane." The soggy tab flipped back out. "I think I need to start as soon as possible."

"I can't tell you how relieved I am to hear you say that." Ever since I'd found out what it would cost us to rent our own apartment — even three moldy rooms in a basement — the crunch of numbers in my head sounded like bones breaking. I didn't think I'd taken my married-into wealth for granted. But never mind new shoes, or tires, or the take-out we shouldn't have ordered that night. There were the mothers I knew from my former support group who were constantly battling the Regional Center for an extra twenty minutes of speech therapy a week, who shook out their purses to find change for the bus.

I had thought myself spared that misfortune after being singled out for others.

But if Val would just get *something*.... By spring, I could work full-time if necessary.... We were already buying generic brands....

I saw a future of second hand clothes from Delight de Bruin's symphony guild thrift store, and it was a bleak landscape.

My mother knew men who would buy us all dinner before they spent the night. Sometimes we'd go to the park when she knew they'd be there.

At the kitchen table that night I forgave her.

"Oh, I know I need a job," Val said. "It's just that it's been such a gift to be able to have this time with you."

"Really." He must mean it. No one had ever spent this kind of time with me. I snatched the chicken back from him. "We'll make it somehow." I started eating, going straight from carton to face. I *was* hungry.

"And I've been thinking about where to start." Val frowned, trying to scrape the last noodle and grains of rice into a pile big enough to pick up without using his fingers. "There's a clinic in the Haight where I know a guy, I bet he'd give me something — maybe there'd even be health insurance."

"Val!"

"Sure, sure — we go way back — to a little village in Germany, but that's a story for another night.'"

"I bet," I laughed, a little histrionically.

"So what I was thinking was, I'm just going to take one last little trip before I settle down for good."

"One last little...."

"Camping trip. It's the perfect time of year, before the weather gets too cold for sleeping outdoors. You're invited," he teased. "This is my last chance. We're going to have a baby and we're going to be in one place for a long time."

"Things are different with a baby," I conceded, in the understatement of the new millenium, "and the first few months are pretty tough, but you'd be amazed how soon they ... they start walking and even putting on their own clothes and before you know it they're out of the stroller. Even with Jack — "

"Honey, if you wouldn't mind, it would make all the difference."

He really meant to go.

"I'm just not used to this — this — "

"This what? Being caught in a trap?"

"Please don't talk that way," he begged.

But it was clear not only that I had described exactly how he felt, but that he would chew his leg off if he had to.

"There's a spot up in Yosemite, near Half-Dome. Me and some dudes — "

"Your road hogs?'

"Road dogs. Hogs are motor — "

"I know." *Fine. Go,* I thought. *If you think I'm going to beg ...* but I thought back to the first nights I'd spent here after leaving Alex and Jack. Without him, Aunt Patsy's apartment felt like the Bates Motel. "Will — " *don't beg!* — "Will you really come back?"

"Ban-Ban! How can you think — ? I won't just come back, I'll come back a different dude." He glanced down at his plate, filled again with putrid meat and fat, smiling a secret smile of triumph.

"Don't come back a dude at all," I suggested, forcing my own smile. "Come back a *mensch*."

***

On one occasion, when Val told me that I worried too much about the future, I had replied, "Someone has to."

His stated goal for the next few days was to get me to stop the worry, "so we can make some memories for when I'm traveling."

He did not succeed in getting me to put Jack out of my mind, but he deserved an A for effort. He cooked lasagna. He rented *Waterloo Bridge* and *Dark Victory*. We watched them with arms and legs entwined as in the early days, but now with the baby in my womb fitting snugly between us.

On the last night we made love. It was sad but sweet, like eating the last cherries of the summer. We'd had our troubles, and like every couple, we always would. But there would be a new season.

On the morning of his departure I carefully applied both cheer and lipstick to my face. When we heard the screech of brakes and the blare of the horn, I whipped out a brown paper bag. "Provisions!" I announced. "I know how you forget those little luxuries — like water? I've got bottled water, granola bars — enough for everyone — beef jerky — "

The horn blared again.

Val kissed my forehead. "I will call *if* I can, okay?"

"Okay. And you'll be back — "

He frowned. "Ban-Ban, we talked about this. You know I can't commit to a date. You're just setting yourself up to be angry."

"I hardly think it's unreasonable — "

"Early October, all right?" He smiled, raising my chin with the crook of his finger so that I would meet his eyes. "It's the last time we'll be apart."

"I'll look forward to squeezing into a dentist's chair with you when I have my next root canal."

For this remark I received a chuck under the chin that was meant as a sign of amusement. Then I watched through the window while Val, reunited with the hogs, or dogs, or whatever species they were (I was voting for anything that wasn't *homo sapiens*), celebrated a festival of fist-bouncing, palm-stroking and one-armed, Tarzan-like pounds on the chest before they loaded the camping gear on the roof of the off-road vehicle.

Elsie was going on this trip, and she ran around each of the men, one at a time, wagging her tail until it was a blur of gold, and barking out her joy. I almost thought I could understand her, like Scooby-Do: "Wank oo wor waking me!" She circled each member of the party, then she sprinted around the van. Val dashed out to catch her. "Whoa, girl!" he cried. "The street is dangerous!"

I blinked, and they were all gone. Val had forgotten my bag of snacks. I held it in front of my chest.

Then I had an idea. If he were going to be gone anyway, perhaps I could use his absence to my advantage.

***

Every Tuesday Alex had lunch with the Mayor at City Hall. That was the place to catch him. I'd never get past the metal detector at Bryant Street: Everyone knew me, from the lawyers who roamed the hallways to the elderly Asian woman at the newsstand in the lobby.

When I found a metered space on Van Ness half a block away, I chose to see it as a good omen. I wore the big black hat, oversized sunglasses and scarf I had used as a disguise at Julius Kahn Park. With the collar turned up Alex wouldn't spot me immediately, and all I needed was that extra moment to prevent his escape before I could confront him.

And if I could get him cornered — just for that moment — I would, as he used to describe it, "go into my act." I would pretend that I had seen the error of my ways and thrown Val out. The proof: Val had left for Yosemite.

I would not try to make out that Val was broken-hearted (that would be pushing my luck), but rather describe how he was relieved to be set free and had seized the opportunity to do more traveling.

Next: I would beg Alex to take me back. I was sure he'd believe that I wanted him back, because he thought just that much of himself.

But Alex wouldn't want *me* back. I was also sure of that. Now that we were apart it was too, too clear we belonged that way.

And so, the balance of power between us would shift. He knew that it was time for the next installment in our soap opera: Millard and Rotwell would love to depict Alex as the cold-hearted bastard who scorned his penitent wife. WRONGED WOMAN WANTED SECOND CHANCE.

Thus Alex would have to negotiate with me — call off the hounds of CPS, agree to keep Val's drug conviction out of our custody fight, *maybe* even consider joint custody. And, by the time Val returned, I would have gained ground he couldn't retake.

I loitered about a hundred feet from the main steps with my back to the security guards, trusting that I would blend in with the crowd, considering the high per capita of oddly dressed people in the vicinity.

Punctual as he was, Alex showed up at five to twelve. But when I strode toward the city-owned black town car I saw that instead of Alex, a svelte brunette was emerging. Sherri Pechner. What was she —?

Then I saw Alex's polished black Oxford stick out from behind the rear passenger door. Sherri started to reach for his hand but stepped back instead and let him wrestle his way out.

Damn, Sherri Pechner. She'll ruin everything.... No, not if I can help it.

She almost did, though.

Once on his feet, Alex regained his aplomb. All he needed was a cigar to be Boss Tweed, Abe Ruef, and Winston Churchill. Sherri handed him a slim briefcase. It was new, and I could see from the way she completed the transfer that it was a gift from her, replacing the old style briefcase he loved.

Sherri took his arm as they went up the steps together. As she murmured sweet strategies in his ear, I bounded up the stairs behind them and then jumped around to block their path a few feet from the revolving door.

"Anna!"

"Anna."

They did not look happy to see me. Sherri turned to Alex. "You said she'd do something crazy like this." To me: "You look like you just came from a clearance sale at Ross."

"Nice to see you, too, Sherri. You getting a lot of responses on Match.com? 'Very rich man, no oral sex please'?"

"*You* should talk. From what Alex has told me about your — *limitations.*"

That was the end of any "plan" I might have had.

I whirled on Alex. "You son of a bitch. A serial rapist-killer is entitled to a defense, but not me?"

Alex patted his face with his handkerchief. "We were following the rules of discovery. But you and Lover Boy don't seem to care much about rules."

"You shot down my own chance at a lawyer! You know damn well that nothing happened at that party. You've bribed people to lie for you. You call that following the rules? And how about all those lies you published in the *Chronicle*? Jack could read that interview some day and see what his dear daddy thought of his mother."

Sherri merely smiled as she let her sinewy arm snake over Alex's shoulder. She had cut her black hair into a sinister, asymmetrical bob. I'd spoiled everything now. My jealousy surprised me even as it blistered my skin.

Alex pocketed his handkerchief. "I suppose you kept a copy for him. You can give it to him for his high school graduation. If he ever graduates."

"If he doesn't, whose fault will it be?"

"Not mine. He'll be off to school next week."

"What? Where?"

Sherri leaned into Alex. "Boarding school, dah-ling. Would you like to borrow my Bloomie's card while we have lunch with His Honor?" She pointed east with a red-tipped nail. "You look like you could really use a makeover."

"*You* shop at that pathetic satellite store." I thrust my pregnant belly toward the pair of them. "Boarding school? Over my dead body."

"Sherri, let me have a minute here." The meekness in Alex's voice shamed me.

We stepped as far to the side as possible, away from the revolving doors, where civil servants heading out to lunch had been scowling as they had to detour around us.

Once there, my angry vision cleared, and I saw that he looked ten years older than he had in his *Chronicle* photo. He'd gained more weight, the gray in his temples reached back over his ears, and his usually bloodshot eyes had sunk deeper into his face.

"What's this about boarding school?" I demanded, folding my arms against the wind.

"I'm out of options, Anna. Child Protective Services has been to my house twice. *Twice.* They couldn't come in because I wasn't there. Now they're harassing me to stay home from work for a week so they can spot-check me. *Stay home from work?*"

I was about to point out that people *did* stay home from work, even men, even important men such as he, when their child's welfare was at stake, but then I realized, "Wait — CPS has been out to see you? I thought you sicced them on me."

"I would not do that. It's Riordan. PROTECT filed an *amicus curiae* brief in our custody case, stating that our parental rights should be terminated and Jack made a ward of the state."

"Can they do that?"

"They did it."

"Are things that bad at home?"

"Worse. I can't do a thing with him. He won't let me touch him. And emotionally.... It's like he's going out on the tide."

"Goddam it, Alex, why did you fire Mairead?"

"I made a mistake, okay? It was — it was — " He did a quarter shoulder-turn. *Sherri's idea.*

"I always told you Mairead was irreplaceable. Not so easy finding good childcare, is it?"

"I tried to get her back two days later and she already had tickets to go to Ireland."

"I know."

"So she *was* talking to you," he confirmed. When he drew himself up he tried to suck in his stomach with about as much success as I would have had.

"Alex, that is not going to fly now. It's too late for us to be slinging blame, okay? If we don't do something quickly — "

"This boarding school isn't bad," Alex apologized. "Some autistic kids thrive in boarding school."

"But it's not right for *him* and you know it," I barked. "Besides, how much research have you done? Is this place even set up for high-functioning autistics?"

"I don't have *time* to do a lot of research," Alex bristled. "It's in Idaho, and no, I haven't been able to visit, but it's expensive enough. I just have to show Family and Children's Services that I can provide a suitable environment." He wavered. "Whatever a boarding school is like, it'll be better than...."

Than a youth detention facility.

He read my mind as I had his. "Marianne has your old friend Lourdes de Leon to testify for her now and — "

"How is she 'my' old friend?"

"She'll say whatever it takes. Her FARE funding could depend on it. She's as good as any autopsy."

"Someone should do an autopsy on her," I said, without thinking, but I must have imagined that he almost smiled. I wondered how it was that I could hate him and feel sorry for him at the same time. *And what do we do when we have no money to keep him in a boarding school? What do we do when the* real *pedophile creeps into his room at night?* "Look." I jumped into the tiny wound that had opened up. "I made a mistake, too. Let me pay for it. Not Jack."

Alex was staring past me, at the phantom Jack drifting out to sea. "We wanted everything for him," he said. "Everything."

Yes, everything. That September afternoon came back to me. My final squeal, Jack on my belly, and then Alex holding him.

Now, without thinking, I put my arms around Alex. "Why him, Alex?" I asked his shirt. "Why us?"

"I don't know, Anna." I felt his noon beard scratch against my scalp as he shook his head. "I wish I did."

"What will happen to him?"

"We have to keep fighting for him," he said weakly, yet with his familiar resolve. But then, in a voice I'd never heard from him, a croak: "I just don't know how anymore."

"Let me see him," I begged. We were still holding onto each other.

"You wouldn't like it."

"Of course I wouldn't. I didn't like seeing him *before*."

"I can't. I can't break my own restraining order."

"Please, Alex. No one has to know."

"Someone will know." His mouth was close to my ear. "Someone always knows. Haven't *I* taught you that?"

"He needs his mother. Hasn't he taught *you* that?"

He didn't let go of me. We rocked back and forth.

Then I pulled back. "Let me find him a place to go to school," I begged, clutching his waist.

"School starts in two weeks."

"Give me two weeks, then. You can bury them in paperwork 'til then. Isn't that what you do?" A note of flirtation, born of mania, crept into my voice, the warmth people feel just before they freeze to death. "You've got nothing to lose. If I find a school, you let me take him back." If I had been Elsie, my tail would have been wagging at one-twenty WPM. "Then if it doesn't work out, you come snatch him back, and I swear I'll let you say I kidnapped him — I swear I won't argue with you or try to get him back ever again. You can put me in jail if you want. Okay? Okay?"

He stroked his chin once. His nails were bitten down below the quick and calluses were starting to form.

"Okay," he said.

CHAPTER EIGHTEEN
PUT THEM ALL TOGETHER THEY SPELL MOTHER

A typical conversation over the next few days:

"I'm new to the city," I said after introducing myself as "Darya Oberhaus," "and I'm looking for a school for my son...." A brief description with key details omitted.

A typical response: "The person to call is Lourdes de Leon. She knows the school district in and out."

"That's funny. She told me to call *you.*"

"Really? I'm flattered. Well, let me tell you where we have Jeremiah...."

Not every conversation went as well. "Your options are fewer than they were last fall," one parent warned me darkly. "There was an incident back in May — "

This led to the much-embroidered tale of this unstable mom and her offspring, the Krazy Kagen Killer.

Parents were excited about the latest rumor, which I hadn't heard yet: that a well-known Hollywood producer was poised to buy the rights from Jimmy Gaines for a movie of the week, *Murder on Minotaur Island.* Gaines was holding out for an indictment, after which the price would shoot up. "Do you read the blog on JoshsSpecialWorld.com?" one woman asked me. "Daniel Radcliffe might play the psycho boy. But if they shoot here there'll be lots of extra work. I belong to the Screen Extras Guild myself."

"What pisses *me* off," another mom complained, "is how this has hurt so many other kids. Sloane had one friend. One. Now the kid's parents won't let them play together any more. Thinks Sloane might get violent or something. 'S bullshit."

I was wading through this *khazerai*, groaning inwardly for coffee and sometimes biting down hard on my lips, when my current interviewee, a woman with a Southern accent, drawled, "Ah'll tell you, the diamond in the rough is Clarisse Heims."

"I haven't heard of her."

"It's a not a *her*, silly," she teased. "Clarisse Heims Alternative. My Harper is in eighth grade there now.

***

Public schools, I was learning from "Darya Oberhaus's" new friends could be surprisingly eager to please, since they were accountable under the Americans with Disabilities Act. I realized now that Alex and I had dismissed them as potential placements too soon and too easily.

Clarisse Heims smelled of pencil shavings, bologna and a classroom's pet hamster, but so had Pathways Academy, with all its fresh white paint, skylights and attitude. Yes, I'd had enough of private schools for a while.

Granted, when I entered the office early that morning, the secretary looked at me as if she wanted to cry out, "No room! No room!" as surely as the Mad Hatter and the March Hare did to Alice.

But the principal, Kitty Seldon, who emerged to greet me in a flaming vermillion polyester pantsuit, had both a kinder and far more penetrating expression. Kitty struck me as someone who would know both the latest news *and* gossip, but neither of us mentioned the possibility of Daniel Radcliffe or his local counterpart playing her prospective student as an autistic-psycho.

Kitty quickly took me back out into the hall. It was the second day of school, but students had not yet arrived, and we'd have more privacy.

"They say nothing else comes close to your full-inclusion program," I told her. Just because you're a kiss-ass doesn't mean you're a liar. "And that you're the best principal in the city."

"We've come a very long way with full-inclusion," Kitty said. She tapped her foot as if to express her impatience with the length of the journey ahead. "When the first kids started in the mid-90s, there was a lot of resistance among the older teachers."

I didn't like the sound of that. "And now?"

"Some have retired, some have seen the light." She moved her head to one side and then the other. "The rest.... Well, it's a new day and they can't stop that." Kitty was an inch shorter than I, with face of a pixie. It was good camouflage, for she had the ambition of a Hillary Clinton. I recognized it from long acquaintance with the ambitious. "We started in '95 with three special needs kids and we've got twenty now. My problem today is that that's our full quota of full-inclusion students."

She offered me a truncated tour as the take home Jeopardy game. The hallway needed painting but most of its surface was hidden by a series of quilts, each handmade by a different class. Kitty showed them off like a new grandparent with a wallet full of baby pictures. "This is my favorite." She stopped in front of the most complicated one. "It's — it's a communal farm," she said, suppressing a forbidden amusement. "The fifth grade did it, in fact, last year. The teacher *is* a champion of the differently abled."

The quilt depicted, roughly, children hoeing a blue cotton earth.

She battled a smile. "Ernest does have rather fervent views ... of how society should be."

I was beginning to glimpse a possible way in here, even though she added hastily, "He has several students with IEPs in his class already."

"May I ask you about them? I mean, how are they doing?"

"They're flourishing. One is hearing-imp — I'm sorry," she cut herself off, "Ernest tells me she's not hearing impaired, she is a person with hearing difficulty."

"It *is* a moving target," I observed awkwardly.

"Another boy has epilepsy. As opposed to being an epileptic. You can't say that anymore, either."

"Why not?"

"If you call someone epileptic, you're defining him or her. 'A person with epilepsy' is just a person with blue or brown eyes.'"

I head the *hoosh* of hydraulic brakes. The first school bus had arrived and my time was limited. "Ms. Seldon, let's be honest. You don't want me or Jack at your school because we're radioactive. Politically."

She looked over at the quilt.

"You've heard *baaad* things about us," I said without drama. "I won't plead our case because I don't want to drag anyone else into this. But if you give us a chance — " I stopped, because I wasn't sure what I'd be getting her into. "He's a kid who needs help, and everyone says this is the place to get it." I pressed my hand against the wall. "Everyone says you 'walk the walk.' That's exactly the phrase they use. Clarisse Heims could be the place where he turns around. That would make quite a story, too."

Kitty was far from heartless, and neither did an appeal to her ego go unnoticed, but she was practical above all things. "I was telling you the truth about our quota. We get funding from the district — "

"If there are kids with special needs in the class there must be an aide there already, too."

"There is."

"Ms. Seldon, I will work for Clarisse Heims. At Pathways — " *God, that still hurt!* — "I put in hours as a room parent, fundraising — whatever was needed."

At the word "fundraising" Kitty could not control the lift of her eyebrows. Now that I had dropped Little Boy it was time for Fat Man. I had nothing to lose.

"Ms. Seldon, my husband and I *are* separated. But he cares about Jack's education as much or more than I. He's close to four of the seven school board members. Even if he's defeated in November, these are people who would be more than happy to help him out on personal matters — as appropriate, of course."

I wasn't completely confident that was true. Many of San Francisco's petty poobahs, both elected officials and the power brokers who put them in office, including those whom Alex had counted as actual friends, had withdrawn their support. The school board members in question might well be — were likely — among them. But — they might not be. Alex would always do his best for Jack in the areas in which he was able.

My final message was in code, but she would know to crack it. "My husband understands the public interest."

Outside, the whine of diesel engines departing accompanied the yelps of children gathering on the playground.

"Well, Mrs. Kagen...." Kitty reached for a shape on the quilt, a dark-skinned child with a yellow quarter moon sewn over his head, evoking a halo. "I suppose...."

I knew that "I suppose" was a formality. Future superintendents of schools did not suppose; they made decisions and didn't look back.

"We can give it a try."

***

Darya held me loosely as she sobbed, her face on Val's shirt. I'd put it on that morning when I could find nothing else that would fit. I felt her tears soak through the chambray.

"I wish you had told me about it before."

Darya had come to me straight from the evaluation at UC Medical Center.

"Callaghan went with me," she sniffled. "Do you have a Kleenex?"

"In the bathroom."

Darya's eyes moved in the direction of the bathroom. "Callie — "

"No, I'll get it." I pushed myself up from the sofa with my fists. I was so relieved that Darya had gone for help, and so busy flattering myself that I might have had a hand in it, that I was willing to wait on her one last time.

"But *I* should have been with you today," I worried, when I returned with the box. "Not Callaghan."

"Tia Anita, can I have something to drink?" Callaghan asked. The line etched between her brows looked as though it would become permanent soon.

"Of course, dear. Help yourself to whatever's there." Our provisions were all pregnancy-and-kid friendly.

"Get something for Kennedy," Darya commanded weakly. "Do you have a tippee cup?" she asked me.

"No, I don't have a tippee cup."

"Well, it's your apartment." She twisted a second Kleenex while Kennedy dug troughs in the dirt surrounding a prayer plant.

"Not really. Now, look, pull yourself together. Tell me what happened."

The two-hour wait just to get to the examining room. Another hour for the resident. By then your child has stuck cotton swabs into every orifice except his ear.

But this is a teaching hospital, and the resident is the one who will really be tested. She taps her pencil against her lips as she goes down her checklist. She pursues a line of questions relating to....

"Something about his big toe?"

"Rubinstein-Taybi Syndrome," I laughed, to lighten the mood. "Now *that's* ridiculous."

"Then they told me it might be Sensory Processing Disorder."

"That doesn't sound right," I said. I smelled Diagnosis of the Month. "Maybe some auditory processing...."

"The doctor said I should sign him up for a playgroup at the hospital."

I put my arm around her. "Yeah, big help, right? But you gotta do what — "

"At least they didn't say he was autistic."

I drew back. "That's a little insensitive, even for you."

"But Anna, you know what I mean.... You've had years to get used to the idea."

"Newsflash. You never get used to it."

"Anna!" She was going to melt into tears again. "*Now* who's being insensitive?"

Callaghan reappeared. "Tia, Kennedy spilled some juice on the carpet. It's — it's grape juice."

I patted her cheek. "But it's *white* grape juice."

"I'll clean it up," she volunteered.

"No, I'll clean it up. Go look at the books. Don't worry about your brother."

Darya put her head in her hands, grieving Madonna, covering her eyes so she wouldn't see the tea towel I held in front of her a moment later. I snapped it against her head. "Get up. Carrying on like one of the Trojan women doesn't help. Whether you like it or not, you've got two children. Just FYI."

"I know ... if it weren't for Callaghan...."

"Speaking of Callaghan, you are going to stop using her like a combination special ed teacher and flesh-covered punching bag."

"I still think he might grow out of it." Darya resumed weeping into a fresh Kleenex. "Can't he just grow out of it?"

"Well, until he does I suggest your get off your ass." I softened. "I'll help you get through this. We'll help each other."

A horn sounded outside and I jumped up. "It's Alex — with Jack," I said excitedly. "And you know Alex, he waits for no man. Or woman. You'll want to see Jack."

I was outside within two seconds.

Alex's white Cadillac was double-parked. He had his hazards on, but double-parking was still a good way to get a ticket, cursed out, rear-ended and, once in a while, shot.

"Can't you pull into the driveway?" I asked, bending over his window.

Alex was amused. "*That* little strip of concrete?" He added, "I have case files bigger than that."

"*Now* you get a sense of humor," I muttered.

Jack must have flung himself across the rear seat, because I couldn't see him through the window.

Alex was already on the street, wheezily removing a hefty black canvas duffel bag from his trunk. "I didn't know what to pack," he said. "I tried to get Jack to help me, but — we can move things over gradually. If it works out, that is."

"I should have given you a list." We fell easily back into our old roles. "Have you got his toothbrush, the *Crime Conquerors* pajamas — the pawn?"

"You have a short memory," Alex chuckled. "He never leaves the house without his pawn."

That night Alex would have the house to himself. The remote. The refrigerator. "Besides, we don't live in the woods here. If there's anything you need tonight, go get it." He dug in his pocket for a wad of bills. His small smile said, *Aren't I* saint *in a made-to-measure Zegna suit?*

With an unexpected feeling of dread, I approached the back seat.

"I had a little trouble getting him in the car," Alex said, adding modestly, "But I handled it. He was excited about seeing you. It's just — I should warn you — I told him you were coming home with us."

I paused in my reaching for the car door. "You told him *what?* Alex, you know — "

"Strategy meeting tonight," Alex said cheerfully. He wouldn't have to worry about finding a sitter now, either. "I hope this Clarisse place lives up to your expectations."

I tapped lightly on the window.

"People talk about how unfair the power of the incumbency is, but D.C. can campaign every waking hour if she wants. *I* have to keep doing my job."

Still nothing. I opened the door to the rear seat where Jack was, as I had pictured, splayed across the leather.

I couldn't see him clearly, but I smelled him right away. He reeked of decaying leaves and chocolate, of milk and orange juice already going sour from his breakfast and even — I could hardly bear to think it — feces. Had he had a bath — had anyone tried to wash him at all — since Mairead left?

"Come out, Boychik," I encouraged him.

"No, Mommy, you come home with us. Come home with us...."

"C'mon, Jack," Alex jollied him along. "Your mom has some good plans for you tonight. I hope you do," he warned me.

"Just help me get him out."

Alex leaned in. It took all his strength to lift Jack from the leather and on the sidewalk where he went deadweight.

"Goddam it!" Alex rubbed his fist into the small of his back. But his good humor returned quickly. He was free, free, free! "Sorry about that." Checking his watch: "I'm on taxpayer time. You got this under control?"

"I have no idea."

"Great."

From the sidewalk Jack moaned, "Mom is supposed to come home with us. With us...."

Now there was just the dullest edge of impatience in Alex's voice: "You know how Daddy puts the bad guys in jail so they can't hurt anyone else? There are some bad guys out there that Daddy has to take care of."

"Mommy, get in the car. The car...."

"Boychik, you're coming with me."

"No! You're coming home with me! With me...."

"You all'll be fine," Alex said. Then he was back in the car, trailing a plume of exhaust. He'd never cut the engine.

Crouching on the pavement, I got a closer look at Jack. He was dressed in clothes I'd bought him: cuffed and pleated black trousers with a striped button down shirt. But the stained shirt was half in, half out. His flopping, untied shoelaces were nearly black. An inch of sock was visible between his trouser cuff and running shoes.

He'd grown.

If that hippie-bureaucrat pair from CPS saw him like this, he'd be in a foster home before nightfall.

I looked from my crumpled-up son to his duffel bag. They both looked too heavy for me.

"Is the coast clear?" Darya shouted from the doorway.

"If you mean Alex, he's gone," I called back. I scanned the block. Val and I had been quiet neighbors, but those days of volume control might be over. I had never gotten to know the other residents and I hoped there were no Mrs. Drs. among them.

"Well, that was close. I was afraid he was going to come in."

Since my back was to her I indulged myself in a melodramatic look up at the heavens.

"I've never forgotten — "

How he wouldn't let you stay with us after you left Steve.

"—and in a house like Hearst Castle — "

His own sister-in-law.

"—I mean, we could have camped out on the *third floor,* for God's sake — "

He knew what a hard time I was going through.

"—and me with two little kids! But it's not worth going over again. We'd better blow this canoe." Darya, having recovered her equanimity with the same speed as Alex, already had her children by the hands.

"It was good to see you, Tia," Callaghan said over her shoulder as they walked away. "Mommy has a date tonight," she added. "With a scorpion."

"*Scorpio*," Darya laughed. "We're studying all the signs, just the two of us. So you see," she mocked me, "I *am* spending more time with her, like you said I should."

***

Ten minutes later, Jack was dancing in place on the same square of sidewalk, insisting, "This is not a good place! I want to go home! No house! Go home!"

I hadn't seen one of these since the morning after St. Seraphina's. But after Alex and Darya's departure, Jack's moaning had escalated to screaming and his deadweight had turned to kicking as I had tried logic ("Don't you want to see your new room?"), bribes ("I have cookies inside. Lots of cookies."), and finally, God forgive me, a threat. ("If you don't get off that sidewalk and into the house right this minute....")

I hadn't had him back for twenty minutes. Never mind what CPS would think — I was about to call them for help.

I had never paid attention to how much foot traffic there was on this street. Passers-by with grocery bags or running with iPods cut wide swaths around us.

As on that other morning, Jack was in freefall and there wasn't much to do until he crashed to earth. Perhaps a big blow-out tantrum was inevitable. He'd been sitting on the top of a bulging duffel, where all his demons were crammed inside along with the *Crime Conquerors* action figures and his cuffed black trousers. Now with me at his side, he could stand up and let everything spill out, because I was there to drive the demons away just as I put would put the trousers in a drawer and the action figures in a sturdy plastic bin — if I ever got him inside Aunt Patsy's front door.

I ran my fingers through his hair. It was as greasy as maple syrup, and I wondered how I'd get him cleaned up: the dirt out from under untrimmed nails, the dead skin off his lips. How I'd get him to sleep in a strange bed. How I'd ever get him to go to a new school.

A woman approached us. A pregnant woman, no less, pushing an umbrella stroller bearing her one-year-old son while her pre-school age daughter dutifully held onto one of the stroller handles.

"A little discipline is all *he* needs," she said, without breaking pace. She made a show of maneuvering both ambulatory child and stroller around us with several resentful grunts.

I wished I could tell her how easily she could have been me. No doubt she measured out her life in hand-sewn Halloween costumes, in the Saturday afternoons she and her husband spent tending the flower beds, and counting these young saplings her just reward.

But I could ignore the pedestrians. The problem was that this was National Dog Walking Hour. Every time Jack's screams softened and I thought I saw a narrow path into the flat, someone came by with another one. Some of those dog owners were nice. "Pink Floyd won't hurt you. Would he like to pet him?" Others were on the defensive before I said a word. "My dog has just as much right to this street as your brat."

I could see no alternative to letting Jack cry himself out, and so I stayed with him, sitting "criss-cross applesauce," as teachers called it now. More neighbors would be coming home, now that the work day was coming to an end. Neighbors who might testify for me or for the county to determine what kind of hands Jack was in.

***

We were still outside when Jack fell asleep with his head on what was left of my lap. I sat until my thighs tingled and then went dead.

The days were shorter now. The sun had set when Jack opened his eyes: Egg-shaped, hazel-gray, large in his face. My eyes.

"I missed you, Mommy," he said. "Missed you...."

I hugged him, filling my nostrils with his stench.

***

We spent the next hour exploring Aunt Patsy's apartment. He wanted to see every dish, book, and houseplant. A few of the last weren't doing too well.

With this first crisis in remission, I began to wonder about Val. How would he react when he came home to see his future stepson living with us? But this was what we had planned — wasn't it? For me to get a divorce, for us to get married and get custody, or at the very least, joint custody, of Jack. Strangely, I could only remember snippets of conversations and brief remarks.

All made by me.

***

Later that night Jack and I watched the *Back the Future* trilogy, all three films, which I had bought as a boxed set as part of my shopping earlier that day. Jack ate pizza in bed next to me. He was gripped by the plot, and I was thrilled — and totally full of myself. I had *known* he'd like something like this, given his interest in fantasy stories, time and dates.

When we got to *Back to the Future Part II*, Jack's questions were perspicacious but inevitably frustrating after much repetition. "Who's Queen Diana?" he asked when the 2015 setting made a reference to the Princess who had died before he started kindergarten. "Why don't we see Biff with the sports book in Part I if he goes back in time later to give it to himself?"

Finally I said, "Time travel stories never hold up if you look at them too closely." *Because things are always the way they're supposed to be, good or bad.*

Omar Khayam had it nailed: "Nor all your piety or wit … nor all your tears wash out a word of it."

But that first night, at least, you might say that Michael J. Fox wasn't the only one who got his future back. And when Jack's perseveration wore me out about halfway through the third movie, I turned on my side, nuzzled into my pillow and said, "We'll talk about it more tomorrow, okay? Have some more pizza. Try not to get cheese on the…."

CHAPTER NINETEEN
LET'S KILL ALL THE LAWYERS

Alex and I left the State Building together.

We had spent the past four hours being deposed by state attorneys. A.G. Marianne Pasquale herself had been present. The last time I'd seen her had been at a cocktail party, and we'd joked about men and sports, but this afternoon she had not spoken my name. I was "you" and "Ma'am."

Golden Gate Avenue was another of the city's wind tunnels; love it or leave it. My coat flapped as hard as a canvas sail behind me. But it was getting difficult to button. At first Dr. Phelps said it was normal to "pop out" earlier in a second pregnancy, but at my last visit she had warned that I was gaining weight too quickly.

"You were good," Alex said.

High praise from him. "Thank you."

"I was afraid you'd get hysterical."

I lifted one corner of my mouth. "And I was afraid *you'd* go schizoid."

He looked startled. Alex still thought that "schizoid" was an abbreviation of "schizophrenia."

"It means withdrawn. In lay-person's terms."

"Indeed." He looked at his watch.

"I'm glad you were there," I admitted. There hadn't been much for him to say, since I had been on Minotaur Island and he had not. I was the one the lawyers asked, over and over and over, as Jack might, for a moment-by-moment account of the field trip up until the time Tyler was found.

The sun. My feet aching. The branch that finally scratched through my jacket.

The rocks that blocked my view of Tyler's body until the end.

"Eyewitness testimony is notoriously unreliable," Alex said grimly. "Most people are pret-ty suggestible."

I didn't think I was overly suggestible but I had gone over that day in my mind so many times that it was as worn out as a child's blankie. Except that it was the anti-blankie, able to send me spiraling down a series of what-ifs.

"I make Elizabeth Loftus required reading for every prosecutor in my office," Alex went on. Loftus was a worldwide authority in the field of memory, and one of a select group of people whom Alex genuinely admired.

In the deposition, I'd used my own doubts as an excuse to say, "I'm sorry, I don't remember," whenever it felt honest enough, which was also whenever the question felt dangerous.

"Were any of the boys acting strangely that morning?'

"I don't remember."

"Was Jack in particular acting strangely?"

"I don't remember."

What was I supposed to say? "Yes, I was worried from the time we got on the ferry that something was terribly wrong"? Because Alex was right. Now it seemed that even as we ploughed away from the wharf and Emily and Sophie placed themselves thigh to thigh with me in the stern, that there was something sinister ... shall we say, afloat? The way the boys ran around the deck, testing how far they could lean over the rail before Ms. Scarborough screamed?

And the less I said, the less likely I was to contradict someone else's story.

"Mrs. Kagen, how soon did you report your son missing?"

"As soon as I noticed."

"How long was that?"

"I don't remember."

A stenographer recorded every word spoken. I could hardly credit such "technology" in the 21st Century. Why not just use a quill pen and be done with it?

"Mr. Kagen, did you notice any aberrant behavior in your son that morning?" Earlier question re-worded.

"No."

"In the days preceding?"

"No."

"But you wouldn't describe his behavior as 'normal' on any day, would you?"

Fuck you.

"His behavior was normal for him. There was no change in his manner, speech or routine."

Alex and I reached the intersection. This was the Tenderloin: by day a neighborhood of liquor stores, panhandlers and Vietnamese immigrants; by night, teenage prostitutes, drug deals on corners, knife fights in doorways.

"Did your son have prior conflicts with the deceased?"

"No. They had no relationship at all."

"How is that possible, attending the same school, and in such a small classroom setting?"

"He had no relationship with any of the other children, beyond the superficialities."

Alex and I walked in silence as long as I could bear it. Then I begged for reassurance, "The A.G.'s case is pretty weak, isn't it?"

We had learned that day, though I wasn't sure we were supposed to, that after scattering Tyler's ashes on Minotaur Island, Margaret Gaines, Tyler's mother, had left dad Jimmy. She could not be located for a deposition.

"This is a setback for her," Alex agreed. "But she has your Mrs. de Leon testifying."

"Again with the 'my' Mrs. de Leon." I took my hands out of my pockets long enough to raise palms to the sky. But today Alex and I were on the same side. "What can she say that's so bad?"

"That she observed Jack's violent behavior in playgroups."

"But would that — isn't that — "

Alex was genuinely patient with me that day. "A lot of evidence that isn't admissible at the trial level can be presented to a grand jury." *Very* patient, because he knew I knew that. "Pasquale only needs to show probable cause for an indictment," Alex reminded me. "The defendant doesn't even have a voice there."

Time, however, had not been on Marianne's side after all. As she let the investigation drag on, hoping to alienate neither the well-organized vigilante voters, nor the citizens who took the trouble to familiarize themselves with the case and were thus sympathetic to Jack, she had only increased the polarization between the two groups.

"How's Jack doing?" Alex asked.

I scraped my shoes against the pavement. "He's settling into the apartment pretty nicely." As soon as I said "apartment" I bit my tongue. The apartment was the den of iniquity I had taken him to. I still couldn't quite figure out why, no matter how passionately I'd pleaded or how much Alex feared Jack becoming a ward of the court, he had been able to swallow the final insult of placing Jack in Val's care. True, Val was gone at the moment, and for Alex out of sight was truly out of mind. Maybe when Val came back Alex would suddenly want to re-think Idaho.

"You could call him," I said, trying to sound kind.

"I've been afraid to. Does he — talk about me?"

"Of course." But Jack didn't seem to miss Alex. "He's nervous about starting school on Tuesday," I confessed.

"Well, that's to be expected. Any kid — "

"Right."

We strolled down Larkin Street toward Civic Center Plaza, where both of us had parked. The city had spent $100 million dollars landscaping the square, installing a playground and the obligatory espresso bar. It had rapidly been despoiled by graffiti, strewn with litter, and enthusiastically vandalized.

"I've got to get back to the office," Alex said. "We're putting together our first mailer. Mailers, if we get the money. But I want to see Jack, um, as soon as I can."

***

Jack *had* been settling in. So much so that he was willing to have Raven babysit him while I was busy with government lawyers. She'd brought her son, his former classmate Philip, and Jack had been thrilled to see them.

Nevertheless, when I returned to Aunt Patsy's apartment, I hurried to the door.

In the flat, I went down on my haunches to gather the day's mail, scattered just inside the slot. I tucked it under my arm just in time to use my hands as a buffer against Jack's standard greeting, which was to throw himself against me. He was anxious whenever I left him, afraid I wouldn't come back. "Mommy! Mommy...."

Raven had been playing Monopoly Junior with the two boys when I came in, but she started cleaning up the moment she saw me. "You should get one of these," she said. "He did a good job. Be sure to make him the banker," she grinned. Then, more seriously, "I told Janis she owes you an apology." Up until now, by tacit agreement, Raven and I hadn't discussed the matter of her partner and me.

"She doesn't. It's a complicated situation. I might not need a lawyer now. *Kine hara.*"

"I've talked to Janis about her temper," Raven said. "She's sorry later, but sometimes the damage is done."

I sensed her embarrassment. "No hard feelings," I said. "And thank you for helping me out today. Can you stay a while?"

"I wish I could. I have a doctor's appointment."

"Check up?" I asked, excessively causal.

"Hey, Pathways can't afford to lose *me*. They get a grant from Dykes on Bikes for letting me be a room parent." She put a hand on my shoulder but did not look me in the eye. "Call me again. Philip had a great time."

"But Jack — " Philip began.

"Philip had a great time," Raven cut him off.

"Bye Philip!" Jack called. He was lying on his back on the floor and cycling the air with his legs. "Bye...."

"You've got the mail." Philip pointed to where I had it tucked under my arm.

"Just junk."

"Maybe Jack's invitation is there."

The word "invitation" swung like a wrecking ball through the air.

"What invitation?" Jack wanted to know.

"I'll check, Boychik." I slung Philip's denim jacket over my arm and had the front door open in a New York second. "So sorry you can't stay."

"What invitation?"

"Do you want to help me with dinner, Jack?"

"No, thanks. What invitation?"

"Philip," Raven said nervously, "you don't want to sit in that awful doctor's office with Mommy, do you? Well, you'll have to if we don't get home to Mama first, and she came home *early* for you...."

"What invitation?"

"To Cesar Ruiz's party," Philip managed to tell him before Raven tugged him over the threshold. "He's going to have Science Matt and a chocolate and vanilla cake. It's in two wee — "

I didn't really mean to slam the door behind them.

"Let's go look for the invitation," Jack said. "We'll put it on the fridge! Cesar is my friend. Friend...."

"Hey, kidaroonies!" I cried, like Chuckles the Chipmunk from *A Thousand Clowns*. "How would you like to start TV time early?"

"Yaaay!"

I wasn't off the hook, but I'd bought a little time. I heard Jack turn on the TV, and the theme song from *Crime Conquerors* came on. I never could have believed that I'd be happy to hear that music again. "I'll watch that with you, Boychik," I called from the kitchen. The forerunner of

Crime Conquerors was a Japanese program and the American version used some of the same stock footage. In every episode a new monster tore down a street full of cardboard high rises. By the following episode the high rises had not only been rebuilt to identical specifications but formed a skyline that rivaled Chicago's. The stock footage made the Godzilla movies look like *Citizen Kane,* but I found it even more amusing that intergalactic villains would choose as their primary target for destroying the earth Bedford Falls, the small Midwestern town in which the series was set.

I'd look through the mail quickly, pluck out anything necessary, hide it, and throw away the rest. I wasn't expecting an invitation from Cesar Ruiz.

There were several offers for new credit cards with **IMPORTANT OPEN IMMEDIATELY** printed on the envelope. I was embarrassed that I had hoped for a postcard from Val during the first week. I didn't hope any longer, yet going through the mail wasn't my favorite time of day.

There was a new PG&E and phone bill. Well, at least I could keep the lights on. Alex's checks also came in the mail, not fat ones, but enough to cover what we needed. For now.

I was just about to toss the rest when I took a closer look at what I had first thought was a promotion for a local real estate agent.

It was a picture of a dead baby. A dead baby with a bloodied and beaten face.

I turned away in revulsion, took a deep breath, and then looked back.

Huge yellow block letters against a black background:
IS THIS WHAT WE WANT TO HAVE HAPPEN TO OUR CHILDREN?

I opened the folded stock. **ALEX KAGEN WOULD LET IT HAPPEN.**

The print on the left was small and the color poorly chosen, for the yellow wobbled against the black. "This year thousands of children were maimed, abused and even murdered. Thousands of juveniles broke the law. Complaints were filed by citizen victims of rape, physical assault, armed robbery and verbal harassment. Hiding behind their chronological age and protected by a broken system, none of these evildoers were brought to justice."

Sure, sometimes charges against first-time offenders were dropped, and pleas were negotiated.... But Alex was *proud* of the diversionary programs he'd nurtured.... "When not only darkened alleys, but sunny parks and grade school field trips are no longer safe then the citizens of San Francisco must take a stand."

The rest of the text accused Alex of behavior ranging from missing court dates and doctoring evidence to not using a coaster. At least the opening paragraphs had been coherent. Whoever had written this *drek* had knocked back a few adult beverages by the time he or she reached the end. He or she. As if I didn't know who wrote it.

The only information that anyone would really absorb was that there was a dead baby, and it was his fault.

In small white print on the back of the mailer was the note, "made of 75% recycled materials."

Campaign season had officially begun.

Jack yelped at something on television. "Honey, can you turn that down?" I called.

"What?"

"Can you turn that down?"

"I CAN'T HEAR YOU."

I dropped the mailer into the trash bag set aside for recycling and went into the front room where I lowered the volume for him. "Is my invitation there?"

"Not yet, honey." My fingers curled into fists and unfurled again. *Damn it, just tell him it's not coming.*

He was zeroing in tightly on the screen. "When it comes we can put in on the refrigerator. Refrigerator...."

I drifted back into the kitchen, and when I next realized what I was doing I was staring at the refrigerator. Since Jack's return to me I had made it his, with photos I had taken with a disposable camera (Alex still had primary custody of the Kagen family camera), and a few pictures torn from *Crime Conquerors Chronicles* magazine.

A long time before, while Val was still on the Ride, Jack had drawn me a page of dark green scribbles when I met him secretly at Julius Kahn Park. I had tearfully attached it the refrigerator back then, at his request. For the first month after that I had felt a sting in my chest every time I opened the refrigerator door. But gradually I had become accustomed to it.

Maybe it was because Jack was finally with me again that my eye fell on it afresh.

It had never looked any different to me than his other drawings, when we could coax any drawing out of him at all. They were always a collection of lines and crude attempts at geometric shapes. He always resisted using more than one color.

And so I had seen it as a document of his future, the future I loved to torture myself about, when he would be taking orders in a stock room from some punk ten years younger than he....

In the southeast quadrant of the page he'd drawn a capital Y.

This *was* a picture of something.

"I'll destroy you!" Jack shouted from the next room.

CHAPTER TWENTY
LAW AND ORDER SPECIAL BIRTHDAY PARTY UNIT

Campaign season had begun, all right. I woke the next morning to find "Coggs signs" sprouting all over the city. Coggs was the company that manufactured and distributed campaign posters, and here they were, in the windows of stores and homes, stabbed in the earth in front of houses, and plastered on light poles from shoulder-level to bulb. There were rumblings in the Board of Supes to ban them from these utility poles soon, but on the way to school that day Jack got to see them in full bloom for his father.

Alex used the same colors as he had before: the San Francisco Forty-Niners' red and gold. His slogan, "…and Justice for All," remained unchanged as well.

***

On his first day of school, Jack accompanied me inside with little resistance. We met Tiffany Chan in the hallway. She was the "full-inclusion teacher," the person responsible for overseeing all the special needs children at the school. "Why don't I take over," she offered. "He might do better without you." She handed me a spiral notebook. "One of us will write you a note every day. And you write back with any questions or concerns."

"Can I write in the notebook?" Jack asked. "Note…."

I went back to the car, where I listened to *Follies* for twenty minutes. Then I drove slowly past the school, quiet in front now. There was no black-haired boy lying on the sidewalk kicking, so I went home.

There I waited all day for "the call." Parents like me know all about "the call." It didn't come.

At 2:45 I was back in front of the school. Clarisse Heims used the same pick-up procedure as Pathways: a long line of cars inching forward, stopping just long enough to upload sons and daughters.

When I reached the front of the line, Tiffany was standing next to Jack. He looked blissfully MIA. There was no time to talk, with a coral Escort crawling up to my bumper, but Tiffany gave him a boost into the pilot seat, waved, and moved quickly down the line with her next charge.

I asked Jack for his notebook, and inhaled his teacher's entry before I put the car in drive. "Jack … doing well … everyone's name and birthdays already … a pleasure … happy to be back with mom."

***

"Has some trouble focusing," and "outbursts of laughter," came back the next few days, but so did, "clearly intelligent" and "delightful sense of humor." His new teacher, Ernest Debard, led a discussion of the idea that the test of a civilization is in the way it cares for its helpless members.

Apparently, while Alex and I were twisting ourselves and Jack into shapes that a yoga master couldn't pull off, trying to make a private school work, the San Francisco School District had been getting its act together. The first few years, Principal Kitty told me unselfconsciously, were a constant battle between parents and teachers, and flare-ups were still common enough. But here in the birthplace of political correctness, the "differently abled" were the newest oppressed minority. I was sure that, in the privacy of the parents' homes, there was plenty of discomfort with Jack's presence at Clarisse Heims. Nevertheless, we had crossed the border from Presidio Heights to the Richmond — though you must consider both neighborhoods a state of mind.

I asked Alex to take Jack on Saturday. He demurred; he was planning to spend it with Maddy and some other close advisors, probably including Sherri, working on this latest round of damage control. Maddy (who had started speaking to me again) told me that Sherri wanted to respond in kind to Riordan's hit piece but that Alex refused to do any negative campaigning, "even if it costs me my office."

But whatever kind of campaign Alex ran, he could have his meeting at his house, where Jack still had many of his things.

Maddy also told me that the grand jury would convene before the end of the upcoming week.

Before that, I was going to crash a party.

***

Cesar Ruiz and his mother lived in a Spanish Revival-duplex, with a roof of red clay tile and an arched entryway.

I stood under that entryway now, facing a door with an ornate metal knocker in the shape of a lion's mouth. I made out that lion's mouth through the leaves of the massive bouquet of carnations that I held in front of my face. With the flowers so close to my eyes I had a decent view out, but anyone standing more than a few feet away would have difficulty making out my features. A leaf from a carnation stem poked into one of my nostrils.

A balloon bouquet tied to the scrollwork on a metal railing announced that a party was going on inside. Long before I reached the porch the party had reached me in the cacophony of a crowd of sugared-up children, but the party sounds were louder here, and if the louder the screams the happier the kids, the party was a roaring success in more ways than one. There weren't just Pathways kids here but Cesar's friends from his after school chess club, computer programming club, and the Gifted Child Learning Center. Who knew that such smart kids could be so noisy? It didn't bode well for the Master Race apparently coming of age.

I raised the lion's jaw and knocked twice. Hard.

Cesar's mother, Nora, answered the door. She was an attractive woman, but I hadn't seen her in almost a year and she had grown thinner and a little drawn.

"Yes?"

"Happy birthday!" I cried in falsetto. It was better than "Candygram."

Nora squinted. "I told you the bastard wouldn't call," she said to someone I couldn't see. She held out her hand grudgingly. "I'll take that."

"You have to sign for it, Ma'am," I said, speaking hoarsely to disguise my voice a little. "I've lost my pen. May I use one of yours?"

Nora looked irritated but she unconsciously took a half-step back, and that gave me an opportunity to push past her. I felt the carnation blooms brush against her shoulder. Now at least she wouldn't be able to slam the door in my face.

"Do you want me to put those in water?" I heard, among the shouts of the young guests, the voice of Laurie Batarski. Laurie, the first woman since my mother to slap me in the face, was Nora's friend, just my *mazel*.

Laurie was also a little sharper than Nora. She probably recognized my distinctive heels: she wouldn't know they were Chloe, but she'd know they weren't from Payless Shoe Source.

She yanked the bouquet out of my hand, shaking tiny leaves to the floor.

"You!"

"Oh, my God!"

"Who is it? Who is it?

Half a dozen kids gathered round us. Past them, in the living room, I saw a man dressed like Professor Frink from *The Simpsons,* with bowtie, pocket protector and nerdy black-framed glasses, holding a test tube. That must be Science Matt, in the middle of his show. Cesar, the birthday boy, was next to him, smiling modestly. "You're a smart young man!" I heard Science Matt say.

"It's Jack's mom!"

Emily, Laurie's daughter, with her sidekick Sophie by her side.

"*You* get out of here," Laurie commanded me. She tossed the carnations to the floor with a broad gesture that had them strewn all over the tiny foyer.

"I didn't come here to talk to you," I said self-righteously.

Laurie glared at Nora. The reason they were friends was because Nora eagerly imitated Laurie and helped her to execute her most evil schemes.

"No one here has anything to say to you or to your killer son." Nora was equally self-righteous. "He's caused enough trouble for *my* boy."

"Yes," Laurie agreed, adding craftily, "Didn't Cesar say that he wished Tyler were here to share this special day?"

By now the rest of the kids had abandoned Science Matt to crowd near the door, trampling the carnations. Cesar and Dylan had not joined us. I could see them, past the Moms from Hell, in the living room, looking at me with a mix of surprise and fear.

"Did he?" Nora frowned, then quickly amended, "Oh, yeah, right he did."

Emily, Laurie's daughter, had first thrown her arms around her mother but seeing that I was the one causing the disturbance she hung back, wide-eyed, then took her friend Sophie's hand.

"Nora, we have to talk. Cesar is hiding something, and I want to know what it is."

This was too much drama for Science Matt to resist. He joined us in the over-crowded foyer. Cesar and Dylan still stayed behind, pretending to examine his beakers and vials.

"My boy? My boy? If he did anything, it was try to include *your* weirdo kid."

Emily had tears in her eyes. She tugged Laurie's sweatshirt. "Mama, don't let Cesar's mom talk about Jack that way."

A couple of the boys stomped on the surviving carnations blooms on the floor; others quickly joined in. Sophie moved quickly to rescue the few still intact, almost getting her own hand stomped on in the process.

Other kids pummeled me with questions.

"Is Jack going to jail?"

"Where is he going to school?"

"Are you having another baby?" one of the girls sniggered. "Or are you just getting fat?"

"We miss you!" Sophie said. Since *her* mother wasn't present she was free to express her support.

"I have something to show Cesar," I said. I swayed back and forth on my heels, but the birthday boy was no longer anywhere to be seen. Neither was Dylan.

"There's nothing you have to say to Cesar that you can't say to Nora," Laurie told me, crossing her arms and tapping one foot.

"Fine. You can all see this, then." I brought out the picture that had been posted on my refrigerator, that Jack had scrawled at the park. I had stashed it in my purse, slung over my shoulder. "Here." I held it out. "I bet that Cesar or Dylan can tell me what it is."

Nora humphed as she took it. She was Laurie's eager hatchet woman, helping the latter maintain her power base, but she bent the rules a little when it came to dress, favoring strappy tanks and items such as the leopard print mini-skirt she sported now, which showcased her trucker's-mud-flap figure. "What the hell is this?" she snorted. "It looks like a two year old drew it."

"Let me see that." Laurie yanked it from Nora's hands. Nora flinched but did not otherwise object. A couple of the boys, already benefitting from early growth spurts, tried in turn to yank it from hers.

"Emily, you used to decipher some of Jack's work for me." Laurie did not take her eyes off me as she passed the paper to her daughter. "When I was grading papers for Ms. Scarborough."

Emily looked at me as she took it. "I can't tell, Mama," she said helplessly.

"Sure you can," Laurie encouraged her. She rarely touched her daughter but she was always eager to boast of her abilities. "It's gibberish, that's why you're having a little trouble. Didn't we always have trouble with Jack's... 'work'?"

"I'll tell you what it is," I said. "It's a map."

"A map," Nora ridiculed me. "Cesar!" she yelled. "Come talk to this crazy woman."

"So you have a fifth-grader, too?" Science Matt asked me. "When he has a birthday party, you might consider hiring professional entertainment."

He held out his card. I took it.

"I don't just do a science show. I can do Professor Dumbledore, a real good Justin Timberlake ... the red Crime Conqueror...."

"Oh, *her* son would just *love* that," Nora said. "Wouldn't Jack love that, Anna?"

"We miss Jack," Emily said sorrowfully. "We wish — " But her mother glared at her and she stopped.

"Cesar!" Nora shouted.

"I wouldn't co-operate with her," Laurie reproached her. "She never came to any 'Macramé Saturdays.' Not one."

Several kids had spread out among what were only a few rooms, and one of them brought back a wary Cesar and an abashed-looking Dylan.

Without further ceremony I grabbed Jack's drawing from Laurie.

"I have no idea what that is," Cesar said.

He might have been smart but he wasn't a good liar. He went through the broad motion of showing it to Dylan who also struggled to look blank. In fact, the paper wasn't decipherable to me. It was just crooked circles that looked like amoebas, a few lines, and marks that were halfway between Xs and asterisks. But Cesar and Dylan had just confirmed my suspicions.

"Come on, Cesar," I said. "Jack drew this for me. I bet I know what it is. I bet you know what it is, too. You, too, Dylan."

Cesar shrugged and mumbled with a guilty stare at his mother.

Even Nora could not overlook Cesar's response. She and Laurie exchanged hardly noticeable glances. Then Laurie spoke up for Nora. "You just get out of here and leave our children alone."

"She's not bothering us, Mama," Emily said.

"You're always looking out for the underprivileged," Laurie said to Emily, "and I'm proud of you. But some people just deserve what they get."

"It doesn't matter," I said. "I'm not leaving."

"Then I'll call the police," Nora said.

Several of the boys *ooohed.*

"This will make a good item for the paper," Laurie agreed. "Call 911," she instructed Nora.

"I got something to do first. Gimme that." Nora took the paper from Cesar and ripped it, first in two broad, noisy strokes, and then, glaring at me, in a frenzy of movement in which she reduced it to confetti.

***

"Please tell them to hurry, Miss," Nora said into the phone. "I think she might be dangerous."

But I wasn't going anywhere. I wasn't exactly panting to see the police, but I had foreseen this possibility.

"Wait 'til they hear about this at the next PROTECT meeting," Laurie gloated.

When a patrol car double-parked in front of the house most of the boys, and some of the girls, rushed to the windows.

"He's coming up the walk!"

"He's got a gun!"

"He's got handcuffs!"

"He's got a club!"

My heart pounded. I closed my eyes, resolved to appear strong even if I weren't feeling it.

Then the policeman blocked the light from the door. He was a big man with blonde eyebrows. A couple of the boys reached out surreptitiously to touch one of the many weapons on his belt, leaping back on contact.

When he saw me he grinned, then quickly forced the grin into a stern look.

It was Officer Armstrong. Back in June I had thrown up on his shoes. But that was after we had spoken in whispers about our ASD sons. I knew from that brief encounter that he was not going to pistol-whip me just to satisfy the rage of two nutty moms. Okay, *three* nutty moms.

"So what's the trouble here, Ma'am?" He sounded as though he were trying to imitate John Wayne. He certainly had a greater gift for mimicry than Val.

"This woman — " Nora cried shrilly, "just broke into my house, and now she refuses to leave."

"Search her," Laurie demanded.

"Yeah, maybe she's packing!" one of the boys said hopefully.

"The dispatcher made it sound much more serious. A 186 in progress." Officer Armstrong regarded me and from the upturned corner of his mouth I understood both that he recognized me and that I was not to say anything about our previous encounter. He grinned for a general audience. "I can see why you might have needed help with crowd management. But it's not really a matter for an LEO. You know, Ma'am — " John Wayne again — "there are fines for making false reports. There are real crimes we have to attend to."

"I only wanted to talk to Nora," I said respectfully.

"Like *that* would ever happen," Nora said. "I wouldn't throw a bucket-a water on you if you were on fire."

Behind Officer Armstrong I saw a stout older woman coming down the sidewalk. It was Celia Shumacher, Dylan's mother.

"Hello!" she called out cheerfully when she saw the open door. "I'm not late, am I? I hate to inconvenience a hostess. You're always so kind to Dylan, Mrs. Ruiz. Oh, dear." She stopped as soon as she saw that there was a policeman there.

"Hi, Mom," Dylan acknowledged her uneasily. They were the first words he had spoken.

"If you'll excuse us, Ma'am," Officer Armstrong said. "Mrs. Kagen," he addressed me a bit gruffly and no one seemed to wonder how it was he knew my name, "maybe you should tell me your side of the story."

I did, quickly, in spite of multiple interruptions. Celia had only been the first of the parents who had arrived in a phalanx now. I was happy to see that neither Raven nor Janis was among them.

"So," I concluded for Officer Armstrong, "I think my son drew a map of Minotaur Island."

At which statement Nora insisted indignantly, "There never was no map."

"Mrs. Ruiz tore it up," I explained.

"That is *so* not true," Laurie defended Nora hotly.

A few of the kids weighed in on my side but their sketchy stories were lost in the general confusion. One dad tried to escape with his daughter, who was whining that Cesar hadn't served his birthday cake yet. Others — parents and children alike — were helping themselves to the same cake, even though the candles remained unlit on the top layer. They sucked frosting off their thumbs and settled in to watch the rest of the drama unfold like Monday Night Football.

"Well, it doesn't really matter," I said. I reached into my purse. "What I showed Mrs. Ruiz was a photocopy. Here's the original."

I pulled it from a zippered pocket in my purse.

Nora and Laurie gasped the loudest. Then silence fell: a silence heavy enough that we could all hear the two boys who'd found their way into Cesar's bedroom trying to guess his password.

Jason Armstrong took the drawing. It was the one Jack had done in purple crayon. He squinched up his face. It could easily have passed as a much younger child's scribbles, and had looked that way to me for a long time — until the shape that might have been a Y caught my attention. Maybe I was trying too hard. Maybe I was more suggestible than I thought. But the more I looked at it, the more I could see trees and rocks.

Jason Armstrong hooked his thumbs over his belt loops. He was a little too burly to effectively jut out one hip but he did his best and his best was good enough.

"Maybe we should go to the station to figure this out."

***

Jason's pronouncement set off a noisy discussion. Nora was defiant at first, but Jason did Jack Webb from *Dragnet.* "These boys are part of an ongoing investigation, Ma'am."

Nora looked to Laurie for support, and was surprised that it was not forthcoming. But Laurie liked rules, and it wasn't her kid who was in trouble.

"Why, Nora," Celia said earnestly. "I know Dylan would like to help out. Wouldn't you Dylan?"

Dylan didn't answer. He stood close to Cesar, looking protective.

Nora protested, "We already know what happened!"

"Then there can't be any harm in talking, can there?" Celia was in her early sixties, with gray hair tinted a pale peach and teased into a bouffant. "Anything we can do to help that poor boy's family, Officer. Dylan's father and I are so distressed about Dylan being there. We know he wants to help." She cast a loving but strict eye on her son. "Why hasn't your friend Mairead been to church lately?" Celia asked me then. The Shumachers also attended Sunset Word of God. "She and her friend Kelly are delightful. I love their accents."

"Officer." Science Matt held out a card. "Do *you* have any children?"

***

The four of us were in the interrogation room at Richmond Station: Jason and me, Cesar and Dylan. The room was cramped, with a rectangular table perpendicular to the obligatory two-way mirror, and a few file cabinets on one wall giving us little leg room. I didn't ask Jason if it were true that the police controlled the temperature to make suspects more uncomfortable. I did know that I felt overheated.

Nora and Celia had agreed not to watch from behind the two-way mirror, so that Officer Armstrong could in all honesty tell their children that the interview was private.

He did fail to mention that I would be there, however.

Another thing Jason Armstrong didn't mention was that he was not going to involve any other police officer nor any of his superiors. What the Captain didn't know wouldn't go downtown. It wasn't as big a risk as it sounded. "This stuff happens more than you'd think," he told me.

We sat, and as hard as it was, I let Jason do all the talking. For now.

"Okay, guys," he said, "just start from the beginning."

"There's nothing more to tell," Cesar said imperiously, "besides what we've been telling everyone from the first day."

But Dylan squirmed.

"We're not trying to get you in trouble," Jason said, removing his nylon jacket to reveal his bearish frame. "Maybe we can make this go away. But not without a little co-operation. Otherwise…."

"Otherwise *what?*" Cesar challenged.

Jason had the end of a pencil in his mouth. "Otherwise we can subpoena you to testify at that grand jury hearing next week. Under oath. You haven't been under oath before, have you?"

Cesar's look said *make me,* but Dylan said, "All right." His voice went from bass to soprano between "all" and "right." Cesar glared at him, but I could tell Dylan had been waiting for this moment.

***

Cesar and Dylan had come to Minotaur Island with a carefully planned agenda. They had been best friends for years; Cesar the brains, and Dylan the athlete. No one was going to pick on Cesar for being a nerd with Dylan as his pal. I remembered with remorse my mistrustful attitude toward Dylan on that first day.

When Ms. Scarborough announced the field trip two months before, Cesar, spurred by his natural intellectual curiosity, went to research the island's history, and learned about the ill-fated occupation by the Healerists and their tragic end. He thrived on just such mysteries.

With Dylan as companion, he went to the library. Then he went to museums and talked to their curators. He and Dylan even interviewed a couple of elderly *Chronicle* reporters spending their final days at Laguna Honda, the city's public nursing home.

Under the Freedom of Information Act, he was able to get copies of Theodore Merrick's journals, and applied the system used by the authors of *The Bible Code* to find hidden clues. This decoding shored up the evidence of his least reliable source: the Laguna-Honda resident who thought he was talking to Edward R. Murrow.

Cesar began to identify with Theodore Merrick, leader of the Healerists, a prophet with no honor in his own country who met such an unjust end. Cesar also became convinced that the Healerists had left behind their communally held valuables, buried at the summit of the island, but never found. Those valuables included women's jewelry, cash, and at least one cult member's rare coin collection.

The culmination of all this work was a map. He had since destroyed it, and he would not admit that it was similar to the one that Jack had doodled. But he did admit to a map.

The path to the treasure was supposed to be marked by symbols carved in either rocks or tree trunks, and then, when the trees ended near the gully, there would be several heavy stones marked with crude notches. But after twenty years it was inevitable that some of the clues were gone; the heaviest rocks and the thickest tree trunk were vulnerable to the elements.

Cesar knew that one of Jack's unique gifts was the ability to pick out details that were invisible to the average observer. And, although Cesar had brought along a compass, he had never been able to determine exactly which was north on the map he created. Jack could orient them, and then Cesar's compass could take over.

When Cesar and Dylan saw Jack head for the bathroom they saw their chance to invite him along. The bathroom was empty except for Jack talking merrily to himself while he splashed pee around the urinal. They told him a distorted version of the story. Early 49ers had buried their gold on the island, they said, like pirate treasure, you know, man, and they wanted him to help them find it. They would give him a share.

I interrupted with a question.

"Where does Tyler come in?"

"He caught us in the bathroom, dude," Cesar said disgustedly. "He made us take him."

"He was in one of the stalls," Dylan elaborated. "We checked the stalls. I still don't know why we didn't see him." Apologetically, "He said he needed money real bad. That his dad needed it for the IRS."

"Blow fish coming up for air," Cesar warned Dylan. To us: "He said he'd go straight to Ms. Scarborough if we didn't take him. *And* he wanted *half* of what we found."

"He was a jerk." Dylan had to agree. "I mean I'm sorry about what happened, but he was an ... a jerk."

"His parents were fighting a lot," Dylan added hastily now, to excuse Tyler. "He was afraid — "

"Dude, his dad wasn't even his dad," Cesar corrected him. "Remember? His parents weren't married and his so-called 'dad' never adopted him."

Dylan sunk a little lower in his chair.

"Tyler was always giving *Dyl* a hard time about being adopted," Cesar explained indignantly. "He said his way was better, 'cause it meant the dude really *wanted* to be his dad, like *that* made any sense." He rolled his eyes. "It doesn't matter, dude," he said, slinging an arm around Dylan's shoulder and then engaging him in a similar series of fist-pounding and palm-stroking that I had seen Val and his road beasts engage in the morning of their departure. "Being adopted is just the same as the regular way."

I might not feel that way in a few months when I was seven centimeters dilated, but otherwise I agreed.

Dylan participated in the hand routines listlessly at first, but then with increasing finesse, concluding not just with a smile but a mighty high-five.

Pleased to see that Dylan was more cheerful, Cesar turned to us again. "Tyler's so-called dad hadn't even been with his mom very long."

And now Mom, the self-styled "Mrs." Margaret Gaines was gone, and no one knew where. How convenient. "So what happened when you left the bathroom?"

First Cesar gave Jack the map to study. Jack committed it to memory instantly. Then the four boys disappeared into the bushes and started up the hill. After one glance at the map, Jack led them, continuing his self-talk, variously imitating airplanes and penguins, and tripping frequently. As they got closer he noticed the first of the markings. It was weathered out to near-undectability — but it *was* a peace sign. On Jack's rendition it had become a simple Y. I must have seen it upside down.

"It was awesome," Dylan said. "There were like a million rocks all over the place and he found just this one."

Jack had identified true north, and their plan had been to send him back to the meadow, but they discovered that they still needed him to detect more clues. Many were gone, but the faded peace sign directed

Jack to where three eucalyptus trees formed an isosceles triangle. He recognized the trees as eucalyptus from the shape of their leaves on Cesar's more intricate map — leaves that were similar enough to some species of cannabis, to inspire Cesar and Dylan's later story. The top tree pointed to the next marking: a ballpoint pen, buried upright halfway along the shaft. No more than a millimeter of the plunger was left above ground.

"I woulda needed a freakin' magnifying glass for that," Cesar said.

The rocks that were supposed to guard the site were nowhere to be found, but the gully that opened up fifty feet away was further evidence that the boys were in the right spot. They had wanted to bring tools with which to dig but feared that anything large or sharp enough to be of any assistance would be seized by the rangers when we were all searched after disembarking the ferry. So they went to work picking up fallen branches.

"The branches!" I interrupted. "They weren't walking sticks, then."

"Well, they coulda been," Cesar shrugged. "We might have used them for walking sticks later."

Jack just kept picking up twigs and pebbles. Tyler was cranky and restless.

"He just kept asking us about the money. How much did we think it would be and stuff like that," Dylan said. "We couldn't get him to help us at all."

Jack wanted to help, but all he could do with the branch they gave him was to make meaningless marks in the dust. His self-talk was getting on their nerves and after a few minutes Cesar told him just to sit down on the biggest rock and wait. Cesar and Dylan worked as fast as they could, counting correctly on the fact that they would be hard to find, hoping *in*correctly that no one would come looking for a while.

Then Tyler snuck up behind Jack and yanked the pawn from his pocket. The situation deteriorated quickly.

"Leave him alone," Dylan said.

"Why? He's just a retard. Here, you want to see him do tricks like a monkey?"

"You're the retard." Cesar was perspiring heavily in the heat. *"He got us up here, didn't he? Knock it off."*

"Squeak, monkey, squeak!" Tyler was only a little taller than Jack, but he held the pawn just out of reach. *"Can you eat a banana with your feet, monkey?"*

Jack whimpered. "My pawn! My pawn.... *"*

The boys stopped their story. Dylan rested his fingers on the table near me. A few hairs sprouted near the joints.

Finally Jason prompted, "And then?"

"Give it back, Dude," Cesar said.

Tyler turned on him. "You think you're hot shit, man, doncha? You are like a total freak."

"Stop it, Tyler," Dylan said. He lowered his head and pawed the ground with one foot, a bull about to charge.

This was a signal to Cesar; Dylan and he were always two halves of the same mind. Cesar dropped his digging stick and grabbed Tyler around the waist. He wouldn't have been able to hold him for more than one second, but it was precisely in the middle of that second that Dylan butted him.

"And Tyler went down the gully," I said.

"It wasn't Dylan's fault, Dude," Cesar complained. "He did it to himself."

Dylan tried not to sound defensive. "He did get all kind of melodramatic, like the dudes at church when they speak in tongues."

"What do you mean?" Jason asked rather sharply.

"He threw his arms around like that demon guy in *HellaTrash*, like he was cursing us. Trying to make Dyl feel bad."

"It was just a *little* sock in the gut."

"We went right down the gully to help him — "

" — and he was unconscious — "

"A carrot."

"That's when we made a plan — "

" — to put the blame on Jack."

"Because we didn't think Cesar was dead!" Dylan's voice cracked, either with emotion or the onset of puberty. "If we'd known *that* — "

Cesar scoffed, "It wounta mattered." He'd been trying to sound tough, and now he tried to sound tougher.

Dylan explained, "We never thought he'd get in so much trouble."

"Because," Cesar sneered, "everyone is always making excuses for him. He gets away with *murder*."

Silence.

Murder, murder, murder. I closed my eyes to block out Cesar's face, but instead saw Tyler stretched out in the gully. I already knew the answer to the question I asked next. "And how did you get Jack to promise to keep all this secret?"

"We said we'd be his friends from now on."

"That we'd have him over to our houses and stuff."

"The movies."

"Birthday parties."

"We'd hang out."

Jason's handgun was holstered at his belt. He edged away from me.

"Well, boys, I think we might have what we need." Jason wrote on a notepad and angled it toward me so that I could read: "They just have to repeat this to the A.G."

I nodded. Our impromptu interrogation wasn't going to get Cesar or Dylan investigated and neither of their families had enough money to interest Jimmy Gaines. But it would prevent an indictment being handed down for Jack. That was enough for me.

But the boys — or Cesar at least — might as well have seen the paper. "You said you'd keep this private," he accused.

"I said we could 'make it go away,'" Jason reminded him. "You won't get in trouble."

"You aren't recording this or nothing?" Cesar asked. "That would be a violation of my fourth amendment rights."

"Ceeze," Dylan said, "this has been bugging me. Let's just do a data dump, huh?"

"No way," Cesar said, with neither anger nor room for discussion. He fixed cold eyes first on Jason, and then on me. "We don't trust you. You tricked us here."

"No, sir, we did not," Jason countered. He had rolled up the blue sleeves of his uniform, and he rested bulky arms on the particle wood table. "We had both your permission and permission from your parents to talk to you."

"Well, we didn't say nuttin'," Cesar declared. "Did we, D-man?"

Dylan looked not just older then, but old. Weary. His skin had gone sallow.

"You protected Jack before," I said, remembering their account of how they tried to stave off Tyler's attack.

"And look what happened," Cesar retorted. "He's trouble, dude."

***

"What do we do?" I asked Jason when the boys had gone home.

Jason Armstrong had been shot at, scaled walls that would have given Spiderman pause, driven a hundred and twenty miles an hour in pursuit of a suspect. But he was unsure what to do about these two pre-teens.

They confessed: they were surprised that the adults in charge did not excuse Jack's behavior and that the incident grew in the both public and private imaginations, and so they said that Jack had the digging stick as a weapon. It was a pure invention.

But this "confession" was really a boast, and they metaphorically took the fifth after that, though we spent another twenty minutes trying to sweat them out. "That's our story and we're stickin' to it," Cesar said. Dylan ambivalently cast his lot with his friend.

"Hang tight," Jason said now. "I guess." He drew a tic-tac-toe grid on his pad. "We can't force them to testify at the grand jury, and we can't force them to let us testify either. I'll pass along what I've learned today, but from what I read about this case, what's-her-name Pasquale will push for an indictment anyway."

I rubbed my chin until I felt the skin grow raw. The defense could subpoena the boys, and if on his own, Dylan would probably tell the truth, but the only thing he might be more loyal to than the truth was his friend Cesar, the boy who had been Copernicus at the age of seven. Cesar, with his innocent face and clear, honest eyes. Then it would be our word against Wally and the Beaver.

"Why did you do this for me?" I asked Jason. "There was nothing but trouble in it for you." A complaint from the parents; a reprimand or worse from above.

He showed me the game he'd drawn. "Your move." I saw that he configured the game in such a way that he could win two ways. No matter where I placed an O to block his X, I was screwed.

"We have to stick together," he said, and I knew what he meant.

CHAPTER TWENTY-ONE
THE RETURN OF THE NATIVE

I pumped the brake to let my van edge forward in six inch increments until we were positioned exactly outside the front doors of the school. There, Tiffany, though rushing as usual, waved to me with one hand while motioning Jack to descend with the other.

"Bye, Mom," Jack said. "See you this afternoon!"

He almost lost his step on the running board but regained his balance in time to waddle after another student. "Hi, Fletcher!"

So happy. So oblivious. Some kids his age read the newspaper. Or surfed the web to learn about something more than the cast of *Crime Conquerors*.

***

When I got home and put the key in the lock, I found that it was already open.

I jumped back from the knob, instinct telling me to flee the duplex and make my own 911 call. Instead, with fibrillating heart, I turned the knob again and went inside. I immediately heard barking. And then Val, crowing cheerfully from the bedroom: "Right in here, Banana Boat Baby. Come and rock *my* boat!"

He was naked, or at least so I guessed; the sheet was pulled up just high enough to cover his navel. He reached over to pat the empty pillow where my own head had been the night before. "C'm'ere, you."

"Jack's here," I said, standing at the foot of the bed. "I mean, he's moved in."

"I kind of figured, from the action figure in my butt." He pulled the green *Crime Conqueror* from under the sheet.

"Are you okay with that?"

"Of course," he cooed. "Where've you been?"

"Dropping him off at school." I actually stamped my foot. "His case goes to the grand jury in two days … grand jury? That ring a bell at all? Or did you scale mountains so high that you suffered some anoxia?"

"Sadly, I did not scale mountains high *enough*," Val said good-naturedly. "My dream is to break the one-mile mark some — wait!" He gripped the sheet. "Did you say the case is finally coming to the grand jury?"

I nodded.

"Oh, my God. You said she'd drag it on past November."

"I said she might try," I corrected him, and I sounded petty to myself when I re-iterated, "*Might.*"

"It has been going on so long," he mumbled to himself. "What changed?" He was all attention now.

"Pressure from different sides, I guess." I leaned over and picked up the action figure, causing Baby to apply her own pressure to several of my internal organs. Suddenly I didn't want to talk about it after all. Going over the details was too much effort for the possible relief it might afford.

He bowed his head. "It sounds like you needed me and I wasn't there."

"What was your first clue?"

"Honey, I am so sorry. How was I supposed to know?"

"How were you supposed to know? Are you kidding? You leave me broke, pregnant, under investigation by Child Protective Services...."

He shook his lowered head. "I'll never forgive myself. But I was gone only a few weeks," he reminded me plaintively.

A few weeks. It had been closer to two months. And it felt like much, much longer.

"Everything's going to be okay. You're the *uberfrau.* And I have a strong karmic feeling about this."

"If non-Hindus actually understood the concept of 'karma,'" I said through gritted teeth, "they would realize that I have to wait for my next incarnation in order to be rewarded or punished for current behavior."

"Anne Banane...."

"Are you going to start with how I 'worry too much?'" I asked. "Just because I'm a worrier doesn't mean there isn't something to worry about."

He looked down at the old chenille bedspread, and he seemed to withdraw into himself. "It was a mistake to leave when I did, wasn't it?"

"That was sort of the point I was making, yes."

"Banana Boat. I don't have a good answer. You *do* take things too seriously. I stand by that. But I guess I don't take them seriously enough."

"You think?" I rotated the green Crime Conqueror. Was it Morgan or Montel?

Val's fingers played with the sheet and he looked in the general direction of the window, but his eyes were unfocused. "I don't blame you for being angry."

"Good."

He finally turned to me. The look in his eyes was unfamiliar — and unsettling. "You know, I'd understand if — if — "

"If ... what?"

"You know." He hung his head.

Now I sighed. "I don't want that."

A smile split his face. His expression reminded me of Jack when I offered to take him to Toys-R-Us. "Will you tell me about the baby?"

I'd been dying to tell him.

I stepped out of my shoes — the heels were getting lower by the day — and crawled on my knees, though with some difficulty, up the bed, where I settled under his arm. "You can really feel her move now." I unbuttoned the chambray shirt, starting at the bottom.

"Really?" He put his hand on my belly and waited. When my skin jumped, Val jumped, too, pulling his hand away. He looked so startled that I laughed. He laughed then, too, and then we gazed at each other with big smiles, and I felt, for the first time, as though we were parents.

"I missed you," I said, when he lay down beside me again. The sun glinted off the downy hairs on his chest. The bed felt like ours again, instead of a piece of borrowed furniture. He stroked my hair, familiarly, and the past few weeks melted away.

I'd lived without him, and I knew I could, but it was so nice having him there, his warm, bare skin and my own bare skin, shivering, when his fingertips returned first to my belly and then traveled south.

***

So this was how it happened: sex and love.

As mysterious a process — to me — as breeding a mandarin orange and a grapefruit to get a tangelo. And the results even sweeter.

After a little while, he amused himself by resting his hand on my belly, waiting to feel the kicks. "It just wasn't very real to me before," he said in a small, awed voice. "This ... this changes everything."

"That's the way it is sometimes." I almost added, "for men." But then I remembered how different my first pregnancy had been. Until I had to push Jack through my cervix, he hadn't seemed very real to me. Not the way this little girl was.

I finally asked him about his trip. He told me about the idiot who fed Elsie s'mores ("Biker and Smith has to stop me from *kicking* his sorry ass"), about the paperbacks he traded with fellow travelers along the way ("I read *Siddhartha* for the first time, and it really got me thinking"), about the dawns and sunsets over stark, uncluttered mountains.

"Are you really okay with Jack being here?"

He better give the right answer.

And then I didn't even hear his answer because the reality of what we were facing swept over me. The glorious morning turned dark. *What kind of mother — ?* I'd let my — my *boyfriend* take me so far out of myself so that I'd forgotten for a good half hour that Jack was part of this picture.

"You believe me, don't you?" Val said.

"Oh ... yes, of course."

From his face I could tell that he *had* given the right answer.

"You've got to try not to worry."

He was so patient with me. I was so ungrateful, always focusing on what he wasn't doing. He'd help me get through the next couple of days. So what if he hadn't been burning with professional ambition over the summer. He was a caretaker by nature. If feeling the baby move could affect him this deeply, then holding her in his arms would complete the necessary change. Alex was helping out, doing what he did best: throwing money at a problem.

We'd get by.

"We'll get through this," he echoed my thoughts.

"There's one last thing — well, I hate to use the verb 'worry,' but... 'concerned' isn't much better."

A short laugh. "You get one last one."

"It's Elsie."

Val sank back down next to me, preoccupied. "It'll be hard for her to go back to city life after all this time in the great outdoors. But don't worry, Banana Boat. She'll be fine."

"Goddam it," I burst out. "I was talking about Jack!"

"Oh, honey, don't worry about that."

"What do you mean, don't worry about that?" I was closer than I had been in a long time to erupting into tears. I was not blaming it on pregnancy hormones. I was always crazy.

"I *hoped* this day would come," I sniffled. "But I've had to get him used to so many new things, I mean, his teacher is really nice and after the first couple of days he really settled down ... so I stopped thinking about it."

"It?"

"Jack. Is. Afraid. Of. Dogs."

Val tucked a clump of my hair first behind one ear, then the other. "You have a short memory. Don't you remember how good I am with him? I got him on a bike in one day. If *Il Duce* hadn't jumped in — "

I winced.

He switched gears diplomatically. "I am trained in desensitization techniques. I can help Jack get over his phobia."

"We tried desensitization — "

"You haven't tried it lately. And you haven't tried it with me. It's so simple ... we start with pictures, then Elsie in the next room.... And then not only can we all live together but it's going to make his life a lot easier."

All live together. I wanted him to wear a t-shirt with those words on it. For however well Jack seemed to be adjusting, I was tired. The dishes. The laundry. Grocery shopping. Planning something for dinner every night. Packing a lunch for the next morning. And why, oh why, couldn't I convince Jack not to stop pouring juice until *after* it overflowed the cup?

And all of this was nothing compared to the homework. Alex and I had both set our sights on keeping him up academically with the middle of the class and surprisingly, we'd come close. On multiple choice or math tests, he did well, and when there were papers to write we helped him a lot. Maybe more than a lot.

But now there were no more tutors or Mairead or Alex. It was no longer "sometimes" me, it was always me, and Jack, yelling at each other across the kitchen table every night: "If you don't stop stimming and start concentrating...." "But I hate homework! Homework...."

"If you can work that out," I breathed, "I will owe you my life."

***

I tapped my fingers against the steering wheel as I waited in the pick-up line. I'd barely made it on time. The school day had vanished into the bedclothes. And Jack could keep time for the military.

Just tell him about Elsie....

Don't tell him about Elsie. Maybe he'll surprise you....

I hadn't even talked about Val since Jack had come to live with me: I was that unsure that Val would return. This was just about the worst possible way to introduce a child to a stepparent. Maybe instead of taking

Jack home we could go down to the wharf and he could watch his pregnant mother try to pick up sailors.

I realized the line of cars hadn't been moving. I looked up from the vortex of the steering wheel. There was a commotion ahead: milling students and parents clogging the main doors. In my rearview mirror I saw that the school bus on the corner hadn't left yet.

Given the dark tendency of my thoughts it was almost natural that I assumed that something bad had happened to Jack, or that history would repeat itself in the form of another disaster: A fire. Valuables stolen from a locker. And Jack accused of being the arsonist or thief.

I jumped from the van, leaving my hazards on, and rushed to join the growing mob at the doors.

"Clear out!" Principal Kitty Seldon's voice was commanding.

A few people obeyed her, steering their children out with them, but most tried to press in through the opening. I was one of the offenders, but I wasn't going to turn around until I had Jack in my crosshairs if not in my hands.

From sidewalk to hall the crowd gathered in a shape like an exclamation point: a fat line leading to a circle. It took me several panicked moments to identify Jack. He was outside the circle, with the same lost expression he had the day Alex had returned him to me. The others, parents and children, were crowded around a disturbing Something.

I became aware of a distant siren, quickly growing louder

"What part of 'clear out' don't you understand?" Kitty bellowed at us all and now that I had Jack clearing out was all I wanted to do. The others obeyed Kitty as well. As the circle dissolved I saw that people had been gathered around the prone body of a child Jack's age. I shuddered. *Not again. Oh, God, not again.*

Outside the paramedics were jumping from the ambulance. I kept my head low. "Get in, Boychik." With the remote key, I got the automatic door to swing open for him

"Kevin waved his arms," Jack said as he stepped on the running board. "Then he fell down. Down...."

As long as it had nothing to do with you.

Call me cruel, call me insensitive. My first thought should have been for the other boy. I would think of him once I got Jack the fuck out of there — and out of there before anyone remembered that he'd been associated with such a disaster before.

As for Jack himself, if he had more to say, it was lost behind the hum of the mechanized door closing. I re-mounted the driver's seat, put the car in gear and my left-turn signal on. Someone in the other lane would let me through. Eventually.

"He has epilepsy. 'Lepsy....'"

"Yes, dear."

Man in blue car, please—? No?

I stuck my hand out the window and waved frantically.

"Will he be *all right?*" Jack pressed.

I didn't answer, though he asked me three more times, until the compassionate driver of a Honda Civic waved me in. Then I said. "You're worried about the boy who got hurt."

It was the perfect opaque therapy statement, but Jack became impatient. "He didn't get hurt. He has epilepsy. 'Lepsy....'"

This second time his words penetrated. "He must have had a seizure, then," I concluded. "The ambulance was there. I'm sure he'll be fine." I wasn't sure; I was woefully ignorant of epilepsy. But there was no point in worrying Jack until it was necessary.

"It was just like Tyler," Jack said. "Tyler....'"

His echolalia flared under stress. I decided to pull over. Jack under stress was not a Jack to introduce to Elsie.

I blocked someone's driveway and tugged on my shoulder harness so that I could twist around. "Jack, remember Val?"

"With the bike."

"Yes. Well, it turns out he has a dog...."

"I don't like dogs! Dogs...'"

"I know, but...." But what? How in the name of God were we ever going to work this out?

"I'll protect you," I promised.

"You can't protect me!" He flapped his hands.

No, I couldn't. Before he was born, I let something go wrong. "Now, Jack, listen to me...."

Wait.

"What about Tyler?" I asked.

"You can't protect me!"

"The dog will be gone." Elsie couldn't be there when Jack first came home. That was all there was to that. "I promise. Jack, what did you say about Tyler?"

"He ... fell down."

"When Cesar held him and Dylan pushed him with his head." I repeated the other boys' description, picturing the *oomph* and Tyler rolling out of sight. "What happened to Kevin that was like Tyler?"

He remembered himself. "I'm not supposed to tell. Tell....'"

I reached for him but the seat belt restrained me. My fingertips quivered in the air six inches from his face. "Jack. Cesar and Dylan aren't your friends."

"Yes, they are! They are...."

"You'll make other friends." *Please God.* "Real friends don't ask you to lie. Not about something like this."

Jack considered, and then his face cleared. I'd seen this look before, occasionally: a moment of pure understanding. It might have been like trying to read by lightning, but each time I saw it I swore that one day that lightning would start a fire storm.

"He made his arms go stiff. Stiff...."

"Did he flail — " No, Jack wouldn't understand "flail" — "did he throw his arms around — " *like that demon guy in* HELLATRASH, Dylan had described it.

"Yeah...." But Jack's focus was slipping away. I had to snatch it up long enough for one final question. "Jack, why weren't you more upset when Tyler died?"

"You said that when you die you go to heaven." He tilted his head to remind me. "There's all the food and TV you want. You said when Grandma died that I *shouldn't* be upset."

"I did say that, didn't I." I twisted back around to put my hands on the wheel. I had said a lot of stupid things over the years.

***

I made two important phone calls that day.

The first was on my cell phone from the car. I told Val that we must find temporary lodging for Elsie, until he could perform the magic of desensitization that he had promised.

He finally agreed. "I have friends with a pretty decent yard...."

Relief that Val-the-man-with-the-bike did not have a canine sidekick overshadowed other issues, and Jack survived his first night with Val — whom he remembered — by talking to him at length about his father's election. Jack knew how many precincts there were and how many people were registered to vote in each one. He also had a lot to tell Val about how he was going to have a new baby sister.

That night I Googled epilepsy and read about tonic and clonic and tonic-clonic seizures and something called SUDEP: "sudden unexplained death in epilepsy."

It was near midnight when I called Alex.

"This had better be important," he growled when he realized who it was. Then he came to attention. "Jack. Is Jack okay?"

"Jack's okay — "

He was disgruntled again. "Then why — "

"Tyler died from an epileptic seizure," I said.

CHAPTER TWENTY-TWO
A DOG DAY AFTERNOON

"I'm grateful that justice was served in the end."

So Marianne Pasquale declared into the lei of microphones that the media had formed on her chest at the press conference outside the state building.

After she failed to get her indictment.

I already knew the outcome thanks to a cell phone call from Maddy but I watched from Val's apartment, squeezing his hand until it turned white. "I told you so," he said supportively and suggestively into my ear.

"Ms. Pasquale, some critics have said that you overreached."

"…you unfairly persecuted a disabled minor…."

"…the charges were never valid…."

"…you turned this into a campaign issue…."

Marianne had not had time to prepare for the toggle switch of public opinion. Jack had gone from cross-eyed drooling serial killer to martyr of the disabled community in one morning.

"What about accusations that your office deliberately hid the autopsy and paid off the doctor who performed it?"

"Absolutely untrue." Marianne had agreed to this conference; she didn't have much choice. But now she looked as though she had just discovered that the window was barricaded.

"How do you explain the sudden reappearance of the medical examiner?"

"Dr. Windbag Liar was on vacation in the Brazilian rainforest and was unable to be reached until last week. Fortunately he returned in time to testify on the side of Mighty Mouse."

She was making slightly more sense than this but her excuses were no less feeble. So many politicians think they can get out of an embarrassing situation by sheer force of personality. Sometimes they're even right.

"How do you explain the medical examiner's testimony that the victim had Dilantin in his system?"

"And the medial malformation in his brain?"

"Is the school guilty of criminal negligence in this case?"

"Our office is reviewing the evidence."

But after this response she retreated to the high ground of "no comment" until a staff member hustled her away.

***

Gaines held his own press conference, at the Boulevard St. Michel, poorly attended. "This is a load of — " *bleep-bleep-bleep.* "I will avenge my son."

Within a few days an investigative reporter from the *Chronicle* drew the same conclusions that I had: During their short relationship, Margaret "Gaines" had never told Jimmy Gaines about Tyler's epilepsy, and she had never married him lest she become responsible for his long-standing debts to the IRS.

Jimmy Gaines continued to make noise for a while as an outraged guest on 1 a.m. radio talk shows. But he neglected the next filing deadline for his wrongful death suit.

***

I heard various bits of gossip surrounding how Patrick Riordan lost his job. Scattered as these bits were, in the end they lined up like the pieces on a newly set chess board, identical but facing opposite directions.

In the Decorrah version, the two confronted each other at campaign headquarters, which also happened to be her living room. She demanded to know by what authority he had sent out the disgraceful "dead baby" mailer. He called her a bitch and referenced the little crack babies she was wasting her life trying to rescue. When he demanded not only his last paycheck but a bonus, she revealed her discovery that he, as treasurer of the campaign, had written a number of checks to himself. "Just who is this 'Mr. Cash,' anyway?"

According to Riordan, the war of words took place in his bedroom, where lesbian Decorrah had cornered him in the past, hoping to find out what all the buzz about heterosexuality was about. He not only rebuffed her advances but told her that he had warned her about the potentially libelous mailer. When he went on to say that he was leaving the campaign, she broke down and begged him to stay, weeping, "I can't win without you!" His dignified exit line, "A man has his self-respect. I don't even want my last paycheck."

Riordan's account originated at The Recount, the first stop on his tour of local taverns that served as City Hall hang-outs.

Behind the scenes, the campaign had been unraveling for some weeks, as Decorrah's top lieutenants, Whitey and Soaring Eagle, conspired to reclaim their original positions of power. Once Riordan started drinking secretly, they were able to close ranks around Decorrah, supposedly to safeguard her, but also to control access. Their intentions were good, but their expertise lacking: They turned away interview requests from newspapers and even our local NPR affiliate.

After the charges against Jack failed to materialize, Alex's coffers swelled. And without Riordan, and without Jack as homicide suspect, PROTECT crumbled into even more fragmented hate groups, then joined the slime crawling on the underbelly of the Internet.

Whether Riordan was fired or he quit, there was only one version of the rest of the story. After The Recount, Riordan made a tour of other local political hang-outs, and on the way home he was arrested for a DUI. If convicted, it would have been his third offense.

He skipped bail.

   ***

Val said, "I've got something to show you."

He stood in Aunt Patsy's doorway. Behind him, I saw Jack and Elsie — standing no more than five feet apart. I started quickly outside.

Val restrained me. "No offense, but I think he'll do better without you."

"But he's out there with — "

"Yes, and I'm going out, too. Will you trust me?"

Now *that* question was a revolver with three chambers loaded, but I went to the front window where the shutters were drawn closed. "Here, try this." Val pulled the central bar so that the planks of the shutters flattened. "Now stand close."

When I followed his direction I had a more than adequate view of the street, only partly obstructed by horizontal wooden stripes. Since Jack was standing far away from the shutters, the effect would be reversed on him and I would be nearly invisible, on the same principle that had kept me hidden from Nora Ruiz.

"Hi, Mommy! Mommy...."

Jack waved. I wasn't dealing with Nora Ruiz anymore. I waved back.

True to his word, Val had already joined them. With my presence revealed, he didn't try to preserve the illusion that they were alone, and he, too, acknowledged me with his own, ever-optimistic, Leo-departing-on-the-Titanic wave.

I opened the shutters, and then raised the windowsill so that I could lean out a little. "Okay, Boychik."

Jack had lost interest in me. He focused on a small light brown object in his hand, studying it until his eyes crossed.

But that meant that he was ignoring Elsie, who sat on her haunches only a few feet away. She made an effort to restrain herself but sometimes failed. Then her bottom would rise from the concrete, and Jack would snap to attention. Val would bark his own sharp command, "Stay!" and the golden dog would slap her rear back down.

Wow. If only you could train your *kid* to do that.

But maybe you could. For when Val whispered in Jack's ear, Jack looked up at me, did a quick hop-footed dance and waved again. "Watch, Mommy! Watch, Mommy...."

"I'm watching, dear," I called back.

"Watch, Mommy! Watch, Mommy!"

With Val just behind him. Jack leaned so far forward that I was afraid he would tip over. "G-good dog," he quavered. He held out his trembling arm, and I saw that the brown object was a doggie biscuit, shaped like a small bone. Elsie leapt to her feet. She barked once, but Val silenced her with a brusque command. Humbled, eager to obey, she contained herself as she took a few steps forward. The bone was just long enough to make the transfer from Jack's fingers to her mouth possible without contact of skin (his) to lips or tongue (hers). Jack yanked his hand back, and Elsie crouched down, chomping her biscuit with a contentment inaccessible to homo sapiens.

"Good job, Jack, buddy."

They repeated the process twice more. At the end, Elsie approached Jack with head bowed, and he patted her on the head, exactly three times.

Both Elsie and Jack had carefully rehearsed this circus act. But since he wouldn't even enter the same house with her before, it was major progress. I would not take it away from Jack, nor let anyone take it away from me.

So satisfied was I with this moment that I didn't even protest when Val came in, leaving Jack alone outside. "Elsie will take care of *him* now." Val assured me. "We can keep an eye on them from here, at least for a few minutes."

We stood together at the window, watching our children. Val put his hand on my shoulder, and I reached across my bosom to press his hand in gratitude. I leaned my head against his side. Hope — the thing with feathers and sometimes fur, which prances on the sidewalk.

Then Val said, "I need to talk to you for minute."

To paraphrase Nora Ephron, when does "we need to talk" mean anything good?

"Yes?" I asked, after I ran my tongue around the inside of my mouth.

"I think we're going in different directions," he said softly.

My skin went cold.

"How can you tell? I thought men didn't like to ask for directions."

"Can we make this easy, Ban-Ban?"

"Yes. Let's make it easy." Neither of us spoke until I said, "I knew this was coming."

Outside, Jack was introducing himself to passing strangers. "I used to live on 'Jacks-own-Street!'" Elsie yapped once at each passer-by, making it clear that Jack was now under her protection.

Yes, I had known that Val was going to leave. I just hadn't *known* that I had known. But I had, the moment he agreed to let Elsie stay with friends, because he never would have let her go if he had thought it would be for long. No one Else for Elsie. I was the dog in Val's life, and this rapprochement between Jack and Elsie was the bone he was throwing me.

I knew long before that. I knew when I found him in Aunt Patsy's bed. I had no one to blame but myself for the many times I'd let him convince me things would be different, but I had wanted to be convinced so badly....

"I love you," he said. "I loved you when I walked out into the waiting room at St. Sair's — "

"No, you didn't," I interrupted. "It just seems like it now."

"It's the day-to-day that doesn't work for me. I tried to make it work. She was the one I really tried for." He nodded toward my stomach. "I can keep trying. Another year — maybe. And then it's going to be so much harder on all of us."

Jack was spinning. Elsie, excited by his movement, was on her feet, barking and prancing in imitation. I had to make sure she didn't get too excited.

"I've never seen the Ganges River. Or the Great Wall of China. Can you understand that, sweetheart?"

Pity me, he was begging. Jack Kerouac without a thumb with which to hitchhike, Charles Lindbergh without a plane....

"*She* has her whole life ahead of her," he said, indicating the baby again. "I have to decide what I want to do with mine."

Edmund Hillary with no mountains....

Oh, grow up, in the name of God.

"I *wanted* to make it work...."

With my free hand I cupped my belly in the universal gesture of expectant mothers. "It's not a question of whether you *want* to make it work," I accused him. "You have a daughter coming. That creates certain responsibilities whether you like it or not." Jack wasn't his son, and I had never been his wife, but the baby.... "She didn't ask to be born."

"I didn't ask her to be born, either."

This silenced me. So I was guilty of the oldest trick in the book, was I?

"*Nobody* asks to be born," he went on. "Aren't most people glad they were?" He smiled condescendingly. "And *her* — she can do anything. Be anything. It's a good time for women." He blue eyes widened with a new thought. "Maybe she'll take after me."

I did not allow myself to speak.

"And how can it be bad to have lived? How can I — we — have done anything but good by making a baby?"

I looked at the chips in the white paint of the shutters and the grit on the wooden planks.

"I always said that the one thing I wanted was to leave the world a better place. Now I know I will."

He put his hand on the center of my belly and smiled. I almost slapped it away. How dare he? So *we* made a baby, did we? He gets his rocks off and four weeks later I start throwing up, and then I go through a month of caffeine-withdrawal headaches, and now I have one tiny foot balanced on my liver and another on my spleen, but *we* did something good?

I did not shout these words aloud because I could not know the baby's mind. What if, someday, she wanted to know her father? It was my responsibility to keep that option available to her by not permanently alienating him.

He apparently interpreted my continued silence as agreement, for he smiled wistfully, and continued caressing the mound that was his daughter, too.

I even forced myself to say, "You'll be in touch."

"Of course!"

Then I wondered why I said it. I knew that there'd be no visits, no requests for pictures, no cards on birthdays. There'd be no money, either.

He would never provide for her, whether he was in my bedroom or in Mumbai. And I'd known that, too, for a long time.

Which left me with one remaining dilemma.

I loved him. I hated myself for loving him, because he was hurting me and because there was no equation between what I needed and what he gave me, or vice versa.

Yes, Val had been correct when he observed (on a day when I still lived in a mansion, on a day when I told myself I could just be his friend), that "we choose who we love." But he had been more painfully correct when he had added, "it just doesn't feel that way."

Being the dog in Val's life was bad enough; my only hope now was to stop myself from becoming a bitch. Once again, it was a classic movie that saved me. This time it was *Singin' in the Rain:* Gene Kelly, as Don Lockwood, sums up his rise in Hollywood to reporters in three words: "Always with dignity."

Hold onto what he gave me. The first man I wanted to talk to and to have sex with, the back rubs, the fun I'd forgotten was possible — the garage sales, the movies, the concerts in the park....

I had finally merged the Daddy and the Stud. But instead of getting a Staddy, I got a Dud....

For everything he did for Jack.

For giving me the daughter I wanted, even if he doesn't.

Val stepped aside from the window and held his hand out like Vanna White showing the prize to be won on *Wheel of Fortune.*

There was Jack: dancing in place, but a happy dance. He reached into his pocket for another treat, and Elsie danced, too.

"You see?" Val asked. "He's fine. He's — himself."

He held my eyes a long time, and I fought hard not to look break contact first. "I guess the 'call of the wild' is louder than 'the call of the child,'" I said.

"We were going to make this easy," he reminded me, but with a grin, and a facetious wag of his finger.

Don Lockwood might help me keep my dignity, but nothing and no one could make today easy. Women weren't supposed to need men anymore. But was it wrong to want someone to come home at night? A face across the kitchen table, the back of a man's head on the other pillow?

"We'll be fine," I said, more haughty than dignified, but it was a start. This moment would pass and become another moment, and then another, until there were no more moments left.

Frederico Garcia Lorca wrote a play cumbersomely titled, *The Love of Don Perlimplin and Belisa in the Garden.* An old man loves his young, unfaithful wife, Belisa. She, in turn, falls in love with a mysterious stranger whom she sees at night in the garden, made visible by his red cape. She doesn't know that it is her own husband in disguise; her love burns for the phantom who will fulfill all her romantic fantasies. Perlimplin stages a murder of his rival — in other words, he commits suicide. When Perlimplin dies and Belisa realizes what has taken place, she falls to her knees, wailing, "But the young man — where is *he*?"

She can't comprehend that he never existed.

"When?" I asked.

***

I found a new place for myself and Jack to live. I was still packing when Val left us, on a rainy morning two weeks later, with his passport and a smile.

CHAPTER TWENTY-THREE
STRANGE BEDFELLOWS

"This is not a good place," Jack said, as he often did when he arrived somewhere unfamiliar. "Place...."

"But we're here for Daddy," I reminded him.

On this Saturday, Stern Grove Theater was being used as a candidates' forum. A half dozen Democratic Clubs had joined together and after a hundred man-and-woman-hours of bickering had decided on the format. It would not be a debate. Rather, the major candidates for the important offices would, in shifts, each have an opportunity to speak, followed by a brief Q & A period from the audience. It was one of the last events before the election.

Stern Grove was another of those little pockets of San Francisco in which you pretend that you were in the wilderness. Almost. The odor and noise of automobiles still penetrated the border of trees, and in spite of the strategically placed garbage cans, there were always a ground cover of discarded Fritos bags and empty beer and soda cans.

The Grove offered two main attractions to the public. The first was this massive amphitheater, with tiers of seats fashioned from granite quarried in China. Unfortunately, the second main attraction of Stern Grove was located just west of the amphitheater: the city's largest off-leash dog park.

Jack and Elsie had lived on peaceable terms during their final days together, as if struggling to maintain appearances the same way Val and I had. I was proud of Jack, but anxious about how his first encounter with a different dog would go.

At the top of the theater, I clutched Jack's hand and scanned the back rows for Raven and Janis. Janis was one of the organizers of the event, and Raven wanted to get us together. I, too, wanted to make one more relationship right.

Alex and the organizers were lucky: after wet weeks in early October, we were now enjoying a late Indian summer. With the amphitheater so large, we could count on a number of empty rows in the back where we could move around, or even leave if necessary, without calling too much attention to ourselves.

"Are there dogs here?" Jack demanded suspiciously.

"Just stay close." I hoped this wasn't as bad an idea as it suddenly felt. I couldn't see Raven. So I started down the granite stairs, moving cautiously, as my center of gravity had shifted. We had timed our arrival as close to Alex's appearance as possible. Jack wasn't much for long speeches.

"Anna!"

I turned and spotted — oh my God — Mairead? Yes, her unmistakable blazing hair.

"Mairead!" Jack forgot all canine concerns and turned sideways to edge along the narrow granite aisle to her. "_{Mairead....}"

"Oh, I love those hugs!" she exclaimed, as they embraced.

"So ... you're back." Seeing her, I felt all over again how I had lost something precious and irreplaceable.

"I t'ought I might see youse," she said happily. Her accent was thicker for her time back home. "I've been trying to find you for three days, but you're not at the old place...."

"I have a new cell phone number," I explained. "When did you get back?"

"Just a few days ago. The craic was great. Hi there, Handsome — you do look handsome!" She hugged Jack again.

"How's Kelly?"

"Grand now," she said. She let go of Jack rather suddenly.

"My daddy's running for District Attorney!" Jack announced. "_{District....}"

"*Sssshhh.*"

Two angry faces turned to look at us from below. Although we were several rows from the main concentration of attendees, Jack's last outburst had been an overexcited one. We settled in quickly, Jack between us.

The stage below us had eight candidates, from the Asian-American incumbent to a high-functioning schizophrenic who'd managed to slip past the angrily-hammered-out rules for qualifying for the forum.

Mairead and I each held one of Jack's hands, and he became a conduit to my past. San Francisco politics ranked slightly behind corn futures on Mairead's list of priorities, and so, I thought smugly, she must have wanted to see me rather badly. Perhaps she missed some things about life in Presidio Heights, too — not the physical comforts as much as a woman and child who adored her. Her second family — and mine, too.

Down below us, another line of men and women filed onto the stage. They were the candidates for the last supervisorial district that was up for grabs this year. I recognized Manfred, last name forgotten or unknown, the author of Manfred's Manifesto, and the perennial candidate whose platform was that all taxes were unconstitutional.

The candidates sat on folding chairs. A standard podium had been moved to the middle of the stage with a base for a cordless mic. The forum was being moderated by a strident, humorless woman in a gray suit reminiscent of a prison matron's. When the candidates were speaking, she held the mic under their mouths as if it were a respirator. She had no qualms about cutting off the speakers when their time was up in a voice that I doubted even Alex would argue with. These forums were perfect examples of the Tragedy of the Commons. There was no advantage to an individual candidate sticking to his or her time if the others weren't going to obey by the rules, for the candidate's sacrifice for the greater good would go unnoticed. Frau Moderator was a good advertisement for totalitarianism.

"You have to tell me about your trip." I took a chance on whispering over Jack's head to Mairead.

"I will." She held Jack's hand up as a sign of the promise, while putting a cautionary finger to her lips.

"You look awfully good," I said anyway. Her hair was longer, and she'd traded her old Catholic schoolgirl look for more typically San Franciscan attire: jeans and a tank top layered over a t-shirt.

But underneath tee and tank I knew she was unchanged. I thought of her meaty chips with the crispy shells, our excursions to buy Jack's clothes, our impromptu picnics at Clay Street Park, where there was rarely a dog to be seen. I didn't mean to leave Mairead when I left Alex; she had just had the same address....

"I have an idea," I said. I glanced down at the heads of the people who'd shushed me, and then went on as softly as I could without being overheard, "Move in with me."

She could still work up a good blush.

"No, wait — wait 'til you hear this." I was quite taken with my own plan. "Alex is helping me find a little house. We could share expenses — I'd pay you, too." She probably needed a new job now, and I'd budgeted for little part-time help once I went back to school. I didn't plan to desert my newborn, but I knew myself well enough to know that I'd need the occasional break. "I know you love babies," I reminded her cunningly.

"I do," she said longingly. But she squirmed.

"What are you guys talking about?" Jack demanded. "Talking...."

"What are you going to do otherwise?" I asked bluntly.

From below: "*Sssshhh.*"

"I can't, Anna." She bent forward and whispered across Jack's lap. "Kelly and I aren't friends?"

"No? You didn't have a fight, did you?"

"No, Anna," she said patiently, even though by now she was maroon. "We aren't *just* friends."

Comes the dawn.

I put my free hand over the lower part of my face. Then that seemed too obvious, so I tried making my face a blank. That seemed disapproving so I tried smiling. I think I crossed my eyes, the way Jack did when he stared at something too long.

"Eee-yaah! Mommy, can we go now? I'm bored. Bored...."

Jack to the rescue! "No, dear," I said with exquisite patience, "we're here to see Daddy, remember?"

"Mairead!" Jack exclaimed. "I'm going to have a sister! A sister!"

"Don't be so embarrassed, Anna," Mairead smiled at me. "I owe some of it to you."

I had no idea what to make of that.

"It's why I left Dublin in the first place. I mean, when I came here? There was a girl down the street, and ... My family ...? I was so afraid they'd find out. And I t'ought, San Francisco, that's where they all go. But then I got here and it felt the same."

"Really." I examined patterns in the stone bench, seeing the distorted faces I so often did, these grimacing more than usual.

"I liked the new church because there was no way I'd talk to a priest? I t'ought God would help me change, if I could talk to Him directly.... Then last summer, you and Val...."

"Please don't. I can't stand to think about what you must have thought of me."

"It's not like that? What I t'ought was, 'If your woman can go after what she wants, with a child and everything, then it's about time you did."

"When is Daddy coming, Mommy? You said Daddy was coming."

"And the others at church helped me see, God doesn't care who you love. He just wants you to love."

Below us, Manfred was railing. A few people got up to leave.

"Well." I finally spoke. "I'm happy for you. Very happy."

"We're happy," Mairead said. "That's why I wanted to see you.'

"Everyone's happy!" Jack concluded. He held both our hands up to the sky, and when he let go, I clasped Mairead's.

***

And then: the candidates for District Attorney.

Decorrah walked out on stage first, regal as always, dressed in a long black robe that made her look like a Supreme Court justice. I could imagine "Pomp and Circumstance" playing in the background.

"This campaign has been muddied with extraneous issues," she began. "I regret that deeply. So I want to spend my short time here with you today talking about my vision for the city...."

Her speech was heartfelt but uncontroversial until she concluded:

"And since every crime is inspired by hate — hatred of self, hatred of God and humanity — that will be a city free of crime."

The applause and cheers, which had come in spurts throughout her speech from supporters concentrated near the front, now came full and resounding, and then swelled and swelled more until the very ground shook like a 3.1.

The finale: Groups of her followers stood up from the front row and threw rose petals at her feet.

"We'll have none of that," Frau Moderator commanded, withdrawing the mic from Decorrah.

"D.C.! D.C.!" her friends and fans cheered.

"I said none of that! Shall I disqualify your candidate from the rest of the forum?"

Decorrah motioned for her supporters to sit down, but it took another three minutes for the two women to restore order. Alex couldn't be seen to be quashing D.C.'s support, so he was forced to sit by ineffectually, ankle propped on opposite knee, examining something on the sole of one shoe.

The fracas at the bottom of the theater was, at least, of personal help to me.

My problem had started during Decorrah's speech. I was reaching into my purse to dig for bobby pins so that I could get my hair off my neck when I saw the black Labrador sniffing around the edge of the seats, just a few rows down.

Jack had stretched out on the granite bench. "Daddy's running for District Attorney, Daddy's running for District Attorney," he sing-songed, beating his sneakers against my elastic-waist pants. Then he isolated the dog's sniffles, and he shot upright.

"We have to go," he declared. "Go!"

The party that had been shushing us got up and moved away.

"Don't you want to stay and hear Daddy?" I tried pulling Jack on my lap, but it was impossible; we'd both grown too much. I managed to get the edge of his bottom on my knee.

"I don't see an owner." Mairead peered around.

I spoke close to Jack's ear. "If you want to hear Daddy talk, you have to ignore the dog."

"I don't want the dog!" he cried.

"I can take care of it, Anna," Mairead said, reaching for him. "Come on, Jack."

He bent toward her, but I held on firmly to his torso. "No, I've got it," I said. "Jack," I whispered urgently. "You can do it. You can do it."

"No!" he cried, but joyfully. "*We* can do it!"

Jung called it synchronicity. That past week I had been playing the soundtrack from *The Producers*. To my surprise, Jack loved the music. He did burst into "Springtime for Hitler" at some rather inopportune moments, but now, at Stern Grove, he began to sing "We Can Do It," another song from the musical. "We can do it, you won't rue it, we can make our dreams come true!" He was dangerously loud and rather horrifyingly off-key, but the Lab, with its own sensitive ears, fled.

So did some other members of the audience. But after that Jack was all right.

Later we had two more canine encounters, one with a German shepherd large enough to frighten *me*, but the second with a dog of mixed breed that could have fit in my glove compartment. Jack huddled behind me and cried, "Get the dogs away!"

At first I was disappointed, remembering how well he'd gotten along with Elsie at the end. Then I was resentful, remembering Val's conceit about his success.

But Jack recovered fairly quickly, and I thought, this is real progress. There's no miracle cure. The miracle is that you can survive it, without either running away or pretending what's in front of you doesn't exist. Val and Elsie had become reconciled to each other. You have to take life one dog at a time.

***

After the Lab left, Die Frau and her staff re-exerted control over the crowd. Jack calmed down in time to watch his father take the podium.

In spite of the extra pounds, Alex made a compelling physical impression. Maybe the sayings, "throw your weight around" and "fat cat" started with men like him.

We had moved back two more rows. I wanted to be able to make a quick escape if necessary.

"Voters and friends, I'm not running *against* anyone," Alex began. "In fact — " chuckle — "you can see that I'm not in shape to do a lot of running, period."

"Is Daddy making a joke?" Jack asked.

"He's trying, dear."

"You're hurting my hand! Hand...."

Thankfully, that was Alex's last attempt at humor.

"What I would like to do today is to revisit my record."

He repeated statistics from his July newspaper interview. Then he retold the story of Gary Bryce Smithson, whose conviction remained his most dramatic triumph. He never addressed Decorrah's hit piece nor took the obvious pot shot at her inability to control her fan club.

He didn't say anything as memorable as *"Ich bin eine Berliner...."* but he had a voice such as Seneca must have had. He even had his speech timed to end about twenty seconds early so there was no risk of being cut off, and his final line, resounding through the speakers, was "I can, and I will, protect you all."

Frau Moderator, who had still not parted with the microphone, withdrew it from its place near Alex's lips, where she had held it motionless for the past eight minutes. "Questions for the candidates," she ordered.

By now she had indoctrinated the audience thoroughly: Raise your hand, wait to be recognized; and let her repeat the question, *citizens,* or this way to the tumbrels.

Every speaker had ringers. Even Mad Manfred, the candidate who would abolish all taxes, had a friend planted among the audience to ask where he could send donations. Manfred directed him to his website.

The first question for D.C. Washington was about the "dead baby" mailer. The voice was male, and definitely familiar, but I couldn't see him. Then I heard a woman below us say, "He's in a wheelchair."

My first thought was that this was a rude remark, and my second thought was that the woman must be referring to Paul Deschiens, the prosecutor who had become Alex's protégé.

"Poor man. So good-looking, too."

And poor Decorrah, too. There was no good way to answer: She could distance herself from Riordan's actions and make herself out a bungler unqualified to manage a Carl's Jr., or try to defend the mailer as a legitimate campaign strategy and turn into Riordan in drag. She tried to do neither and ended up doing both.

But her people weren't completely unschooled. They had something for Alex: "Mr. Kagen," began the question, asked by someone I couldn't see, "you say you can 'protect us all.' But you seem to have, shall we say, some personal problems with women and children? You've given up custody of your son and made some very ugly and very public accusations against a woman whom you *now* say is a capable parent at what seems like a convenient time for you."

I closed my eyes. Just a few months ago I would have loved to hear a stranger embarrass Alex over what he was doing to me, and to Jack, but now....

A little advice. If it ever comes up. When you are watching a child — and especially a child like Jack who is less predictable and more volatile than most — don't close your eyes.

Jack was running down the stairs in the middle of the amphitheater. My clumsy son with his awkward gait had turned into Jesse Owens, going down, down, down, down, down....

"I am not a good family man," Alex said decisively. "I failed completely as both husband and father, and if I had it to do over again, knowing everything I know now, I don't think I would do any better."

This admission was so unexpected that it took longer than it otherwise might have for the audience to realize that a young boy was running down the center stairs. Only a few people nudged each other and pointed while others kept their attention on Alex, who was still speaking.

"I've got to go after him," I said, trying to get to my feet but having trouble getting my balance.

"Shall I?" Mairead volunteered uncertainly.

"Do you think you can catch him?" If I fell down stone steps....

Alex's voice on the loudspeaker: "But the complete collapse of my personal life was due in large part to my dedication to my work."

...down, down, down, down, down....

"No," Mairead admitted.

"I can pay attention to my job or to my family. If you want to hear about how your D.A. unplugs the phone every night so that he can sit down to dinner and have quality time with his loved ones, *do not* vote for me. If you want a person in office who will give up everything else in his life to enforce the law and safeguard the residents of San Francisco, then *do* vote for me."

He paused. In that pause two things happened: reporters wrote down his words, and the audience noticed Jack. Indeed, Jack was hard to miss. He was almost at the stage, and the steady low-level noise that was always audible in a crowd of this size grew louder.

I sank back. "We'll leave it in God's hands," I said, almost sincere, resigned to an enraged ex-husband and an all around embarrassing situation.

Alex was too far away for me to see his face in detail. I sensed more than saw when he first became aware of the boy, then how he recognized him, and then ... I wasn't sure anymore.

By now Jack was trying to heave himself on the stage, which was at the level of his head. He did not have the upper body strength for such a task but he applied himself with vigor, pulling first with his arms, grunting loudly enough for me to hear in the back rows, and then trying to jump, flapping his arms, giving the strong impression that he believed he could fly.

The curious murmurs and buzzing of the crowd became laughter.

"They think he's cute," Mairead said. "I — I think."

I wanted to cover my face, but I had to watch.

"C'mere, big guy," Alex said. He reached down and like the mothers of legend who lift cars to save their child's life, he was able to pull Jack up onto the platform.

The laughter began to recede.

"Daddy!" Jack always could make himself heard.

Alex raised him up, evidently with some idea of hoisting him on his shoulders, but that was not going to happen. So instead he took him firmly by the forearms and swung him around in a circle.

"Vote for my daddy!" Jack shouted, as loudly as anyone with a microphone, as he spun. "Vote ... for ... my ... daaaaddy!"

***

"Once more and your old dad's going to be sick."

Alex had been spinning Jack around again. But now it was a few weeks later and instead of Stern Grove in the afternoon, the venue was a dimly lit hospitality suite at the Mark Hopkins Hotel on election night.

"But Daddy!" Jack whimpered. "You're losing! Losing...."

Alex sank into the yellow chintz Rococo armchair that was the closest furniture that would have him. He was the main attraction at his victory party. At least, for now it was a victory party. Every candidate was having a "victory" party tonight. Sometime before morning, most would turn into "receptions" to thank volunteers and contributors.

The immediate cause of Jack's distress was the most recent update posted on the Internet which showed Alex trailing by two percentage points.

Maddy had booked the suite. The main room was in the corner of the building, so that we had nearly a 180 degree view of the Bay Bridge and the East Bay hills, the lights providing a sweeping candlelight vigil for our wait.

A second smaller room had been turned into a "command center," with Paul Deschiens and two other ADAs set up at three different laptops on folding tables. In both rooms there was a television bolted to the wall near the ceiling. Each was tuned to one of the local channels covering the election, with the volume kept low.

Every other available space was packed with Alex's campaign employees and volunteers, lawyers and support staff from the D.A.'s office, and consultants and freelancers who had done such varied jobs as graphic design and research. Alex even had one or two real friends, old study partners from law school. And so did I — now. I had not only invited Mairead, Kelly, Raven, Janis and Darya, but half a dozen single moms and a few couples from Jack's new school.

Then there was the political crowd — consultants and press — making their rounds. Bo Hanks and Ray Shimmie had repented of their earlier desertion. Perry Millard had the chutzpah to show up. He'd tried to kiss me on the cheek when he came in, and when I expressed my indignation to Alex, Alex had said, "If you wrote off everyone who ever disappointed you, you'd lose every single ally you had."

Yes, Alex could be forgiving when it was expedient.

The day before, Alex had emptied his campaign war chest into a final push to "get out the vote." He had joined his volunteers in distributing door hangers in the precincts where the highest percentage of his supporters lived.

He thought his donors deserved to have their money spent on winning the race, not on "frou-frou hors d'oeuvres," but for tonight, behind his back, Maddy had funneled money into lush finger food, deli trays, and gorgeous French pastries — *mille feuilles* and fruit tarts — their sugary glaze turning crusty as the evening went on. Jack could position himself at the food table and eat steadily without taking his eyes off the set.

The television coverage that interested us was minimal, since there had been many other offices and propositions on the ballot. The way to keep track of the results was, *naturellement,* the Internet. Paul Deschiens was the designated precinct monitor, but a few moments ago a murmur had traveled among those with handheld devices.

Paul then reluctantly faced the unavoidable, making the official announcement, "We've fallen another two points behind." He hunched a little over the wheeled tray-table that Alex had given him as a gift the previous Christmas.

"Daddy, that's bad, isn't it?" Jack wailed. "Bad...."

That was when Alex picked Jack up from just below his armpits, the same way he had at Stern Grove, raised him halfway to his chin, and declared, "Don't you worry about your old man, son." For the benefit of the nearby guests, "Those are the most liberal precincts in the city. We didn't do well there last time, either."

Didn't do well. Half the people who bestirred themselves to go to the polls at all would use their stylus to punch the dot next to the name that sounded most familiar. Alex's world hinged on those tiny round punched-out pieces of paper, but he did not appear to be thinking of them as he moved from room to room with exceptional grace — a pat on the shoulder here, a compliment on a new suit or hair cut there — while I kept taking off ill-chosen clip-on earrings to relieve the pain in my lobes and tried to remember my statistics class, the better to predict the final outcome of the evening.

I was his acknowledged consort that night. Passing by me now, he bestowed both a nod and an almost ingratiating smile. Then he clasped his hand formally in front of himself, and asked, "Could we speak for a moment in private?"

I instinctively looked for an emergency exit.

"Sure."

We slipped quietly out of the suite, where Alex headed away from the elevators to the end of the hall. We would have privacy here, as not many people would climb the stairs to the 15th floor.

Alex pawed the floor once with his shoe. "I wonder if you'd consider coming home. You and Jack."

"If this is a joke, Alex, it's pretty cruel."

He responded in his deepest bass, with no awareness of the parody he was performing, "I never joke about marriage."

My first memories of home were tactile: the rubbery leaves of the orchids we had delivered every Tuesday; the nap of the carpet, the surrender of the mattress when I went to bed.

"We were a good team once," Alex said.

I was wrong about the stairs. A waiter approached, balancing a large silver tray on splayed fingers. I couldn't tell if it was a man or a woman: The person had buzz-cut hair, a boyish figure, and features not yet come into maturity. "Excuse me," the person said as we had to part to let him or her pass between us. I snatched the opportunity to look at the gold name tag on the black vest. It read, "Tyler."

I stared after this Tyler for a moment before asking something else. "Tell me, Alex. How did you know that Val would leave me?"

"I know his type. They blow through my courts every day."

"*My*" courts.

But just think what it would mean to Jack. He talked about his father constantly. Could I do this for him after all, in spite of my mistakes? Might the baby be better off, too?

Alex had offered to raise this other man's child before. But that was when an expanding family would improve his image, and it couldn't help him now that the polls had closed.... Such an offer came either from the greatest love or the most frightening indifference.

"I need some time to think."

"Of course. And you might like to wait to find out if you'd be the wife of the District Attorney again, or just some putz."

I almost touched him. "Oh, Alex, that doesn't matter. For me, the pressure wasn't worth the perks. I just wanted it for you, because you wanted it."

***

The crowded rooms of the suite made Jack anxious. Periodically I took him out into the hallway and offered to take him home. But he insisted, "I want to wait until Daddy wins. Wins..... What if he doesn't win? Doesn't win...."

I didn't know what to say because I didn't want to add a broken promise to his disappointment if Alex did not win. To distract him I took him for a walk around Huntington Park, but then it started raining. Indian summer was over.

***

Disheartening news. Due to a glitch in the computer at the Department of Elections, the counting of the absentee ballots, begun when the polls closed, had to be started again. Usually the absentee ballots could be tallied within the first hour. We'd been expecting to get the results by 9:15, but the media was quoting spokespeople predicting that it would be 11 p.m.

I had to get out again for a few minutes. I didn't want to leave Jack, but Alex didn't want me to take him, either. I told myself that that was just the protectiveness I loved. Even the night I told him I was having Val's child, Alex had stayed home to defend the perimeter.

Even in the best of relationships, one must pick one's battles. I had started the evening by bringing Jack in his new denim jacket, an item of clothing that Alex had not let him wear before. Alex had remarked, "He looks like he's on his way to Juvy after all."

So this time I let Alex have his way and went out alone.

When I left the suite, Jack was holding court, entertaining Alex's staff by calculating what days of the week that their birthdays would fall on in 2015.

I took the stairs at the end of the hall, where Alex and I had had our tete-a-tete, though it would make for a difficult descent. I wanted to make sure I didn't run into anyone.

It was a slow journey. At the even-numbered floors I wanted to reconcile with Alex. At the odd-numbered floors I did not.

At the mezzanine I didn't know what to think.

The meeting rooms were on this level, but the only events scheduled for the evening were two seminars: "Selling Short in Bad Times" and "Weight Loss with the Lord." It would be a good place to rest and think for a few more minutes.

Except that Sherri Pechner was there, too.

She sat in a chintz-upholstered chair, a sibling to the one that had caught Alex. She crossed her long legs, and the toe of one red patent leather stiletto moved rhythmically up and down. She looked as though she had been waiting for me.

"I guess it's over," she said.

"'It ain't over 'til it's over,'" I said. Yogi Berra's oft-quoted saying was never quoted so oft as on an election night.

"That's not what I was talking about." She uncrossed her legs. She had on a red dress to match her heels, a form-fitting sheath with a low, square, bust-enhancing neckline, the kind of dress that you can never, ever imagine wearing again when you are more than four months pregnant.

"Then what are you talking about?" I asked.

"Alex."

I hadn't forgotten Sherri Pechner. I had just put her out of my mind.

Looking straight at my navel, she asked, "Does Alex ever talk about me?"

"No." But on a charitable impulse I appealed to her practical side. "There are plenty of rich and influential men in the city for you to choose from. If you don't mind marrying someone a little older, like Alex, you can practically take your pick."

"You've been out of circulation too long," she told me in a world-weary tone. "They have egos like rock stars, the brains of inanimate objects, and the bodies of Samoan wrestlers."

Alex wasn't exactly Brad Pitt, *or* the Dalai Lama — but he was a brilliant man in the areas in which he was brilliant.

"And after everything I did for him ... *saved* that campaign."

"He valued your contributions," I said ambiguously — and generously, I thought. The stairs had been a bad idea. I needed to get outside.

She said dreamily, "What we could have done together. You were such an idiot to let him go."

***

In the Mark Hopkins courtyard, the rain came down harder than before. As usual, I hadn't brought raingear: Umbrellas were for pessimists. But I came out from under the awning anyway and tilted my face into water falling from the sky until I felt cool and a little cleaner.

Once Alex berated me in the foyer of the Pathways Academy for not having a raincoat.

...Alex's answer at the candidate's forum was brilliant. I couldn't imagine how *he was going to get out of that one ... but he did. He admitted he always put work first.*

...But I guess he's planning to change....

...He never said that....

...What do I care? I don't like *having him around....*

...I don't like having him around ... but for Jack's sake....

...He'll still let me go back to school. He was all for it when we were making up a budget....

...He might not want me to do that anymore, if I move in with him again....

...So the denim jacket makes Jack look like he's going to Juvy, does it?....

...And that's who I'm doing it for, for Jack....

...That's who I did it for before....

...And I'd do it again for you, Jack, if there were any chance we could make it work....

"Are you all right, Ma'am?" one of the doormen asked. "Do you need a cab?"

"I'm fine," I lied. "Say, did you vote today?"

***

The hospitality suite had emptied a little by the time I returned. Some guests were scrambling to make one or two more parties before the night was over, taking advantage of the night artificially prolonged by the City Hall computer failure.

Mairead and Kelly had waited for my return. "Couldn't leave wit'out saying good-bye," Mairead said, hugging me. "Jack's holding up really well, isn't he? It's late for him."

"He's a fine boy," Kelly said. "Don't be forgetting it. *Slan go foill.*"

***

The final precincts came in. "Kagen 98,487. Washington 101,359," Paul told us through the sliver of glass in his throat.

"So," Alex said blandly, "it's all on the absentee ballots now."

There were just a few of us left, huddled in the main room on the yellow-patterned chintz, facing a fake fireplace. We were the family of a patient in surgery waiting for the doctor to come out with the news, with the added pressure of the patient waiting with us.

Besides Alex, Jack and me, we were Maddy, Bo Hanks and Ray Shimmie, Paul, Darya, and three volunteers I hadn't met before that night.

Bo and Ray had helped Paul re-establish himself here, for it was accessed by two stairs. He sat motionless, intently focused on the screen, as if there were a cone around his neck, like the ones they put around dogs to keep them from biting their own wounds.

I took Jack for another walk during an earlier break in the rain. We talked about the new season of *Crime Conquerors*: Queen Verminix, the new villainess, had new heroes to fight: Manuel and Marcus. Montel and Morgan had been replaced because the hairlines of the actors who played the roles were receding a little too much for them to pass as high school students any longer. Their departure was causing Jack a great deal of consternation.

"People come and go in our lives," I said. "It's hard." I pulled him a little closer. "It's very, very hard."

"I *liked* Montel and Morgan! Montel and Morgan...."

Now, almost two hours later, Jack lay under the buffet table, which was stripped down to half-eaten pastries and congealing grease from the cold cuts.

Alex was holding forth about cases currently before the California and United States Supreme Courts. In the background, Jack was re-enacting yet another destruction of Bedford Falls. He used the scraps of some popped helium balloons to represent Verminix and her armies of the night.

"Here we go." Paul interrupted his boss in the middle of a comment about equal protection. His voice cracked. "Final ... final ... Washington, 109,376." He sucked in his breath. "Kagen ... Kagen...." He gasped. "111,051."

Then he broke down sobbing. No one moved. I got up and put my arms around him.

"I'm okay," he said, collecting himself quickly.

"It's been a tough night," Alex said gruffly. He sounded as though he might express some emotion himself. But he knew how to shift the mood. "It was the absentees!" he said in a voice that mocked Santa Claus. *Ho-ho-ho.*

Maddy punched numbers into a calculator. "Yep. The absentees came in for you almost sixty-forty. Couldn't-a done without them. Little close for you, Alex, honey." *She'd* survived the night because there was a balcony where she could go out to smoke.

So, it was over.

I collapsed against the back of my chair, unnoticed by the others. My limbs shook as though I'd finally set down three heavy pieces of luggage I'd been carrying for months. As the trembling subsided, I found that I had spoken the truth: I had wanted it for him because he wanted it. I felt happy for him, for the man who was Jack's father, the kind of happiness I rarely felt for anyone except Jack himself.

Alex cleared his throat. "I couldn't have done it without you all," he said hoarsely.

Ray Shimmie stood up. "Yeah, it's all good," he said. "Bo?"

Bo shifted. "You go on ahead. I'll call you tomorrow. Tomorrow, okay?"

Damn. Darya had taken me aside to ask me about Bo's marital status about an hour before. She was disappointed at my answer but apparently had recovered.

Darya and Bo did leave separately, about ten minutes apart, but I had seen both of them use that strategy at other events, with different people.

Maddy's cell phone rang. "O'Reilly." Pause. "Great." Impatiently: "Yes, of course we'll wait. Doesn't Muni run 'til midnight?"

She slapped her phone shut. "Fucking assholes."

"Madeleine," Alex said, "we've talked about language."

"It just sucks — that absentee thing. We missed the media the first time around, and half the lazy fuckers have probably gone home — "

"*Madeleine.*"

Her phone rang again.

This was one of the few San Francisco contests too close to call until the very end. The media had visited us, but they had moved on. Now they would return to what looked like a frat party gone very wrong.

"When the phone stops ringing, then we can worry," Alex said. "You're like a bride obsessed with the perfect wedding. It's one night. What matters is the next four years."

"Maybe they'll use some of the earlier footage." Maddy squinted. "I'm going to see if I can get a hold of Sherri and get her back. She'll know how to work this." She stood up. "Alex, you'd better shave. Paul, make sure you're next to Alex every second. Anna … h'm.... Don't take this the wrong way, but...."

"She stays," Alex said.

This was going to be hard.

"I want to stay," I said to Alex. "But later, if you have a minute, we need to talk about — "

He flapped his hand at me without turning around. "Later."

"Daddy, did you win?"

Jack crawled out from under the table. He must have fallen asleep. It was two hours after his bedtime, and he had school tomorrow.

"I won, Jack," Alex said. It hit him then. *I won.*

"My daddy won!" Jack was groggy but happy. "Won...." He reached into the pocket of his trousers. "You won because of me! I brought you luck. Luck...."

He let his head sink down to the carpet again, overtaken by exhaustion. But his fingers did not loosen their grip around the black pawn in his small hand.

EPILOGUE
THE (ALMOST) HAPPIEST PLACE ON EARTH

OCTOBER 2006.

Tiffany Chan leaned into my window, sparing a rare extra minute for us when she brought Jack to the car.

"She's getting so big!"

She was talking about Marissa, now 21 months old, sitting regally in her car seat. "Hi, Diffy."

"So, today's the special day," Tiffany said.

I pressed the button that opened the second row passenger door. Jack usually took the special ed school bus now, but I had arrived to pick him up early. Tiffany helped him heave up his back pack.

"I'm sure he hasn't let you forget it." Tiffany and I had stopped using the communication notebook when Jack started seventh grade, but Jack had probably been repeating, more often than the news station reported traffic and weather, "My dad's taking me to Disneyland!"

"Oh, it's been on his mind."

"I know how a plane gets in the air," Jack said by way of good-bye. "How does it *stay* in the air?"

Tiffany's attention returned to Marissa. "When am I going to have a little doll like this?"

"Very soon," I assured her. She was dating someone promising.

"I can't wait!" Tiffany reached to tickle Marissa under the chin.

"'Top dat!" Marissa protested, shoving Tiffany's hand away.

"That's not nice," I told Marissa, for form's sake.

That afternoon, as I sat behind the wheel of my aging Town and Country, it seemed that the past two years had gone by quickly. But I knew that as I was living them, many long nights of breast-feeding every two hours and trying to figure out *wtf the baby wanted* had seemed to go on forever.

Now I knew that those mothers with their "easy babies" were liars. I had gone for eleven years thinking that the Hell Months of Jack's infancy were a symptom of his disability.

Either that, or God really had it out for me.

As a toddler, Marissa was high-strung and demanding, with her own set of rules. But she was a typically developing child, and whenever she had a tantrum over bedtime or a toy I wouldn't buy her, I only had to remind myself of that.

"Disneyland gets 40,000 visitors a day!" Jack chimed in.

"And your orals are next week, right?" Tiffany asked.

"I'm defending my dissertation," I specified grimly. "That's why Alex said he'd take Jack for the weekend. So I'd have more time to cram. He doesn't realize what a handful *this* one can be."

Tiffany would know that I spoke in the *faux* put-upon voice of a mother who feared that it was bad luck to express too much pride.

    ***

At home we didn't have a lot of time. Jack's notion of a weekend bag was one stuffed with as many action figures and DVDs as it would hold. I'd done most of the packing while he was at school, but I was still rehearsing the application of toothpaste to a toothbrush on his toothbrush with him when Alex arrived.

Alex didn't just honk, but arrived early enough to park and come in.

"We're going to Disneyland!" Jack fairly screamed at the sight of his father, as if it were news to all of us.

"Take lots of pictures," I reminded Alex. I had bought my first digital camera and taken up photography as a minor hobby. Pictures of my children and their artwork covered the walls of my Sunset split-level. But the whole house looked like a daycare center: The entryway had a coat rack for the kids' outerwear, and I lined up their shoes underneath. The living room was entirely turned over to their toys, games and books. Wire baskets were crammed with stuffed animals (Marissa's obsession; most of them had been acquired "pre-loved" at garage sales), and *Crime Conquerors* action figures. We ate off of melamine dishware. But on melamine or Wedgewood, I was still a rotten cook.

I did have a few adult-sized chairs, and Alex seated himself in one now.

"I go too! I go too!" Marissa demanded shrilly at his feet.

"We'll call you, Marissa," Jack promised. "Don't be sad."

"Maybe we should make this quick," I said, lifting her up from under her arms. "She hasn't had a nap."

"You can go next time," Alex said kindly.

"Want Daddy! Want Daddy!" She reached out for him.

I always flinched when she called him that. At least he didn't correct her. He didn't seem to mind, in fact. Now he let her scale his lap and plant herself there, secure in her belief that she could prevent his leaving.

"I would take her if I could," he apologized, ruffling her wavy black hair the way he used to do with Jack when he was younger. She was a mini-me with bigger eyes. "I just hope Jack's okay."

Jack was a few feet away, spinning with arms out. We watched him in silence for a heartbeat and then I chirped, "You got the pass, right?"

"I got the doctor's note." Alex patted his breast pocket. "I keep it close to my heart."

With a note from a medical doctor explaining Jack's condition, Alex and Jack could avoid the hour long waits that wound around even the least popular attractions at Disneyland and its neighboring theme park, California Adventure.

I wished I could express my gratitude for this personal "California adventure" that Alex was undertaking. He hadn't taken a weekend off since … since … no, our honeymoon had failed to straddle the weekend.

But Alex took a compliment about as well as I could catch a ball, so for now I kept my thanks to myself.

"We'd better get going," Alex said, looking at his watch.

"No go, Daddy! No go, Daddy!"

Alex looked down my daughter with an odd expression. "I'm sorry to leave you like this."

I shivered unexpectedly, wondering if "you" were me or Marissa. "I'll deal with it," I said.

    ***

I couldn't study until Alex called my from his cell phone as they strode down the jetway in John Wayne airport. "Jack was fine," he reported.

"We got 30,000 feet high!" Jack declared when he got on the phone. "My ears hurt!"

After Alex and Jack signed off I had to entertain Marissa until her bed "time." Marissa resisted all routine, and I spent longer getting her to bed than I ever had Jack.

And, unlike Jack, who was mesmerized by television from the time he was a year old, Marissa could not be babysat electronically. I spent Saturday morning snatching twenty minute periods of study between changing her diapers, handing her cookies and reading *Goodnight, Moon.*

That was, until I had a visitor.

"Waid!" Marissa lurched toward Mairead's arms.

"I didn't forget your exam," Mairead said, "as a matter of interest. And I thought maybe that Little Miss and I could go to the park for a few hours, give you time to concentrate?"

"You — you have to let me pay you."

"No, I don't have to let you pay me. It's my graduation present."

"I don't qualify for any presents yet," I said, gloomy as Eeyore. The past two years had been a little too busy even for me, between Jack, a baby, school and not much respite care. Jack was no longer hard to find a sitter for. He was eccentric but easy to manage. But Marissa ... well, she was comfortable with Alex and Mairead, having known them since birth, but otherwise it was a difficult age for introducing new caregivers.

I wasn't complacent about successfully defending my dissertation on this first round, and I was eager to get one step closer to earning my own living. A long, long time before, I'd been a *wunderkind* myself, but now I was staring down the double-barreled shotgun marked with the numbers "four" and "zero" and I still had post-doc hours and a licensing exam ahead. Once I passed that exam, it wouldn't matter very much that my degree would be from a small, independent school that geared its classes for students who had day jobs and/or children. Out in the real world, it would be my work that mattered.

My ambitions had altered, though. I had abandoned my dream of becoming not just a psychoanalyst, but a counselor of any kind. I still believed in Freud's distinction between "neurotic misery" and "ordinary unhappiness," and the supremacy of unconscious motives over unconscious ones, but I had lost my faith in the ability of therapy to triumph over Life. I still loved the theories; it was the practice that was problematic. Everyone knows you can be a good clinician and have neurotic problems of your own, but I simply didn't want to be in the position of role model. So I'd go into testing or research, and let others — younger, more qualified, more devout — put their healing hands onto people's psyches.

"Sit down for a cuppa first." In my kitchen, I kept a box of Lyons, her favorite brand of Irish tea. She didn't believe anything manufactured in the United States deserved the appellation "tea."

"That'd be grand."

Marissa sat on her lap and pulled on the ends of her hair. "Ahnge." *Orange.*

"How's the trip going? To Disneyland?"

"Until I get a call to fly to Anaheim and to rescue either of them, I'm counting myself lucky." I put the kettle on. "I don't want to even *think* about the junk food he's stuffing him with."

"There's a pair of them in it," Mairead tittered.

"Tell me how things are *chez Mairead et Kelly*?" I asked.

"Grand."

"Want cuppa!" Marissa demanded.

As I made Marissa warm milk in a tippee cup with a little sugar, I prompted Mairead, "Sounds like there's more."

Mairead blew on tea that must have already been cool but finally said, "She wants to get married."

"Congratulations!"

"I'm not sure I'm ready."

"Take it from me, you're never ready," I said "But you have to do as I say, not as I do." My own "World's Best Mom" mug was a present to myself during the week I became infatuated with Cognitive Behavioral Therapy, but the infatuation was really with the hottie professor who was himself a devotee of CBT, and the fever had spiked and passed quickly. I was still not only unprepared for romance, I was outright paralyzed with fear.

No Daddy, no Stud, no partner at home. I was lonely, but I'd been lonely before. And after all, the modern woman isn't supposed to need a partner. The key word here is "partner." Not a Daddy, not a Stud.

"'S so ironic," Mairead said, and even she had to grin. "A few years ago we *couldn't* get married, so I wouldn't have had to deal with this?"

"Well ... tell her you need more time."

"Your woman's a little insecure. She thinks I don't love her now." She looked down suddenly.

I paused uncomfortably, then sighed, "'Love's never easy.' *Bombay Dreams*."

"You and your musicals." She clamped her mug on the table. "We'll be off, then?"

"Wait." I put my hand on hers. "I want to tell you something."

She looked anxious. Classic Mairead. People don't change a lot.

"You're one of the good people."

She could still work up a blush.

"There have been five, six people like you — maybe. People who really get it and hang in there. People like me rely on people like you."

"'Whatever you do unto the least of these, you do unto me,'" she quoted. Her eyes misted over. "I do want a baby someday," she said.

***

Darya showed at around four. Unlike Mairead, whose unannounced visit was an anomaly, Darya never called in advance, because she knew that I'd find some excuse to tell her not to come.

"My orals are Monday," I said. "I've got about half an hour before — "

"That's all I need. Less." She'd been crying.

I let her in.

She picked up a pink bear that Marissa had left lying on the floor. "This brings back memories." Callaghan was seven now.

Darya had sent Kennedy to the UCSF playgroup, where he'd received a more appropriate diagnosis: Conduct Disorder. A short time later they'd asked him to leave after he bit another child, which, by the way, is what kids with Conduct Disorders do.

Darya next found a psychopharmacologist who sent him cycling through a medicine cabinet full of the latest drugs.

Darya had tried. I knew she had. But at the beginning of the previous school year Callaghan and Kennedy had gone back to live with their father. Darya had her children over the summer, and during winter and spring break. She bemoaned their absence, but when the children were due for their visits she did not seem to anticipate their return with any especial pleasure.

Darya held the pink bear while she updated me about her latest romance. He was separated from his wife, had joint custody of his three children and had recently launched his own construction business.

"...He's a Virgo like you, and you and I have always gotten along. If I could find out the time of his birth I could get a real chart done."

"You know, Dolls, I kind of need to get back to work here? My orals? What if we got together Tuesday?"

"Oh, right. One kid in Disneyland and the other strolling in the park with your nanny of twenty-seven years." Darya stroked the bear's stomach. Suddenly she threw it up in the air. She let it fall to the floor were it lay face up, the way Marissa was born.

Marissa was also almost born face up in the suicide seat of Darya's leased BMW. Jack had been a fast delivery, but I was unprepared for how much faster Marissa would arrive, though I should have been prepared for how late Darya would arrive when I called her, as prearranged, to drive me to the hospital. She made several wrong turns ("You're making me nervous with all that screaming!") on the way to St. Seraphina's, and I was fully dilated by the time she pulled into the ambulance driveway.

"...meanwhile, a man to pay the bills...."

There's a clichéd but appropriate analogy therapists like to use with their clients, about how you have to put on your own oxygen mask before before you put one on the person depending on you.

And if I'd had a therapist *à ce moment cà*, that therapist might have advised me to let Darya go now — to abandon her to a future of wretched men and the troubled teens that even darling Callaghan would likely turn into.

But if I'd learned anything these past few years, it was that it's luck as much as choices that govern our lives. Darya didn't have the best record on the second, but neither had she had much on the first.

"Just give me this weekend," I said, "then we schmooze all you like."

"I could use some attention now," she said huffily.

***

CPS finally closed its Kagen file. After Alex was re-elected, and a few face-saving months passed, he made a phone call on an unrelated matter to the director of State Social Services, who sat at the top of a tall tree of government with many branches. One of those branches was Child Protective Services. And the director owed his appointment, in large part, to Alex. Very much behind the scenes, but ... to Alex.

After about a year, rumors of treasure left behind by Merrick and his followers resurfaced. The Park Service began to come across solitary explorers with shovels. Sometimes there were couples, and more than once there were little parties of seniors with metal detectors. Then the *Chronicle* did a feature on the story, and the real chaos began. People arrived in their own sail or motorboats, sometimes chartering transportation. Within a month, Minotaur Island resembled the surface of the moon. The Park Service closed it down again, and organized its own search.

The government treasure-hunters found two large metal containers, only a few feet below ground, within a yard of the spot that Cesar had pinpointed and that Jack had helped the boys locate. Between them, the boxes held valuables almost identical to what Cesar had been searching for, and worth over half a million in today's dollars.

Within hours claimants came forward, describing themselves as relatives of either the leader, Theodore Merrick, or one or more of his dead followers. Most of the money would go to the attorneys who were filing the class action suit.

**

Sunday morning I hit my mojo, alternately scanning the DSM-IV-TR and some of the books in my bibliography. My dissertation addressed a narrow aspect of the difference between situational and characterological depression. Marissa, perhaps sensing my urgency, was entertaining herself unusually well. At noon I got up for a fourth cup of coffee and was on my way back to the computer in my bedroom, when the doorbell rang. I knew who it was. Alex observing this courtesy, although he had a key for emergencies, was a stinging reminder that we were no longer married. In many ways we had created the illusion for ourselves that we had never divorced; we were simply a couple with a few quirks in our relationship. We both knew married couples who maintained *de facto* separate residences. Nobody expected, for example, a congressman or woman to travel home from Washington every night when the House was in session.

"We got an earlier flight," Alex said. "I think that Jack reached his limit."

Marissa joined us immediately, and she loaded stuffies on Alex's lap. "Your babies," she explained.

"*I* didn't want to leave early!" Jack protested. "I was having fun!" He clutched a wrinkled map of the park. "We didn't get to see 'Mike and Sully to the Rescue!'"

"Next time." Alex, who had lost about fifteen pounds, leaned as far forward as his stubborn remaining bulk would allow. "I heard from Paul early this morning," he tried to say too softly for the kids to hear. Paul was now his chief assistant and Alex's choice as his eventual successor. "Triple murder-suicide in Seacliff. It'll be on the front page tomorrow."

"I *swear,* the lengths you'll go to get out of an actual vacation," I remarked as I sipped my coffee. I raised my Mom-mug. "Want some?"

"I have to get going in a second. I need to know ASAP how big this is, who should take it over — "

"I think Jack is old enough to understand the real situation," I said. *That you had to get back to your safe place — work.*

"I was hardly going to tell him about a grisly murder." Alex was indignant.

"A murder!" Jack cried. "Cool!"

"Okay, it was getting a little much for me." He was conciliatory now. "But it was getting pretty over-stimulating for Jack, too."

"Let's go out and come in again," I apologized.

"More babies," Marissa said, adding three stuffed animals on his lap.

I inhaled through my nose. "You *are* a great dad," I said.

He tensed.

"I know" he said. "You think I'm being sarcastic. I deserve it. I'm whatever the smart-ass woman's version of the boy who cried wolf would be."

He was going to get another compliment whether he liked it or not. "But you *are* a great dad. You got him on a plane. You got him to sleep in a strange city."

Alex brushed this off. "I knew he'd be fine. He's come a long way."

"Bye, Dad!" Jack said, picking up the remote.

"Well, that's my cue."

"Jack, you can wait five minutes until your father leaves."

"No, I can't!"

"No go, Daddy!" Marissa wailed.

It was so gut-wrenching to hear her say that. I'd withstood it Friday, because I'd been distracted by my anxiety about how Jack would handle the trip. Now I told myself that I was projecting, reliving my own father's disappearance. But like it or not, a lot of fatherless girls grow up to marry men like Alex Kagen and get knocked up by men like Alex Valentine. She was too young to hear about Val yet, but the time would come when she had questions.

Alex Valentine ... the man in the red cape. Christian from *Cyrano*. I'd thought I was over him a long time ago. But even now, when I saw a tall fair-haired man on the street (and God help me if he were on a bicycle), I thought it was Val for a moment, until I blinked and he transformed into someone older, or heavier.

Val *would* be a little older now. Maybe he was even heavier. Often I prayed that he'd never came back to San Francisco. Often I prayed that he would, so that I'd be able to tell him what a prick he was. So that I'd be able, one last time, to lie in his arms.

He did send three postcards the first year. He even asked, in one, what I had named the baby. No return address, and no communication after that. I just had to wait for strangers to look like strangers again. They would.

"I'll take you out next weekend." Alex interrupted my blast to the past. I saw that he was ruffling her hair again. "Here, let's put the babies back in their bed." He scooped up three of the stuffies.

"You'll take her — " I stopped. If he were setting her up I'd kill him. As slowly and painfully as possible. No jury of my peers — ex-wives — would ever convict me.

"I don't think I'm ready for diapers again, but — "

"What do you mean, 'again,' dear?"

"—but I bet we'd be safe for a couple of hours. Or you could come with us."

"That's very sweet of you." I didn't trust him. I twisted my fingers together, absently feeling for the ring I had only removed once the divorce had become final.

If my rejection of his offer to reconcile on election night had hurt his pride, he'd recovered very quickly, and I knew that he was glad that I hadn't accepted after all. We had a practical and mostly affectionate arrangement now. If another man or woman came on the scene, we would have to reconfigure again, but I didn't see that in the near future.

Every functional family is the same; each dysfunctional family is dysfunctional in its own way.

"By this time next year I'll be campaigning for attorney general," he said. "I bet she'll be ready to leaflet and go door-hanging by then."

His predecessor in the D.A.'s office, Marianne Pasquale, had lost her re-election bid the same night that Alex had won his, and she still blamed him.

As for Alex, he wondered if the people of California would let a second San Francisco D.A. follow the same career trajectory, but Maddy was drooling over the prospect of breaking out of local races and into the state arena.

Decorrah was out of elective politics. Within a few months, she and Alex's office, and sometimes she and Alex personally, were working together on child abuse cases his office was prosecuting. Like Gilbert and Sullivan, they made a productive team, without ever liking each other much.

For a man who had a homicide case on his hands, Alex was taking his own sweet time getting out the door. "Alex, is there something on your mind? Jack's perfectly happy. Marissa will have a tough time when you leave but — "

"There has been something on my mind."

"Well?" I hoped it wasn't money. "You know, if I pass the exam tomorrow, I might be able to take the licensing exam as early as spring." I couldn't wait to be able to support myself.

"I beg your pardon?"

"Sorry — just my own little train ride. What is it?"

"You know I'm not a liar."

But I am. Jeezus, will I ever live it down? The plump proof of my ability to lie was determinedly re-filling Alex's lap. "Of course not. I mean, of course. You're not a liar."

"When you're dealing with criminals...." he motioned with his fingers, prompting me to help him with the precise term. "Sometimes you learn certain habits, almost...."

"There's something you want to tell me."

"Yes." Pause. "I never had a vasectomy."

"You — " He was joking — screwing with my head in his old, nasty way. "But I remember — you told me it was St. Patrick's Day, and I remember you limping up the stairs."

Alex rubbed one hand vigorously over an anxious face. "Anna, do you remember, too, how we talked about eye witness testimony?"

"Yes...."

"And how — " *cough* — "unreliable it is?"

"Yes." Not too friendly.

"Well, you see," he said in a fatherly tone, "this is where I have to admit that you psychologists really have it down." He went on in an uncharacteristically fast and frightened voice. "It's very easy to plant memories in people's minds."

He pulled Marissa on his lap again, dislodging some of her animals in the process. "Want stuffies!" But Alex held on to her with his arms around her waist, so tiny in his thick arms. "Daddy! Stuffies!"

Alex tilted his face against her cheek. "Owie!" She recoiled at the scratchiness of his noon beard.

Still he held on to her. "You see any resemblance?"

Alex and Marissa's foreheads were suddenly aglow. The shape of their hair lines and their brows, dipping slightly over the inside corner of their eyes, matched exactly.

"You never had a vasectomy?" I asked stupidly.

"No."

When you look back on an earthquake, it always seems that you knew it was coming the moment before. You didn't. But when the ground steadied beneath me I was stupefied no longer. "You — you bastard!"

"Anna, the chil— "

"Don't you start with 'the children'! You tricked me!"

"Mom," Jack interrupted, "are you guys fighting?"

"Well," Alex said sheepishly, "you *had* tricked me."

"Tricked? What the fu-heck — *tricked*?"

I sputtered for another minute. Alex waited, composed now.

Whether he intended it or not (and my bet was on "intended"), in that minute I let sink in, deeper than before, what I'd done to him. Of course, he'd ... but I'd....

"I'm so sorry," I said.

There was a pause and then he said, "I'm sorry, too."

There was another pause, and for the first time since we'd met, Alex was the one who ended the awkward silence with a little bit of sass. He leaned toward Marissa without letting his face scratch hers again. "What did you just say? 'Can we go out and come in again'?"

He'd been thinking this for a long time, perhaps waiting for her features to give him some evidence. Or maybe I didn't give him enough credit. Maybe it happened in reverse: once she called him Daddy and tugged on the hem of his suit jacket, he started searching, hopefully, to find himself in her.

"I suppose — " I grabbed my coffee, which was tasteless and cold. "We should get a DNA test. That's easy enough."

"No." He kissed Marissa's temple, and when she batted him away he just held her more tightly. "If by some chance she's not mine, I don't ever want to know."

So many things we're better off not knowing.

"Don't you have to go, Dad?" Jack asked. "I want to watch TV. TV...."

***

Mothers, I understand that we all must cope in some way. You will hear no more judgments from me about JoshsSpecialWorld.com or heavenly beings who emerge from your womb.

I was never a big believer in recurring dreams. But now I have one. It's short, barely more than an image, but so vivid it might have been produced by Lucas Sound and Light.

I'm on an island standing next to Jack. It's really no more than a rock jutting out of the sea. The water is bluer than anything I've seen in the real world, and I can make out each curlicue of white on the foam as the waves break against us. There isn't room for either of us to move without falling into the freezing water. I hear the taunting caws of seagulls and smell fish and salt. I hear Marissa crying, but I don't know where she is.

It is still dark the morning of my oral exams when I wake up from the dream, and this time I hear a man's voice. A grown man's voice, but it's Jack's. It says, "We're odd, by God. Get used to it."

And I'm back on The Rock, dreaming awake. Water, waves, seagulls, rotten fish. But now I know we're not abandoned; we're waiting for help. This is hope. It's all we can expect and all we need.

**THE END
of
THERE'S MORE THAN ONE WAY HOME**

ACKNOWLEDGMENTS

Prominent New York editor and writer Nancy Nicholas is generous with her many gifts: her talent, her time, her encouragement, and various cat tchotchkes.

This book benefited from the counsel and direction of poet and editor David Groff, always given with patience and good cheer.

Among those who helped me on research for the book: Drew Johnson, Nelson Lum, Laura Shumaker, and Michael Bernick.

This may not be the best of all possible worlds, but somehow I got into the best of all possible writing groups. This sisterhood includes, in alphabetical order, Sheri Cooper, Phyllis Florin, Terry Gamble, Suzanne Lewis, Mary Beth McClure, Alison Sackett, and Linda Schlossberg. Before I met them I did not believe that such women existed.

Elizabeth Pomada and Michael Larsen are dedicated agents who daily add to the quality of life for writers and the quality of books for readers.

Steven Drachman is the visionary publisher of Chickadee Prince Books, whose commitment to craftsmanship recalls that of the fabled literary editors of the past.

Donna Levin
October 2016

CPSIA information can be obtained
at www.ICGtesting.com
Printed in the USA
FSOW03n0252200517
34190FS